MAGICK

Book Two of
The Dragonfly Chronicles

ELERI DRAKE

McCollum Creative Endeavors, LLC

McCollum Creative Endeavors
P.O. Box 1712
Apex, NC 27502

Cover design by Najla Qamber
Editing by Melinda DeJongh

E-Book ISBN: 978-1-962436-02-1

Print ISBN: 978-1-962436-03-8

Manufactured in the United States of America

*First Edition published by The Wild Rose Press under the name Heather McCollum, April 2015 *Second Edition, March 2025

For more information about Eleri Drake and Heather McCollum books, please check out her web site. https://www.heathermccollum.com/eleri-drake/

Eleri Drake Website

CONTENTS

DEDICATION

For Irena, my mom,
who also has the amazing ability to heal souls. Mom's powerful warrior
spirit, through everything life has thrown at her, inspires me and those
around her. She is my everyday example of a kickass heroine.

Love you, Mom. Thank you for always believing in me and for teaching
me to trust my instincts.
A woman's instincts are her magick.

TRIGGER WARNINGS

Norse and Danish warriors, now known as Vikings, raided Britain numerous times in the 9th century. They were notorious for their brutal ways while stealing provisions, valuables, and even people to sell into slavery. Life expectancy was between thirty to thirty-five years old, and many children died. To keep historically accurate in MAGICK, some of my characters may seem cruel. Of course, my hero has more respect and honor, but please understand the setting in which he lived.

I want you to thoroughly enjoy this Enemies to Lovers tale but be aware that there are threats of rape and killing. The heroine is captured as a thrall (slave). There are discussions of child death from illness and a difficult birth. However, there will never be a rape on page in my books, and the animals always survive. Also, the characters smell much better than they did back then.

FOREIGN WORDS IN MAGICK

Celtic (C), Danish (D), Old English (OE), Old Norse (ON), Scots Gaelic (SG)

bacraut – anus (ON)

cac – excrement or dung (C)

daingead – damn it (SG)

Danmǫrk – Denmark (ON), means Danish Marsh

for helvede – hell (D)

hā – interjection expressing surprise, interest, or distress (ON)

Hel – Hell, the location (ON)

kærasta – darling, used for girlfriend (ON)

kerling – old woman (ON)

màthair – mother (SG)

mathkr – grub or worm (ON)

ormstunga – snake's tongue (D)

pintle – penis (OE)

sæla – happiness, name of dog at Spring House (ON)

ve! – expressing dismay or surprise (D)

PROLOGUE

"Will she live?" Merewin whispered to the chilled air as she watched her sister's body melt and elongate into a thin, red thread, twisting like crimson honey until she couldn't discern any of Serena's lovely features. Merewin held her breath as the thread stretched across the dim room and up through a crack in the broken thatching.

"Come Merewin, you go next," Merewin's mother, Gilla, said, causing the girl to suck in a breath. Gilla knelt and placed a green stone in Merewin's palm, a sad smile on her lovely face. "I will hide you, like each of your sisters, in a different time and place. I will thread you backwards two hundred years."

"Two hundred?" Merewin swallowed hard.

"They will not find you then."

A low hiss came from behind Gilla near the door, and Merewin's younger sisters screamed. Gilla turned, cutting fingers in the air, and several thin snakes writhed as she sliced their venomous bodies in half.

"The demons who killed your father can't break through my wards that protect us in our stone circle, but they can send their beasts."

Wind gushed around the eaves like storm-driven waves. Did the demons already rule the sky? Flakes of debris filtered through the frigid air, making Merewin cough.

Gilla brushed fingers against Merewin's cheek, and the girl relaxed into the familiar caress. "I, too, am frightened," Gilla said in a low voice.

Merewin was seven years old and scared beyond any nightmare that had ever tortured her. The world had been safe before, and happy. Their father would laugh with them and spin his girls around in the wildflowers growing within their stone circle. All that had changed in a handful of days. Now she would be sent somewhere away from family, somewhere two hundred years ago. Merewin swallowed past the scratchy ache in her throat. "Will...will Serena be whole when she lands?" Her voice trembled.

Gilla nodded as she glanced at the rear wall. It shook under the assault of some large object, a boulder perhaps. "I'm using another of Drakkina's tricks. My ancient master may not have known much about love and kindness, but Drakkina certainly knew magick. And she taught me the ways of threading through time."

A shriek of wind shook the west corner of the home, making Merewin's two young sisters huddle closer together.

Gilla tied a small bit of fur around Merewin's wrist. "You go with a friend, Merewin. One who, like you, is fiercely protective and curious."

Her mother pulled her into a hug. The warmth of it enveloped Merewin, soothing with the sweet smell of honeysuckle and spice. "You're so strong and beautiful. And stubborn like your father. And like him, you could never let an animal or friend go unaided. So to you, I give my power to heal."

Merewin's eyes filled with tears. "I'd rather you keep it and keep me," she whispered, not wanting her little sisters to hear the quavering in her voice.

"You will die here, Merewin," Gilla said with quiet determination as she pulled back and searched her young face.

"Then so will you."

Gilla's gaze remained riveted, but she didn't say anything.

Merewin knew she was the bravest of all the sisters. Hadn't her father always said so? She looked straight in her mother's eyes. "Màthair, we will fight them together. I won't let them kill you."

Gilla took a deep breath as tears pooled, restrained. "As long as you live, I live." Her voice rose in strength. "One day when you've grown strong, you can come back with your sisters to kill this evil, but right now you must go. You must take my powers to safety."

Merewin shook her head and opened her mouth, but Gilla spoke first. "I cannot battle them when I fear for you." Gilla's gaze pleaded. "I must thread you away as Drakkina taught me." Merewin gave a slight nod and Gilla smiled, though a tear slipped.

Gilla spread Merewin's fingers open so that they could see the jade stone in the center. There were coils of thread ingrained in the depths of the deep green hue. Gilla spoke over the stone, lips hovering above the shiny surface.

"I freely gift you with my power to heal. On the currents of my blood, on the currents of my love, on the currents of my power given by the Earth Mother, send her now within my thread of healing."

Gilla took a deep breath, closed her eyes, and blew gently for several long moments. Merewin could almost see the power blowing out of her mother's lips, like invisible smoke. The coils inside the stone glowed softly.

Gilla smiled as she stood back from Merewin. "Tha gaol agam ort."

"I love you too, Màthair," Merewin said over the pounding of her heart.

Gilla smiled. "Go now and live a long life."

Merewin grasped the stone while her sisters hugged her numb body. The walls began to ripple as if they were merely a reflection in a pond. The heat in the stone coursed through her until she felt as if she were melting into a warm pile of wax. Instead of pooling, her supple body twisted and stretched. Merewin gripped the jade so firmly that she couldn't feel her hand anymore, only the solid jade at the center of what had been her palm.

The green thread of energy shot across the room, up through the narrow chimney and out into the sky. Merewin watched their small cottage grow distant as she sliced through the gray swirls of demonic fury.

Up above the roiling terror the threaded shape twisted as the sun and moon arched along their paths across the sky. Faster they moved until the flashing of sun and moon melted into one orb of blinding light.

Merewin tried to close her eyes but didn't know if she had eyes. A scream tore up through her, but she didn't have lips to open.

She watched helplessly as the flashing light streaked across her view. She held tight to the hot stone, knowing that she didn't have a hand to hold it. The flashing continued until there was only an illuminated smear. Merewin's essence lay along the long green thread suspended under the blurred celestial lights. She thought about Màthair, about her three sisters, about the ancient master, Drakkina. Who was she? Where was she now? Couldn't she help them?

After what felt like hours, the flashing ceased. Merewin saw the full moon stare down, and she fell. Her gaze fastened on the solid moon as she knifed down through the air back toward earth. The wind stung as the thread coils wound together, first into toes and feet, coiling up into legs. Merewin felt the breeze currents as they billowed under her robe and slid along her expanding form. She clung to the jade rock, funneling faith into it. Hair re-formed and whipped at her ears. She had a face again, and eyes, so she looked down. Mistake.

"Aaaaaahhhh!" she screamed, as her mouth formed. Trees stood below like pikes, waiting to impale. Arms flailing, hair wildly dancing, she fell through the tall oaks. Merewin's cry followed like a howl in the wind as bare branches washed across her face. A soft mound of fur skittered up her arm and wound around the back of her neck, but Merewin had no time to worry about it. With a thick *whump*, she landed, barely jarring her head. Her empty hand flew outward, curling around the edge of a woven basket. The softness at her neck squeaked and tickled a path down to her hand. A little pine marten blinked her beady eyes up at her. A friend?

Torchlight flickered and cut across a forest of trees surrounding Merewin. She was in a clearing edged by a small circle of boulders. Bits of animal fur and herbs lay scattered in patterns around the clearing. Clay jars stood at even intervals near the stones. Merewin turned her head slowly to take in what looked like one of Màthair's more serious summoning ceremonies. As she twisted to see behind her, Merewin's gaze locked with that of a woman.

The woman peered with sharp eyes, her brows raised, giving her a curious look. As if Merewin was an herb she'd never seen before that she might stick in one of the little clay pots. The woman's hair looked dark in the waning light and lay in a long braid that fell in her lap where she sat cross-legged near the torch. Her clothes were neat with pretty embroidery around the collar. The dancing firelight revealed small wrinkles around her intelligent eyes, making her look a little older than Màthair. A dark mole sat on one cheek. She smiled then, and Merewin saw little crooked teeth.

"Well, Navlin," the woman said, glancing up to the sky as if checking to see if anyone followed Merewin down from the heavens. "Ye did ask the Earth Mother for a lass." Her words came clear, and although Merewin had never heard them before, she somehow understood them. The woman indicated the basket Merewin sat upon, and Merewin realized it was a woven bairn's cradle. "I suppose I should have specified that I wanted a *wee* lass."

CHAPTER ONE
ICE

Port of Ribe, Denmark
Meeting House of King Ragnar Lothbrok
15 Years Later— August 841 A.D.

Drakkina peered out from behind the crystal blue eyes of the old pagan priest, or guþi, whose body she temporarily inhabited. Eldgrim's mind fought against the intrusion. Drakkina, a powerful Wiccan spirit, gripped his consciousness, urging it to slumber while she controlled his tongue and body. But the thoughts of his gods and demons warred against her, trying to expel.

Shut up, you old man. She pressed against his internal protests.

Drakkina surveyed the Meeting House of King Ragnar Lothbrok's home through the old man's rheumy eyes. *You're distracting me.* The tight pressure of two consciousnesses in one body was expected but still unpleasant even when she was the one in control.

Drakkina had found another of Gilla's hidden daughters, Merewin, in Northumbria near Lindisfarne, in what would become southeast

Scotland. By the blessed Earth Mother, Drakkina had found Merewin before she'd had to call Merewin to help her save Serena. Now that Gilla's first daughter had been bonded to her mate, it was time to nudge Merewin toward hers. Unfortunately, he lived across the sea in Denmark. So she'd had no choice but to interfere. *For the greater good and my peace.*

Drakkina focused the guþi's eyes, her eyes, on the arched stone entrance. Danish warriors stood around the perimeter of the central fire pit where venison turned on a spit. The smell of unwashed bodies and wood smoke made Drakkina wrinkle the old guþi's nose. He apparently thought nothing of it.

"I hope Merewin's mate smells better, else it will take more than my magick to bring them together," she mumbled through the man's thin lips.

"What do you say, Wise One?" King Ragnar asked from his chair next to Drakkina. King Ragnar was a commanding man, full Dane to the ends of his long red mustache. Despite the rough exterior, Drakkina felt the deep sensitivity of the man's heart, especially toward his wife and child.

"Nothing of consequence, my liege," Drakkina forced through the seer's vocal cords. "Are you sure he comes?"

King Ragnar grunted and swallowed a gulp of mead from his carved horn. "He comes. He's loyal to me." The king looked over. "And you're certain, Eldgrim, that he's the one who must find the healer?"

"The gods have shown me his face. To save your son's life, Hauk Geirson must bring the witch."

"Do the gods know how much Hauk despises healers?"

Drakkina pursed Eldgrim's leathery dry lips together. "The gods know the purpose more so than we mortals."

The oak door screeched on iron hinges, hitting the stone wall with a resounding *bang*. A swirl of wind dashed in around the muscled legs of a large man. Drakkina held her breath. Could this be the one?

"There now, he comes," Ragnar said, raising his calloused hand toward the front of the hall.

"Hauk Geirson of Spring House to see King Ragnar Lothbrok," one of the king's men called from the door.

The giant called Hauk strode across the room with all the presence of a glacier carving through rocks and earth. The room nearly trembled with his spirit. Drakkina saw a brilliant aura around him; such spirit she hadn't seen before. The man looked every bit the Dane raider, except cleaner. Drakkina smiled. Merewin would surely appreciate that.

His wheat-colored hair was shot with blond and left to hang in gentle waves to his shoulders. Several war braids flashed within the waves. Bands of braided gold curled around his massive, bare biceps.

The man exuded confidence in each step. His shoulders were broad, and the muscles in his arms showed evidence of hours of war practice with the heavy battle-axe. Drakkina's gaze followed the length of his body to his narrow hips hidden by the fine tunic. She smiled mischievously. Gilla's second born would fall right into this brawny warrior's arms, no doubt. Drakkina's gaze moved back to his face.

Narrowed eyes returned her stare. He had one scar across his forehead and one on his strong neck near the jaw, both turning the warrior's handsome features dangerous. Drakkina stared back at his blue eyes, and Hauk raised one eyebrow in question. She looked away. Had her approval been so obvious? Even behind the face of an old man?

"Hauk, welcome to my fire pit," King Ragnar boomed.

Hauk bowed his head. "I come as requested by my king," he looked up, "and by my friend." The two clasped forearms and the king gestured toward a serving woman to bring Hauk a horn of mead. The two talked casually for several moments while Drakkina concentrated on tamping down the guþi's will within. She had to make sure that the king convinced Hauk to find Merewin. Drakkina's mission to save the worlds depended on it.

"How is Ivarr?" Hauk asked.

With one last shove, Drakkina subdued Eldgrim. He would have a headache when he woke but shouldn't remember the possession as more than a nightmare.

Ragnar's eyes dimmed, and Drakkina felt his spirit clench. "That's why I've called you to me, Hauk." The king nodded at Drakkina. "Wise Eldgrim has seen a vision from the gods. There's a woman that I need you to bring to me. A woman across the sea."

Hauk's piercing gaze fastened on the guþi's, and Drakkina swallowed past the dryness in the seer's mouth. There was a power about him that made her feel like he could break into the guþi and pull her out by the throat. She had to gather her wits.

Drakkina cleared Eldgrim's throat. "Aye, I've had a dream and also a vision. There is a young woman who can heal the king's son, and you must be the one to bring her."

Hauk's lips curled back from his straight teeth. "A healer," he said, nearly spitting out the title. Hauk snapped his gaze to Ragnar. "You send me to fetch a healer?" Although the words held more respect when he spoke to the king, they still dripped venom.

Ragnar nodded, reluctance evident. "I know, I know Hauk, ever since Ingun and the others died, you don't trust healers."

"It was the false promises of the false healers that tore Dalla's heart apart," Hauk said between clenched teeth. "She has yet to recover from her family's deaths."

Ragnar lowered his voice. "And you, friend, have not recovered either." The king shook his head. "It wasn't your fault that they died."

"I brought the healers into my home. I believed their words."

Drakkina saw guilt, loathing, and pain reflected in the mighty warrior's aura. Such weight must weaken him.

"Hauk," Ragnar sighed. "'Tis terrible what happened, your loss, your daughter's loss, but 'tis more than merely losing her mother that turns your daughter wild."

"Aye, 'tis losing her brother, her uncle and aunt, her grandparents, and her mother that has turned her wild. Those ormstunga healers tortured my family instead of healing them." Hauk's voice was granite as he crossed arms over his chest.

"Friend," Ragnar said, "I do not ask this of you to torture you further. But I must try to save Ivarr. He seems to grow weaker each day, and I fear that he will follow his brother and sister into death before his second year. He shows the same signs." Ragnar glanced around toward his wife and spoke low. "I fear Aslaug will not survive the burial of another babe. Each time Ivarr drops his arm in weakness, she goes crazed with weeping."

Hauk's gaze softened even though his face remained in stone. "I'm sorry for that, Ragnar, but no woman can work magick to cure."

Drakkina spoke up. "This one can. She has great magick to heal. You can find her in the forests of Northumbria. A witch in the woods."

Hauk's gaze iced over again. "And the gods say that I must go. Me?"

Drakkina nodded.

"Why me?"

Drakkina clasped her hands before her and bowed. "I do not pretend to understand the gods' reasoning. I only bring the message."

Hauk snorted. "You pretend to understand the gods' reasoning all the time, Eldgrim."

Ragnar stood. "Hauk, if there's any chance…" He hesitated. "Any chance to save my boy and my Aslaug from hysteria…" He breathed deeply. "I must try. Think, if it were Dalla who grew weak, wouldn't you do anything to save her?"

"I tried running down that path, and it led to Hel. The pain is worse when you have hope."

The king stood straighter, donning the cloak of authority. "Then I order you, Hauk Geirson of Spring House, as your king whom you have sworn to defend and obey, to bring me the great healer from Northumbria."

Without missing a beat, Hauk bowed stiffly. "Then I leave at dawn."

"Take enough men to fill your longship. If you bring the woman back to me, you can keep all the riches you gather there. If she can save my son, the healer is worth more than her weight in gold and silver."

Hauk nodded abruptly and pivoted with smooth strength. He pointed to several warriors on the way out of the hall, and they followed.

Drakkina let out a long breath. Her job to bring Merewin and Hauk together would be harder than she'd anticipated. And she must bring them together to take the next step toward the ultimate goal. She'd find all of Gilla's daughters and unite them with their soul mates before the final battle to save the temporal worlds.

Drakkina watched Hauk stride off into the night beyond the open door. Couldn't the wise Earth Mother have picked a more pliable mate for Gilla's second daughter?

"He will do it?" she asked through the guþi's tight lips.

Ragnar sat. "Aye. He honors his responsibilities. But I hope the gods know what they are doing, sending him."

Drakkina couldn't agree more.

CHAPTER TWO

FIRE

Ironically, fertility rituals were Merewin's specialty. Ironic, because Merewin never wanted to have a child of her own. Children were nearly impossible to heal, and she hated failing.

But this couple wanted a bairn so badly that they had traveled through war-stricken Mercia to find help. The wind tugged at Merewin's long, heavy hair, and she pulled it to one side. She placed an ivory-colored moonstone in the woman's hand and a gray, smoky quartz crystal in the man's hand. She closed their fingers around each gem. "They will grow warm," she said.

They nodded in unison, their eyes wide with hope. Why they even wanted to bring a child into this turbulent life, Merewin couldn't fathom. With the Danes attacking the monasteries and villages along the coast, stealing their provisions and lives, a child was an added vulnerability. She exhaled long and forced a smile across her mouth.

"I feel it," the woman said, a look of wonder on her freckle-strewn face.

"I do too," the man said and clasped her empty hand with his. That was their own body heat since Merewin hadn't begun, but she let them think what they may.

A prickle spread across Merewin's back, making chill bumps rise on her arms. She let her gaze roam the cheery forest surrounding them. Soaring oaks stood rooted into the rich earth like protective sentries. A gentle stream warbled by, collecting in a deep, clear pool surrounded by sun-warmed boulders. The golden rays sliced down between the leaves onto the blue tent that waited for the couple. No eyes watched, even though at times Merewin thought she felt them. It seemed more so since Navlin had given up and died two months ago. *'Tis nothing.*

Merewin inhaled the soft earthy smell of the forest to center her concentration and then turned back to the couple. She held their fisted hands in each one of hers, closed her eyes, and wiggled her toes into the rich Northumbrian dirt. She took a deep breath and expelled the unease with an exhale. Calm, confident, she felt the power surge up through the earth beneath bare feet, power from the earth. It warmed her legs, womb, and chest, and radiated into her arms. The stones warmed as she funneled the earth's energy into the elements.

Merewin pushed more heat into the man's quartz. "Mother of all Earth, bless these people, bless the seed that creates life." She funneled more heat into the woman's moonstone and heard her soft gasp. "Bless this womb that holds and nourishes life." Merewin channeled a steady stream of power up through both of them. "Bless the union of this man and this woman, so that life may form between them." Merewin let the healing power in the rocks and her own magick infuse both people. It was draining to do both at once, but in this case, it made sense since they needed to be in harmony.

"Now," she looked at the woman, "ye will follow me into the stream. Roland, ye will wait for Eileen under the tent. When she comes to ye…" Merewin hesitated… "ye will enact what ye must do in the marriage bed."

Merewin stepped into the cool stream. "Come, the water will cleanse yer womb." She gestured to Eileen to follow. The churning water pulled heavily on the long thin drape of Merewin's robe around her calves.

"I cannot swim," Eileen whispered as they waded into the rippling water.

"I can," Merewin said confidently and grabbed the woman's arm. Navlin had taught her to swim. *'Tis foolish for people living near the ocean not to know how to stay afloat.* But Merewin was sure Navlin taught her in case any of the monks threw her in a pond for being a witch.

⬦◯⬦

The sun slanted through the trees on its evening descent as Merewin walked back toward the cottage. She pulled out her soaked skirts to dry as she meandered. The fertility ritual had proceeded as usual. If all went well under the blue tent, the couple would have a bairn in nine months. Merewin smiled to herself. The couple had looked so happy, so hopeful.

"Aye, they will have a wee bairn soon, a crying, spewing, helpless bairn." She shook her head. "No bairns for me."

Merewin's smile faded as an ache pushed at unbidden tears, burning and making her blink. She pictured a chubby little face. He was the only bairn she'd ever tried to heal—several years ago now. Still, the anguish pressed against her chest making it hard to catch a full breath. "Nay, I will never have a bairn."

Merewin caught a tear and flicked it to the ground, shaking away the babe's image. "Navlin, why did ye have to go?" Merewin let her voice rise into the surrounding oaks. The woman had been her mother since the day she'd dropped into Navlin's plea to the Earth Mother for a child. As Navlin lay dying, Merewin had tried to heal her, but the old woman didn't want to be healed. "Stubborn," Merewin mumbled and continued to walk.

That was the one thing Merewin hated about the magick her mother had given her. It needed the cooperation of the sick, hurt, or dying. Without consent, her powers were useless. She'd seen it when Drakkina had called Merewin to heal her sister, Serena. She'd seen it when trying to heal those in mourning who only wanted to join their spouse who had died. She ground her teeth thinking about it. Merewin hated to fail.

A chattering scampered up behind, and she smiled. *Ellette.* In a flash, the little pine marten climbed her skirts and huffed softly.

Merewin laughed. "Ye were asleep ye lazy beast, and I know how irritable ye are when ye're disturbed." She scratched along the creature's head, marveling at its softness.

Ellette pushed into her palm to increase the pressure. At least she had Ellette. Fifteen years, and the animal still ran and leapt like a kit. Merewin sighed into the fur, pulling support from the length of brown fluff. Her birth mother had sent the animal. If it weren't for Ellette, she would be completely alone now. Merewin sighed.

As rays of waning sun darted around the thick trunks of trees, Merewin glanced at the quietness. The hairs at her nape prickled, and she turned in a circle, her gaze ducking in and out of the many layers of trees and bushes. Someone or something watched. Was it the evil that had killed her birth mother? Surely those demons would attack, not stalk.

"If that's ye, Drakkina, show yerself or begone," she said softly into the silence. Merewin turned in another circle, catching the slight breeze in the wet skirts. She stopped. "Smoke." The word had barely left her lips when Merewin yanked her wet skirts to her knees and ran along the familiar path. Ellette gripped onto Merewin's shoulder beneath her hair.

Merewin slowed as she entered her clearing except... The leaf she'd left in the crack of her cottage door was gone, blown away. *The door's been opened*. And then reclosed.

Merewin unsheathed a thin dagger as the door opened again.

"Merewin of the Woods?" the man asked. She recognized the voice of one of the merchants in the nearby village and lowered her dagger.

"Kendal? What's happened?"

"'Tis my son," the man pointed toward the cottage. "He's hurt. The Danes have returned."

Holy Earth Mother! The Danes, the brutish raiders from the sea who looted, raped, and burned. "Is that why there's smoke in the air?"

Kendal nodded, and she strode inside, seeing the older child on the bed. Blessed be, he wasn't too young. Ellette leapt off to sit in her nest of wool and scraps by Merewin's bed. Merewin lit several lamps from the glowing coals in the hearth.

"The Danes attacked a child?" She was so tired of hearing the fearful tales of the looting raiders along their coast. King Eanred had paid them to leave, but they always returned with new threats. Perhaps they'd heard that Eanred had died, leaving the land in the care of his son, King Æthelred, who was always somewhere else when needed.

Kendal hesitated. "Nay, actually...the one Dane, a giant... He stopped the band before my lad."

Merewin placed a purple amethyst on the boy's head and pulled power up from the ground, through her, and into the stone.

Kendal continued. "My lad backed away and turned. It was then that the village attacked. A large rock caught my lad in mid-run. I dragged him out from the battle that started. And brought him here."

"The Danes are still at fault for coming here to steal and burn." Merewin closed her eyes and hovered her hands above the boy, spanning the entire body. She stopped at the head, feeling the trickle of blood flowing inside the boy's skull against the slippery folds of brain matter. The injury was serious; he would never wake on his own.

"Ye did the right thing bringing him to me," Merewin whispered and directed her full attention on stopping the slow trickle of blood inside the boy's head. Amethyst was very powerful for head injuries. Merewin moved the gem to focus and channel her gift.

The blood stopped, so she redirected the energy to the bruised tissue of the brain and its lining, making the clotted remains contract into tinier and tinier particles until they disappeared. Merewin breathed deeply and set one hand over the side of the boy's head. She channeled magick through the entire body, flooding it with energy to wake him.

"Jacob?" She heard Kendal whisper and opened her eyes.

The boy stared at her. She smiled. "There now, ye're fit again. No more jumping in front of Danes."

The boy tried to sit up, but his father held him in place.

"He's well now, Kendal. He can stand." Merewin returned her gem to the bag and gathered supplies in another bag: linen wraps, poultices, some foul-tasting but strong concoctions she brewed. If there were injured, she'd be needed. Navlin taught her how to disguise her powers in the healing nature of herbs and common sense. She turned back to Kendal as he hugged his son, who stared at her.

"Are ye well?" she asked. Merewin bent to study his soft brown eyes. They were round and large like a doe's eyes. He hadn't yet grown into them.

Jacob blinked several times. "Aye," he said. "But the Danes...the giant one who leads them..."

Merewin nodded while her mind raced to the other things she needed to gather before sneaking into town to heal the villagers.

"He spoke some of our words."

"Oh," she said and tried to hold on to her patience. There was so much to do.

"He asked about ye."

Merewin's attention snapped back to search Jacob's face. "About me?"

"What are ye talking about lad?" his father asked. "How would a Dane know Merewin of the Woods?"

The boy's wide eyes moved between his father and Merewin. She called upon the practiced patience she used with the sick. Inside, she wanted to shake him into telling her everything at once. "What did he say, exactly?" She enunciated with care.

"He asked if I knew where the healer in the woods lived."

Merewin's stomach tightened. "And what did ye answer?"

Jacob swallowed hard, then grinned. "I said that the Witch of the Woods was named Navlin, and that she died two moons past."

Kendal lowered his hand to his son's shoulder. "Clever lad."

Merewin continued to stare at him. "Aye, clever. Thank ye." But that didn't explain how the Dane knew about either of them, here tucked among the oaks of Northumbria. Navlin had been discreet and Merewin even more so. How would word of her or Navlin's healing reach the Danes? She looked again at Jacob as he prepared to leave with his father. "And what did he say when ye told him Navlin was dead?"

The boy frowned. "I don't know much of their words, but I think he said..." he scrunched his face in confusion. "I think he said 'good,' but that doesn't make sense. Why would he come looking for something and be happy that it wasn't here?"

"What will ye take in payment?" Kendal asked. "And don't say he was not hurt much. I saw the boulder that knocked him down and the blood under his eyelids is no longer."

Merewin met the man's gaze. "Where would they keep the injured from the fight today?"

"Don't go there. 'Tis too dangerous."

"My payment is the information." She squeezed his hand. "And yer silence about me and what I did for yer son."

He exhaled. "They were setting up a tent next to the stronghold. Most likely for the injured."

Merewin nodded. "Go carefully. May the Earth Mother bless yer family."

Kendal and Jacob headed out into the deepening night. The smell of woodsmoke lay heavy on the breeze. Merewin turned back to the comfortable little cottage. Ellette chattered from her nest. "It doesn't make sense, Ellette." Had they come all the way from Denmark for Navlin or her?

The unease of guilt lay in her stomach. If people had been injured because the Danes had come looking for her, she must help them.

Merewin stripped out of her damp skirts. She donned thin black trews that Navlin had sewn for her to wear when she helped the ill and injured at night. The material clung to her legs so that she could run fast and free. The black bodice fit snugly over her form, so no material would brush against anyone or anything, giving her away. She put on a pair of soft leather boots that tied up her legs. She could run silently in these without cutting her feet.

Merewin tied the bag of stones to her belt and tucked the dagger securely in its sheath. She plaited her long hair into a thick braid.

Ellette jumped onto Merewin's leg. The little pine marten skittered up her body to lie near her ear. Merewin threw a cloak around her shoulders in case she needed to blend in with the villagers.

"Not a sound, little one," Merewin whispered to her friend.

As she left the house, she touched the jade stone hanging on a cord. The stone had been the one to bring her to Navlin, and it still held the ability to translate any language. If the raiders spoke Danish, she would be able to understand them, and they would understand her. Although she didn't plan to speak to any of them.

Merewin ran through the shadows to reach the edge of the forest where flames licked dark paths along the encircling fence. Several warriors stalked around the perimeter. They looked every part the cruel giants she'd heard of and had hidden from in the past. *May demons feast on their souls.*

These grisly men, with long unkempt hair and beards, looked six feet tall. They walked with swords and battle-axes strapped to their massive forms. Their sweaty arms were slashed with ash from burning logs. When they drank, wet rivers coursed down their beards. They used the backs of filthy hands to wipe their lips. She could hear them belching and farting.

"Filthy murdering thieves," she whispered. Ellette squeaked softly in her ear and leapt from her shoulder. "Nay," she said under her breath as her friend skittered toward the men. Ellette was small for a pine marten and danced amongst the barbarians, distracting them. They made a game out of trying to squash her, but she was always an inch on the safe side. "Be careful, Ellette," Merewin whispered as she crept from shadow to shadow toward the tent.

Hauk Geirson silently lowered himself to the pallet next to his unconscious friend and brother-by-marriage, Gamel. Stretching his uninjured arm overhead, Hauk rolled the tiredness from his shoulder. He leaned over Gamal, pulling the blanket higher. "Bera will carve the skin from my body if I let you die." The only movement was the shallow rise and fall of Gamal's chest. "You must live to see your first born," Hauk said. His nephew or niece was due in about one moon.

Hauk exhaled and leaned back against a stump, his long legs crossed at the ankles. He could see the bruised lump evident above Gamal's ear where he'd been struck by a large rock.

"You mathkr," Hauk whispered from behind clenched teeth. "Don't you die, Gamal." Hauk checked Gamal's pulse. It was much too weak, but there was nothing he could do to help him. If his nephew or niece were deprived of a father, it would be Hauk's fault. He leaned back, closing his eyes. Yet another death to carry around his neck like a satchel of rocks.

For helvede. There was always death. How many men had he killed in his life of raiding? Raiding and exploring had been his escape in a world of binding responsibilities to country, king, and family. But he'd lost the lust to conquer. When had that happened? Hauk ran his hand down his face. He knew when it had happened. When he'd lost his family to death, when he'd lost his son. Toki couldn't have been much younger than the boy he'd spoken to earlier. Hauk had failed to keep Toki alive, and his failure had weakened him as a warrior.

No killing, unless necessary, he'd told his men before they'd landed. No destroying by fire either, as fire was never fully controlled. They'd come for the healer. His men could take property of the rich overlord, but they were to leave the locals alone. Perhaps find a willing woman to bed, but no killing, no raping, no burning. But the villagers had expected the worst and attacked.

The gods were angry. They'd taken his family, after all. Hauk inhaled the smoky air. In the smoke he could smell burning flesh from his memories of his family's funeral boats burning at sea. Their images blurred his sight.

Gamal wheezed as if he too coughed in the billowing smoke. Hauk leaned forward and adjusted his friend's head. Must he torch another boat with his sister's husband on it while she wailed from the shore, ripe with Gamal's child?

They should never have come to Northumbria for the healer, but Ragnar had ordered it. "She doesn't even live," he said to the unconscious Gamal. "Died of age." They would find her cottage in the woods before they left this fool's errand. He needed more than the words of a youth to tell Ragnar his miracle healer was dead. Hauk needed proof that the guþi's prediction was merely gossip spread through continual raids along the Northumbrian coast. Old Eldgrim was wrong. He'd said the healer was young, and yet she'd died of old age. The guþi had been wrong before when he'd recommended healers for his family.

Hauk leaned forward to peek under Gamal's eyelids. Blood flooded the whites. He shook his head. "Fool's errand." Hauk had been a fool before when he'd brought the healers to Spring House three years ago. Dalla had only been seven when her mother died, despite the assurances of the healers. Their false hope had broken Dalla's heart when death took her mother during the night.

Hauk squeezed the bridge of his nose and leaned back. He stilled when he detected a movement in the shadows at the back of the tent. Perhaps a brave wife or son came to rescue one of the fallen villagers. They were welcome to it. As the fallen littered the road before the stronghold, the villagers took to their homes or ran into the woods. Hauk had ordered all the injured to be tended regardless of who they were. Of his own men, only Gamal had been injured badly. Hauk had a gash along his arm where a sharp rock had sliced him, but he'd cleaned and sewn it, and it would heal.

The cloaked figure moved between the men on the ground with lithe grace. *A woman.* Her hood hid her face as she bent low. Was she stooped with age? As the figure knelt and touched the first man, Hauk watched the confidence of her movements, the strength of her hands. Hauk lowered his lids again as her head turned toward him. After several silent moments he cracked his eyelids open.

The woman had lowered her hood, and the torchlight fell on a face of finely formed features: high cheekbones, perfectly arched eyebrows gathered in concentration, full pouting lips. His gaze followed her braid down into the back of the cloak. How long was it? It looked dark. Would it be black like midnight or a warm brown? So different from the yellow hair of many in Denmark. Her arms looked slender and her fingers agile as she plucked objects from a bag and laid them on a man battered and sliced.

Hauk frowned. Who was the man she tended? Her lover? She placed her hands on the man's wound across his chest. Was she praying to their god? After several long moments, she pulled back the dressing his men had applied to the deep cut. The Saxon moved. Hauk nearly lurched when the man pushed up to sit. Only his honed discipline kept him still.

"Merewin?" the man rasped. The woman touched a finger to his mouth and pointed to the side of the dark tent. The man wasted no time in following her order to escape. As the man rolled under the tarp, Hauk shifted his weight to stand, to stop her, but she went to a second man. Hauk's gaze followed her from man to man as she patiently and quickly revived them. His men had reported that the injuries were serious, yet these men woke under her hands.

After all the villagers had fled the tent, the woman stood. Her cloak slipped off her shoulders. She was tall, very unlike the other Northumbrians. Hauk kept his eyes lowered and waited. He would stop her, question her. Exactly how was she doing what she was doing? And what was the true color of her hair?

Instead of following after the last villager, the woman walked toward him. She made no noise that he could discern. Her steps were silent as a shadow. Did she even breathe?

Hauk cracked his eyelids and saw her kneeling on the other side of Gamal. She slid her hands above Gamal's bruised temple, her eyes closed. After a moment, she sat back on her heels and dug deep into her pouch. Would she strike the man lying unconscious? Hauk was ready to grab her arm if she pulled a weapon. Instead, she produced several pebbles. She laid one at the center of Gamal's forehead and one on the pulse that beat in his throat. She placed one in his ear near the bruise.

Turning toward Hauk, she leaned over and placed a small stone on his head. He made certain not to move, but her attention returned to Gamal immediately.

Hauk watched, barely breathing, as she touched the stones on Gamal with her hands and bowed her head. She was so close that the faint smell of woods and flowers and spice came to him as he breathed. He had the irrational urge to bury his face in her hair.

She took two stones away but left the one on Gamal's head. Feeling the warrior's pulse, she nodded. Had she helped him? Impossible. Could she be the guþi's healer?

Hauk was about to move when the woman's warm fingers brushed against his arm where he had bound his slash. She spent a long time running her hands over his bandages before she untied the binding and slid it free. Her touch sparked through his body, waking all his senses.

She pulled some stones out and placed them along his arm. Her fingers were warm and soft against his skin. Hauk breathed in more of her scent. A piece of hair had come undone from her braid and fell across her forehead as she bent over him. It brushed his bare arm.

You are mine.

CHAPTER THREE
THE CHASE

The woman called Merewin touched the stones, staring at the gash, studying it. He felt a whisper of her breath on his skin.

"Why don't ye knit together?" Her accent was local, making the Danish words she spoke sound odd, foreign. Unnatural.

After several more moments of her teasing touch, Hauk opened his eyes. She was so absorbed with her work that she didn't look up. Hauk watched her choose different stones and start over. Finally she sat back on her heels.

"Bloody barbarian, ye must not want to heal." She plucked the stones off his arm. Without looking up at his face, she whipped the stone off of Gamal's forehead and dropped it into her bag. "Ye'll wake soon," she said to Gamal, "but yer friend with the slashed arm," she began and turned to Hauk.

Her words froze on her lips as her almond-shaped eyes locked with his. Hauk could almost see her mind measuring the distance to the tent wall and the severity of his wound she hadn't healed. Hauk shook his head, casting the stone from his head to the dirt.

"My wound will not stop me from catching you." The woman's eyes grew large. "You understand Danish," he stated, hoping for a response.

He didn't get one. The woman watched as if he were a wolf. "You're a healer," he said unable to completely keep the chill from his voice. She remained mute. "Your name is Merewin." The name felt good in his mouth. Much better than the word "healer." "Merewin," he repeated.

Silence. His frustration grew as they stared at one another waiting, waiting for one of them to move. Did she think she could escape him? *Mine.* The possessive thought coursed through him again. The fire burning on all three torches flared at once, illuminating her head. He reached to touch the slip of hair that fell along her cheek. She jerked her head back before he could catch it, leaving his hand in the air. "What color is your hair?"

His question startled her, but she continued to stare with no movement of her luscious lips.

Behind her Gamal groaned and pushed himself into a sitting position. "What happened?"

Gamal? He'd been near death. "How—?"

Fire ruptured through the slash in Hauk's arm. He stared down incredulously at a small dagger sticking out of the wound. The woman leapt up and ran to the side of the tent.

Hauk's roar filled the empty tent, and he yanked the dagger out of the fresh wound.

"Who is she?" Gamal asked, standing. The two guards rushed in and stood stunned, looking around at the once overflowing tent.

Hauk whipped the binding back around his freshly bleeding arm. "She's the healer," he said, tying it off with his teeth. "And she's getting away." Hauk tucked the dagger in his belt and leapt after her.

I stabbed him, I can't believe I stabbed him! Merewin dashed across the bridge. The guards out front had left their post, running into the tent. Merewin stretched long legs to their full stride, plunging into the woods along the familiar trail. Her limbs ached with exhaustion from all the healing, but fear pulsed through her muscles, adding strength. He wouldn't catch her through the woods. They were her woods; she knew them blind.

Merewin cursed softly as the clouds revealed a nearly full moon whose light slanted down between the leaves of the trees. She dodged a fallen pine, jumped behind a wide oak, and threw her back against it. As she stood listening past the drumming of her heart, she tried to slow her breaths. *Think. Don't panic.*

Merewin's chest heaved. She needed to focus, but all that kept popping into her head was the barbarian's intense gaze and the way he'd rolled her name across his tongue. *Merewin.* She had heard her name a thousand times, yet coming from him it sounded sensual, rough against soft skin. And he wanted to know the color of her hair. Why?

Breathe! She strained to listen. The sounds of the night were familiar as if nothing out of the ordinary were happening, as if she weren't hiding from a furious Danish raider, who also happened to be the most gloriously dangerous man she'd ever seen. His hair had been long, almost to his shoulders, and light-colored like many Danes. But unlike other barbarians, he didn't possess a long bushy beard. His beard was short, close-cropped, neat. She'd been able to see the firm set of his jaw behind it, the fine structure of his cheeks. The man's nose had been straight except for a small bump that showed it had been broken before. The scar on his forehead added more danger to his stare. Then there were his eyes.

They were intense, curious. They had widened when the dagger sliced into his wound. Yet he hadn't yelled or flinched at the pain, as if pain was a daily occurrence, something part of life like breathing.

Merewin still couldn't believe she had done it, injured someone. Her whole life revolved around healing, not hurting. *I had no choice.* Her gaze darted around the trees, her heart still pounding hard. *Must escape.* His look, the way he'd said her name, it all felt possessive. She shivered and wrapped shaking hands around her arms. A man like that could eat one up, body and soul. He would enslave her.

Merewin glanced around the silvery woods. There was too much light for hiding. Where should she go? The path to her cottage was too well-worn. *Not home.*

Snap.

Merewin held a breath and pressed herself against the tree. *Please be Ellette, please be Ellette.* Nothing more came, but instinct screamed at her to take flight.

Run! Her mind shrieked as she tried to fight the panic. It surged through her, renewing her strength. Merewin pushed off from the tree and broke into a run through the woods. Her tight-fitting clothes allowed her to dodge limbs and snarls as if she were naked.

Crack!

It came from behind, but she didn't dare turn to look. Instead, she concentrated on stretching her stride, leaping over fallen trees and narrow streams, ducking under limbs, and changing the course in hopes of losing whatever pursued.

After long minutes, an ache stitched in Merewin's side, and she slowed to a jog. Where exactly was she? She felt the constant tug to the west on the right, the tug that had pulled at her since she'd first landed in these woods. One day she would journey west to find the standing stones that were probably the source, once she escaped these bloody Danes if they were looking for her.

Merewin hesitated, scanning the terrain left to right. She had run beyond her cottage, past the blue fertility tent. Along the shore, there were rocky hills dotted with caves. She could hide in one of them until the raiders left. If they left.

She turned her gaze. *Cac!*

The barbarian's gaze locked with hers where he silently jogged to match her stride, not twenty paces behind. His arm was bandaged, but he didn't seem hindered by it. In fact, the bloody man didn't even look winded.

"Halt, Merewin," his voice washed over her, full of confidence. Was he actually smiling? "I've already caught you."

She took off like a deer flying from a wolf. Bounding over trees, under limbs, dodging between small places he wouldn't fit. These were her woods; she could lose him. But if that were true, how had he followed her? She pushed the traitorous thought from her mind and focused on the narrow paths.

She couldn't hear him, but she knew he was there, just as he had been the entire time. Had he matched her pace, waiting for her to tire? Clever, and she'd always thought the raiding Danes were dumb brutes.

Merewin's chest burned with each shallow breath. *Holy Mother!* She heard him now. His breath came out in deep, even huffs. His legs thumped against the leaf-littered ground with each stride. She heard him crash through the leaves of a low-hanging branch. He was close, too close. Merewin saw a large oak and headed toward it. His hand brushed her braid. She could hear his breath. *I'm almost to the tree.* As if the tree could somehow save her.

Fingers grabbed at the end of her hair. The warrior's large body slammed into her from behind. As they flew through the night air, he turned them together, so that they smacked the ground with him on the bottom. Still, the breath flew out from Merewin as she found herself staring at the moon through the tree limbs, her back against the man's hard chest. He tossed her to face him so that the tips of their noses touched. In one smooth roll, the Dane pinned her beneath, clasping both wrists in the hand of his good arm.

"I said, halt, Merewin," he ground out through white teeth.

Merewin twisted and kicked until the man pinned her legs and lowered his weight, limiting her breath. She was helpless as a mouse in the falcon's grasp.

"If you cease, I'll let you breathe. If you continue, I'll let you pass out."

Even though the thought of being insensible sounded alluring at the moment, she couldn't fight while unconscious. Merewin stopped struggling and stared him full in the eyes. She wouldn't retreat no matter what the man threatened.

As soon as she ceased her struggle, he lifted so she could inhale. Her chest heaved, her body begging for air. Stars danced before her eyes, but she refused to acknowledge them. The Dane stared down. He lowered his face, daring her to look away, but she wouldn't. His eyes were intense and full of curiosity.

He smiled then and raised one brow. "You're furious." Her only answer was a glower. "More furious than afraid, I think." He was so close. She smelled honey mead and pine. The Dane lowered his face to her hair. Was he sniffing her? He pulled back and with barely a grimace he moved his injured arm up to her face.

Merewin felt a pang of guilt at causing the injury, but it quickly vanished as she felt his erection bulge against the juncture of her legs. *I'll stab his wound again or lower still.*

He touched the side of her head gently, like a caress. Merewin turned her face toward his hand and bit down on the fleshy ball of his thumb.

The Dane wrenched back his hand and Merewin squeezed her eyes shut, waiting for him to strike. Instead, she heard a low chuckle. "Ferocious beastie. Do I need to gag you?"

Merewin's eyes blinked open.

He leaned over her face, his lower half still entrapping her body. "If you continue to poke holes in me, I will gag you, little fox." He stared and shook his head. "No more."

The Dane lifted his hand, and Merewin flinched briefly before she stilled. He moved toward her face, palm open, like a man trying to tame a wild animal.

Merewin frowned, putting all her searing anger into her gaze. She wasn't some wild animal to be gagged and tied. She wouldn't flinch or react. *He is nothing.* Merewin tried to turn inward, assessing her body and strength level. The healing of all those men and then the run had worn her out. Even if she could fight him, she had little left.

His hand touched the side of her head, gently but firmly. Moving down the length of her braid that lay to the side, he pulled the leather tie from the end and ran fingers through the tight weave, freeing it from the braid.

"Merewin," his voice sounded husky, like a soft caress, and Merewin's stomach flipped. This man was the enemy, someone who could use her and crush her when he was done. But the way he studied her felt different. He looked at her like a person and not something to be used.

"You haven't answered my question."

She looked blankly. What question was he talking about? The moonlight slicing down shadowed his face, though she knew he must be able to see her clearly. His hand fingered downward to release the curls.

"I asked you before. What color is your hair? It smells like," he hesitated, "wildflower and spice." Was the man muddled?

His face came close to hers again. Would he kiss her?

Merewin's heart pounded, and she realized she could move her leg. With a rush of energy, Merewin punched her knee upwards toward the bulge. Her aim was off, but she managed to surprise him enough that he reared back. She rolled out from under him.

She only had time to put feet beneath her when his vice-like hands grabbed her hips, lifting her easily from the ground as he stood. His strong fingers dug into the intimate bend that connected her legs to her hips. She kicked with her still-numb legs and threw her arms this way and that. *Bloody evil hair!* Its length tangled around her as she fought with all her strength.

"Be still, woman," he threatened, his voice cold as he turned and pushed her back up against the oak she'd been trying to reach. His good hand gripped her wrists and raised them up high. With a strap from his waist, he bound them. He lifted a dagger, her dagger, its blade still dark with his blood. Merewin closed her eyes as he stabbed it into the tree over her head, through the strap holding her wrists.

"'Tis dull enough," he said. "It might hold." Then, with a predatory stance, he slowly pushed his large body against her, pinning her between his rock-hard length and the thick oak. His legs braced against her own so that they could not move even an inch. Every inch of him threatened her.

He lowered his head, the gentleness she had glimpsed now gone. His breath came out warm against her lips, and his close-cropped beard brushed her chin. "If you're going to attack a man's stones, Merewin of the Woods, you'd best disable him. Otherwise you will only anger him beyond his self-control."

The threat was there. She'd pushed him too far. Merewin swallowed hard and closed her eyes to hide the fear she knew lurked behind them. He could kill her with her eyes closed. She wouldn't give him the satisfaction of watching her terror.

They stayed thus for several more moments, the sound of her rapid breathing heavy in her head. She tensed when she felt fingers touch her cheek, and she tried not to squeeze her eyes further shut.

"So brave," he complimented softly and brushed lips against hers.

Merewin's eyes snapped open at the touch. Fear reared up inside her, fed by the fact she couldn't move, couldn't escape. *Breathe. Think.* Would a man bent on rape bother with a gentle kiss?

His curious gaze searched. "Aye, brave and beautiful." He touched her parted lips with the tip of a finger.

Brave and beautiful? No one had ever spoken like that to her before. She was pinned to the tree, hands overhead, his hot, hard body pressed intimately against hers. He'd called her brave and beautiful. Was that true? Was she beautiful? She was so tired, not only from tonight, but from living alone. Tired with no one to help. How could someone think her brave when most of the time she felt frightened and alone?

His hands came to the sides of her face, and he tilted her head for a kiss. It was warm and deep, like hot cider running smooth into her belly.

The giant pulled back, and the cold night air hit her body. She blinked, her world righting itself. He stared for a moment, then frowned and turned away.

Merewin closed her eyes in mortification. She hadn't even tried to kick or move her face away. Oh no, she'd let him kiss her, had actually relaxed into the warmth of his body. Was she so needy of company that she'd fall into this Dane's arms? *Never!* The flush of anger, anger at herself, scorched her skin.

Cracking her eyes open, she saw him turn away. She pulled down on the blade in a sawing action and felt the thick leather move, but it didn't snap.

Merewin couldn't help but gaze down his broad shoulders and back to his muscular backside and thighs. He was magnificent, even if he was deadly and her enemy. A gentle heat winding down through her clashed with the ice of fear, making her shiver. Her reaction made no sense to her.

Foolish! She lifted her gaze to the trees, moving above with the night breeze. He was the enemy. It didn't matter if he thought she was brave and beautiful. She continued to move the leather shackle along the blade until he turned around.

His eyes had narrowed slightly, his jaw hard. "That was for mangling my stitches," he indicated his arm and pierced her with his stare.

She didn't dare close her eyes again, and she wouldn't look away. *No fear.* The stare became a challenge. *Do not blink.* She concentrated on the sting of her eyes instead of the way he seemed to look deep inside, down to her core as if he were trying to figure her out.

When he turned and sat down on a stump, Merewin exhaled softly in relief. She blinked long to clear her fuzzy sight.

"Now, some answers," he said. "I tire of listening to my own voice." He scanned the woods. "First, there's the color of your hair, woman." He studied her in the moonlight then glanced at his arm.

Merewin could see a spot of blood seeping through the binding. It would need to be re-stitched if her magick wouldn't work on him. And for chasing her down and pinning her to a tree, Merewin wasn't about to try again even if she were the one to rip open his stitches.

"I know your name is Merewin as I heard it spoken, but are you the fabled Witch of the Woods?" He yanked a long rag from his belt and added it to the first bandage, tying it off with a tug of his teeth. Standing, he began to pace before her. "You don't look like a witch, although you're wearing strange clothing." He stopped as if waiting for an answer. "Like a man's trousers but slim, close to your skin."

Merewin had no intention of answering. She didn't even know who he was. He had chased, tackled, kissed her against her will, and now had her pinned to a tree. Merewin pursed her lips tightly together.

"Mute? Nay. I heard you speak to the injured in the tent." He frowned and waited. He would be waiting a long time if he thought she would suddenly start answering questions. "You play tricks like other healers." His lips pulled back as if he'd eaten a rancid mushroom. The glare, more than his scars, turned his expression deadly. He stood tall. "Stubborn? Aye, you are." He moved to touch the wisp of hair that fell across her cheek but stopped. Perhaps he was afraid she'd bite him again, although Merewin couldn't imagine this brute being afraid of anything.

He paced around while she remained staring straight ahead. "I need to know if Navlin is the famous healer, and if she is truly dead." He paused for her to answer, but she didn't, and he continued. "The Witch of the Woods we have heard about in Denmark is young, so perhaps you are the healer I seek." He stopped and leveled his gaze with Merewin's. "If you are, my king has need of your services."

So he wanted more than her body and life. He wanted her magick. How had the Danes even heard about her?

The warrior ran his good hand through his tousled hair. "I know you can hear me, and I think you understand me."

She said nothing, but her eyes cursed him with every sharp glare.

"That's another trick, how you understand me. You speak your words with the same inflections as the villagers, but the words are mine, Danish."

She liked the way her silence irritated him.

The Dane snorted and walked back to sit on the stump. "Very well then. If you can't understand me, I guess I can say out loud what it is I plan to do with you." His gaze slid along her body stretched against the tree. "But first... Are you still a maid, then, dear Merewin?"

CHAPTER FOUR
STOLEN KISSES

Without a hint of a smile or frown or any expression the barbarian asked his question.

Merewin's heart thumped up into her throat, but she showed nothing but smoldering fury. She raised her gaze to stare off into moon shadowed forest.

"I think you might be a maiden from your kiss," he said.

She wanted to kick dirt in his face but stayed passive and leaned against the tree.

"Don't fret, Merewin of Northumbria. I don't rape like some warriors." He spit on the forest floor. "Those who take what isn't freely given are monsters who deserve to have their ballocks gnawed by rats. I only bed women who beg me to."

She opened her mouth to say she hadn't begged to be kissed but closed it again. He was trying to trick her into speaking. He couldn't win this contest of wills, but his assurance helped her breathing to even out.

"When you ask, I will teach you all you need to know. Starting with your mouth." His voice remained even, as if he were telling her how to saddle a horse or milk a goat.

Merewin's fingers tingled on the verge of numbness. She laced them together and looked to where he sat on the stump as if he had all the time in the world. He picked up one of the plentiful acorns between his fingers and then threw it at a tree.

Crack! They remained quiet while he picked up a few more, throwing them with exceptional aim in the dark forest.

Foolish pig. He was stronger and faster, but he didn't know how stubborn she could be. He was a stupid barbarian who didn't even have the courtesy to tell her his name.

Her anger made her glare natural. Although it didn't matter since the bloody barbarian kept his gaze elsewhere. *Look at me, ye demon. See how I glare at ye.* Thoughts screamed behind gritted teeth. She pulled against the leather binding and felt the knife cut a bit through it.

"I think..." he drew out "...first I will teach you how to kiss me, using that sweet mouth of yours." He tossed the acorn high up in the leaves and waited until it descended, thumping the ground next to him. "I will slip my tongue inside to stroke you and teach you to stroke me in return. I doubt you've kissed a man like that. 'Tis a mating of the mouths."

The man was mad. What were they doing out here in the forest?

He kept an even voice. "Then when I feel you lose yourself a bit, relaxing into me like before," he paused to glance at her for a brief second.

Daingead, was she still glaring when he looked?

"Then I will send shivers down you as I run my hot tongue along the sensitive line of your lovely neck, down to your perfect, round breasts."

Blessed Mother, he was talking about her breasts! *He doesn't rape, and I'll never ask him.* The reminder helped her stay calm.

"I will lick those lovely white mounds and tease them with my hands, my mouth, graze them with my teeth." His gaze raked her body stretched against the tree. "I will peel that cloth," he indicated her tight-fitting trousers, "from you."

Even more than his words, the gaze caused a rush of heat to wash down through her, suffusing her with a jittery feeling of languidness, like she could run a mile, but also wanted to lie down and stretch.

He brought his gaze back up to hers.

Holy Earth Mother. What horrid reaction was this?

"Aye, and you will like it. You will moan as I suckle you, my hands roaming down across your soft, hot skin until I find that lovely pelt between your legs." His look held hers, and she couldn't tear her gaze away. His sensual lips formed the words that promised pleasure she had never known. What was he doing to her?

"You will be slick and hot there." He swallowed and Merewin's breath hitched in time with her heart. "I know how to touch you to make you moan. All you have to do is ask."

She swallowed too, watching the way his gaze sank to the juncture of her legs revealed by the tight-fitting trews she wore. She felt naked and crossed her legs, pressing against the traitorous ache there.

"Since you cannot understand me, I am free to tell you what I will do to you next." He watched her and waited. "You will thrash beneath my fingers, thrusting your mound into my hand while I tease and excite your flesh."

Merewin's lips parted, and she realized her glare had melted away as his words invaded, shocked. She clamped her mouth shut. *Think of Navlin.*

She narrowed her gaze and stood tall, focusing her mind on Navlin's lined face.

"You will moan as I touch you, rub you, lick you."

Navlin's face kept melting away as Merewin's body registered the images of this powerful man pleasuring her. 'Twas true she was a virgin, but she had heard and even seen enough mating after her fertility rituals that she could imagine what he wanted to teach her.

Nay. I will not think of that. As she straightened up against the tree, her breasts thrust out more, and the Dane's gaze moved back to them.

Merewin felt a chill and her nipples hardened beneath his stare. How could he control her body without touching it? What dark magick was this? She looked away, out at the silver-washed trees standing like massive sentries. She needed to escape. This man was more dangerous than death.

His voice began again, low and insistent. "You will be wet and quivering as I run my hands and tongue down your body. You will moan my name, begging me to touch you."

Moan his name? She didn't even know his name. Merewin opened her mouth to rant about his rudeness, but then snapped it shut. She clenched her teeth. This was a mere game to make her talk and reveal that she understood his words, but she was too clever to fall for his tricks.

His voice was a rough whisper in the night. "I will memorize your scent and inhale it as we come together. We will move as one, your pleasure reaching higher than you could ever imagine."

Merewin closed her eyes against the look in his gaze. Raw hunger blazed, a hunger that made her tremble. Not with fear, Merewin wouldn't allow it. But with some other emotion that threatened to consume. So she shut it out, closed her eyes to him. But she couldn't shut out the sound of his deep voice. Passionate images of his body against her own penetrated her mind as he spoke of penetrating her aching body. She pressed back against the tree to still the wobbly feel of her legs.

"I'm a master at bringing out the heat in a female. I will do everything to make you quiver with pleasure."

She licked her drying lips, and his words ceased in mid description. Merewin opened her eyes to find him staring at her mouth, open desire changing his face to match the one in her mind, the one that loomed over her straining body. For a long moment he merely stared, and she noticed that his breath also came quicker. Was he as affected by his words as she? Her gaze dropped to his trews, to the very large bulge there. The sight made her clench. Would he come over to her, touch her and realize that his words had affected her? He'd said he didn't rape.

Without moving his eyes, he began again, his voice stronger. "Have you ever taken a man in your mouth, Merewin?" Merewin closed her eyes again. "Nay, probably not," his voice hardened, "and since you are mine now, I will be the only man you will touch."

Her eyes widened. She was his? When had that happened? Ridiculous. She wasn't his. She was no man's, and as soon as she escaped he would never see her again.

His voice softened again. "Once I bring you to your woman's joy, you will learn to take me in your sweet honey mouth."

Merewin's lips opened in shock as she was no longer able to control her reaction. She wasn't supposed to understand his words, but this was too much.

"But first I will taste you. I will lay you back and spread your long legs apart, baring your core, opening you first with my fingers," he bent his fingers. They were long, strong fingers. "Then when you are dripping, I will lower my mouth and..."

"My hair is brown," Merewin yelped, drowning out his words. "A medium shade of brown, perhaps with some lighter golden spots, I've been told." The Dane stopped. Daingead! She wanted to groan, but he'd probably think it was with lust. He had bloody won.

Merewin looked away while the words rolled out of her mouth. "Navlin was the Witch of the Woods. She raised me. She died two moons ago." She opened her eyes again. "And ye will tell me yer name, demon," she demanded with as much dignity she could pretend to have. "Now."

⬧◦⬧

Hauk Geirson stared at his captive. He had won this battle, but the look in her eyes—it was sad, embarrassed, self-loathing perhaps. Hauk always won, but this woman didn't know that. And somehow his victory felt bitter. No, he didn't assault women, not like some of his crew. But had he not done that to her with his words? What was this sinking feeling under his ribs? Remorse? Never. He had a mission, and it had been a tactic to make her talk, nothing more. And he hadn't harmed her body. Others may have tortured her, ravished her. He thrust the bitter feeling aside.

"I am called Hauk Geirson of Spring House, and I've journeyed from Denmark to find the famous healer from the woods of Northumbria." Regardless, he didn't like this look on her face, as if he'd crushed her spirit somehow. He much preferred her glares.

"But you can call me master," he said arrogantly and grinned when he saw the fire light her expression once more.

"I think I will call ye barbarian," she spat. "Release me. I have answered yer questions."

Hauk looked at her lips closely. "How is it that I hear you speak my language, but your lips form other words?"

"Magick."

Hauk felt his stomach tighten, and it had nothing to do with remorse. "There is no such thing. You're an illusionist."

"I am the daughter of a Wiccan priestess."

"Navlin."

"Nay, she found me. My birth mother was a powerful Wiccan priestess."

Hauk couldn't hide the anger that laced his words. "There are only false healers. There is no magick here in Midgard, only with the gods in Asgard." He had made that mistake before, believing tricksters claiming to be able to heal, offering false hope and deadly remedies. He'd been fooled before and lost nearly everyone he loved. Only Dalla and his sister remained. He wouldn't be tricked again. "You use illusions."

Merewin shrugged her shoulders. "Very well then, 'tis all an illusion that my lips form words native to Northumbria but ye hear the tongue of yer homeland," she said with obvious sarcasm.

Hauk snorted and pulled the dagger out of the tree. Her arms fell, and he saw a small grimace cross her features. He cupped her bound hands in his large ones and worked the blood back into each digit. With a quick slice of his own sharp knife, he snapped the strap.

She kept her gaze straight ahead, level with his chest. This woman was taller than most but still stood a head below him. She would match him well.

Several guttural shouts came from a distance behind them back toward the village. "Those would be my men searching for you." He felt her stiffen, but she didn't say anything. "Although I claim you, it would be better if they did not see you dressed," he paused and looked down her sleek length, "so tightly. Do you wear other clothes?"

Merewin pulled her hands back from him and crossed her arms over her breasts that were pushed upward by the hugging material. "Aye," she snapped. "I only wear these when I wish to run through the night without making a sound." She gestured behind him. "I have a cottage, back and slightly to the west."

Hauk turned and took her wrist. "Show me." She stood mute, staring at him with defiance.

Shouts came again, and her gaze shifted uneasily. The woman huffed and walked quickly through the moon shadows of gray and silver. The light touched her hair, gliding along the waves that fell to her waist. Her legs were incredibly long. No wonder she'd been difficult to catch. They led up to gently curving hips, perfect for a man's hands. *My hands.*

She was his by right for leading the mission. Ragnar only wanted her to heal his son. After she failed, Hauk would take her to his home, as a slave, a thrall. He wouldn't force her into his bed, but eventually she would come to it. He barely had to notice a woman to have her fall into his bed. They had all come willingly before. And this one was brave enough to help care for Dalla. It would restore calm at Spring House. Aye. He would have Merewin, and she couldn't quit when Dalla became troublesome and wild. By Odin, perhaps this had been a worthwhile mission after all.

The shadows were thick inside her cramped cottage. She refused to stir the fire to light and dressed in a dark corner. She emerged in the long skirts and modest bodice that he had seen on the village women. "Pack the black costume with your things. Perhaps you can run through the dark in Denmark." His humor fell on the floor before them.

"I'm not packing because I'm not going anywhere," she said firmly. She did have spirit. That would serve her well with Dalla.

"Aye, you're going to Denmark."

"For what reason?"

"King Ragnar Lothbrok has summoned you. 'Tis my mission to bring you there."

"Ye said he wanted the Witch of the Woods. She's dead."

"Ragnar needs a healer and was told the Witch of the Woods was young and living in Northumbria. I saw you in the tent." He frowned, thinking of what he'd seen. The injured villagers must not have been so bad off, but Gamal... Hauk cleared his throat. "You are the one."

"I said, I'm not going with ye." She brandished another long dirk that she'd drawn from a cupboard. The woman must have weapons hidden about. He took a step forward.

"Do not touch me, barbarian, else ye'll feel my blade again."

Her strong spirit would serve her well when winter covered Denmark. In one fluid motion, Hauk knocked the dirk to the floor and grabbed Merewin to him. She gasped as she hit his chest hard. He held her arms to her sides and bent his face so that they looked eye to eye in the dim light.

"If you keep trying to maim me, I will keep you tied." His face was purposely rigid and cruel. Better for her to understand and stop trying to escape. She'd only harm herself, something he wouldn't allow.

"You have no choice, Merewin. You're coming with me." He watched her swallow and felt a tremor run through her. He couldn't see the woman's face clearly, but her shoulders seemed to slump a little. He reached one hand up to touch her face, and she jerked it away.

"And if I come with ye, are ye going to," she stopped and turned her head as far from him as she could. Her voice was soft, "do what ye said out there? To me?" The undercurrent of fear was unnerving, and Hauk forced her chin back around with one finger. She looked him in the eye, the anger back in place. "Because if ye touch me like that, I'll kill ye," she said with venom.

Hauk didn't let go of her chin. He answered slowly, succinctly. "I will never take what isn't freely given. You have my word."

"Ye kissed me. That wasn't freely given."

"True." He nodded slowly. "I grant you the same thievery."

Her brows pinched in confusion, so he explained. "You can steal a kiss back from me. To make it fair."

She snorted softly. He liked the little sound, maybe because it didn't sound like fear.

"But I won't steal anything more than a kiss." He waited until she nodded and then let go.

With a cracking of wood, the door flew inward off its hinges. Hauk pulled Merewin into the protection of his chest then pushed her behind him. His wound shot fire through his arm as he hefted his war axe, but he ignored it.

Bjalki, one of his men, stalked into the cottage. Hauk kept his axe in place as the arrogant warrior brandished a torch.

"It was not barred, Bjalki." Hauk's tone was cold. This one irritated him, his brash ways, his desire to destroy without provocation. He played the part of leader because his sister was widow to the king's brother, but he hadn't earned the title.

"It is you, Hauk?" The fire came farther into the cottage.

"Aye, and I've found the healer. We're coming out. Back up." Hauk felt Merewin's fingers curl into the back of his leather vest. Lowering his axe, he reached behind him for Merewin's hand. It was cold, delicately boned. With all her bluster and stubbornness, she was fragile. Hauk pulled her into his side as they walked out into a group of ten of his men.

"Gamal, what are you doing out here? You should be resting," Hauk said.

Gamal pummeled his chest. "I'm fit enough to fight alongside Thor," he bragged, his easy smile in place. He ran a hand along the injured side of his head and looked at Merewin. He bowed slightly. "I send my thanks to you, healer."

Hauk felt Merewin bow her head. "My name is Merewin."

"The witch speaks our language," Bjalki said.

"Merewin was trained by the old Witch of the Woods," Hauk said irritated over the title. "The crone died two moons past. We'll take Merewin to Ragnar."

Bjalki lifted his torch higher into the night air, illuminating the circle. The men peered closely at her. Hauk watched Bjalki's gaze travel her length. Didn't the short wit see that she rested under his protection?

A lustful grin split along Bjalki's face and turned Hauk's irritation blacker still. Even with his one arm drained of full strength, Hauk could still hack through him. The woman was his, would be his thrall after she met with Ragnar.

Hauk dipped his axe down, swinging it back with enough momentum that it swung high over his head. With little effort he threw it to land a foot in front of the leering Bjalki and the others. Hauk pulled Merewin around in front of him. There was no time to explain to her what must be done, or why. His gaze took in her large eyes as he descended on her open mouth. She pushed her hands against his chest as he kissed her roughly, thoroughly until he heard Gamal laugh loudly behind him. Several others joined his brother-in-law, and Hauk released Merewin.

Her lips looked full, swollen from his kiss, parted and wet, and he was tempted to bend his head again. Shock changed to outrage, but before she could retaliate, he pulled her back up against his chest, pinning her arms to her sides.

"Merewin of Northumbria is under the protection of Hauk the Broad. She is taken in the name of King Ragnar. None shall touch her," Hauk proclaimed.

"Except you," Bjalki said, the slight sneer barely concealed.

"As is my right for leading this mission. I claim the woman," Hauk said, his gaze meeting first Bjalki and then slowly moving to the others who had been equally interested, some of them adjusting their cocks rising in their trousers.

Gamal stepped next to Hauk to face the men, his hand at his sword. "By law, 'tis Hauk's right."

Bjalki spit on the ground near Hauk's axe. "So be it. Let's return to the village. Mayhaps I can find a little woman to take back with me."

"Strip the stronghold, but leave the village in peace," Hauk commanded.

Bjalki shook his head. "You've become soft, Hauk the Broad." He turned to leave.

"If you wish a challenge, state it Bjalki."

Bjalki ignored Hauk and continued to stalk up the trail. Several men followed him while Gamal retrieved Hauk's axe.

"Loki rules him," Gamal said.

Hauk felt Merewin wiggle against him, and he eased his hold.

She turned to him. "That's two stolen kisses," she snapped.

Hauk ignored Gamal's raised eyebrows. His brother-in-law stepped away to talk to some of the others. Hauk kept his voice even. "I had to claim you, Merewin, for your safety."

"So I should be thanking ye for touching me again without my permission."

Hauk was tired. His arm ached, and if he didn't tend it soon, it would become tainted. His patience with Merewin's anger was thinning. His gaze turned cold as he looked down. "Aye, you should be thanking me, woman. I may not rape *helpless* women," he said, stressing the word, "but that one does." He indicated Bjalki.

Merewin held her ground, her chin high.

Hauk shrugged. "Feel free to steal two kisses from me. Now go grab what possessions you wish to bring. Gamal, stay with her. I need to tend this arm," his gaze narrowed at Merewin, "again." Hauk turned, dismissing Merewin.

"Hauk Geirson," her soft voice stopped him. She had said his name. If he ignored her, would she say it again? He waited. "Or Hauk the Broad."

He turned. "Just Hauk."

She glanced at his arm. "Even if my magick doesn't work on ye, I know the ways of traditional curing."

Her voice lacked the spitfire from before. It was humble. An apology? He doubted it. But perhaps it was gratitude as she realized what would have happened to her tonight if Bjalki had tracked her down instead of him.

A fierce chatter came from the deep woods behind the cottage as a small line of fluff darted straight for Merewin. As it leapt for her arm, Hauk caught it by the end of its tail.

"No, don't scare her, else she perfume ye," Merewin warned as she grabbed the flailing creature from his outstretched hand. "I'm sound, Ellette. Where have ye been?" The woman actually cuddled the small scrap of pelt, letting the animal nestle around the back of her neck, hiding in the thick mane.

Gamal laughed. "I think your little beastie there was perfuming," he used her word, "Ivan and Kieven out front, Hauk."

Merewin didn't say anything but scratched the little head. "Ellette comes with me," she said, her look daring him to contradict.

Hauk nodded, wondering when she'd decided to come willingly. His gaze followed the gentle sway of her hips into the cottage.

CHAPTER FIVE
FAREWELL GIFT

The day dawned like any other late summer day with misty rays of sunlight streaking through the trees. Merewin glanced around the small home she'd grown up in with Navlin and pushed at a tear that wouldn't obey her will. Nay, this morning was different. She was being forced from her home, captured by Danes, and headed toward a foreign land as a thrall. Merewin pushed her hair behind her ears and bent to pick up part of the door that had been shattered. She placed it against the wall and looked up at the rafters.

"Will I ever be here again?" Disobedient tears washed out her eyes and down her cheeks. She brushed at them.

Someone coughed at the doorway, but Merewin kept her back to it.

"We leave soon," Gamal said. His voice was quiet, respectful, making Merewin's eyes blur again. She held up a hand to indicate she'd heard, and he moved away.

Merewin wandered around the cottage gathering her herbal tinctures and salves, her stones, and small clay phials of powdered herbs. She wrapped them in the black clothing she'd worn the night before, not because Hauk had ordered her to bring it, she told herself. She might need the dark clothes to escape in this foreign Denmark.

Escape: the thought of it checked her tears and straightened her spine. *No more tears*, she could almost hear Navlin's gentle rebuke.

"One must always look forward," Merewin whispered Navlin's favorite saying. She stepped to the hearth and kicked at the gray charred wood. "Oh Navlin, what am I going to do?" A tingling sensation itched at the birthmark on her inner thigh, and she absently rubbed it.

"She's not in the chimney, child," a woman's familiar voice came from the other side of the cottage.

"Ahh!" Merewin screamed and spun around.

The misty form of an ageless woman in flowing iridescent robes stood near the door. A dragonfly-shaped pendant hung low on a golden chain around her neck. Barely visible dragonflies darted and hovered. *Drakkina*. Merewin instantly dropped the bag on her foot and yelped.

Gamal shoved through the doorway brandishing a sword. "Healer?" His gaze searched the room, but he looked right past Drakkina.

"He can't see or hear me, Merewin," Drakkina said. "Not unless I wish it, which I do not."

"What is it, Merewin?" Gamal asked again as he scanned the room.

Merewin smiled timidly, her hand at her chest, and shook her head. "Nothing Gamal. Ellette," she said, and gestured to her pet, who sat on the bed baring sharp little teeth at the spirit woman.

Ellette chattered loudly until Drakkina put her finger to her lips, and the little pine marten stopped. So, her pet could see the Wiccan priestess.

"Ellette startled me. I'm almost finished."

Gamal's gaze circled the room once more before he nodded and walked back out.

"What are ye doing here?" Merewin whispered. The last time she'd seen Drakkina, the crone had the stain of blood and the stench of trickery on her.

"I said I would visit," Drakkina said. "When the time was right."

Merewin caught her breath. "Can ye help me? Help me escape these barbarians?" She flapped a hand toward the door.

Drakkina frowned. "Why?"

"They're forcing me to leave here, leave my home."

"As you should."

"Ye're mad, crone."

"'Tis your fate, Merewin. You're meant to go with the Danes, with Hauk Geirson."

Merewin felt nails digging into palms and forced herself to unclench her hands. "How do ye know this? Did ye have a part in sending him after me?" Merewin's low voice barely hinted at the storm building inside. Her stomach twisted, coiled like her nerves, ready to strike.

"He's your soul mate, and as a child of Gilla, you must be connected to him." The apparition waved in and out of solid form. Light blue eyes shone nearly white, giving an unearthly look. Lines marked her face, making her appear wise, yet her proud stature gave the appearance of youthful strength. Hands came before her as if in prayer, the dragonflies making a halo about her head. "You two must be together, blessed by the Earth Mother."

But this was no saintly angel as the monks liked to paint in their tomes. This meddling witch had sent Hauk and his men to hunt her. "Ye meddlesome witch," Merewin said through gritted teeth.

"You should thank me," Drakkina continued with a wink. "He's quite breathtaking to look upon, and he smells nice too. Something not easily found in your century."

Merewin whipped a clay pot toward the apparition. The vessel flew through her form to smash against the far wall.

Gamal jumped inside again, his gaze ricocheting from wall to wall, sword drawn.

"Ellette knocked over a pot," Merewin snapped before she could calm herself enough to act like nothing was amiss. Gamal studied her, his brows furrowed, and grunted before stepping back out.

As soon as Merewin saw him reach the edge of the clearing she turned, keeping her voice a low hiss. "I can't believe ye sent a hoard of barbarians after me, to steal me away from my home."

Drakkina opened her arms to indicate the cramped little cottage. "Away from all this?" she said sarcastically.

"Aye, 'tis my home."

"What is left here for you? Nothing. You're all alone." Drakkina pinched her lips. "The woman who raised you rests with the Earth Mother, the villagers revere your power but, out of reverence, they fear you. The monks threaten to burn you. What is so important here that you can't leave it?"

Merewin stared at Drakkina. Her words rang eerily true, and Merewin felt her face flush. She narrowed her gaze. "I don't like being forced, captured against my will, enslaved, and at the mercy of strangers. Strangers who steal, murder, and rape."

Drakkina tilted her head to the side as if inspecting. "Yes, you have your father's pride, now don't you." She crinkled her eyes, judging. The old crone held a bent finger out toward Merewin. "Be wary of that trait, child. Too much pride is dangerous. It can trick you into believing you're always right, and when you find out you're wrong it can destroy you. It killed your father."

"Why didn't ye save him, or even defend us when the demons came?"

Drakkina sighed, her voice gentle. "I was not aware, was not even in your time when the attacks came. I found the ruins in the aftermath."

Anger faded from Merewin's voice as sorrow weakened her words. "My mother," she swallowed, "she died after she sent me away, didn't she?"

Drakkina stared back. "Yes, she did."

Merewin closed her eyes and leaned against the hearth. "I should have stayed to help her."

"You would have died, too. The demons stole your father's powers. Even at full strength your mother could not stand against Semiazaz and his pack of demons for long. Once her protective wards fell, the evil descended. If you and your sisters had been there, the demons would have killed you all and stolen all Gilla's powers." Drakkina's face was grim.

"Why did they attack?"

"They want the combined magick of your parents to be powerful enough to rip the temporal web," Drakkina said while absently clutching the pendant. "Once that falls, all times will crush into each other, creating mass chaos. People will be brought back to life only to die again, gruesome, suffocating deaths. Those who survive will live under the rule of evil so perverse they will seek their own deaths until this world is barren."

Drakkina rubbed at her forehead. "If you had stayed with your mother, the demons would now have one of Gilla's threads of power." She met Merewin's gaze. "She sent you and your siblings away. In so doing, she could die in peace knowing you were safe. And for the time being, so was the world."

"Do these demons hunt me now?"

"Doubtful. They can traverse time, but Gilla hid you all quite well. More likely they wait until you come back together to conquer them."

"My sisters and me?"

Drakkina nodded.

Merewin stood to pace. "Then if we stay apart, stay hidden, the temporal web you talk about should be safe." She waved her hands. "No need for this 'find yer soul mate' nonsense."

Drakkina shook her head, causing the dragonflies that had landed on her silvery hair to alight. "The demons grow stronger as they learn how to use your father's powers. Eventually they will learn to shatter the web. The world needs all Gilla's children and their soul mates to stop them."

Merewin stared into the empty space in the room, while all the information filtered through her mind. Absently she asked, "and my sisters? They are well?"

"I've only tracked down Serena and you so far. She and Keenan Maclean had their first child, a lad they named William."

Merewin smiled. "A wee boy?" Merewin sat down on the edge of her small bed. "I would like to see them."

Drakkina's image faded a bit. "They won't live on this plane for another nine hundred years." Drakkina shrugged. "Perhaps we can manage a temporal visit after you and Hauk are married."

"The bloody hell I'll marry the—"

Hauk barged into the cottage, his body walking through Drakkina's form. He stood still, his battle-axe hefted and ready to strike. Merewin watched with wide eyes as the wisps of Drakkina dissipated like scattered smoke. Hauk shook himself, and Merewin noticed gooseflesh all along his bare arms.

"Someone is here." He rotated quickly until his blue gaze fell upon Merewin. "Who is in here with you?"

"Ellette," she said softly. "Only me and Ellette."

"Who were you talking to?"

"Ye listened?"

"Who, Merewin?"

Merewin pointed at her little pet that sniffed around Hauk's leather boots. "I spoke to Ellette."

Hauk eyed her pet. "You were having a conversation."

"Did you hear another voice besides mine?"

He frowned. "I'm not certain."

"Then I must have been speaking to Ellette," she said, as if reaching a conclusion.

Two strides led him to where she stood by the bed. His massive frame obscured the rest of the cottage from her sight. His knees brushed her legs as he loomed. The man's mass should have frightened her, and her heart did start to race. But it wasn't fear that rushed through her blood. Excitement perhaps? A preparation for battle?

"You're not a good liar, Merewin. Who did you speak with?"

Merewin huffed, sat abruptly and leaned back on her hands so that she stared up at him, letting her hair fall behind her to pool on the bed. "Very well then, I was speaking with the spirit of a great Wiccan priestess whose body faded into mist when ye barged through her." She paused and stared. "She's here to save the world, and she's the one who manipulated events so that ye would come to find me."

She left out the part about them being soul mates. It didn't seem like the right moment to mention it. "Oh, and she says ye smell nice," Merewin added with a sarcastic lilt to her voice. She took in a long, exaggerated sniff, and detected the fresh scent of mint mixed with leather.

He continued to stare, brow furrowed.

"Actually, ye do smell good. Why is that?"

His words came slowly as if his mind churned through something completely different. "My mother had an aversion to the smell of humanity. She taught us to bathe every day and freshen our breath by chewing mint that she grew." He paused. "A Wiccan priestess?"

"Aye," she answered. "I chew mint when I have an upset stomach." She continued in her half-horizontal position to stare up at him while he held her gaze staring down.

"And she appeared here and then vanished?" he asked. "When I walked through her?"

Merewin nodded. "Magick," she whispered and smiled mischievously.

Hauk snorted and spun on his heel. "We leave now. Follow me or I will carry you."

Merewin breathed deeply to slow her racing heart. Was it wise to bait a barbarian? He had promised not to take what wasn't given, but she'd be wise not to tempt his word. Merewin grabbed her bag and wool cloak and followed him out the door. She wouldn't stand the humiliation of being carried.

Ellette jumped on her skirts, skittered up her body, and curled into a ball at the nape of her neck. Her usual traveling spot.

Back in the village, the full contingent of Danes waited to march back to their longship by the sea. Most of the homes remained barred. Nervous eyes peeked out of an occasional crack.

She walked stiffly along the line of men, her chin held high. She would never let them see fear in her, nor the sadness she felt at leaving the closest thing she had to a home. Perhaps Drakkina was right about her not fitting in here, but it was familiar. Even if she didn't feel kinship with these people, she was content with them. They revered her healing powers, and now they watched through cracks at her humiliation as the raiders led her away. At least Hauk had allowed her to walk without chains or ropes.

The Danes carried treasures from the king's stronghold: gold and silver plates and drinking goblets, jewelry, and fine cloth. The new king, Æthelred, would be furious when he returned to find his fortress stripped.

Merewin stepped in line with the rest of the treasure. As she turned to follow the path down to the sea, she heard a door bang open and a startled cry. She looked back to see Kendal's son sprinting toward her. Kendal raced after him, and the boy's mother clutched her apron in the doorway. Merewin turned and Kendal's son jumped in front.

"Ye need to go back to yer home, Jacob."

"I will," he said and swallowed nervously as his gaze wandered down the line of frowning warriors. "They're taking ye away?"

Hauk walked up near them, but he wouldn't be able to understand the youth's words, only hers.

"Aye," she said calmly. "They have someone who needs my healing, a king in fact."

Jacob raised his eyebrows. "They did come for ye."

"So it seems."

Jacob held out a small bag. "I gathered these for ye to take...when I heard."

Merewin took the bag and spilled small, capped acorns into her open palm. "Acorns?"

"From around yer cottage. In case there are no great oaks where they take ye. I thought ye could plant these and one day have yer own grove, like back here."

Tears burned behind Merewin's eyes. She drew a ragged, deep breath before she could find her voice and smiled past the blurred vision. "I thank ye, Jacob. I've never received such a thoughtful gift before."

He blushed.

Merewin tucked the precious gift into her bag while Jacob jogged back to his family. What sadness to realize that she did have friends here, only when it came time to leave. Merewin turned back to the path, tilted her chin upwards so the tears could not flow out of her eyes. They would just run down the back of her throat. The taste of regret was bitter.

She heard heavy footsteps, and Hauk came to walk beside her.

"Acorns?" he asked.

She stared straight ahead, trudging on, step after step even though her legs felt numb. "To start my own grove of oaks where ye take me, so I can have a little bit of my home with me." She kept her voice strong, until the end when it dipped, giving her away.

"Ye grieve leaving here?"

Merewin snapped her watery gaze up to him. "Aye." She glared and then turned back to the path ahead.

"Then we will plant them when we reach Denmark," he said with a nod and walked up ahead, leaving her alone to grieve.

⚬

It would take a day and a half to cross the sea to Denmark if the wind stayed with them. Hauk watched Merewin where she sat clasping her seat at the dragonhead prow of the ship. He stood at the tiller in the stern, steadying the massive back oar that controlled the direction they moved. They flew along the waves a few degrees off due east as the wind filled the rectangular, striped sail. His men sat relaxed, joking and polishing their treasures. When the wind died down, which she always did, they would row. But now they rested.

Gamal stood beside him. "You took no treasure for yourself?"

"Nay, I have no need," Hauk answered, his gaze followed the snapping ends of Merewin's golden-brown hair. She'd been right. There were gold strands like honey woven into the deep brown mix.

Gamal laughed. "There is always a need for treasure, friend." Gamal handed him a delicate gold chain. "For Dalla then. You know women always want a little gift to make up for your absence."

Hauk smiled wryly at Gamal. "Thank you. How could I forget little Dalla."

Gamal laughed out loud. "How indeed. She has a bit of Loki in her heart, I fear." It would have been an insult from anyone else, but Gamal's easy smile and true affection for his niece made the truth easier to swallow. Hauk nodded. "Aye, she has spirit."

Merewin kept her face to the brisk wind. She would burn her delicate skin that way if she weren't careful.

Gamal spoke softly. "Perhaps your mind rests on someone closer at hand?"

"She is but a mission," Hauk said without thought.

"Hmm..." Gamal said, staring at Merewin's straight back. "A nicely displayed mission."

Hauk turned narrowed eyes to Gamal. The man was, after all, married to Hauk's pregnant sister. But only laughter lurked in Gamal's gaze, no lust or wandering thoughts.

"Of course, nothing is more beautiful than my Bera," Gamal countered Hauk's glare.

Hauk grunted and turned back to the view. "She will freeze up there, or burn her face in the wind," Hauk said. "Take some furs up there. Warn her of the risk."

Gamal grabbed some pelts and kicked at the outstretched legs of the crew as he walked toward Merewin.

Hauk watched as Gamal stood with her, totally at ease. She even turned to smile at him.

Gamal was completely in love with his sister and therefore safe. Still, Hauk frowned. Merewin would never offer him a relaxed smile, not when she blamed him for stealing her away.

Gamal helped her wrap several long, stitched furs around her, tucking in her hair and bringing the covering up around her face. Now she'd be sheltered from the elements and the leers of his men. It was his duty to protect her and bring her safely to Ragnar.

As Hauk predicted, the wind died on the second day. Stagnation sat upon the water, warning of a possible storm ahead. The men took up their oars and rowed, their built muscles used to the exercise.

Life on a longship was cramped, cold, and often treacherous. Hauk didn't mind the discomfort, for he'd grown up alongside his father, uncles, and brother on the narrow decks of ships. However, for a woman used to earth beneath her feet, and quite a bit of solitude and privacy, the trip must be distressing.

Merewin snapped at one of his men for coming too close. "I curse yer pintle will shrivel and fall off." She then made a sign with her hands that made Knud's eyes widen, his cupped hand pressed over his cock as he backed away. Most of the men seemed to hover toward the stern of the ship when they weren't tied to their oars. Away from Merewin. She might be slight, but her tongue and cold stare could slice through a warrior. They believed she had some otherworldly magick. Hauk knew better. There was no magick in the world of man.

Hauk ordered them to stop when the mist off the ocean obscured the fading glow of the setting sun. Clouds covered the expanse of sky shielding the stars. Without stars or sun, there would be no way to navigate. Hauk frowned as he sucked in the heavy air. Aye, a storm was growing. He glanced toward the prow head where Merewin leaned against the side of the boat, watching the fog engulf them.

Gamal and his cousin, Svein, wove their way to Hauk while the others dispersed with rations of cooked venison, bread, and vegetables prepared in Northumbria. Through the dense cloud, he saw Merewin eat some bread and cheese that Gamal had brought to her earlier.

Gamal crossed his arms before Hauk and inhaled. "The air is heavy."

Hauk nodded. "A storm comes." He watched the woman stare out at the mist. "I must get Merewin to Ragnar safely."

"We can't row in this," Svein said, waving his hands before his face, swirling the mist.

"There's nothing to guide us," Gamal agreed.

In the still water, over the sound of men chewing, Merewin's voice floated in on the moving fog. "I can guide ye."

CHAPTER SIX
SACRIFICE TO THE SEA

With her soundless tread, Merewin looked like a goddess from Asgard walking out of the mist. She stopped directly in front of Hauk and looked up, her face framed by fur. "I always know where west is." She raised her arm straight and pointed behind. "West." She windmilled an arm forward to point in the opposite direction. "So that would be east. If ye want to travel slightly south of that..." She moved her finger a bit to the right.

They stared at her in the darkness. When no one spoke, she lowered her hand. "Or we can sit here waiting for the sun." She turned to head back to the prow where a carved dragonhead stared outward as if seeking land.

"How do you know where west lies?" Hauk asked.

She turned her face to him. "Magick."

Hauk snorted loudly and several men laughed around their food. She taunted him with that word. Would she if she knew his past?

Merewin began to melt once again into the dark mist.

"Wait," Gamal said and turned to Hauk. "I feel a storm, too. If she can help—"

"By steering us all over the sea?" Hauk said. He would not be made a fool of again.

Gamal lowered his voice. "Hauk, I know you hate magick in any sense, don't trust it. If I were you, I wouldn't either. But she healed my head somehow. I don't know the how of it, but I know that I was hurt, and now I'm not. Perhaps she knows something that will help us. I would get back to Bera and our child."

Hauk watched the misty form of Merewin looking out at the dark nothing around them. "If you know how to steer us, what stops you from steering us back to Northumbria?"

"I thought of that," she said, her voice even. "But once we arrived, I would have to go through this miserable voyage all over again from the beginning. Nay, I want to get off this freezing, rocking log." The men laughed, several quite loud, but she ignored them. "Even if that means we're in Denmark. As long as my feet touch earth."

A bit of the fur around her face moved, and her weasel stuck its nose in the air. It chattered and hissed as if agreeing.

"Fine, woman, prove your powers," Hauk said and handed the tiller off to Gamal. "You will tell Gamal how to steer slightly south of east." As she walked up past him, her arm brushed his. He felt the contact course down into the pit of his hard stomach.

Hauk looked to Gamal. "I row," he growled, not caring how bad-tempered he sounded, and found a seat far from Merewin's softly directing voice.

The dead calm followed them through the night. The fog rose off the surface of the water, as if the water breathed smoke. Hauk worked his muscles, conditioned from long rows, through the black of night.

Usually there were stars glittering overhead, a gentle breeze to wick the sweat from his brow, strong voices belting out rhythmic songs of conquest to the beat of the small animal-skin drum they took turns hitting. Tonight, only the drum sounded to keep the men in rhythm together.

Hauk knew they were moving, but the sensation of being suspended in an eternal otherworldly cloud was chilling. The men felt it, too. Their silence, broken only by the slice of the oars through the water in time to the steady drumbeat, added to the unnatural feel. It was nights like this that spurred tales of serpents and falling off the edge of the world.

Merewin's voice floated to him, correcting Gamal at the tiller every so often. If it weren't for the feel of a storm, he would have anchored for the night, waiting for the edge of the sun to guide them from a horizon. But a storm at sea in the black of night meant death. So there was no option but to blindly row, hopefully toward land.

A rotation of two men began and proceeded through the night, allowing two at a time to rest their muscles and capture a few minutes of sleep. His turn at rest came hours later. He passed the oar to Svein, stretched his arms overhead, and walked back to the tiller. Merewin sat on a box of treasure, eyes half closed. He almost thought her asleep, but she suddenly pointed slightly to the left and the tillerman pushed the tiller a bit in response.

Merewin looked drained, like one of Dalla's woolen dolls that couldn't sit exactly upright without a spine. Exhaustion shrouded her like the murky fog. He knew she hadn't slept much the night before they left. Although he'd allowed her to stay in her cottage after tending and rewrapping his arm, he'd heard her throughout the night, pacing across the wooden floor.

She had slept fitfully at the prow head last night, and now she forced herself to stay awake as their guide throughout another night. A mortal woman couldn't possibly be that strong.

"Merewin, take your leave," he said. She didn't respond. He bent down so his face was level with hers. "You'll lose consciousness from fatigue. We all must rest, so must you."

She didn't bother to open eyes. "And let ye row off course? Not while there's breath left in me. I wish to touch land again."

He smiled and clapped his hand over her knee, engulfing it. She opened her eyes more. "You will touch land again Merewin. I will hold the tiller steady while you rest for half an hour."

She frowned at him. "If I wake to find myself on the shores of Mercia, I'm staying there."

"I agree with your terms, woman." He took the tiller, looping a strap around it on both sides, adjusting it when she pointed once more before lowering to the deck floor. He heard her even breaths within seconds. Hauk was glad he'd strapped the tiller to keep the ship straight and steady as the waves began to swell. Swirls of mist undulated like thick serpents, no longer stagnant. A breeze picked up, tearing through it, only for it to reform. Aye, she would need her rest, because the storm barreled toward them. He peered out through the moving fog. Somewhere out there Denmark waited.

Long hours of watching the mist, listening to the drumbeat for the rowers, and lack of sleep played on Hauk's senses. This was why he told his men not to look out at the water, because imagined sea creatures could grow fear in a warrior's heart. Hauk didn't believe in anything fantastical though. Magick and otherworldly creatures belonged with the gods, not here in Midgard with men. He ignored the mist that looked like rising tentacles and hovering clouds that resembled the backs of sea monsters.

'Twas hard to find the rising sun through the murk, but the blackness melted gradually to gray. Hauk turned in each direction, bracing himself as the deck pitched one way and then the other. He watched the spot where the sea should meet the sky. Which direction lightened quicker? It should be the one nearly before him if their course were true. The swells chopped against the sides of the boat, sending up spray. *By the gods, let the sun rise before me.* The ship pitched and heaved in the increasing waves.

"By the Earth Mother," Merewin groaned as she pushed up from the planks. Her shadowed face turned toward him. "That's right. I'm in Hell." Her voice was pained as if she felt sick.

"Are we still headed east?" he asked above the shouts of his men as they put their remaining strength into their oars. Every one of them must pull hard to control the ship in the tossing sea. Hauk didn't worry about them. He'd trained most of them himself. He did worry about the woman hunkered down before him. She turned to stare out at the angry gray air and dark waves.

"Aye, east, but adjust slightly to the left."

Hauk unlashed the tiller and moved it slightly left.

Merewin stood and immediately fell against him as the ship rocked hard.

She turned her face up, and his stomach seized. Fear, raw and unspoken, reflected in her eyes. Hauk pulled her closer, shielding her in his one good arm while the other steadied the tiller. He had never before feared the ocean. He respected it, honored it, but he saw it as a challenge, something to make him stronger or take him to Valhalla. Either way, it did not matter.

True, if he died, Dalla would mourn, but she would live with his sister. Perhaps she would be better without him anyway. But the fear in Merewin's gaze snapped something inside him, something that made his stomach turn. He was suddenly vulnerable. Her life was his responsibility, and she was delicate, fragile, and very much afraid.

He leaned down toward her ear, trying not to slam his head into hers as the sea pitched and heaved beneath them. "Can you swim, Merewin?"

He felt her stiffen, and she nodded with jerky hesitation. "I've never swum in the ocean, but I know how to swim in a river or pond."

"In case we take on water, I needed to know." He tried to dispel the growing panic on her face. "But we should be there soon. We've rowed all night. We may not be able to see it, but Denmark lies somewhere close."

She ducked her head against his chest to shield it from the pelting rain.

Gamal fought his way across the slippery deck to them. "Perhaps we should give Odin a sacrifice, appease the gods with our treasure?"

Hauk looked to Gamal. His sister's mate wasn't afraid, being seasoned as well, but he had a babe on the way, his first, and he wanted to reach land.

"Feel free to offer your treasure to the sea," Hauk yelled against the wind. "I'm holding onto mine."

Gamal laughed and caught himself from falling into Hauk and Merewin.

Hauk watched through the gray light as several men dumped gold goblets and spoons over the side of the ship and continued to row.

The rain pelted down like small rocks. Hauk strapped Merewin to him and tied himself to the base of the tiller. To be swept over in this fury was certain death.

Gamal took Hauk's rotation at the oars so Hauk could continue to steer with Merewin strapped to his side. His stitched arm throbbed after the grueling night, but he ignored it. He felt the warm spreading of blood under his soaked tunic.

Merewin would complain that she had to sew it again, but it couldn't be helped. Odin was furious, and the men's offerings hadn't appeased him. Instead, the ocean seemed infuriated.

Bjalki came to stand near Hauk. "Perhaps Odin needs a blood sacrifice to release our lives from this storm."

Hauk stared at him. "And you're volunteering, Bjalki."

Bjalki frowned and glanced at Merewin braced where she stood against Hauk.

Hauk's stare filled with cold, calm promise, promise that Bjalki would die in the sea before he allowed anyone to throw Merewin into the jaws of the ocean.

Bjalki stared back. Was the mathkr accepting the challenge?

Blood pumped through Hauk, warming him. He would relish this.

"Land," Gamal yelled from the bow of the ship.

"Land ahead."

Hauk continued to stare at Bjalki until the warrior turned his hawk-nosed face toward Gamal.

Land. A gray strip appeared and disappeared ahead of them in the shifting fog and washing rain. As they neared, he could see trees spiking tall along the rocky coast. A torch burned bright under a covered rock outcropping. A beacon. He squeezed Merewin. Not only had she found land, she'd found Denmark.

Merewin looked up at him. He smiled, water dripping from his hair and face. A drop dripped from the tip of his nose onto her forehead, making her blink. "Land is ahead," Hauk said, "and it seems to be Denmark."

Hope lit her eyes, and she tried to turn in his arms, but the lashings held her to him.

"You won't have to swim today," he said and loosened the straps to allow her to turn into the wind and rain as the men pushed hard to reach the shore with the increased tempo from the drum.

They landed north of Esbjerg. Horses were provided for some of the men, some doubling up on the larger geldings. It was at least an hour's ride south to Ribe. Hauk and half the crew would stay with the longship to row it south to port once the storm blew out. The others chose to ride through the storm to Ribe where Ragnar waited.

"I'll take the healer to the king," Svein called from his horse, his red hair darkened by the rain.

Hauk watched the man's appreciative gaze run over Merewin. She still seemed weak and fragile standing near him, her eyes trained on the ground. The fur hood was soaked, and escaped tendrils of her hair lay plastered against her chest. A tremor of cold shook her shoulders every few seconds.

"Nay," Hauk said and pulled her against the warmth of his body. "She needs to rest and get dry and warm."

"I can keep her warm against me," Svein urged, making Hauk wonder at the young warrior's intent. The man was a cousin of Gamal's, but he'd spent time talking with Merewin during the trip. Perhaps he was foolish enough to think he could take Hauk's treasure.

"I care for what's mine," Hauk said.

Svein gave a curt nod, his look lingering on Merewin for a second before he turned his mount.

Hauk paid an elderly merchant several Northumbrian gold pieces for the use of an empty cottage on the edge of the small town. He lifted Merewin's sodden body and jogged with her through the muddy streets until he found the small shack. The rest of the warriors would find shelter in the town's common longhouse. Merewin needed privacy and quiet. Otherwise, illness would overtake her, something he knew too well.

Hauk laid her on the floor, wrapped her in blankets and started a fire with the flint and wool the old man had given him with the cottage. After the sparks caught on the dry tinder, he crouched before her, touching her cheek. "Merewin, we need to get you dry." She nodded, though her eyes remained closed, dark lashes against the paleness of her skin. Thank Odin she was still responsive.

She licked her dry lips. "I need to...have privacy, to relieve myself."

Hauk leaned back on his heels as she opened her eyes and pushed up into a sitting position. The woman was strong.

She frowned, her gaze circling the one-room shelter. "Ye may be able to piss over the side of a longship, but I cannot, will not." She tried to stand, the weight of her wet clothes making her sway. "I still feel the sway of that blasted boat."

Hauk's frown relaxed. "You can use the woods outside. Don't try to escape," he added as she walked slowly to the door. Rain slanted in, wetting the dry floor. She looked back at him as if he were insane.

"I'm freezing, hungry, exhausted, and in a strange land. Rest easy that I'll return to yer fire," she said with a toss of her limp hand at the flames.

Smart woman. Hauk shook out two blankets near the fire to warm. Several minutes later, she returned, going directly to the fire. If possible, she was even more sodden. Merewin swayed as she held her hands out to the dancing flames. He needed to get her dry.

Hauk managed to strip the heavy clothing down to her smock before she noticed. "Cease." She crossed her arms over her chest to hide the peaked nipples from his view.

By the gods. Her curves were bared to his gaze as the wet linen stuck to her. He tried to ignore the bountiful beauty of her, but his body reacted without his consent. He shifted in his stance and adjusted the tightness that strained against his wet trews. "You need to get dry, woman, before illness takes you." The gruffness of his words made him sound surly.

She looked at him, weighing his words. "I'll remove my smock." She pointed to the back corner. "Ye can stand over there with yer back to me."

By Odin. She would soon be his thrall once he gained her from Ragnar. Yet she ordered *him*. He should be allowed to see her naked. He opened his mouth to say as much, then saw her shoulders tremble as a cool breeze flew around the drafty room. *Hā!* He shut his mouth. She would stay in her wet smock if he didn't comply. And unlike men like Bjalki, Hauk would never rip it from her.

He'd been taught to conquer, but Hauk also honored the souls of all living creatures, including a woman deluded into thinking she possessed magick. *She healed Gamal.*

Hauk ignored the thought and stomped off to the back of the small room, grabbing a dry blanket. Stripping away his tunic, he inspected his freshly opened arm. He'd clean it and bind it a third time.

Hauk froze as he heard Merewin remove her smock. The soaked fabric sucked against her skin. "Ye're wet too," she said, making him almost turn, but then Hauk heard her little weasel squeak. He'd forgotten about the wee beast that had remained tucked under Merewin's hair through the journey on the sea.

He heard the dry rub of the blanket covering her like his body craved to do. Was her skin as silky pale as her face? Like moonlight splashing against her? Her nipples would be peaked from the chill. Even though she belonged to him, he would hear her breathless pleas before he took her. The thought of what that would sound like nearly made him groan.

Several more minutes passed without a sound. "Finished?"

No reply. He turned.

Merewin lay on her side, her body wrapped in the blanket, curled inward so that her entire front faced the heat of the fire. Eyelashes lay against the deep circles of exhaustion. Breath came in even draws through gently parted lips. Sleep had claimed her, curling around her soft form like a protective lover.

Hauk stared a long time as the firelight flickered across her delicate features. Damp tendrils of hair dried into curls around her face. How had she healed Gamal? How had she guided them home through the fog?

"Magick." He frowned, his back rigid. "Illusions." But she only answered with a whispered sigh. He walked to the door of the hut to stare out at the slanting rain. He would never allow illusions and false promises to harm his family again.

CHAPTER SEVEN
TO SLEEP & DREAM

"Must we get back on the boat?" Merewin murmured as she stood on the rocky shore before the longship, holding her damp boots. "The world has finally stopped swaying beneath my feet."

The Danes continued to board, but Gamal stopped beside her. "We must bring Hauk's ship to its home mooring, plus 'tis the swiftest way to Ribe."

"I'm in no hurry."

Gamal laughed. "Nay, I suppose you aren't." He squeezed her hand, catching her attention. "You have my thanks from me and my family for healing me on your land, especially when you knew me only as the enemy. I still don't know how you did it."

She said nothing but felt his gaze upon her. Gamal lowered his voice. "If I thought you were walking into danger, I would stay you."

"I'm a captive, Gamal," she turned to look directly at his merry blue eyes. "Danger ensnares me."

"You're a thrall," he corrected.

"Which means slave."

"Not exactly." Gamal waved his hand toward Hauk. "And you are a thrall to Hauk the Broad."

"And this should make me feel safe?" Merewin followed his gesture to Hauk, who stood surveying the loading. His broad shoulders and height were intimidating, but so far he hadn't as much as bruised her. He'd tricked her to speak with his heated descriptions, but then swore he wouldn't act on them unless she asked. She snorted softly at the thought but still followed the lines of his body. Everything about the man marked him as a warrior and leader, from his mounding biceps to his honed war axe. It was his strength, though, that had protected her from the fiend Bjalki.

Gamal offered Merewin his arm and pulled her toward the wooden side of the longship sitting in the shallow water off the coast. "Hauk protects what's his to the death." Gamal's tone was serious, sending a chill to tickle the back of her neck where Ellette lay like a wrap. Merewin stopped with Gamal on the pebbles before the lapping water touched the tips of her bare toes.

She looked down at the cold water at the same time Gamal did. He bent to pick her up, his arm brushing the backs of her knees, when another set of strong arms lifted her into the air.

Hauk pulled her away so suddenly that Gamal nearly fell into the water. "I'll carry her aboard." Hauk's voice thrummed through Merewin, the deep cadence hammering with the beat of her heart. Merewin held onto his shoulders as he sloshed through the shin-deep water.

Ellette peeked out and hissed. "Ellette doesn't like the idea of boarding any more than I do," Merewin said above the thudding in her ears. Could he hear her heart beating so hard?

"Your pet is free to remain here," Hauk said.

Ellette ducked behind Merewin's hair, her long tail hanging down over her shoulder. "She goes where I go, always has."

Hauk grunted and placed her on the deck near his station at the tiller.

"Haven't ye ever had a pet, a faithful animal that followed ye wherever ye went?"

"Nay," he paused and looked out at the men climbing aboard. "But I've seen it before. My son had a dog, followed him everywhere."

"Yer son?" Merewin couldn't hold back the question nor the horror in her tone. "Ye're married?"

Hauk glanced back. Sadness edged the deep blue of his eyes. "Nay, not anymore."

Relief surged through Merewin, not that it mattered much if he was married. But he'd kissed her. Betraying a wife would have made him even more the barbarian.

"I'm sorry that ye lost her." She sat on a crate strapped to the side of the hull.

His gaze followed her, turning cold. "I wed to seal an alliance for my father. 'Twas not a love match." He turned away and walked to the side of the boat to help the other men push long poles against the rocks to move the ship away from the rocky shore.

Merewin held the seat as the vessel rocked. Hauk pulled the lines of the rectangular sail, making his biceps contract into muscular mounds. Even with the gash in one arm, his strength was great, frightening if he were an enemy. She frowned. *He is the enemy.* He was the master and she the captive. Once recovered from the voyage, she would plan an escape. Curse Drakkina and her plans to bring Merewin to Denmark, bring her to this Dane. The thought caused her head to ache, and she rubbed it.

As the sails filled with wind, the boat moved along swiftly. Hauk wove his way back to the tiller. He stood a long time in silence. Merewin watched him adjust the course to keep the boat along the land, headed south.

"We will land in Ribe before the sun reaches its zenith," he said. She rested her aching head in her hands.

After nearly an hour of silence and continual swaying, Gamal walked over to her. "You look green, Merewin."

"I've been watching to see if I need to hold her head over the side," Hauk said from his stance at the tiller. Merewin glared at him, and Gamal laughed.

"I've never been to sea before, and I don't like it," she defended.

"You didn't purge during the storm," Gamal said.

She shook her head. "I was nauseous the entire trip and vomited once during the night over the side."

"You're a healer. Can't you heal yourself?" Gamal asked.

Merewin tilted her head in a long stretch from one shoulder to the other. "Somewhat, but the energy I use to heal can weaken me. If I'm the one I'm healing, I can weaken myself more than help. 'Tis best to suffer," she said.

Ellette peeked out her nose out from her hair, chattering like she agreed. Seeing her friend hale and safe, Merewin smiled for the first time in days. Her mother had sent the small animal with her, and she'd remained with her through the years. She was smaller than a common pine marten and had outlived them by three times over, showing no signs of aging. *You won't be alone.* Her mother's words warmed her.

Gamal stared at her. "Whew, you could win Odin's love with that smile, woman," he said, causing Hauk's face to swivel toward her.

Her smile faded despite Gamal's friendly gaze. She was still their prisoner no matter how she was treated.

"You should smile more," Gamal said and looked to Hauk. "You may need to claim her again once we reach port, very publicly."

The thought of the last claiming made Merewin's heart pick up pace again. She looked back out over the gentle swells and pushed her hair to one side, lifting the weight to lighten the strain on her neck. Ellette ran down her arm and scampered under Merewin's skirts.

Gamal reached out a hand to lift her skirts. "Your pet likes to hide."

Hauk stepped in front of Gamal's hand like a sentry, a mountain in trousers that hugged his arse. The wool followed the tapered muscles down his thick, long legs. She looked away when she realized she was perusing him.

Gamal mumbled an apology for nearly lifting up her skirts and walked off to check on the crew. Hauk stepped back to the tiller, and the silence ensued.

She sighed into the salty air. "What is wrong with this king of yers that he must send all the way to Northumbria for a healer?"

"Ragnar is not ill; 'tis his son."

Merewin's stomach contracted. She curled her fingers around the edge of the hull, waiting for the meager ration she'd eaten that morning to come back up. It took her several long breaths of cool air before she could speak. "A son?" Her voice was a little higher in pitch than normal.

Hauk turned his stormy blue eyes to her. "You are ill."

She waved his concern off. "How old is this son?" The answer was more important than her volatile stomach.

He continued to watch her. "He's about halfway to his second year. Will you need to purge?"

Merewin's eyes grew round as panic consumed her. She nodded helplessly as Hauk grabbed her, rotating her so that she faced away from him. In one step he held the top of her body over the side of the vessel.

Merewin threw up into the frothy sea. *Bloody foking hell.* The king had sent for her to heal a young child. Something she couldn't do.

The throbbing in her head peaked violently, and Merewin pushed her forehead into cupped hands. What could she do? These brutal warriors had been careful with her, had treated her with more respect than she would have imagined after the tales of their cruelty to victims and prisoners. But that was when they thought she could help their king's son. What would happen when they discovered she couldn't?

Merewin vaguely heard Gamal's concerned words nearby. She drew in a gulp of air. It burned on the way down, and she coughed at the smooth planks. They would take her to the king, parade her before him with promises of healing, of saving his little boy. Hope and relief would flood the king's gaze, like when she'd reassured the parents of the eighteen-month-old bairn who had fallen from his papa's horse. And then her healing stones would remain cold beneath her touch. The magick would hit against an invisible layer of apathy, and the child would still die. She would fail. Again.

The tips of leather boots obscured the strangely comforting view of the worn planks in her line of sight.

"Merewin." Hauk's calm voice ordered her to look at him. "Merewin," he said again as he squatted.

She coughed and swallowed, the ache in her throat growing worse. Merewin's nose began to drip. She sniffed.

He touched her hair, gently, and a warm flutter uncurled in her stomach, easing the terror that lay knotted there. "Look up." It wasn't the order that made her lift her head, but the strength in the words, a strength that sounded like protection. She was his, as Gamal had said. And for the first time, that didn't sound so bad. Not if he could protect her when she failed.

She looked up and wiped her nose with the back of her hand. Their gazes locked. So much strength filled those gray-blue eyes that some of it flowed back into her. She breathed deeply. "Hauk, I cannot heal the king's son," she whispered above the rush of wind.

He held no expression. "You admit that you're not a healer, that your magick is an illusion." His lips tightened.

She shook her head and glanced to the side where Gamal also crouched. "Nay, I am a healer, but I cannot heal children, not young ones anyway." Gamal and Hauk glanced at each other, their brows furrowed. "If ye bring me to yer king to heal his son," she swallowed against the burn, "I will fail."

Gamal moved closer because her words were so soft. He handed her a leather pouch of weak ale. "But you healed me. I know you did. The men said I should never have woken from the hit I took." He touched his temple. "I don't even have a bruise now."

The drink soothed her burning throat. She had to explain, at least to these two. They were her only chance of survival. If she could convince them, maybe they would give her a means of escape.

"I can only heal those who want to be healed. If a person loses the will to live, my magick can't counter that. Not if they want to move on to the Earth Mother's embrace."

"The Earth Mother?" Gamal asked. "Is that the god the little monks talk about?"

Merewin almost smiled at the reference. "I don't know for certain. Navlin thought that their Father God and the Earth Mother might be the same. One power that created all life, that holds the spirit after the body has died."

"You think Ragnar's son will not want to live?" Hauk said bringing her gaze back to him.

"'Tis not that he doesn't want to live. 'Tis that he doesn't know yet that he's supposed to fight for life." The two men stared.

She clasped her hands together, squeezing. "Have ye ever seen a young child fall underwater, completely?" She looked between them.

"Your cousin's child, Gamal. Didn't her babe fall in a pond when you visited last summer?"

"Aye, little Devon fell in."

"How old is Devon?" she asked.

"He had only begun to walk. A year perhaps."

Merewin nodded, her voice gaining strength. "Did he thrash around fighting to reach the surface?"

Gamal shook his head. "Nay, he merely lay under the surface, his eyes wide. He moved a bit, but didn't thrash. It was very clear water, and I saw him before I scooped him up."

"Exactly," Merewin rubbed her temples. "He thought that suddenly being underwater where he couldn't breathe was part of life, he didn't yet know to fight. A young child remembers the bliss of being in the Earth Mother's arms before being born into this cold, wet, cruel world. If he thinks he's supposed to go back, he won't fight against it."

The two men continued to watch her.

"Bairns aren't old enough to forget Her touch. Once they do, they don't accept what is happening to them, like yer cousin's son did when he was suddenly under water. Once they are old enough to forget what 'tis like before they were thrust into this world, they fight to stay in it, no longer accepting that they're supposed to return."

Gamal plopped down on the deck, sitting to face her. "So—"

"I can't heal a child so young." Merewin lowered her gaze back to Hauk's boots. "I have failed before."

Looking down made her nose drip again, and she wiped it. Her throat hurt, her nose tickled, and her head ached. On top of everything else, she was becoming ill. She sneezed loudly.

Leather boots thumped on the deck as another warrior approached. "What's going on with the healer?" 'Twas the warrior with the solid chin that he liked to stroke. Merewin had heard him called Garrett.

Gamal exhaled. "She can't heal Ivarr—"

"Can't heal him in the condition we've put her in with this voyage," Hauk finished.

As if brought on by Hauk's words, Merewin sneezed again.

"Our healer has taken the ague," Hauk said and draped a woolen blanket around her shoulders.

"Aye," Gamal said nodding vigorously. "The cold long nights made her ill. She needs to get well before she can heal Ivarr."

Garrett chuckled. "Our healer needs healing? Can't she do that to herself."

"Nay," Gamal said, wrinkling his nose. "Something about the energy to heal would make her weaker. She suffers like the rest of us."

"Best keep her warm," Garrett said. "Wouldn't do to have her die before she's of use to the king."

Merewin snuggled into the scratchy woven blanket. Perhaps that was her best option. To die and go to the Earth Mother before being forced to fail again. If she would die anyway, best that it happened before another child died in her arms.

With the surrender of someone not willing to fight, she slumped, nearly falling off the seat. Hauk caught her and slowly lowered her to the deck. His warm, rough hand cupped her forehead. "You don't feel overly hot, but you need rest."

She looked up into his face. "I can't heal him, please don't take me to heal him. I will fail." Her words were even. Emotion took too much strength, strength she no longer possessed.

He frowned. "Rest now."

Merewin closed her eyes to the feel of Hauk tucking the blanket around her body, the salt wind brushing against her face.

Nightmarish images swirled through Merewin's unconscious mind. Visions of her mother being torn apart by leather-winged demons, the accusatory yelling of the parents of the boy who had died, an image of a ferocious dragon holding a limp Dane child. "Nay," Merewin mumbled against the tormenting scenes.

Shh, child. A calm voice overrode the cries and curses. *Your body needs to rest peacefully to fight your illness.* Drakkina's misty face smiled at her in another dream.

"Too tired to fight," Merewin murmured.

Drakkina's face pinched. *Stop talking nonsense, Merewin. You don't give up. You're a fighter, like your mother.*

What did fighting bring her? Death. In the dream, Merewin opened her eyes to see the spirit woman sitting cross-legged on the deck of the longship across from her.

Your mother died saving her children. She never stopped fighting for your lives. If you give your life up so easily, then she died in vain. Didn't you say these same words to your sister, Serena? Remember!

Drakkina's presence became larger in Merewin's mind, almost taking up every little space. *If you die, your mother will have failed, Merewin.* The crone's face moved closer, her brows rising. *You will live and get well and do what you must to save this world, because that is what your mother died for.*

Merewin cried in her dream. "Màthair."

She is in the Earth Mother's embrace, but you can't go to her yet. You must fight to keep this world from falling apart. And the first step is to live!

Merewin rubbed her legs together where her dragonfly birthmark itched on her skin.

Now let yourself fall into a deep slumber, child. I will guard your dreams. Drakkina shook her head. *Dragons and demons,* she muttered and looked directly into Merewin's unconscious mind. *Sleep, deep,* she said, and Merewin found herself relaxing into the bottomless depths of comforting darkness.

CHAPTER EIGHT
WARRIOR MOTHER

The smell was intoxicating. The sea mixed with wild wind, leather, and something else warm, exciting. Hauk, full of power, stared at Merewin intensely like he had when he'd pinned her to the tree back home. A stare full of raw promises of pleasure. He caught her against him. She didn't struggle but wound her hands in his long, wavy hair that blew around him in wild disarray. He lowered his mouth to hers and...

"Merewin," his voice penetrated her dream. But how could he be kissing her and talking at the same time? "Wake, woman." The dream Hauk dissolved as Merewin turned her head.

She flicked open her eyes against the high sun. Hauk's face was so close to her that she almost continued the dream and kissed him, but the foul taste in her mouth stopped her. Merewin tried to swallow but her tongue stuck to the roof of her mouth. She groaned.

"Time to go, Merewin," he said and gently hoisted her up to sit. Hauk pushed a leather flask into her hand. "Drink, to clear your throat."

Merewin took a sip of honey mead past the rawness. The honey soothed it.

Hauk handed her a small chunk of cheese and a hard piece of flat bread. "You've gone all day without food. You won't get well that way." He watched her until she took a small nibble.

At the taste of the tangy cheese, her stomach growled, remembering the instinct to nourish the body. Hauk nodded and stood as she chewed the bread.

Merewin took another drink and then noticed that they were the only two on the longship. Where had all the warriors gone? And the boat was blessedly still.

She peeked over the side. People in colorful garments and furs strode and meandered along the wooden wharf, talking, laughing, arguing. A group of old men with long beards sat at a table outside a building with a sign hanging from a chain. It had a carved illustration of the large drinking vessels that sat before each of them. They gestured wildly at one another with fierce frowns until suddenly they broke into laughter.

Long tables lined the wharf where fishermen sold fish, mussels, and oysters. Children ran after large, shaggy dogs while others carried buckets and sacks that looked too heavy for their bent backs. Thatched houses sat back from the wooden walkways leading around the water's edge. Piers jutted off the walkways, one of them leading to Hauk's ship.

"Where are we?" Merewin asked.

Hauk looked up from gathering the food remains together. "Ribe." She looked back out over the steady throng of people. "'Tis one of the great Danish ports and where King Ragnar and his followers have taken up residence."

"Ye live here?"

He nodded in a direction. "Some ways out through the forests to the east, away from the smells of humanity." Merewin wrinkled her nose at the odors floating with the breeze.

"Where are all the others?" She indicated the empty ship. "Gamal?"

Hauk leaned down and hoisted her up under both elbows until she found her feet. "They left hours ago when we docked."

"Hours ago?" she looked overhead at the sun that was beginning to descend.

Hauk handed her a soft cloth. "For your face," he said indicating that she had some dirt or worse on her face.

Her eyes widened, and she snatched the cloth from him, turning to scrub at her face. Had she drooled? Not that it mattered. Her goal was to look as ugly as possible to keep any of these murdering barbarians away from her.

"We stayed behind?" she asked, setting the rag down and fingering through her hair even though she didn't care if she looked wild.

"You were asleep, and you needed it to get over your illness."

Merewin glanced at him. "You stayed so..." she paused, "I could sleep?" She blinked, astounded.

"But now we must go," he said and picked her up easily, one arm under her legs and the other behind her back.

She stiffened. They would bring her to the sick child. "Let me down."

"Your boots are still damp, so I will carry you to Ragnar's hall."

Merewin twisted, pushing against his hard chest. "I said put me down."

Hauk let her slide to the planks, her worry and anger making it easier to ignore the effect of that slide down his body. "I am ill," she said and took the boots dangling from his fingers. "I don't wish to cause rampant illness. Think of that. Would it do to bring a healer who infects the whole royal court with the ague?"

He looked hard at her and spoke low. "'Tis not my choice, Merewin. A runner came right before I woke you. Despite your illness, Ragnar demands the presence of the healer. Ivarr must not be doing well."

"The child's name is Ivarr? And he's the bloody king's son?"

Hauk stared hard at her. "Your eyes are green like sunny forest moss."

Merewin's eyes opened wider. Was that a complement?

"But fear lurks there, more fear than when the sea tried to swallow us." He frowned like she was at fault for the emotion.

"I can't heal him, Hauk." She shook her head. "He's too young. Your king will...be angry."

His face darkened enough that she took a step back. It was easy to imagine this huge warrior breaking a body in half or knocking someone's soul right out of them with a punch. "You belong to me, Merewin. When you fail, I will protect you."

The reminder of her low status raked against Merewin's nerves, straightening her spine. She'd always been in charge of herself. She wasn't property no matter what this ogre thought. She glared at him. "I belong to no man."

Hauk grinned. "Good, I prefer your anger to your fear, woman. Adds spark to the green."

Before Merewin could snap a retort, Hauk leaned in and kissed her, briskly, possessively. Surprise held her rooted while warmth flooded down to her toes in one huge rush.

"Hauk!" a woman yelled.

Hauk pulled away but smiled down at Merewin's wide eyes. He ran hands through her waist-length hair, working fingers through the tangles.

"Hauk! What's taking you so long?"

He glanced behind Merewin, and she smacked him in the chest. Her hand made a thumping sound. "I hope ye catch my ague," Merewin said.

Hauk chuckled, the sound like a rumble.

"Is this the healer?"

Merewin turned to see a tall woman, full with child, lumbering toward them. She waved but frowned with impatience, causing the family resemblance to jump out.

She stopped next to Hauk's arm and grabbed it for balance. She spoke to Hauk but smiled at Merewin. "Svein and Gamal told me what she did for him, how Gamal would have died or remained asleep if she hadn't healed him, and that she healed all the villagers, too." The woman barely took a breath as the words poured out.

Luckily the Danes had allowed Merewin to keep the stone around her neck. It warmed as it aided Merewin to understand the fast roll of foreign words.

"I must thank her." The pregnant woman smiled with teary eyes. "If Gamal had died you would have had to take me in to live with you, Hauk. You need to be thanking her, too."

The woman looked closely at Merewin. She spoke louder and slowly, enunciating each word. "I wish to thank you." She grinned broadly then turned to Hauk. "Can she understand me?" Neither Hauk nor Merewin had been given a chance to get in any words. "Hauk, speak." She smacked his arm and frowned. "You never talk."

"And you, sister, talk enough for the whole village."

Hauk's sister kicked toward his shin, but he easily sidestepped the leather-clad foot, making her wobble. Hauk's hand shot out to steady. "If this child wasn't making me so awkward, you would have felt my revenge."

Merewin couldn't help but smile at the comfortable banter and felt a small pang of jealousy. She'd grown up without her siblings, without the support and love that seemed to emanate from these two.

"Bera, this is Merewin, and she can understand our words."

Bera turned toward Merewin, her arms open as if to hug. "You saved my Gamal."

Hauk stepped between them as Bera's body fell against him. "Merewin is sick and doesn't wish to infect anyone."

Bera peered around Hauk. "If she does, she will heal us."

Hauk snorted. "You are as bad as Ragnar, Bera. You know that there's no magick to heal, not here in Midgard. That is only for the gods."

Merewin ignored Hauk's words and peeked around him at Bera. "Yer husband has been very kind to me. I am glad to have helped him return to ye." Merewin turned her head to the ground and sniffed. "But I'm afraid I am sick and cannot heal until I am well." She would go along with the misinformation Hauk had devised to give her some time to figure out what to do.

Bera stepped back, her hand resting on her rounded midsection. Her smile remained. "I will honor you with a feast once you're well."

Merewin felt a blush and lowered her eyes. "I'm a slave now, not a guest to be honored with a feast."

Merewin heard Hauk grunt and caught a glimpse of Bera's foot making contact with Hauk's shin. "You're a thrall right now, Merewin, but thralls can buy their freedom," Bera said as she glared at Hauk.

Merewin tilted her head, inspecting her large captor. "I can buy my freedom?"

"Aye, you can," Bera supplied.

Hauk's voice rumbled as he pulled away from the pier. "You're worth far too much for you to ever pay for your worth, Merewin," Hauk said.

Merewin let the wind flip her hair back as she tilted her face up to Hauk. "Ye set my worth?"

"Aye," he said, his gaze running along her face and hair.

"Then set it low," she said, through clenched teeth.

"Nay," he countered defiantly.

"I am but a fake, remember, an illusionist with no true magick. What then is my great worth?" She smiled through her temper as she turned his own words back on him like a stolen dagger.

He leaned close to one ear, his hot breath sending tingles down her neck. "Your body is molded for a man's hand, Merewin. Your hair is soft and rich. Your eyes gleam with the spirit of a warrior. And your taste sets fire to a man's loins. You have great worth despite your delusions."

Merewin gulped past the constriction in her throat and numbly allowed Hauk to drag her toward a long, double-storied structure. Her rapid pulse revived her even though the illness and the horrors of the last few days made her steps heavy.

Your taste sets fire to a man's loins. Were Hauk's loins on fire from kissing her? Did the traitorous ache in her affect him too? Heat infused her face.

Merewin felt the familiar tug of her skirts as Ellette caught up to them and climbed to rest across her shoulders. The familiar softness under her hair fortified her. She wasn't alone.

Several warriors stood outside the door of the huge wooden longhouse with swords, daggers, and shields close at hand. Hauk pulled Merewin through the opened doorway into a dark interior and took her boots to set on the planked floor. After the bright sunlight outdoors, the darkness blinded. Merewin felt the stuffed humanity in the room. The smell of smoke from a central fire pit mixed with the aroma of cooking meat and the tang of unwashed bodies.

Hauk's voice boomed out, making her jump. "I present Merewin from Northumbria, daughter to the Witch of the Woods, and reputed healer." He pulled her forward, still talking. "I claim her as thrall, as is my right as commander of the raid." He pulled her up before him, back pressed against his chest, his hands clamped tightly over her slender shoulders, showing his mastery.

Somehow this blatant show of dominance didn't annoy Merewin as much as it should. In fact, it calmed her somewhat. As she adjusted to the dimness, the faces of curious Danes came into view. Warriors and women shooed children out the door. Those remaining stared, waiting. Merewin put her hand to her mouth and coughed.

A man with a long mustache stepped forward. Those around him parted, allowing him to walk freely. His stride was purposeful, strong, his mouth grim. He stopped.

"Welcome to my fire, healer from Northumbria. I am Ragnar Lothbrok, the one responsible for bringing you here."

What exactly was the proper response to that? Merewin wasn't sure so she just stared into the man's tired eyes. His physical need pulled at her. She felt his exhaustion and worry like it was a disease weighing against his whole spirit. He seemed to hold his breath as he measured her.

Hauk's voice once again jarred her. "Merewin is ill from the cold and exhaustion of our difficult voyage."

On cue, Merewin sneezed, glancing down at the last moment so as not to spray the king. The king stepped back.

"She cannot heal until she is well," Hauk explained.

A shrill voice bit out through the hush. "If she were a true healer, she would not be ill. She is useless to you, Ragnar." A woman, approximately Merewin's age, stepped out of the gloom. Her long blond hair fell in a tight braid over her shoulder. A predatory expression made her fine features twist into an ugly visage. She smiled at Hauk, her eyes raking along his form. "I'm sure Hauk will agree with me."

Hatred flashed through Merewin. She didn't even know this woman, but every bit of intuition Merewin possessed labeled her an enemy.

"Svala, you don't know that yet," another woman said and walked forward. This second woman was plumper, with soft features and dark circles below red-rimmed eyes. As she neared Merewin, the heaviness of the woman's heart nearly took her breath away. *The mother.* Merewin swallowed hard. It was the same pain she'd felt in the other mother years ago, pain born of intense worry and guilt.

She stopped before Merewin and her dry lips pushed up into a tired smile. "I am Aslaug, wife of Ragnar Lothbrok, and mother of Ivarr. You're here to save my son, and I welcome you with all my heart." She reached to take Merewin's hands, but Ragnar pushed them away.

"She is ill, Aslaug. Don't touch her until she's well," her husband said.

"Again," Svala called from behind the royal couple, her hand gesturing. "I must protest. This woman," she said eyeing Merewin with disdain as if the word wasn't worthy of her, "is an illusionist. No healer would be ill."

Merewin watched Aslaug stiffen. The pain the woman, Svala, caused was cruel. Or was it? Was it not crueler to give Aslaug hope?

"I am a healer in Northumbria," Merewin said evenly, staring into Aslaug's eyes. Hope flared there and Merewin's stomach rolled. "But I have limits." She had to warn them. She'd rather die than build up hope in another set of parents only to watch them crumble, consumed by pain, when their child died.

"Limits," Svala scoffed. "Illusionists couldn't heal my husband and couldn't heal your family, Hauk."

Ragnar held up his hand, and the bitter woman stopped.

Merewin took a deep breath. "I have healed many adults, but not children. The younger a child is, the harder they are to heal."

"He is past a year," Aslaug said quickly. "Halfway to two."

Ragnar squeezed his wife's arm.

Merewin nodded because it felt impossible not to respond to the desperation in Aslaug's voice.

Ragnar studied Merewin. "Hauk has told you our history?"

"Nay," Hauk said. "I thought it best coming from you."

Ragnar bent to Aslaug's ear. She nodded and walked away as Ragnar spoke quietly.

Merewin followed Aslaug peripherally as the woman glided over to several others near a raised platform against a wall. A child lay under a heap of furs there.

"Aslaug has born me three children, Ivarr being the last. Each of them seems normal when they are born, but each one weakens over time. The other two only made it to two years before they died. Ivarr shows the same weakness. I fear when," Ragnar paused, and ran his hand over his forehead. "If," he corrected. "If he dies, Aslaug's mind will die with him." He cleared his voice thick with emotion. "So I sent for you because the gods have foretold that you can save my son and my wife. You're the healer who will do what others could not. You will save my son—" he stopped to stare intensely at Merewin "—because you must."

Merewin tried not to lower her eyes, but it was difficult under such intensity. For a moment, she glimpsed the strength in this man, this king. A strength that could build a man up or crush him. Aye, he could crush her in his retaliation against nature and what it was doing to his family.

Still looking in his eyes, Merewin gave a brief nod. "I will do all I can for yer son. That I can promise. The results will be up to the Earth Mother."

Ragnar looked above her to Hauk's face.

"Her god," Hauk supplied.

Ragnar gave a brisk nod and turned in dismissal.

"I..." Merewin called, "I would like to see the child." Even though her feet were cold and her body aching, she wanted to gather some idea of what ailed the child.

"She will only make him ill," Svala said.

Who was this woman? Her sneer had a strangely familiar cast to it.

Hauk leaned down so his lips brushed Merewin's ear. "Bjalki's sister and sister-in-law to the king. Her husband died of disease three years ago," he said, and it took Merewin a breath before the words registered past the sensations his touch thrummed through her body. Bjalki's sister. Now she saw the familiar wicked sneer.

"I will not harm him," Merewin added. "But I must know what I will need to bring with me once I am well. I would like to prepare." Perhaps she could use herbs and techniques she had learned from Navlin to help him. Traditional, non-magick.

Ragnar nodded and pointed to where Aslaug stood, holding a small limp hand. The pale fingers lay like a dead bird in her palm.

Svala huffed loudly and addressed Hauk. "I didn't think you would claim a thrall who lies about being a healer, Hauk, not after—"

Bera's voice interrupted Svala. "Enough of your venom, Svala. Your voice wears on us."

Svala's mouth closed and opened and closed again like a mackerel gasping for air.

Merewin tried to take a step toward Aslaug, but Hauk's hand on her shoulder still pinned her to him. She glanced at his face. It was tight with displeasure, but she wasn't sure if it was directed at her, Svala, or the whole sad situation.

"I can't walk pinned to a mountain," she said. He relaxed the hold on her shoulders, letting her slip from his grasp. Ellette wiggled as if peeking out from her hair to get a view too. Merewin stepped off the wooden entryway to walk along the hardpacked dirt floor.

Some of the other women stepped back as she approached. One nursemaid sat next to the boy while Aslaug held the small hand.

Merewin noticed a small twitch in the boy's other hand. He laid with his eyes open but blank. His expression was not pained or happy. She imagined he was asleep except his eyes were open.

"We wonder sometimes if he can still see," Aslaug said, as she ran her hand down his cheek.

Merewin nodded. "Can ye pull back the fur so I can see him better?" She held up her hands. "I will not touch him."

Aslaug nodded and the nursemaid pulled back the fur. The child's stomach was distended.

Merewin lifted her hand to touch it but stopped before anyone could grab her and lowered it. "Did the bloating happen recently?"

Aslaug nodded, tears in her eyes. "It was the same in my other babies," she said. Guilt laced her voice.

"My Lady," Merewin said softly. "Ye know ye're not at fault for this."

Aslaug's eyes filled, the tears overflowing her lashes. "Of course 'tis my fault. I am cursed to lose all my babies. The gods are punishing me." Tears leaked from her eyes. "Why else would this happen three times?"

Merewin shook her head and kept her voice even. "Nature is cruel, sometimes without reason, at least a reason we can understand. But if ye have done naught to intentionally harm yer children, ye are not at fault for this. 'Tis beyond yer control, and it has nothing to do with yer goodness as a mother." Merewin nodded to emphasize her point. "In fact, from what I've seen of ye so far, ye have done all ye can to help yer child."

Aslaug closed her eyes, and Merewin looked back at the little boy. He was so still, except for a twitch here and there. "A bad mother would abandon him, but ye fight for him." Merewin looked back to Aslaug. "Like a warrior." Merewin smiled reassuringly. "And he needs yer strength, Aslaug." Merewin looked behind them to where Ragnar watched closely. "And I think yer husband needs yer amazing strength as well."

Aslaug's voice was soft but steadier. "I am weak. I have put two babes in the ground, and—"

Merewin cut her off, "and ye are still standing. That makes ye a very strong woman indeed."

Aslaug wet her lips and ran a hand up over mussed hair. She nodded slightly as if conceding the point. "Warrior, you say?"

Merewin smiled. "Brave and willing to sacrifice yerself to save yer son."

Aslaug wiped the tears and gave a small smile still filled with sadness. She looked back to Ivarr. "I will pray to the gods then and thank them for sending you."

Merewin tensed and breathed deeply. In helping this woman hold on to her sanity was she raising her hopes?

Merewin's lips were tight, but she bowed her head. "I will do what I can to help him." Looking up, she met the mother's eyes. "Meanwhile, as all good warriors do, pray for strength, too."

Aslaug tipped her chin forward as if in prayer.

"I will not touch him," Merewin said and moved her hands several inches away from the boy's skin. She closed her eyes and let the magick of the earth beneath her feet flow up. Like opening a floodgate, the power rushed up her legs, through her hands. She needed to touch the disease that filled the wee body.

Her attuned mind coursed over the lines running through his small frame, through the muscles, along the bones. It was as if the normal energy that gave the body movement was blocked, deadened, so the energy couldn't move. It stagnated in spots causing the twitching, Merewin thought. The belly distended because the muscles of the stomach and intestines were not working properly. The boy's heart still beat, but its pulse was being weighed upon. There was no doubt this boy would die if nothing was done.

With the power pulsing upward, Merewin reached out to pull some of the thick coating of disease from his muscles. She slid the invisible thread through the boy, twisting it around the blockage. Nothing released. She pulled harder and felt her force slip, falling away from the disease. Merewin's breathing increased as she fought for hold on the disease wrapped around and through his entire body. But she couldn't get a good grip. She looked at him.

Ivarr's gaze remained expressionless. He should feel the warmth of her magick in him, feel the tingling along his small muscles. Yet he laid still, an occasional twitch in his hands.

Merewin's strength seeped out as she tried once more to pull at the heaviness in the boy. She grew weaker, until her legs buckled. She pulled her arms back as she plopped on the dirt floor next to the ledge.

"Merewin!" Hauk bent to pick her up.

Ellette, jarred from the fall, pawed her way out of Merewin's hair.

"A rat!" the nursemaid screamed, causing shrieks to run through the ladies nearby.

Several ran away as Ellette jumped up on the ledge to sniff the little boy.

Hauk helped Merewin stand. "She's my pet and quite tame," Merewin spoke over the commotion and reached for Ellette.

When Merewin pulled her pet away, the child turned his head in the pine marten's direction and smiled. It was slight, but it was there. A curious grin.

Ellette scurried up to sit on Merewin's shoulder as Hauk led her toward the door. Merewin watched the boy's gaze track her pet as they walked away.

"Merewin will recover at my holding," Hauk said.

"Bjalki challenges you for her," Ragnar said. Merewin's look snapped up to the king. She hadn't seen the cruel-looking man in the hall, only his sister.

Svala stepped up in his place. "For some reason my brother has an interest in the thrall," she drawled, looking down her nose at Merewin. Svala dripped dankness like a diseased beast. If Merewin weren't the obvious target of her bitterness, she would have pitied the woman.

Svala eyed her as if she were nothing more than a dirty mongrel. "I suppose we can take her in until she is recovered enough to tend Ivarr."

Hauk's voice was low, belying the tightening of his arms as he pulled her in contact with his solid body. He looked directly at the king. "I meet his challenge, but first Merewin goes to my holding. She is weak, and I am responsible for her health."

Merewin's heart slammed in her chest. If Bjalki and his vile sister took her, she would die a slow, cruel death. Merewin leaned closer into Hauk's body, her instincts making her shrink back from Svala until she remembered her courage. *I am Merewin, healer and daughter of Gilla, Wiccan priestess.* Her shoulders straightened.

Hauk stared into the king's face until Ragnar nodded. "As much as I would like to witness the challenge to my arrogant brother-in-law—"

Svala gasped but Ragnar ignored her "—there will be no challenges until the healer is well enough to heal my son. Then you two can slash each other to bits so the gods can choose where the healer will live."

Aslaug stepped into the tight circle and touched Ragnar's arm. She whispered something fierce in his ear.

Ragnar's bushy eyebrows arched upward. He looked at Merewin. "To add to your incentive—" he stressed the word "—to save my son, if you bring him to health, I will pay for your freedom."

Svala muttered something like a curse and turned away.

Hauk's arms squeezed a bit tighter. "Her price will be set too high, even for you." Ragnar's eyebrows rose higher. Hauk turned to step out into the light, his arm around her back.

"Wait," Merewin said, straining to meet the mother's eyes. "Yer son, he likes animals?"

Aslaug nodded. "He has a dog and loved to play with him before, when he could."

"Ye still have the dog?"

"Aye," Ragnar said. "We keep him out of the hall."

Merewin's earlier thoughts began to solidify in her mind. She shook her head. "Don't keep them apart."

Ragnar and Aslaug looked confused.

Merewin tempered her words, not wanting to add false hope. "Yer son is very ill. But I think having things around that he loves will help...help remind him why he wants to remain in this world."

Aslaug dropped Ragnar's arm. "Asta, find the pup," she directed one of the ladies. "Bring him here to Ivarr," she said and strode to her son, her steps forceful.

Ragnar watched Aslaug go and then looked at Merewin. "Whatever you said to her," he indicated the direction where his son lay, "over there. She seems stronger."

Merewin stroked Ellette's tail, which curved around her neck like a collar. "The strongest people I've ever met are mothers fighting for their children, King Ragnar." Hadn't she seen that in her own mother who'd sent her daughters away with her powers, leaving her to face the demons as a helpless woman?

Merewin had certainly seen it in Northumbria whenever a mother came to beg Navlin's services for her child. Merewin looked toward Aslaug where she kissed Ivarr's forehead. "When mothers lose hope or turn their hatred from the sickness toward themselves, they punish themselves as if they're the ones to destroy. I merely reminded her that she is not the enemy, and yer son needs her to be his warrior."

"You've healed her with mere words?" Ragnar asked softly.

"There'll be time to question her later," Hauk said, frustration edging his voice. He scooped her up, his strong arm securely under her legs, and turned without giving her or Ragnar a chance to say more. He stepped with her out into the crimson glow of the lowering sun.

She squirmed in his arms. "Put me down, Hauk. I'm not a child to be carried about."

"Nay, you are weak."

"Not weak enough to be carried."

"Weak enough to fall on your arse."

He approached a tall horse and pushed her upon it. Merewin sat with both legs on one side, her bare feet having no place to rest. She braced her heels against the horse's warm belly. Twisting, she grabbed the mane, her fingers winding in the bristly hair. The horse's head raised, turning its large eye toward her. She'd only been on two horses her entire life and both times she'd feared for her life.

Hauk swung up behind her and pulled her into the *V* made by his powerful legs. Her fingers slipped from the mane, coming away with a few dark strands. Ellette scampered out from Merewin's hair, leaping from the height of the horse to dodge the people. Merewin clutched Hauk's arm before her as he tapped the horse's sides, making it leap into an easy run. Merewin's heart lurched, and she pressed back into his chest.

Together, they wove around villagers and animals, until they broke out onto an open field. "I won't let you fall," Hauk said.

"Because ye protect yer property." Anger laced her words, but she continued to hold tight to his arm and press against him as if he were the only thing keeping her from death. Perhaps he was.

The wind whipped against her cheeks, washing through, cleansing her after the drain of Ragnar's hall. They loped to the edge of the woods, and Hauk slowed his horse to a walk. As they stepped from the deepening dusk behind them into the shadows of the great trees, Hauk leaned forward, his voice a deep whisper against her ear. "These groves are sacred. We walk through them."

"Magical trees? I thought ye don't believe in magick." She tried to ignore the sensation of his breath against the delicate skin of her ear, tried not to will his warm breath to move down her neck.

His jaw rubbed along her temple, then across the top of her head to the other side. He paused and she heard him take a long inhale before his lips touched her other ear.

"I believe in the magick of the gods, not of humans."

Merewin dared not move, afraid she'd break the contact. As his open lips brushed her ear, warmth poured over, down to the pit of her belly, down to the junction of her thighs where she rubbed with each slow movement of the horse. Fie! Was she actually attracted to this barbarian? Damn her body's instinct to mate, for that's all this was. Like two young foxes in the forest in the spring.

Merewin focused on Hauk's large hand casually holding the reins of his horse. His other hand cupped under her ribs as he tucked her tight against him.

"Are you then?" he continued and Merewin tried to recall what he'd just said. "Freyja, goddess of passion and love?" he asked.

Merewin wet her rapidly drying lips. "Nay, no goddess of love. I am yet a maid." She spoke softly and felt a flush prickle the skin of her neck.

"If you were a Dane, you'd have been wed years ago, had six children by now, and possibly be a widow." He lifted his mouth from her ear so she only felt his chin brush her hair.

"Navlin kept me hidden from most. She was afraid someone would harm or steal me from her," Merewin said, her voice hinting at the irony. "No suitor braved the great Witch of the Woods for her daughter's hand."

"A land of cowards," Hauk said.

Merewin frowned, tipping her head back to stare upward at his face. "A land of people who respect magick," she countered. His jaw looked even stronger as she peered up from underneath.

"You mean *fear* magick," he said arrogantly, as he steered the horse over a large log covered with mushrooms.

Merewin leveled her head and twisted in her seat to see him right side up. She raised her eyebrows in mock innocence. "And doesn't the denial of magick indicate a fear of it?"

Hauk's slight grin faded, his expression turning to stone. "I have seen trickery called magick worked before." His eyes grew distant as he scanned the woods ahead of them. "I've smelled the burning herbs, heard the thunderous chants to expel wickedness and disease, watched the sacrifices made, and yet none of it worked."

His stormy blue eyes looked down into hers. "The hope their false magick brought only added to the pain once the disease won. The *magick* I saw tortured those who eventually succumbed to death. The survivors of the disease were tortured as well with the promises of their recovery." His teeth stacked upon each other. "All lies."

Merewin blinked but couldn't pull her gaze away from his. She knew the peak of hope the helpless loved ones climbed. The higher they climbed, the harder they fell if their family member died. "Yer wife?" she whispered.

Hauk looked away into the trees as he continued guiding his horse along the trail. "And others."

Merewin turned back to watch the yellow-tipped leaves fluttering like butterfly wings. Autumn was already descending. Ellette scampered ahead of the horse, hopping over the roots that broke the ground.

As they came to the edge of the woods, Hauk tapped his horse back into an easy run. They flew across another meadow towards a large home with a growing grass roof, the front of the house built of heavy wood planks. The door was large with a swooping, carved lintel. Smaller structures sat around the large one in the shade of a small mountain. In the valley, a stream wound before the large house and ducks and geese pecked at insects in the yard. Several women and men worked along the lines of ripe gardens, harvesting plump vegetables. A boy ran and laughed with a large dog near the front of the dwelling.

Their joyous sounds made her think of Aslaug's son and his reaction to Ellette. Ivarr loved animals. Maybe she could convince him to fight to stay here and not return to the Earth Mother's arms. His disease was immense and intertwined through every bit of his small body. Even with his desire to live, it would be difficult to strip the clinging vileness from him. Without his desire to live, her efforts would be futile.

The misty face of an old woman came to mind. Drakkina. The witch could read thoughts, desires. She could read Ivarr's. Perhaps Merewin could summon her.

As they stopped before the dwelling, a blond-haired girl of about ten years ran out, her cherub-like face radiating happiness. "Papa!" She ran up to them and wrapped her hands around Hauk's leg. Merewin felt him unwrap his arm from her waist. The absence of his heat chilled her.

"Dalla, you get bigger each time I come home," Hauk said and threw his leg over the horse's rump to jump down. Merewin watched from her perch as the child immediately hugged him. It wouldn't be too many more years before she left this home to marry. The girl was on the verge of being considered a woman.

"Did you bring me something, Papa?"

Merewin watched Hauk check his bag. He frowned. "I had a necklace, but I may have left it on the ship." Finally, he gave up and turned to Merewin. He reached for her, his large hands settling around her waist to pull her from the horse's back. Merewin's feet ached as he sat her on the ground. The journey and whatever illness had taken hold in her had weakened her.

"Therefore," Hauk said and turned away to look at Dalla. "I've brought you this woman to care for you. Her name is Merewin."

CHAPTER NINE
SPRING HOUSE

Merewin's heart dropped into her stomach. She was a gift for Hauk's daughter, like a rag doll or a puppy? Anger poured through her, making her stomach churn and her jaw harden. How could she have forgotten, even for a moment, that she was this man's thrall.

Dalla raised one eyebrow at her and then turned a frown on her papa. "I don't need a new mother." Merewin straightened up and stepped back.

"She's not to be your mother."

Hauk seemed to look everywhere else but at Merewin. Could he feel her subdued fury? It was white hot inside her, like an iron poker left too long in a blazing fire. If she had it now, she'd stick it up his arse.

"Then she's a thrall." Dalla smiled. "A slave for my very own."

A chill of unease raced along Merewin's spine.

"I brought Merewin here under orders of the king. She is known as a healer in Northumbria," Hauk said.

"Another healer?" Dalla asked, looking Merewin up and down. "She doesn't smell like one."

What was a healer supposed to smell like? Herbs perhaps.

The dog ran up to them and Hauk scratched the beast's large, gray head.

Dalla continued to frown as she examined Merewin. "I would rather have had the necklace," she said petulantly. Then smiled as her gaze locked onto Merewin's jade stone hanging from a cord around her neck.

"I can have that one then, if she's mine," Dalla pointed to the stone from Merewin's birth mother.

A flush prickled up Merewin's neck into her cheeks. She would not relinquish her only connection to her mother. Merewin grasped the stone in her hand, covering it from the spoiled child's view. The stone also allowed Merewin to understand the Dane's language.

"We'll discuss it later, Dalla," Hauk said.

Dalla gave Merewin a challenging look but turned to go inside. "Come Papa, I want to show you what Svala brought for me."

Merewin hoped 'Svala' was a common name in Ribe. If Bjalki's sister visited Hauk's farm often, Merewin would need to escape as fast as possible. Otherwise, she might stab her. Then she'd have to endure whatever death these barbarians meted out to a thrall killing a citizen. Death, by being eaten by some wild Danish animal during her escape, was preferable.

Hauk motioned Merewin to follow his daughter into the hall. It was a longhouse, smaller than Ragnar's but of the same structure with a loft. A central fire pit warmed the interior as the smoke drifted up and out through a vent in the ceiling supported by heavy beams. Raised ledges ran on both sides of the room so people could sleep close to the fire. Cooking utensils and tools sat in organized groups. Woven mats lay on ledges along with colorful baskets, which held some of the vegetable harvest.

Would she sleep on one of the pallets set upon a ledge? She desperately wanted to sleep. Needed it if she were to improve. Merewin glanced at Hauk, who strode to the back where three doorways were set. She swallowed past the tightness in her throat. Or would she be sharing Hauk's bed instead? Her stomach flipped at the thought. *He doesn't rape.*

Dalla pushed past a curtain over one door and came back out with something in her hand. She lifted it up for Hauk to inspect. "'Tis a silver pin to hold my cloak closed. Svala brought it last week," Dalla said breathlessly as she showed the treasure to her father.

Hauk nodded and fluffed her hair. He looked around. "Where is Vivien?

Dalla shrugged her shoulders and looked down at the pin in her hand. "I have no idea where she hides herself. She doesn't seem to like my company."

Merewin didn't doubt that. How many children did Hauk have? Were they all spoiled like Dalla? Would she have to take care of them? Feeling the tickle in her nose, Merewin looked down at the stamped dirt floor and sneezed.

Dalla jumped and grabbed onto Hauk. "She's ill!"

"She caught the ague on the voyage over. She's here to rest and grow healthy so she can help Ivarr."

Dalla's face paled, her eyes wide as she backed up farther.

"Merewin has a simple illness, Dalla, not a pox."

The girl nodded, but fear tightened every line of her stiff body.

"Papa, you shouldn't touch her, just in case." Dalla pulled Hauk's hand as if to guide him into one of the back rooms.

Merewin took several deep breaths and rubbed at her itchy nose. "Perhaps I could lie down."

Hauk strode to her, his gaze assessing. "Aye." He bent to pick her up, lifting her like she weighed nothing more than a child even though she knew she was tall and sturdy. "You will sleep in a small room between Dalla's and mine."

"I don't want her in my closet," Dalla called, still keeping her distance.

He ignored her and carried Merewin toward the rooms at the back of the longhouse.

"I can walk," Merewin said.

Hauk slowly released her legs, and she slid down close to his body while he still held her firmly behind the back.

A thin woman of medium build and brown hair walked in, followed by the dog from the yard. "Welcome," she said, bowing her head to Hauk. Was this Vivien?

The large animal trotted over. His lanky body was covered with coarse gray fur, and his tongue lolled out, but it was his large brown eyes that made him look friendly. Merewin scratched the dog's head, and he turned his sloppy tongue to lick her hand. Merewin grinned at him. "Yer son's pet?"

"Aye," Hauk said and gave a quick command to send the dog on his way. It listened well to its master.

"Where is yer son?" she asked.

"Dead," Dalla said near the door to her room. "Dead with the rest of them." She tilted her head, her gaze like a dagger at Merewin. "The healers let them die, all of them. Toki, Grandpapa and Grandmama, my own mama, and Uncle Hector and Edwyth too, and she with child..."

"Enough," Hauk said, his voice cutting across his daughter's list. Merewin stared at Hauk's back.

"All dead," Dalla's little voice continued. "The pox made them boil with fever and waste away. But it was the healers who killed them."

"Vivien, take Dalla to the kitchens out back until she remembers to listen to her father," Hauk said and pulled Merewin past Dalla.

The healers had killed them. The words charged through Merewin's mind like battle-hungry warriors. *The healers had killed them. All of them.* No wonder the dwelling was so large if it had been built for a large extended family. And now it stood nearly empty.

Hauk held her hand, and she followed without trying to yank it free as her mind created horrible scenarios of death. "You will sleep in here," he said as they pushed through the curtain into a small room where furs covered a ledge built into the side of the wall. The spongy tick of fresh-smelling hay made a comfortable, if not large, bed.

In the front room, the dog barked, and Hauk poked his head back out. "Your pet has come inside, and Sæla is trying to eat her," Hauk said.

"Is she on the ground?" Merewin asked.

"Nay. In the rafters."

Merewin waved his concern off. "She's survived in the forest for three times the natural life span of a pine marten. Ye should fear more for yer dog."

"Sæla," he yelled, and the dog stopped barking.

"How many died?" Merewin asked.

Hauk leaned against the door and kept his gaze out in the front room. "Six, including my son."

"Only ye and Dalla remain?"

"And my sister, Bera."

"When?"

Hauk straightened and finally met her gaze. He studied her for long seconds before speaking. "Three years ago come winter."

"And ye had healers come to cure them?"

Hauk turned to the doorway. "Rest Merewin. You'll need your strength." He strode out without another word.

———— ◄O► ————

Hauk followed the snapping flames as they licked black char along the logs in the pit. Shadows danced in jagged splinters against the walls of his home. Dalla was finally asleep in her large chamber off the back of the house. It had once belonged to his parents before the pox roared through Ribe and the surrounding countryside, before Hauk's life had crashed around him. Leaving him to play mother to his remaining child, a headstrong girl who grew into more of a terror every day. He loved Dalla, her strength and intelligence, her endearing laugh still edged with innocence. But how to raise her? He ran his hand through his unbound hair.

Was it self-pity he felt gnawing? Hauk shook his head in disgust and took another swig of strong ale. He hadn't let self-pity break his soul before when he'd laid his son's limp body in the funeral ship. Self-loathing, aye, but not self-pity. Anger at his foolishness had strengthened his arm as he held the torch, lowering it to light the ship carrying his entire family out to burn in the sea. His father and mother, his younger brother, Hector, and his new wife, and Hauk's ten-year-old son, Toki. They traveled to Asgard across the rainbow bridge. The body of his wife, Ingun, had been returned to her parents near Esbjerg where she was buried with her possessions.

Right up to the end, he'd hoped they'd survive the pox outbreak. On his darkest nights he could even admit he had hid in the promises of the so-called healers who tortured those he loved until their poor bodies surrendered to death.

The night stood guard around the house. 'Twas so unlike the cacophony of snores and nighttime movements the house once held during the dark hours with family and visiting friends sleeping against the walls and in the lofts of the longhouse. Now the silence taunted him, depriving him of sleep. No wonder he preferred to roam these days. His house was no longer a sanctuary. It was a lonely shell that held ghosts.

Hauk leaned against the wall, his feet hanging over the ledge. A whisper of movement alerted him to Merewin's presence in the room, there in the back where the shadows sliced haphazardly. It was the end of the second day since he'd brought Merewin to his large, empty, silent house. Could she be trying to escape? Where would she go? If Bjalki, or one of his ilk, found her she may not survive the night.

"You should be asleep, Merewin," his low voice filled the space, and he heard her bump something.

"Ouch," she whispered. She came into view, rubbing her shin. Her long, wavy hair swayed toward the ground as she bent over. "I slept most of the day, but ye should be asleep now."

"I require very little sleep," he said, as he dragged his gaze from the woman who looked like a tousled lover. He took a sip of the warm brew. His eyes remained on the fire, yet his senses caught her movement out of the corner of his sight. *Graceful.* Her tall form, draped in a linen sleeping rail from Bera, came closer, until she stopped at the edge of firelight.

She sat on a stool close to the warmth but said nothing. Hauk's gaze drifted over to her despite his somber mood. By the gods, Merewin was beautiful. He'd known she was comely when he first saw her staring at him from the shadow of the healing tent in Northumbria. But having watched her strength and courage through the ordeal of her capture and journey, her beauty shone even brighter to Hauk. Over the normal tang of wood smoke, he smelled the faint floral spice of woman's soap. She'd requested a pitcher of warm water earlier to wash herself. He'd brought in his mother's bathing barrel for her to use instead and enjoyed her shocked expression when he filled it with warmed water.

Hauk's look traveled up into Merewin's face. Her profile was delicate, with fine lines and high cheekbones brought into sharp contrast in the shadows. Even with her mild illness she had the vitality of one properly fed and full of health.

Her lashed eyes tilted slightly at the corners. In the sun they would be a warm mossy green, deep and knowing, thoughtful but also easy to spark into irritation. Those eyes had sparkled with laughter when she smiled at Gamal. Full of fury or full of joy, or even soft with calm, Merewin's eyes were beautiful. Windows to the soul, his mother had said often. But was it true with this woman who called herself a healer, who swore she could summon magick to cure? How could her soul be so beautiful with such lies inside?

"I will not have you lie to Dalla about your magick." Hauk's abrupt command caused Merewin to twitch forward. The fire in the central pit leapt upwards and then settled back down.

Merewin pulled her shawl around her shoulders and turned to glare at him. Spark, there it was in those beautiful orbs reflecting orange flame.

"I don't lie." Merewin spoke evenly, proudly, as if she could boast about a thousand incidents where she could have lied and hadn't. Perhaps she believed she could heal, like a person plagued with madness.

"You couldn't heal me." He glanced at the bandage wrapped around his bare bicep. Merewin's forehead crinkled, and he had an impulse to rub the lines away with his thumb.

"I don't understand why I couldn't. I know the limitations of my powers, and I should have been able to heal ye."

Hauk uncrossed his ankles and sat up square to look closely at her. Threat evident in his voice, he spoke low. "There is no power in chants and sacrifices and foul-smelling incense." He slowly lifted the battle-axe he kept near him, watching the light shine against the polished steel. "There is only power in this."

Instead of respectful acquiescence or even awed silence, Merewin snorted a sardonic little laugh. "That would make men the most powerful creatures in the world, with their iron and steel and war."

"Some of us are more powerful than others," he answered arrogantly.

Her indignant glare almost made him smile. *She's easily baited.*

"All I've seen in yer blades and war," she said, "is more work for me, more bodies to heal."

Hauk frowned again at her unwavering pretense. Perhaps she was mad.

Merewin continued as if warming to her subject. "War is declared over an imaginary boundary or some slight to a man's pride. And what does it bring to the land?" She raised her hands in royal flourish. "More war is what it brings. Nay, yer blades don't hold power; they hold destruction."

Merewin's eyes flashed with suppressed anger, her cheeks flushed deeply, and her hair fell like a curtain. But what intrigued him even more was the passion and intelligence of her words. Also, his obvious physical mastery didn't frighten or subdue her. Merewin of Northumbria was unique. But even in her exquisiteness, she was still lying about the power she couldn't possibly possess.

"I've seen destruction at the hands of women," he said. "Men are not the only harbingers of death and torture, Merewin."

She held her tongue for a moment, the fire cracking between them. "Ye speak of the pox that took yer family?"

Hauk stared back into the brightness, feeling its heat wash over him. Why should he answer her? He didn't speak of it to anyone, and no one brought it up to him. No one until Merewin.

"This house was full of life once," he said evenly, glancing about the tomb-like hall. "My brother had married the year before, and his wife was growing full with child." Hauk looked over to Merewin. She sat still and watched the flames.

Good, the words came easier if she didn't look at him. "My parents were still strong, helpful, never a burden. And Toki, my son..." He stopped to take a slow breath, letting it out in a rush as his face broke into a sad grin. "Toki, loud and full of skinned knees and bumps from climbing trees and chasing his dog. He was so full of laughter and brightness..." His words trailed off, and he cleared his throat. "He was eager to grow into a warrior." Hauk would have trained his son to be the mightiest warrior in Danmørk.

Hauk tipped his ale horn up but found the vessel empty. It thumped the packed dirt floor as he dropped it. "Even Ingun, my reluctant wife." He grunted slightly, remembering her initial wailing when her family made the arranged marriage between them. "Even she had warmed to the constant hum of our life." As if an afterthought he added, "she was an accomplished weaver and loved her children greatly."

He followed Merewin's gaze back to the flames, watching as they cracked and popped in the hearth pit. The bright swirls and flickers took form before him, shaped by memories, nightmares.

"First my brother and his wife became ill. We heard news from Ribe how the port had shut down as pox invaded the town. Ships trying to dock were shot at, forcing them away." Hauk looked over at the silent woman, her spine straight as she sat tall. She pulled her hair to one side, tucking it behind one delicate ear. Perhaps it was the sight of Merewin that made the words come more easily.

"Ingun and my mother nursed them and became ill, as did my father. The morning I packed Toki and Dalla up, ready to send them with Gamal to Esbjerg..." Hauk's words felt like ice on his tongue. "Toki collapsed by the stream. Dalla screamed, but I wouldn't let her touch him. I tied her to a horse with Vivien behind her and sent them flying toward my sister and Gamal."

"Ye stayed," Merewin's voice held the edge of respect, respect he didn't deserve. He balled his hands into fists.

"I stayed." He dropped his head in his hands, scratching along his skull. "I slept outside and continued my rituals of bathing, training, and eating fresh food I found outside. I guess it was enough to keep the illness from me."

The worry and fatigue those days had brought upon him—no battle had ever been more difficult. Hauk looked around the shadowy room remembering the bodies strewn out on pallets around the fire. He'd tried to keep them warm, fed them, and rubbed them, trying to treat their pox blisters.

"They grew worse no matter what I did." He looked at Merewin, and she met his gaze. "You are right when you say my blade and arm are not all-powerful. I couldn't kill this enemy as it raided my home."

Her deep eyes held his, without pity, without judgment.

"So..." He swallowed. "I rode to Ribe for help."

"And ye found healers?"

His expression hardened. "Old Eldgrim said there were a dozen healers who'd come from Uppsala, and I sought them out. They said they knew of this pox and could cure it for enough gold and silver."

Merewin's eyes narrowed, but she stayed her tongue.

"I paid them, bought their promises, and brought them to Spring House." The ache in his chest made it hard to take a full breath. He stood, walking to grab a bladder of stronger mead. He uncorked it and took several long pulls off the honey-sweetened drink.

Sniffing, he looked back at Merewin. She didn't ask, but he brought the mead over for her. She held it to her lips and took a long drink, as a man would. He waited until she'd capped it to keep talking.

"Four of them came, their tinctures and poultices, their chants and burnt offerings to the gods. They heaped foulness on the fire, making the air black and choking. They poured poisons down the throats of my family to make them purge until they lost the remains of their strength."

He stopped, his confession on the edge of his mouth. Would she hate him as he hated himself? "And I let them. I begged them to, anything they could do to save them, to save Toki."

Merewin's face remained the same, listening, taking in what he had to offer as she stared at the fire. Were his nightmarish memories playing out before her? The only change was a tear, which leaked from one of her eyes, trailing unheeded down her cheek.

Hauk tore his gaze from the tear. "And with each painful cure I asked for more." Self-hatred boiled up from deep within him. "They lied to me until every last one of my family had died. Toki was last."

Merewin's words were choked. "Perhaps they couldn't do anything but tried everything they knew."

"They knew nothing!" he roared, standing to pace abruptly before the fire which flared up, tossing and spitting in an unnatural dance as if his anger fueled it. Merewin leaned back from the spontaneous inferno.

"I found out later that others in Ribe had healed on their own with rest and broth and fresh air. Instead, I let the healers," he snarled the word, "heal my family into death."

Merewin stood up. "It wasn't yer fault, Hauk."

"I paid them to torture my family."

"Without knowing it. Ye're not to blame."

In two large strides he stood looming. How dare she make excuses for his crime? "If I am not to blame, then I blame the healers, their ignorance, their self-righteous delusions of power. There are no healers!"

Contorted, he glared down into her glistening eyes, challenging her to deny it.

Merewin stood and brought her slender hand up to his face. She laid it against his hot cheek. Her touch was soft and cool, calm and firm. Slowly she ran it down the stubbled side and brushed his lips with her thumb. She didn't say anything but stared deeply into his eyes. It was as if she poured her calm spirit into his soul, cooling his fever, untwisting his stomach. Was she healing him? She had said she couldn't. The fire beside them shrank back down.

For long moments she stood there, and he realized she wasn't going to refute or defend something she had not done. Her eyes shone, without pity, without scorn, but with feeling, a mirror of his loss.

Hauk moved closer, his arm circling around her back. She stepped before him without blinking.

He placed his large hand around her bare neck, feeling the pulse leap, but she didn't pull away. Instead, she brought her other hand up to cup his other cheek, holding his face. Courage, calm gentle insistence, despite his condemnations about her craft.

Merewin parted her lips, wetting them with the tip of her tongue. The smell of her warmth, mixed with the clean scent of flowers and spice, spun around him, mixing with the spirits in his gut.

Hauk ran his hand up the naked column of her neck and into her hair as she closed her eyes. It was an invitation he could not refuse.

CHAPTER TEN
DESPERATE NEED

Hauk's mouth descended with the force of his pain turned to passion, and Merewin met him fully, slanting her mouth against his assault, drawing him towards her. One hand coiled in her long hair, the other roamed the curves of womanly hips molding her to him, ignoring the tug on his healing flesh.

She moaned softly, crumbling his walls of restraint. He would touch her everywhere. Her hands slid down to run across the front of his chest, dropping lower to dip under his linen shirt. A shiver of heat tore through him as cool hands branded hot skin across his stomach. The muscles of his chest jumped under her caress.

Her mouth was of the gods, and he wanted more.

Hauk moved his mouth to her ear. "Merewin, I want to taste more of you."

He wasn't sure if she nodded, but she didn't push him away or even stiffen. *Permission granted.* He moved to her neck, tasting the doe-like skin down the side to the collarbone exposed above the night rail. Merewin was all soft and curved and womanly. *And she knows my shame.* And she hadn't turned away.

Hauk began to lose himself in the feel of her body, the soft moans, the pressure of her hands kneading his muscles. He would take her, make her truly his, lose himself inside her. Forget.

Hauk reached under her lovely long legs, lifting her into his arms, and turned toward the doorway leading to his large empty room. She clung to his neck where his pulse throbbed with want. But he stopped.

"Hauk?" Merewin asked. She raised her head and turned to look where his eyes focused. A small dark shadow stood in the doorway to Dalla's room.

"Dalla," he said, letting Merewin slide down the length of him to stand once again. How much had she seen? How much had she heard? He had never spoken to her about the deaths, about his part in them. Her little face seemed pale in the depths, lost.

Her voice was soft like that of a small child. "I want Mama."

Hauk stood frozen.

Merewin took a step toward his daughter, but the bite in Dalla's voice stopped her. "You're not my mother, thrall. Stay away from me, stay away from all of us."

"Dalla," Hauk said as she turned to flee back into her room.

The bark of Toki's dog out front saved him from having to act toward either female, Dalla in her bitterness and Merewin in her...whatever she might be feeling.

Without looking at her, Hauk turned to the door where he heard horses' hooves. He adjusted his erect cock, which sought release from the prison of his trousers. Grabbing his axe, he stepped out into the fresh night air.

Svein and Bjalki pulled their mounts around, the hot breath of the horses puffing out under the moonlight.

Bjalki looked down at Hauk. "Bring the healer now. My brother-in-law commands it."

"The boy is near death and Aslaug cries for Merewin," Svein added. "Even if she's not well, Ragnar demands her presence."

Hauk turned toward Merewin as she hurried back into the house. Bjalki spit on the ground next to his horse. "She runs."

The courage Hauk had felt in her, seen in her this night, told him otherwise. "Nay," Hauk said coldly. "We will come."

Merewin's bare feet slapped the earth as she dashed into her small room. There was no time to think now as she pulled the night rail over her head, no time to think about what Dalla saw and heard. No time to wish she'd been here three years ago to save Hauk's family, to spare Hauk the pain she'd seen in his eyes, felt under his very skin. And definitely no time to think about what might have happened between Hauk and her if they hadn't been interrupted.

Merewin shivered in the cool air as she pulled on the second day gown she'd brought. She stopped for a moment as she fastened the brooches at her shoulders to hold up the soft green material. Merewin ran a hand up her bare neck, remembering the feel of Hauk's hand against her skin. She touched her lips, still feeling the pressure of his kiss.

Male voices out in the hall jolted her into motion again, and she grabbed a cloak and the leather bag of stones. By the holy Earth Mother, she hadn't even had time to call Drakkina, having slept most of the day away.

Merewin looked around the cramped room. "Drakkina, ye old spirit. I know ye've followed me." Nothing moved in the room, no transparent form wavered in a corner. "Fine mess ye've gotten me into," she raised her voice a little louder. "Come help me get out of it."

She breathed in deeply and imagined her internal warmth rising. She focused on it, growing it and stretching it out into long thread to send it flying out to the ethereal witch. *Drakkina! Drakkina!* She yelled in her head, the thread vibrating with her need.

I am here.

As she opened her eyes, a mist coalesced in the corner. *Thank the Earth Mother!*

"Merewin, we go," Hauk's voice broke through the curtain to her room a scant second before he did. Merewin glanced between Hauk and the transparent form of Drakkina. "I...I was changing."

Hauk didn't notice the apparition.

"And I needed my stones."

Hauk frowned. "Let's get this over with." He stepped in, blocking Merewin's view of Drakkina. Hauk caught her chin in his hand. "This situation, it could be," he paused, "unpredictable."

Was he warning her? Merewin knew her life would be in jeopardy if the boy died, but that didn't scare her as much as the mere act of failing and being forced to witness up close the terrible death of another innocent child. She was on the edge of plunging into her nightmare.

Hauk hadn't let go of her chin, forcing her to meet his eyes. "And when we come out of the other side of this...we will finish," he stopped, his gaze dipping to her lips, "our discussion." He dropped her chin abruptly and turned, pulling her behind him.

She clutched her stone dangling against her collarbone. *We?* He'd said "when *we* come out." That's what he'd said. She was sure of it. *We.*

Merewin rolled the word around as she ran to keep up with his long strides. He lifted her up onto his large horse and mounted behind her. Merewin repeated the simple word, giving her something on which to focus, quelling the fear. If there was a "we" then he wouldn't leave her behind when she failed, he wouldn't let them kill her.

Merewin leaned back into the cradle of Hauk's body. She needed to think fast, needed a plan to save Ivarr. She'd leave the saving of her own life to Hauk.

Moonlight flickered down through the ghostly trees and Merewin closed her eyes. She felt a core of strength warm down in her belly and she focused on it, a glowing ball of power deep within her. But power would do nothing for a child who wasn't old enough to fight for his life.

Drakkina! Merewin yelled inside the cell of her mind, calling the witch with her thread of magick. *Drakkina, follow me, I have need of ye. Drakkina!*

The horse moved under her body, pulsing over the ground. The dragonfly birthmark on Merewin's inner thigh tingled, making her rub her spread legs against the horse.

I am near, Gilla's child. The witch's voice dipped into Merewin's mind, snapping her eyes open.

Moonlight sliced along the trees as they blurred past. Merewin glanced at the lit torches on the perimeter of Ribe and panic squeezed her heart. *I need yer help, crone!*

"Are you well?" Hauk's breath warmed her ear. The sensation shot through Merewin, bringing back to life the heat of their kiss. Between the panic of riding toward her nightmare and the sensual energy of Hauk's nearness, Merewin could barely breathe to answer him. "You tremble," he said simply and tucked her tighter into him. He leaned closer so his rough cheek brushed against her own. "I will not let them kill you when you fail to save Ivarr."

His words, though positive, didn't comfort her.

"I," she began and then stopped to breathe. "I hate to fail, and I hate death." She wondered if he could even hear the words before they were snatched away in the wind that raced past them.

His warm whisper sounded in her ear. "We have much in common, then."

The three horses stopped short before Ragnar's longhouse. Was her birthmark still tingling? There was hardly time to notice as Hauk whisked her off the horse. He didn't even set her down but carried her in through the heavy oak door.

The hushed sound of weeping and deep murmurs coupled with the whine of a dog chained at the back of the room. The fire roared, making the room feel like an oven. The thick, incensed smoke made Merewin stifle a cough. At least twenty men and women hovered about the room. Their gazes turned toward her.

"Merewin!" Aslaug jumped from the side of Ivarr's platform and ran. "You've come. Please," she said. Hauk set Merewin down, and Aslaug dragged her past Ragnar toward the little form under the furs.

The boy's face looked slack and slightly purple, probably from the strain on his little heart. The disease that engulfed him had finally come to claim the life-giving organ, which struggled to pump blood through him.

Merewin took a deep breath and pulled back the furs. She rested her hands on the little boy, running them along his distended stomach and up to his chest where she felt the faint thud. He still lived.

"He's turning blue," Aslaug said, as she wiped tears from her eyes. "Like my other babes, just before they..." She sobbed, her hand going to her mouth.

Merewin turned to the terrified queen and gripped her free hand, pulling the second one away to squeeze them together. "Aslaug," she bent down so she could catch her eyes with her gaze. "Aslaug, hold on to yerself," Merewin said with soft firmness. "I may need yer help, and ye need to be calm."

Aslaug nodded vigorously, pulling at the core strength of a woman willing to do anything to save her child. Her tears dried, and a determined look strengthened her features. "Aye, Merewin. I will do whatever you tell me."

Merewin nodded and turned back to Ivarr. She laid out several stones along his body. *Drakkina*, she called silently.

I am here. Drakkina's voice came in her mind, and Merewin looked up to see the ghostly figure hovering at Ivarr's head. Merewin glanced at Aslaug and the men who had come closer: Hauk, Ragnar, Svein, and Bjalki. They didn't seem to notice the spirit.

They can't see me. Drakkina indicated the child. *You better heal him quickly before he passes. Even you can't bring him back, then.*

Ye think I don't know that! Merewin's mind screamed, and she stomped her feet. *I can't heal him, crone.*

Why not? Drakkina's confident grin faltered.

He's not old enough to desire life. He remembers the arms of the Earth Mother.

Then you need to convince him, Drakkina said as if it were a simple task.

He needs to realize that if he gives up life, he loses everything he loves here. Merewin's plan began to take shape in her frantic mind.

Yes, yes. Drakkina tapped her unmoving lips. *What does he love?*

Merewin passed her hands over the cold stones. She curled her bare toes in the dirt.

"Give the healer room," Ragnar said, his voice gruff, and all but Hauk stepped back.

Even as Merewin funneled the power of the earth up and into the stones, they barely warmed. She sighed. She could not heal him this way. She glanced back at Drakkina. *Ye need to enter his mind and tell me what he loves and tell him to live.*

Me? Drakkina's image wavered. *I do not enter the minds of children. What?*

Drakkina waved her hands back and forth. *Their minds are like quick pictures instead of thoughts, more like those of animals, mostly thinking only of the present, disjointed. Makes me dizzy trying.*

Try anyway!

Drakkina's form took a step away. *I'm not good at it, either. I would just frighten him with my intrusion.*

Just as Merewin was about to scream some obscenities in her already pounding head, Drakkina smiled. *But I know someone who is good at it, reading animals and probably children.*

Merewin looked at her expectantly.

Serena, your sister.

Merewin's sister lived hundreds of years in the future. Drakkina had threaded Merewin over a temporal bridge to heal Serena. Merewin's birth mother had gifted Serena with telepathy.

"Merewin?" Aslaug whispered. "Is there anything I can help you with?"

Merewin realized then that she'd been standing still for some time while she conversed with Drakkina. "Call her," Merewin said out loud and turned to Aslaug.

"Call who?" Aslaug asked.

Merewin glanced at the curious occupants of the room.

Hauk stood frowning, legs braced as if preparing for battle. His hand rested near the hilt of his sword.

Merewin looked back to Aslaug. "I need to converse with my god."

Aslaug's eyes widened, and a murmur rippled through the room. Merewin ignored the onlookers and the growing scowl on Hauk's face. Merewin cleared her throat and spoke louder. "She will need room. She and I. The Earth Mother and I need room to work on Ivarr."

Aslaug turned to the room. "I want most of you gone, out," she ordered.

Ragnar pointed at the door and the hushed crowd filed out.

Aslaug turned her attention on the men close by. "Back up. Give Merewin more room."

Merewin breathed deeply. She didn't like to lie and hoped the Earth Mother wouldn't mind her insinuations that Serena was a goddess. But in case Serena's form was visible, Merewin didn't have time to explain who she was.

Merewin moved her senses back over Ivarr. The boy was nearly paralyzed with the clinging darkness pushing against his heart. "Stay here with me, Ivarr," Merewin whispered near his little ear. His arm twitched and she rubbed it, waiting. Waiting. Waiting

The dragonfly birthmark on her thigh warmed and Merewin's gaze snapped upward.

Drakkina stood against the wall, her arms outspread. No one noticed her invisible form.

Where is she? Merewin asked in her mind.

Drakkina held her finger to her lips to shush. The image warped then glowed. Another image of a thread wavered into the space next to

Merewin. The thread expanded into long red hair, tousled, laying across naked shoulders.

Aslaug blinked. "I see something." Aslaug squinted her eyes. "In the smoke."

The rest of Serena's body, draped in a linen sheet, solidified. Merewin's sister blinked several times, glancing around as a murmur rose from the remaining Danes. A few people looked in Serena's direction. Others looked around as if trying to see something.

Serena smiled. *Merewin.*

Merewin smiled with relief. *I need ye.*

Drakkina has screamed that you do, Serena answered. *I would have preferred a more appropriate time for our reunion.* She looked down at her near nakedness.

Merewin remembered the kilted warrior who had fought for her sister's life. There was no time for explanations or apologies.

Serena's gaze washed over the audience, and she pulled the sheet up higher over her breasts.

Can ye read in my mind why Drakkina brought ye here? Merewin indicated Drakkina's wavering form nearby.

Serena glanced at the crone and nodded.

"I see her god," Aslaug said, falling to her knees. "A goddess."

Hauk waved his hand through the smoke and stared at the corner, squinting. Could he see Serena and Drakkina?

Merewin looked back to Ivarr. *Then read me, sister.* Merewin opened her mind. Serena's image moved to her, touching her bare arm.

"The Earth Mother," Aslaug whispered.

"'Tis someone who can help," Merewin answered and concentrated on her plan to save Ivarr.

"What is going on in here?" Svala's voice scraped along Merewin's concentration, making Serena's eyes move in the woman's direction.

Ignore her, Merewin thought.

Her sister turned away and moved to Ivarr, touching the boy's cheek. Merewin joined her and moved her hands back over the stones.

Live, Ivarr. Live, child. Serena's words sounded like a whisper of breeze in the room.

Aslaug's small sob came muffled as if she tried to hide it behind her hand.

You want to live, little boy, for all the wonderful things this world can offer you. Serena pressed her thoughts into the boy's mind.

"His eyes," Ragnar said gruffly from somewhere behind Merewin, and her gaze snapped to Ivarr's face. The child's eyes had opened.

Merewin pushed her toes into the soil, sucking the earth energy up through her and pressing it into the stones, channeling it into the little body under them. The stones warmed slightly, but only slightly. She focused her healing energy on the gunk smothering his heart, tugging it from him.

Live, child, Serena crooned, and the boy's eyes moved as if searching for his mother.

Yet the stones would not grow warmer. Merewin squeezed her eyes shut. Telling him to live wasn't enough.

"He needs to see all the things he will leave if he dies," Merewin whispered. "All the things he loves."

Serena nodded and ran her hands along Ivarr's forehead, through his hair. She smiled, tears gathering in her eyes. *His mother.* Serena looked at Aslaug. *She needs to sing to him, his favorite song about the dragonship on the sea.*

Merewin's gaze snapped to Aslaug. "Sing to Ivarr about the dragonship on the sea."

Aslaug's eyes widened, and she nodded quickly like a bird pecking. Words tumbled out of her mouth.

"With joy in the words, not sadness," Merewin said.

Aslaug took a deep breath, her tear-filled eyes looking at Ragnar.

Ragnar nodded to her firmly, urging her on.

Aslaug wiped red, watery eyes. "Yes, of course."

There's more. Serena spoke into Merewin's mind. Serena ran her hand along Ivarr's lips. *Honeycomb, the taste of it. A dog. The sunshine on his face. Another woman, a nursemaid, perhaps. The sight of his father's shining sword.* Serena looked puzzled for a moment. *A Nini?*

Merewin took a big breath. "We need things to tie him to this world. Honeycomb on his lips, his dog, a nursemaid he loves." Merewin looked to Ragnar who stood in a battle stance, his legs braced as if ready to pull his sword and slay the dragon trying to kill his son. "He needs to see his father's shining sword." She looked at Aslaug. "And something called a Nini."

Aslaug's breathless words held the edge of hope. "Aye, his doll."

"It isn't a doll, woman," Ragnar said firmly as he hefted his sword. "My son doesn't have dolls."

"'Tis a babe made of cloth," Aslaug said, ignoring her husband. "Olla, get his doll." Her arm flew out toward a door off the back. "And bring Edwyn here, and tell her to stop sobbing," she yelled at the running woman. Aslaug looked to Svein, "get honeycomb."

"Where?"

"I don't care, man, find some!" she ordered as he ran toward the door, passing a frowning Svala.

"This is ridiculous," Svala said from her spot and took a few steps toward them. "Magick didn't save the others when the sickness came three years ago. Magick doesn't work. The thrall is tricking us with herbs in the smoke."

"Is the sun rising?" Merewin asked ignoring the woman.

One of the warriors guarding the door nodded. "Some time ago."

Merewin turned back to Serena's form. It looked dimmer, as did Drakkina. *Is there anything else?*

Serena continued to caress the boy's arm. *The smell of flowers, sweet smell. And wind on him, clean wind without smoke. He hates smoke.*

Svala stepped up to Ragnar. "She is an illusionist. Hauk, you of all people must see through her tricks. You would not let another fool you."

Serena and Merewin both looked at the serpent who snaked her arm around Hauk's. The fear that had raged through Merewin turned to fury against this she-beast.

Serena looked between them, her face concerned. *Beware of her, Sister,* Serena said as she faded. *The more he loves you, the more she hates you.*

"Loves?" Merewin whispered, but Serena's body dissolved into the smoky air. She glanced toward the wall. Drakkina had vanished too. Merewin was alone.

She swallowed down her fear and turned around to the mesmerized group. "Quickly," Merewin ordered, looking at King Ragnar. "Wrap him up and bring him outside."

"Outside?!" Svala gasped. "Surely you will kill him."

Merewin turned toward the woman, her eyes narrowing. "Ivarr loves the outdoors, the sun on his face. He hates this smoke." She waved her hand in the murky air. "I mean to give him everything he loves."

"Pah!" Svala said. "You speak of a false god and cast illusions."

Merewin noticed several of the warriors shift their stances. Were the woman's words making them doubt what they had seen hovering in the smoky corner and over Ivarr?

"Freyja," one of the women said. "Her beauty...she was Freyja."

Svala rolled her eyes and opened her mouth, but Merewin cut her off. "Yer sword, King Ragnar." Merewin ticked off on her fingers. "The dog, the nursemaid, the doll, honeycomb, and sweet-smelling herbs and flowers, if ye have any left from the summer."

No one moved. It was as if they waited for a decision. Support Svala and her disbelief or Merewin and her Earth Mother.

"The smoke in here will kill him," Merewin said waving her hand before her face. She looked at Aslaug. "He doesn't have much time. We can try my plan, or we can do nothing and watch him die." Harsh, but some situations required a slap in the face.

Aslaug stood tall, her voice commanding. "Move, people, get everything on Merewin's list."

Merewin removed the stones while Aslaug wrapped her limp son in furs. Ragnar lifted him in his arms, striding through the crowded hall.

"Evil, she is evil," Svala called. "Hauk, can't you see she means to torture the child, a boy like Toki."

The fine strings of control holding Merewin's patience across her like a mask snapped, her tolerance shattered. It was one thing to attack her, but to attack Hauk after all he'd been through, bringing up the name of his son? *Cruel bitch!* Merewin rounded and strode over to stand before the creature.

The fire in her anger smoldered under each succinct word, and she tried once more to shield her disdain. "I am not evil, Svala. I will not torture an innocent, sick child."

Svala scoffed and crossed her arms over her chest. "You cast illusions to fool us." She shook her head as Ragnar carried his son out into the sun, Aslaug following, prayers to Freyja and an unknown Earth Mother streaming from her lips.

Hauk stood behind Merewin; she could feel his presence, but he did not defend. Did he believe Svala's words?

"I cast no illusions. I only wish to heal the child." Merewin took a step to follow, but Svala opened her arms to bar her way. "Let me pass," Merewin spoke low. Did the woman not hear the edge to her voice, the warning?

"Nay, if these warriors are too chivalrous to stop you from harming the king's heir further, and Ivarr's parents are too wrapped in grief to see through your performance, then I will stop you."

"Merewin, come out now!" Aslaug called, the urgency in her voice fueling the flames in Merewin's blood.

"Move, ye saklauss witch," Merewin said, her empty hand clenched into a fist. Exactly how Navlin had taught her, thumb on the outside.

"You're a lowly sla—" Svala began.

Merewin didn't let her finish as she swung her fist with all her strength. *Crack!*

CHAPTER ELEVEN
DISEASE OF THE HEART

Svala screamed as blood gushed from her flaring nostrils. Flustered hands cupped her nose as Bjalki jumped to his sister's aid.

Merewin pushed past her out into the sun. The satisfaction of stopping Svala's rantings made up for the pain in Merewin's knuckles. She shook her hand as she ran toward the small group gathered around Ivarr where he lay wrapped in furs on the ground. Everyone was still, watching. *Is he dead?* Merewin's heart sank, and she felt hot tears in her eyes. *Nay, don't let me lose him.*

"What do we do now?" Ragnar asked, watching her closely.

Merewin blinked several times and looked at Aslaug. The woman's gaze was concerned but lucid. The boy wasn't dead yet.

Merewin tried to grab her bag of stones and realized someone gripped her hand. Was she being bound for what she'd done to Svala? Merewin looked up. Hauk held her hand and gently wrapped a torn linen around her bleeding knuckles. His gaze held something, something she couldn't quite place.

He tied off a knot. "You're a warrior." A small grin broke on his face, only a trace, but enough to melt the tension in Merewin's body. It was respect she saw in his eyes, and maybe a hint of trust.

With renewed strength Merewin turned to the soul-bruised people and started issuing orders. When Svala's scream came from the house, Merewin looked at Ragnar. "Yer son will die if she comes near us while I perform my healing."

Aslaug gasped and Ragnar motioned to three strong warriors who took off toward the lodging.

Merewin threw off her cloak and found a soft stretch of grass to sit in.

To pull as much strength as she could from the earth, she would lie upon it. She pulled her skirt up so her bare calves lay on the ground. Several murmurs of disapproval came from the crowd, but she ignored them all.

"Lay his body on mine, his back against my stomach." When they did, she met Aslaug's gaze and pointed at the sack of stones. "Lay the green stone, the agate, on his heart. Lay the purple stone on his head. Lay the yellow crystals just above his naval and one below."

Merewin tried to see where the woman placed the stones on the outstretched boy. Ivarr was turning bluer, the weight on his heart so heavy. "Bring the green stone closer to the center of his chest, not quite over his heart. That's it." She leaned her head back on the grass.

From her position, the sun shone down on them, its warmth a blessing. A gentle breeze blew fresh air to ruffle their hair. "Loose the dog and bring the doll."

The dog ran to them and licked the boy's hands and feet. Aslaug first tried to stop him.

"Nay, let the dog lick. If the stones move, center them again." After a minute the dog lay down against them, his head on the boy's leg.

Merewin's mind ran down the list. "Honey, on his lips by his nurse." A young woman with red, puffy eyes knelt beside them and ran her finger along Ivarr's lips.

She leaned in to kiss his forehead. "Stay with your mother and me, sweet boy," she whispered and pulled a rag doll from her apron. "And here is Nini, holding some flowers for you." The nurse set the doll and flowers in the crook of his limp arm.

Merewin sensed something in the little body on top of her, an awareness. "Aye child, wake and look at all ye have here," she said calmly then looked to Aslaug. "Sing his favorite song, sweetly with all yer love and happiness, not sadness."

Aslaug nodded. She turned away slightly so she didn't see her little boy so limp and gray.

"Listen children to the story that was written long ago,

About a warrior, on the waters, rowing to the rocky shoal..."

Aslaug's sweet lilt carried on and on through many verses while Merewin spoke low above Ivarr's head. "Ivarr, if ye want to hear yer mother's song and play with yer dog again, ye must remain here with us. Ye can't leave this life, ye must fight to keep the things ye love." Merewin closed her eyes and focused her mind on the solid earth beneath her, the cool feel of the soil, the fresh smell of the grass as it tickled at her ankles in the breeze.

"The sun is warm here, Ivarr, the grass and flowers smell wonderful. Yer mama's arms are here to hold ye."

Had the boy stirred?

"Listen to yer mother's voice. Don't leave her, Ivarr. For she can't follow ye if ye leave this world. Live, Ivarr. Want to live, child. Taste the sweetness of life on yer lips."

The power pulsed up under Merewin and gathered in her center until its enormity was too much for her to hold. Never before had Merewin tried to summon so much power from the earth. Little by little, she fed it into the small body. If she let it all go at once, it could burn him or worse, so she concentrated the flow, channeling it up to the stones.

The dog moved its head to set it on Ivarr's stomach, knocking one of the yellow stones.

The nurse touched it. "Ahh," she yelped, dropping the stone. "It burns!"

"Hauk, replace the stone," Merewin murmured, her mind completely engrossed in releasing a constant stream of energy into the boy through the stones. She knew at once when Hauk had re-settled the stone, for the flow grew strong once more. The stones were hot. Joy flooded Merewin's closed eyes, the tears flowing down her temples and into the grass. If they were hot, her magick was working.

"Aye Ivarr, live child." The flood of energy burned inside Merewin as she released the stream but kept the dam strong. The boy moved.

"Ragnar, talk to yer son while Aslaug sings. Talk of yer strength, of the strength of yer sword and how it will be his."

The king's voice droned on, and the boy stilled, listening to the deep inflections of his father's words.

The disease clung to every bit of Ivarr's body, inside and out. Merewin had never felt such an all-encompassing disease before. 'Twas as if it squeezed around and through every muscle in his body.

Painstakingly, Merewin extracted it, pulled it, wiped it, cut it with her focused threads of energy. First around his heart, then his lungs, his stomach and intestines. All the while she murmured reassurances to him under the words of his parents.

There were murmurs around them, and Hauk's strong voice moving people back. Merewin continued, her breathing becoming labored, as she pulled at the foul sap around Ivarr's leg muscles. The grass grew damp under her, her clothes sticking to her hot skin. She heard the dog bark and Aslaug stopped singing.

The child wiggled where she held him.

"Ivarr! My babe!" Aslaug's screech was joyful, but Merewin couldn't open her eyes.

The child laughed and tried to roll off her as the dog leaped around them.

Merewin heard words near her ear and had to focus on them to understand.

"May I take him?" Ragnar's voice pulled her from her concentration.

It was time. Merewin had rid the boy of the gray stickiness within him. She loosened her grasp on the boy's little shoulders.

"Take him," she said weakly and felt a chill as the breeze washed over her drenched body when they picked the child off. The foulness, which had lain within the boy, now soaked from Merewin into the ground beneath, but its stink remained. She took an even breath to try and cleanse herself more.

In the distance she heard voices. "Dear Freyja! Is she sound?" Bera's voice cried somewhere nearby, talking nearly without a break between questions and concerns.

Hauk was right. Bera liked to talk, and Merewin focused on the lilt of her words. "She's not moving, Hauk! Quick, check for breath."

Murmurs and questions from others hummed behind her closed eyes. Through the ups and downs of inflections, Hauk's strong, even voice gave her something to hold onto. "Wake, Merewin, else Bera will talk us to death." His words were light but edged with concern.

Concern? Serves him right for stealing her away from Northumbria. She kept her eyes closed for a moment longer.

"She looks blue. Like Ivarr," a man murmured.

"Did she take his disease into herself?" Bera breathed.

Interesting question. Had she taken Ivarr's disease into her or had it only used her body as a pathway into the ground? She'd never before attacked a disease so strongly rooted in a body. A stronger breeze blew, making her tremble, and the weight of a blanket lowered across her.

"Where is she," a distant screech pierced the hushed air. *Svala.*

Merewin opened her eyes and blinked up into Hauk's stormy blue orbs. Yes, there was concern there as Hauk looked back and forth from one of her eyes to the other. His hand brushed her hair back.

"You look terrible," he said.

"I need a bath," Merewin answered softly.

"You smell terrible, too." Hauk scooped her up easily in his arms. She grimaced with the aches gripping her. "Like sickness."

The small crowd of people parted. "The grass beneath her! 'Tis dead!" someone yelled as Hauk carried Merewin away.

Merewin could hear the ranting words of Svala coming closer.

"Merewin, are you well?" Bera asked but then continued before Merewin could answer. "I hear you punched Svala right in her pointy nose." She lowered her voice. "She's a snake."

"Bera," Hauk said low. "Svala's had great loss, too."

"Hauk, I demand the life of your vicious thrall," Svala yelled, her voice altered to a nasal whine with a rag clamped over it. Bjalki followed on her heels like a well-fed hound.

But Hauk continued his swift gait toward his horse. "Bera, I'm taking Merewin back to Spring House. Tell Aslaug and Ragnar."

"Aye, Brother," she said, but continued to walk next to them.

"Halt!" Svala insisted and ran in front of them.

"Step out of the way, Svala. Merewin is weak," Hauk began.

"From healing Ivarr," Bera finished.

"I don't care," Svala hissed. "I demand retribution. Your thrall maimed me, Hauk. She must be taught a lesson, her place here."

"Svala, I will compensate you for your discomfort," Hauk said trying to step around the vicious she-beast.

"Nay! I want retribution!" Svala insisted.

Merewin tried to sit up higher in her perch, not wishing to appear the invalid. The effort caused her stomach to roll. A large bubble tumbled up her throat. She put her fingers to her mouth.

Hauk stepped around Svala and continued to his horse. "Can you stand?" he asked.

Merewin took an even breath to quell her stomach. The bitter taste on her tongue didn't help. "Aye." Whether she could stand or not, Merewin didn't want to look like a weak babe in front of Svala.

Svala snaked her hand around his arm. "Hauk, you can be the dominating barbarian all you want in my bed, but out here, I'm in charge. I'm the king's sister."

"Sister-in-law," Bera countered.

Merewin's stomach clenched and flipped. The thought of Hauk in Svala's bed, pressing his lips to her, dominating her, tore a pain through her chest. The world swam and more noxious gas bubbled up her throat.

"The same king whose child now laughs," Hauk countered.

"Put me down," Merewin ground out. She wouldn't be held like a bairn before her enemy, for that's what Svala was, an enemy.

Hauk let her slide down his body to stand between him and Svala, so close to the woman that the straight wool of their gowns shifted against one another. Svala refused to give any space, leaning even closer.

"I will see you pay for your crime," Svala threatened. The evil woman wrinkled her nose. "By Thor, you stink."

The oily bubbling Merewin had clamped down broke from her control, rolling up her gullet. In one great heave, Merewin leaned forward and vomited. The churned-up remains of Vivien's porridge washed all down the front of Svala's fine gown.

Svala took a small step back, silent horror contorting her features.

Merewin felt Hauk's strong hands clamp down on her shoulders, supporting her. "Now ye stink too," Merewin said, wiping her mouth with the back of her sleeve.

Svala screeched as she stared down at her ruined dress. Bjalki unpinned her brooches to shed the outer layer of gown.

Merewin turned in Hauk's hands. "Take me home, Hauk," she said loudly.

Bera's shoulders shook with hushed laughter, and most of the onlookers hid their amusement in coughs and hasty retreats.

"Drink some water," Gamal said, coming up beside Merewin with a bladder.

Merewin took a sip and let the cool liquid wash her mouth and throat. "Thank ye," Merewin said, handing it back.

Hauk lifted her onto his horse and swung up behind. Svala continued to rage so he talked loudly over her tirade. "Gamal, let Ragnar know of this," Hauk said, gesturing to Svala, and his friend nodded.

Bera smiled at Merewin, and speaking loudly, said, "you don't look so bad now."

"A good purging can do wonders," Merewin replied and fell back against Hauk as he tapped the horse forward.

"I'll visit soon." Bera waved as Hauk spurred them to the forest's edge.

As soon as they ducked into the tunnel of trees, Hauk slowed. Merewin ached all over. She sighed in the silence.

"You feel better?" Hauk asked.

She nodded. "Aye, since I purged. I'm merely tired and dirty."

"You wretch a lot." She felt Hauk's breath touch her head. Was he grinning? She almost heard it in the inflection.

"I didn't before I met ye," Merewin retorted. His deep chuckle rumbled as he steered the horse through the sacred woods along the path to Spring House.

They rode slowly, and Merewin's mind moved from Serena to Ivarr to Svala's anger. "Svala hates me," she said. It was an easier topic than her healing magick. The old trees bent slightly inward with age as if they listened. Looking upward, Merewin watched the sway of colored leaves, lit by morning sunlight.

Hauk remained silent for so long Merewin didn't think he'd acknowledge her observation.

"We...mated once," he said. "I was drunk and grieving, and she was mourning the loss of her husband. I don't plan to repeat it."

The tension in Merewin's chest relaxed. But why should she care? Wouldn't it be better for her Danish master to find his way into other beds to ease his lust, leaving her alone? Merewin knew the answer before she had finished thinking the question. Nay, it wouldn't be better. It would be awful.

"She's jealous of you," Hauk said, lifting one strand of Merewin's long hair.

"Jealous? I am merely a thrall while she is the king's sister-in-law."

"You are beautiful and a warrior."

He thought her beautiful?

"Svala is a headstrong woman." Hauk pulled Merewin tighter into his lap as they leaped over a small creek. "Most women back down from her anger. She didn't know she barred the way of a warrior."

Merewin sniffed, raising her hand to rub her nose. "Warriors don't vomit in battle."

"Quite a few do," he countered. "Good ones, in fact."

Merewin shook her head. "I'm a healer, not a warrior. Ye're a warrior."

They broke out of the forest, the view of Spring House in the valley below. "We but fight different enemies, Merewin."

She turned in her seat to look at his face. The sun slanted against him, casting gold in the waves of his hair. He studied her, and she noticed lighter blue specks in the deep blue of his eyes.

"I fight enemies with my axe and sword, and you fight illness and injury with your..."

"Magick," Merewin finished before he could. "With my magick."

Hauk stared at her for a moment and then shifted his gaze beyond, above her head. "I don't believe in magick, Merewin." He tapped the horse into a run down the slope as if that was the end of their conversation.

"Ye don't believe in magick? Were ye not just there to see me save Ivarr? I did it, me, with my magick." Merewin yelled over the wind and thudding hoofbeats as she grabbed hard to the fringe of mane.

He pulled up short in front of the house, scattering chickens and setting off the dog. Jumping down, he reached up. "A warrior doesn't win a battle completely on his own," Hauk said. Questions warred with stubbornness in his gaze.

Merewin leaned forward so he'd catch her as she slid off the horse. "I came up with the plan, convinced Aslaug to follow it, hit Svala..." she held up her bandaged hand, "and stripped the disease from the king's son."

His strong hands caught her around the waist. "And your Earth Mother and the other one?" Hauk said, watching.

Merewin's eyes widened. He'd seen Drakkina? No one else had seemed to notice her at all. Had the crone let him see her?

"So obviously," Merewin said softly, "there was magick involved. My magick and their magick."

Hauk shrugged his broad shoulders. "Or an illusion. A trick of light and smoke, some herb you put in the fire so we would see things that weren't there."

"How would I perform this illusion?"

Hauk untied the sack of stones from the horse and pulled his sword and axe from their straps. A boy took the reins of the horse, and Hauk nodded to him before turning back to Merewin. "I've seen many strange things in battle," Hauk said.

"But..."

"I don't believe in magick." He turned his back on her to walk into the house.

Merewin followed, her body feeling so heavy she wanted to sink to the ground. But her anger held her upright. "Just because ye continue to say it, doesn't mean ye're right."

Hauk pivoted without warning, and Merewin walked right into him. He looked down at her, the humorous glint gone. "I did not say there is no magick, Merewin." His voice was low, commanding. "What I said was...I do not believe in its existence in Midgard." Challenge evident in his eyes. "I choose not to believe in it."

The house servant entered from a back room. Without moving his gaze from her Hauk said, "Vivien, send for a bath for Merewin and let her rest. She's in need of more sleep."

He turned and strode down the longhouse and through the arched doorway of his own room.

CHAPTER TWELVE
SIMPLE DENIAL

Hauk arched the heavy axe in a smooth circular motion. *Thwack!* The log split evenly under the assault. The sun lowered behind the small mountain shading Spring House, and the chill of autumn cooled his sweating body. He placed another log on the block and used momentum and muscle to swing the axe again. *Thwack!*

Simple. The act of breaking logs was simple. Hauk liked simple, at least in his home life. Complexity in battle strategy was another thing. Difficult sieges strengthened the mind as well as the body. But he was home, not circling a fort in Mercia.

Merewin.

Thwack! Definitely not simple.

Hauk had avoided her for the last two weeks since he watched Ivarr fill back up with life while sprawled on top of Merewin. As if a dark heaviness had been sucked out of him into Merewin to purge. Hauk wiped the back of his hand across his brow. He squinted at the sunrays as they streaked past the mountain peak. Aye, he believed in the magick of the gods, but Merewin was not a goddess.

Oh, she looked the part with her brilliant golden-green eyes, which turned up slightly at the corners, her full lips and proud chin, and her seductive form, one he was almost unable to resist. She had the cleverness of Snotra, the goddess of wisdom. Merewin's intelligence intrigued him, made him want to talk to her and hear what she had to say. He'd never felt as much toward a female before.

Thwack!

Aye, Merewin looked the part and had the intellect of a goddess, but she was not an immortal of Asgard. Why then did she seem to possess the magick to heal? And who were the two spirit women who'd helped her? The crone had stood silent but watched him. The other could have been Freyja, but he swore he'd heard the apparition call Merewin "sister."

Hauk hadn't asked Merewin anything further about the events of that day. He'd been too busy discouraging Ragnar from buying her freedom. Hauk had finally won the battle when he'd reminded Aslaug that freedom meant Merewin would find a way to return to Northumbria. She'd no longer be available for miraculous healing.

Although he wouldn't admit it out loud, Hauk had also avoided Merewin to avoid another debate about magick. He'd sworn never to put faith into magical healing again the day Toki laid dead and cold in his arms. A woman from Northumbria wouldn't change his mind. But the vision of Ivarr waking in the morning sunshine on Merewin's outstretched body haunted his convictions. If she'd been here when Toki was sick, would his son still be alive?

By Odin's stones, he couldn't let his mind go there. He'd spent the last years wallowing in regret. He couldn't do so anymore. "I still don't believe in magick," he said and swung the axe. *Thwack!* It fell neatly in two.

Aye, chopping wood was simple. A certain act, set in motion, had the same result—a split log. Now and then the log had a variance or might wobble, but Hauk's power, his mighty axe, still sliced through the knotted wood. Simple. And completely in his control.

Thwack!

Unfortunately, nothing with Merewin seemed to be in his control. She was his thrall, but even now she worked in an outbuilding she'd claimed yesterday for her own. Calling it her curing cottage. Pounding plants, straining foul-colored concoctions into vials and bladders, and boiling bits in an iron pot. When he'd stopped in to see her earlier, she'd been covered with sweat, her sleeves rolled up, her hair curling wildly around her trim waist. Beautiful, absolutely, tantalizingly beautiful.

Until he'd smelled the air.

Thwack!

The aroma of healing. It twisted his gut as the memories of sickness and death washed over him. The faces of his parents and brother, his sister-in-law, his wife, and then Toki thrashed against his defenses. Memories he thought he'd crushed so hard they'd disintegrated. And one sniff of Merewin's cures brought it all back. He'd retreated immediately, riding off to clear his nostrils in the fresh air.

Thwack!

Nay, Merewin was not simple, and he needed some distance from her to think clearly. Ragnar's orders to help his ally tamp down hostilities in Dalriada sounded like a good way to find that distance. He'd deal with Merewin's craft when he returned.

"Papa?" Dalla's voice cut through his thoughts.

Thwack!

"Aye, Dalla."

There was silence, and he lowered his axe to look at his daughter. Her lovely little features lay dim on her face as the breeze caught at her blond hair. Even sad, she was beautiful, and not such a little girl anymore. She would marry within five years. He remembered when she laughed often and smiled all the time. When was the last time he'd seen her smile?

Dalla walked up to him as if waiting for permission. Hauk set the axe against the block and opened his arms. She jumped into them, clinging.

"Now, now," he said under the attack. "What's this?"

Her words were muffled against his stomach. "I missed you, Papa."

He looked down. "You have Vivien and Diarf to play with when I'm gone."

Dalla frowned. "'Tis not the same," she whispered, and Hauk knew she meant it was not the same as when the house milled with family. Hauk was able to escape the loneliness that lay heavy on the once loud and happy house by going on raids and voyages. Dalla could not. He exhaled. He had no answers, no solutions to fix the past. He'd rather ignore it until it was forgotten.

"I'm here now," he said gruffly, messing the top of her hair and picking up his axe. "And now you will have Merewin to talk with."

"I don't want her," Dalla spat, giving him a glimpse of the hellion others warned him about. "You brought her home for me," she said, reminding him of his foolish words upon arrival when he was void of a gift. "And I don't want her. Send her back or give her away. I overheard from Vivien that Bjalki, Svala's brother, wants her in his bed."

"Dalla, you're too young to be discussing such things." He'd have a word with Vivien.

Thwack! The axe began a rhythm again, concluding the subject.

"Send her away, Papa," Dalla insisted.

"She is staying, Dalla. Make friends. She can help you prepare yourself to be a proper wife."

"I want her gone! She's not a wife, only a whore for your bed!" she screamed.

Hauk stopped in mid swing. "Dalla Geirson, you will not say such…" but she turned and ran off, golden hair trailing behind. Should he follow? What would he say when he caught her?

When she was out of sight, Hauk returned to the pile of logs. Dalla would outgrow the stubbornness. She would learn to like Merewin.

Thwack!

Simple. He liked simple.

⬤

Svala shielded her eyes from the sun and watched Hauk. She sat atop her mare at the ridge above Spring House. A thick stand of trees blocked her from sight. Svala's gaze followed the swing of his axe down on the log then trailed over the muscles in his flexing shoulders. She squinted and wished she could hide closer. Hauk shook his head, sending his waving blond hair to graze his bare skin.

Svala touched her upper lip with the tip of her tongue. "He's magnificent," she whispered from behind the thin shawl, which hid the bruising under her eyes and around her nose. She still remembered the feel of his large hands roaming her hot body the one night she had coaxed him to her bed. She missed his power, the feel of his hard thrusts impaling her, his hot breath on her nipples and neck. She craved it.

"Look at his strength." Merely watching, the moisture grew at the juncture of her legs. She licked her upper lip again, remembering the taste of the huge man when she took him in her mouth.

"I'm stronger than he," Bjalki said gruffly. His horse sidled closer to his sister's.

Svala absently ran her hand down his arm. "Now, now big brother. Do I detect some jealousy?" she mocked.

"Never." Bjalki's gaze searched the yard.

Svala laughed lightly, but her chest tightened. She needed Hauk. Her marriage to Ragnar's brother had given her a position in the king's hall. And as long as Aslaug's children kept dying, it would have been Svala's future child who ruled next, or even Svala's husband if something dreadful happened to Ragnar during a raid. But now with her husband dead, Svala felt her position slipping.

Some whispered that the warriors would support Hauk as ruler if anything happened to Ragnar. Svala needed Hauk to ensure her position once more, to ensure a child from her loins would rule. Hauk's only son had died, too, and Dalla would soon be married and sent away. It was a perfect plan, if only Hauk would cooperate.

"Let me go down there now and challenge him. I'll show you I'm the more powerful warrior," Bjalki said, jerking Svala out of her musings.

"Nay," Svala snapped, her teasing tone crystalized to ice. "You will stay," she turned her gaze to him. "I don't want him damaged."

"And Merewin?"

Svala frowned, her eyes narrowed, one still pooled with blood. Hauk's mathkr of a slave had broken her perfect nose, and she'd hidden her face for the last two weeks.

"You'll have her once I have Hauk," Svala promised, and ran her hand along her brother's thigh. "If by chance she dies due to your," she paused, "your vigor," she flipped her hand in the air, "well, she's not sturdy enough for living in Danmørk." Svala turned her attention back to Spring House and her warrior chopping wood. "I want Hauk with no distractions, so she must be gone, one way or another."

A low growl came from Bjalki and Svala's gaze snapped back to him. "I would like to keep her as a slave," Bjalki said and leered. "I am the man of this family. I have a say in this plan of yours."

Svala raised her hand to slap him, but he caught her arm easily, bringing her eye-to-eye. "Listen to me, Bjalki. I am the smart one. I have the plan to bring our family to power. Without my cooperation you will remain a lower-class raider."

He stared at her, his fingers tightly wrapped around her thin wrist. She refused to acknowledge the pain his grip inflicted. "In payment, I get Hauk Geirson without his little healing thrall." She spoke slowly. "Do you understand?"

Bjalki dropped her arm, his gaze falling back to the scene below. Dalla ran behind the house toward the stream. "What about the girl?"

Svala shrugged. "She's not a concern." Svala glanced at the girl sitting with her face in her hands on the stream bank. "I'll make sure the little brat is married off soon."

"Dalriada?" Dalla whined.

Dalriada? Merewin's thought echoed the child's cry.

Dalla leaned up against Hauk across the fire from Merewin. "Why, Papa? You only just returned home."

Hauk breathed deeply, his gaze burning into Merewin.

Merewin glanced back down at her trencher of venison, barley, and greens. She chewed at the seasoned meat, which had been delicious moments ago before Hauk's news. Now it took force to finish it. She should be happy he would be gone, but instead dread clutched inside her chest. It had been a fortnight since she'd healed Ivarr, and Hauk was already leaving her alone in this strange new land. Who would protect Spring House with him gone?

"King Ragnar's ally has settled Dunadd on the coast, but the locals have organized and are causing problems," he said delicately. "Ragnar's promised his finest men to help him regain control. So he's asked me to go."

Merewin looked into his eyes, still locked with her own. She swallowed the thick meat but refused to look away. "And what of me?" she asked, ignoring the fear trickling along her spine behind the calm words.

"You have become popular with the hurt and diseased. I'm sure they will keep you busy while I am away."

Of course, she was easily left behind, as a thrall should be. Merewin frowned, anger making her voice strong. "Do I live here, then? Perhaps Bera has need for me, and I could live in Ribe."

Hauk frowned, their eyes in silent battle. "You are mine, Merewin. You will stay at Spring House unless you are needed in Ribe for an emergency. Then Gamal will escort you there."

"Gamal isn't going?" Merewin asked.

"Nay, Bera's time is too close. He should be near her and the babe."

"Svala's brother, Bjalki?" Dalla asked with a glance at Merewin. Did the girl know he'd threatened to take Merewin away?

Hauk's frown deepened. "He will be with me on the mission."

Merewin exhaled. "Good."

Even though Hauk's frown relaxed back into his normal gruff look, the room felt stagnant, gripped in webs of silently screaming emotion. Merewin wondered what it must be like to have her older sister's power to read minds. She looked at Dalla's tight features and shivered, pulling the fur pelt tight around her shoulders. Perhaps it was best not to know.

Merewin studied Dalla from under lowered lashes. She had Hauk's strong features, straight nose and stubborn jaw. Gentle waves of golden-hued hair tumbled down her back. Without the sneer the girl could be beautiful. Unfortunately, every time she looked in Merewin's direction, her pretty face contorted into something close to rage with a hint of "I'll get you" in it. And Merewin would be left behind with her at Spring House and Svala a short ride away in town.

Svala, the evil serpent, continued to spout lies about Merewin in Ribe. Lies about Merewin being a lying illusionist, that her healing was not real and those she healed were still, in reality, sick. Nonsense! Merewin looked back down at the meal she no longer tasted while Dalla continued to whine about Hauk's mission.

True, Merewin hadn't used her magick to heal everyone who came to Spring House. But she still restored them to relative health. She used the traditional remedies Navlin had taught her, extracting healing powers inherent in the Earth Mother's plants to use in poultices and tinctures. Only when the natural remedies failed, or there were dire circumstances, did Merewin use her stones and magick. Failure was something she wouldn't allow in herself, even if the healing exhausted her. She was not a fraud, and she proved it each time she sent someone home feeling stronger.

Hopefully in time, the rumors of her magical healing of Ivarr would fade. So far only two children had been brought before her since Ivarr's healing. And they were several years old, old enough to respond to her stones. Before starting, she had warned the parents of her limitations, but their belief that she could heal anyone was too strong for them to doubt.

"I leave at first light," Hauk said.

"On the morrow?" Dalla screeched jumping up from her little stool. It thumped on the rushes.

Merewin's heart sank. *So soon.* He was leaving her in a house with a banshee in an unknown land where Svala roamed free. *At first light.* He hadn't even tried to kiss her again since the night they were interrupted. Several times she'd awoken at night, Ellette gone to hunt, to the slight smell of leather, soap, and man. But no one stood in the shadows of the small room. Two nights ago, she'd braved a look into his room where a large bed stood empty. She hadn't dared to look further. Perhaps she wasn't as desirable as he had at first thought. Merewin pushed against the ache in her forehead. Perhaps he was afraid of her magick. She sniffed, sitting straighter.

Dalla quieted where she cuddled against Hauk's chest. She looked smaller sitting on her father's large lap.

Merewin met his stare. His gaze, dark and expressionless in the shadows, moved over her face as he spoke. "'Tis but a mission. I will return soon."

Merewin raised her chin slightly, willing the ache in her throat to dissolve. "We will be well," she said evenly, her expression distant and tight. She rose and walked to her small room.

CHAPTER THIRTEEN
TO BATTLE

The odor of dead fish and salty low tide mixed with the guttural sounds of the crew readying the longboat for their journey across the sea and around to Pictland.

Hauk stood, his arms crossed over his chest as Ragnar reviewed the route. They would travel due west until they reached Northumbria, then keep the shore in view as they sailed north and then west and south around the head of the country to the land once ruled by the Picts.

Hauk nodded as Ragnar repeated his warnings about the painted locals plaguing his friend. But Hauk's gaze followed the gentle sway of Merewin's hips as she walked among the tables set up with fresh fish. The soft blue gown that had been let out to accommodate Merewin's height lapped along her legs. She smiled easily with the people of Ribe, many of whom had visited Spring House for her healing talents. Several women passed packets of dried plants to Merewin, herbs meant for more smelly concoctions. She'd already found a place in their society.

Hauk forced his gaze back to Ragnar. 'Twas good he'd accepted the mission. He needed to be away from the stench of sickness. It brought back memories that needed to be forgotten. Aye, the decision was a sound one. He turned to survey his ship, his resolve back in place.

Merewin's laughter filtered to him through the clangs and shouts of the crowds. Without conscious thought, he turned towards her as if drawn. Bera walked with her arm linked through Merewin's, Gamal nearby. Bera's lips moved non-stop, and Merewin laughed now and then. The light sounds pulled him, and her smile caught at his breath.

His brows pinched. *She doesn't smile like that at Spring House.* Nearly every night since Ivarr's healing Hauk had watched her sleep, wondering why she thrashed and frowned. Did she also have demons to chase, memories to forget?

Hauk watched her now beside Bera while his sister haggled with some local fishwives about the morning's catch. Soon they were all smiling and nodding in agreement over some price. By the time he returned, he imagined Merewin would have mastered the art of negotiating a fair price for fish and wares along the wharf. She had intelligence and a natural ability to jump in and take charge. Aye, his Merewin was a leader despite her current status. Hauk rubbed the close-cropped beard along his chin. Even with the connection to magick, Hauk admitted he respected her. Probably more than any woman he knew.

"Hauk, there you are," Svala called, swinging her hips in a provocative walk toward him. Her arms and neck were adorned with polished gold and jewels. She wore a thin shawl over her hair, which she held across her face. "You wouldn't leave without saying farewell, would you?" Svala asked.

The shawl dropped enough that he saw the bruising around the woman's nose, which now had a slight bulge in it. "I understand Merewin has success in fixing broken bones," he said indicating her nose.

Svala's gaze sharpened. "Your slave did this to me. I'm not about to let her touch me again." Her look shifted to where Merewin and Bera laughed, and she pulled the shawl up higher under her eyes. "I still demand punishment against her."

"You will not pursue this while I'm away."

Svala shrugged her shoulders. "I'm a patient woman, Hauk. I can wait." Her look brightened, and she wrapped a hand around his bicep. She lifted onto her toes toward his ear. "But I won't wait forever," she said, her voice syrupy with carnal insinuation. "When you tire of the slave, I may not be available anymore, Hauk. You have been without a wife for three years now."

Merewin glanced toward them, her smile fading.

Bera followed Merewin's gaze and fired off some unladylike retorts he could read from her lips. His sister could be considered a fiery warrior, too.

Svala squeezed his arm. "I know you have not remained celibate," she said, to remind him of their tryst after his family died. "But 'tis time you found a wife again, someone to warm your bed. Someone to train Dalla to be a wife. She is nearing the age."

"She is only ten years, Svala."

She shrugged. "Some marry at twelve."

"Not my daughter."

Svala's eyes darkened, and her voice contained an edge of anger. "I will not wait forever."

Hauk looked into Svala's blue eyes. Why hadn't he seen the ugliness there before? Had he ever really looked in them? "I understand, Svala," he said evenly. She began to smile behind the shawl. "You are free to find a husband elsewhere."

Surprise flitted behind her gaze before prideful anger obliterated it.

"Excuse me, while I see to my ship." Hauk extracted his arm from her grasp and strode toward the docks.

Bjalki met him at the gangplank. "I'm surprised you agreed to go on this raid," Bjalki said, his look wandering over Merewin as she and Bera walked toward the ship. "I was to lead it until you agreed to go." Bjalki spoke without moving his stare from Merewin. "Ragnar favors you over his own blood. 'Tis unnatural."

Hauk stepped into Bjalki's line of sight. "You and Ragnar share no blood. He's a wise king. He knows the strengths and weaknesses of his warriors."

Bjalki's eyes narrowed with open hatred. "Yet time and again, Hauk, you show weakness in letting those we conquer live."

"We can debate the strategy of reaping the rewards of live, contented people over corpses some other time. Right now, you have my ship to help prepare," Hauk said as the women stopped next to him.

Bjalki smiled and bowed his head. "Bera." She nodded her head in return, though she did not smile. Then he turned to Merewin. "Fair healer," he said but did not bow. "My dear sister swears she will have your lovely head on a platter." His grin turned into a leer. "I promise though to have your head in a much more pleasurable place, at least for me."

Bera gasped as Hauk's hand grabbed Bjalki around the neck and shoved him backward against a pier timber sticking out of the water along the wharf.

Bjalki's look held no fear, only mockery, and Hauk wanted to slice it off his face. He drew a short sword and brought it to rest against the man's pocked cheek.

"You would kill the king's brother by marriage in front of a hundred witnesses outside the boundaries of a challenge?" Bjalki asked evenly.

"Not kill," Hauk spoke low. "Maim."

Bjalki's confidence slipped, and Hauk ran the edge of his dagger along the side of Bjalki's beard, sending bristly hairs sifting to the ground. One movement, and he would press a bit harder to slice a layer of skin from his cheek. One crude comment. Hauk waited for it, searched for it.

"Nay, Hauk," Bera's plea barely registered in his revenge-soaked brain.

Bjalki had also desired Ingun, Hauk's first wife. The arse had dogged Hauk ever since, coveting anything he had. Blood pumped through Hauk, ready for action, ready to finish what had started so many years ago.

Soft and steady, Merewin's words beat through the rush of blood in his ears. "If ye maim him, I will be obliged to heal him."

Hauk continued to watch the blue orbs of his enemy. Neither moved. By Thor, Hauk wished Bjalki would move. The fool couldn't possibly have enough brains to listen to his threat.

Merewin's cool fingers touched his arm. Only the control of a seasoned warrior stopped Hauk from springing into action and slicing Bjalki's throat. "If ye maim him," she said softly, "he may be left behind. Here in Ribe while ye are across the sea."

Bjalki smiled. "Aye, Hauk, slice me and I'll stay behind to protect your thrall."

Hauk yanked his blade back, shoving Bjalki. "Get on the ship." Hauk turned, and Merewin's hand slipped away.

Ragnar stood behind him and watched his warrior saunter onto the longboat. Bjalki's trailing laughter held more than an edge of evil.

"He may be related by marriage to an honorable king," Ragnar said and turned to Hauk, "but don't trust his honor, Hauk. I would watch your back on this voyage."

"I always do," Hauk said and turned to Merewin. Fear sat heavily in her features.

Bera wrapped an arm through Merewin's. "We should find a second large dog. He and Sæla will keep Bjalki and his evil ilk away." The bright woman smiled.

Merewin managed to produce a tight grin, but unease sat in her brilliant green eyes. Hauk reached out and ran his thumb over the thin lines of her pinched brow and leaned in closer.

Hauk moved his lips near her ear as Bera stepped away. "You will be protected no matter what becomes of me. Ragnar and Aslaug will protect you themselves, and Gamal."

"Thank ye," Merewin said, her eyes cast on his throat.

"You do not seem thankful." He tried to catch her glance.

Merewin met his gaze. Her green orbs snapped with suppressed ire. "I am not used to needing protection. In Northumbria I had no need of it."

Before Hauk could remind her that she'd needed protection when he ran her down in the oak forest, he saw her blush, gaze lowering again to his neck. There was no need to state the obvious.

"We are a passionate people," he said, his voice low. "At times the passion can run violent." It was true, but he would not apologize for it. He respected and believed in his way of life.

She reached a slender hand up to grasp a charm of Thor's hammer he wore on a leather cord around his neck.

"Does this protect ye?" She rubbed her fingers along the smooth lines.

"Some say it does." Hauk glanced at the common ornament worn by many warriors but then turned his attention to Merewin's bent head. His hand ran along the deep browns and golds of her hair where the sun warmed it.

Merewin reached into a pocket and pulled out a stone. "Carry this then, close to ye." She set it in the center of his palm. The smooth oval rock felt hot to the touch, alive, as if it had a heart and blood. *Magick?* He almost dropped it, but Merewin wrapped his fingers around it. Fear and sadness swam in her eyes, he recognized them and wondered why they plagued her.

Merewin worried at her bottom lip. "I would have ye come back, Hauk. Whole and alive."

By the gods, was she worried about him? She adjusted the leather straps over his arms and smoothed the front of his shirt. When she reached up to run fingers down one of his war braids, he caught her hand and drew her up against him so their bodies touched. He cupped her face in his two large hands so her eyes were level with his. Yet she looked away.

"Merewin." Her stare flicked to his but retreated. "Look at me." Her gaze slowly met his own. "I have always returned. The painted men of your land will not change that."

"And Bjalki?"

"I'll keep my guard up as usual. I know my enemies."

"But Gamal won't be with ye."

His hard mouth relaxed into a grin. *She is worried about me.* "Gamal isn't my only friend or faithful supporter."

She gave a brief nod. "Keep the stone close to ye anyway."

Hauk brushed the sides of her fragile jaw with his thumbs.

"Ready to sail," Svein called.

Hauk ignored him and continued to search Merewin's eyes. How could he banish that look? As he closed the distance between their faces, Merewin stared, eyes open. She didn't blink as he moved his lips against hers. He deepened the kiss, tilting her head to fit intimately against him, and her eyes closed. Only then did he give himself completely over to the warmth of her mouth, the feminine taste of her breath, the spicy sweet smell of her skin. Hauk kissed her like he wanted to lure her inside him, devour her so she rode safely next to his heart.

He heard the whoops of laughter from the men behind him, and he slowly released Merewin from the kiss. Her eyes fluttered open. Passion made the green orbs more like the deep green of the forest. Why hadn't he woken her during the nights these past weeks? Those long nights when he'd watched her? Why hadn't he carried her back to his bed?

"Ready to sail, Hauk?" another man called, laughter in his voice. "Or must we give you 'til midday to say your farewell?" Several others chuckled.

He touched his thumb to her kiss-parted lips. "I will return, Merewin." The tip of her tongue slipped out to wet the small space between her lips and Hauk nearly groaned out loud. She nodded and stepped back.

Hauk turned reluctantly and boarded. "To the oars," he shouted, his voice fierce. The quicker they arrived and subdued the Picts for Ragnar's ally, the quicker they would return and the quicker he could bed Merewin. Then his mind could focus again and no longer imagine mating with her. He would focus on battle and conquest, not on remembering the specific smell of one woman's skin.

As they pulled away from the wharf, Merewin watched. Hauk saw her standing there until her body grew small and slipped away with the view of land. "Spicy sweet," he mumbled to himself then looked up at the sun to confirm the course. Due west.

✦

Merewin rode Hauk's horse beside Gamal as they descended into the valley where Spring House sat along the stream. Tired, she was so tired and alone, even as Gamal's lively tales coaxed smiles. A hollowness sat heavy inside her, similar to the empty feeling she had when Navlin had died.

"I will visit every few days, but send Diarf or Vivien for me if you're in need," Gamal said, as their horses splashed through a narrow crossing of the creek before the large house. "With all the able men from Ribe at sea, there shouldn't be any danger to you out here. Hauk made certain the people know that you're under his protection by..." He waved his hand, "his farewell. And I'm sure townsfolk will keep visiting for your remedies." He smiled broadly. "Between them and Dalla, you should stay busy."

Speak of evil and ye summon evil. Navlin's words tumbled through Merewin's mind as Dalla stepped out the front door, familiar sneer in place. Her eyes looked red and puffy, like she'd been crying. *None of my concern,* Merewin thought. Best to stay away from the little devil.

"Thank ye, Gamal," Merewin said, as he lowered her off the huge beast. "I look forward to yer visits. Perhaps Bera could come with ye."

"Aye, she wouldn't stay away. I think she considers you a friend."

Merewin's smile was genuine. "I would like that." She ignored the tightness in her throat. A friend? She'd never had one other than Ellette before. "Please tell her to come unless she's feeling too uncomfortable."

Gamal nodded and remounted his horse. "Farewell," he said to Merewin, and then waved to Dalla. "Farewell, Dalla. I will return in a few days."

Merewin turned toward Dalla, who abruptly stalked into the house. Merewin drew a long breath. Hauk traveled toward battle, but somehow Merewin felt that the real battle was before her here at Spring House. Merewin had stood defiant before a Dane horde, but one little girl had her nearly trembling. With another long breath, Merewin braved the dark interior.

Dalla sat before a large wooden loom where she pulled a shuttle back and forth to weave the dyed wool into a colorful blanket. Merewin walked toward her small room, barely making a sound.

"He leaves me behind at Spring House but takes you to see him off." Dalla's voice overflowed with subdued hatred. "His own daughter he doesn't take, but his thralllll..." she drew out the title as if it meant something much worse.

Merewin stopped. "He took me to check on the king's son, the one I healed a fortnight ago."

Silence swelled in the stagnant room until it shoved Merewin toward her room. As she let the curtain fall, she heard Dalla's whispered curse above the clicking sound of the loom. "I hate you." The words were so simple but more pointed than all of Svala's clever innuendos. *I hate you.* They cut through Merewin's stomach. Why did this girl of ten years hate her so badly? But Merewin didn't ask. She didn't want to talk to Dalla. *Let her stew in her hatred.*

Merewin had work to do in her curing cottage, and she could make her plans to leave. With Hauk away, this would be the perfect time to escape. After all, she was a captive even if Hauk and most of Ribe treated her like a valuable guest.

Merewin snorted as she sat down on her pallet and rubbed her mother's stone at her neck. *A guest with no rights, who can never go home.* Where exactly was home anyway? Northumbria, in the forest, all alone with Ellette? Some place in the west that seemed to pull her? And how exactly would she get back across the pitching sea? Her mind whirled, creating and rejecting possibilities.

Then there was Hauk. Merewin sighed as she leaned back on the pallet and looked at the hewn logs bracing the ceiling overhead. She felt her cheek where he'd touched not two hours ago. She ran a finger over her lips. His sensual power overwhelmed her, truly capturing her will. Merewin spread fingers through her hair. Aye, she'd have to start making plans, for if he returned from this mission, she may never leave.

CHAPTER FOURTEEN
CIVIL WAR

Unfortunately, during the following week, Merewin spent more time avoiding Dalla's tricks than formulating plans of escape. Crickets and slugs in her bed, toads in her room, honey under her pillow. Dalla had declared all-out war with her simple curse the day Hauk left.

Week two, Merewin thought as she peeked out of her curtained room. Autumn had fully descended on Denmark. Frost bit the air in the large room, bringing all toward the warmth of the central fire pit. Diarf, Vivien's eleven-year-old son, hauled logs indoors. Vivien carried in fresh baked loaves of bread from the stone oven outside. Dalla poked at the central fire with a long stick.

"Get out," Dalla's words rang through the room as Merewin stopped before the fire. "I free you to leave," she said, and then looked up, meeting Merewin's eyes. "My father is not here, so I'm in charge. He gave you to me, and I'm telling you to leave."

Merewin glanced at Vivien. The woman's flustered, wide-eyed stare didn't help.

Merewin looked back at the girl who sat with her shoulders rounded forward. "Yer father bade me to stay." Merewin's mind reeled around Dalla's dictate. Hadn't she wanted a way to escape? Why then did she feel her heels dig in against the child's latest plan to get rid of her?

"He won't know where you've gone." Dalla flapped her hand toward the doorway. "You can return to your country."

"How? I haven't a boat, nor money, nor help."

Dalla shook her head, her face growing red. "I don't care how you go. I just want you gone." She stood up and pointed at the door. "In fact, I order you out, now. You and all your things." Dalla pulled her hand from her pocket and hurled a fistful of round objects across the room toward the door when Diarf unexpectedly walked in.

"Hā!" he yelped, dropping the wood to cover his face from being pelted. One of the objects rolled across the dirt to rest against Merewin's shoe, and she picked it up. *An acorn.*

"Where did ye get these?" Merewin asked past the lump in her throat.

"Out!" Dalla's finger pointed toward the door where Diarf gathered the fallen logs amidst the scattered nuts.

"These are mine." Merewin held her ground, her fingers clamping around the little nut Jacob from Northumbria had given her the day she was taken away. "Ye were in my room."

Dalla's face flushed blotchy and red. "'Tis my home, my room. Your little nuts are mine. You are mine."

Merewin's heart pounded in her chest. Stubborn anger warred against uncertainty and humiliation. She kept her words low, a telling sign to anyone who knew her that she neared the breaking point. But there was no one who knew her anymore, not since Navlin. "I belong to no one. I am a thrall captured by Hauk Geirson of Denmark. I am no one to Dalla

Geirson." Merewin kept her stare even, refusing even to blink. She barely noticed Vivien gathering up the acorns.

Merewin sat down and forced herself to take a bite of the warm bread even though her stomach clenched. She kept her gaze on her adversary. "Hauk Geirson said to stay," she said and chewed lightly. "So I stay." The child didn't know her demands had deterred Merewin from escaping.

Dalla growled low in her throat, not willing to give up. "I will throw you out."

"I don't believe ye can lift me."

Dalla glared. "I will throw your things outside and bar the door."

Merewin made herself shrug nonchalantly even though blood rushed in her ears. The bread sat like a lump in her stomach. "I will go to yer Uncle Gamal. He will house me until yer father returns to hear what ye've done."

"If you don't leave Denmark, he will only drag you back here," Dalla said with the hint of a child's whine. Her eyes narrowed. "Or do you like being his whore?"

Merewin straightened. Vivien stood still, her mouth gaping open. If she had been eating, the food surely would have rolled out. "I am no one's whore, little girl. And ye should not be speaking about matters ye don't understand," Merewin whispered. One more insult and she'd snap. She tried to breathe calmly. *She's an angry little girl. Let her words go.*

Dalla's gaze moved from Merewin's down to the green jade pendant she wore on a leather cord around her neck, her mother's jade, which had carried her to this time and helped her understand every language. "Did Papa give that to you?" Dalla asked. "Was the necklace my gift from his trip? The one he misplaced?"

"Nay," Merewin answered, fingering the familiar weight resting below the hollow at the base of her neck. "'Tis always been mine."

Dalla shook her head. "You're lying."

Thuds from a horse drew Dalla's attention. Diarf ran to the door to look out.

"Svala, sister-in-law to King Ragnar, has arrived," the boy announced. Could the morning get any worse? Vivien shooed the boy toward the back of the house. Dalla ran outside to greet the she-beast.

Merewin had seen her talking to Hauk in Ribe before he sailed. The woman hid her face behind a veil, no doubt to hide the bruising of a broken nose. A twang of guilt tightened Merewin's stomach. She was a healer, not someone who caused injury. Yet in the short time she had known Hauk, she'd stabbed his arm, tried to injure his manhood in the woods, broken Svala's nose, and was about to throttle his daughter. Though her temper was easily lost, Merewin did not consider herself an aggressive person. The Danes obviously brought out violent passion.

"Merewin," Vivien whispered loudly and flapped her hand toward the back where Diarf had disappeared. "Out through here." Maybe Vivien was right, maybe it would be best to avoid what possibly could be another violent confrontation with Ragnar's sister-in-law.

As she rounded the corner toward her healing cottage, she heard Svala's grating voice soothing Dalla as the girl complained about Merewin's presence. Merewin rolled her eyes and stepped inside her refuge. "The devil consoles the demon," she muttered rubbing her arms. She trembled against the door and realized tears ran down her cheeks. She wiped at them quickly. She didn't cry easily, yet somehow the words of this hateful child felt worse than any mortal fear she had experienced so far.

Merewin pushed away from the door and moved woodenly around the small room, checking that her warding stones were still in place around the edges of her doorframe and in each corner. Navlin had taught her basic Wiccan safety measures against evil. If the warding held, those with evil intent should avoid her cottage. Nevertheless, Merewin kept her attention on the flimsy door until she heard Svala's horse clopping lightly out of the valley. Merewin let a long breath escape. Had she held it all day? No wonder her body felt beaten, exhausted by the tension and darkness here at Spring House.

Two evenings later, Merewin sat on the end of her pallet and picked nettles out of her woolen hose. "Hate-filled little fly," she mumbled at the biting thorns that Dalla had hidden in her clothes. Merewin rubbed at her birthmark and pulled the blanket up around her shoulders to ward off the night chill. Ellette had taken off into the darkness to hunt, leaving her to jump at every little noise, expecting another torturous surprise. Two weeks of attacks had made Merewin as jittery as a mouse living with a falcon.

"She needs a beating." Drakkina's voice shot out from the corner. "Or a good dose of poison."

"Ahh!" Merewin jumped up, dropping the hose.

"Shhh..." Drakkina drew out, her bent finger to her lips, as her body coalesced into a more solid form. She floated toward Merewin. "You will wake your master." Drakkina smiled but then frowned. "Actually, I would have thought to find you in his bed. No?"

Merewin grabbed up her hose. "Nay, his bed is empty, and this is where the thrall sleeps."

"Empty? He doesn't seek another?" Drakkina sounded astounded by the possibility. "True, I haven't seen him near you when I've checked in. Only his mischief-filled child."

Merewin frowned at the mention of Dalla. "Hauk's left." She thrust her hand absently toward the west. The pull she'd felt since arriving in

Northumbria as a child hadn't dimmed since reaching Denmark. The westward sense of direction still pulled.

"Left?" Drakkina's voice rose, and she smacked her palm against her lightly wrinkled forehead. "Why can't you girls keep your men with you? First your sister can't keep her man from going to battle and then yours up and leaves." She looked at Merewin. "Where did he go?"

"To battle."

"Battle?" Drakkina shouted.

"Shhh..." Merewin chided but felt a bit lighter. Drakkina was more upset than she about Hauk leaving.

Drakkina flapped her hand toward the curtained doorway. "They can't hear me, only you. What do you mean battle? Where?"

"Dalriada, to battle the Picts." Merewin didn't like to think about him fighting the fearsome painted men from the scary tales Navlin had told her as a child. At least he'd taken one of her warding stones.

Drakkina began to pace around the small quarters. "Dalriada...near the stones then." She huffed. "I suppose I must go protect him."

Merewin stood, the hose dropping in a heap on the earthen floor. "Ye can protect him?"

Drakkina pulled up to her full height, even floating a bit off the floor. "I am a great Wiccan Master. Of course I can protect him."

"Ye haven't protected me from Dalla's wickedness."

Drakkina waved her hands in the air, dismissing Merewin's complaint. "She's but a girl."

"A girl with cruel cunning and a vicious nature."

Drakkina raised her eyebrows "I don't see her wielding a blade."

"Not yet," Merewin mumbled.

"Punish her."

"Punish her? She's in charge," Merewin drawled out. "I'm merely a thrall without my captor to protect me."

"Another reason not to have let him leave."

"I didn't *let* him leave. He's the bloody master." Merewin's words dripped sarcasm.

"You're his soul mate."

Merewin rolled her eyes. "He doesn't agree."

"Well if you'd kissed him—"

"I have, several times," Merewin cut her off and then felt heat creep up her neck.

Drakkina smiled wickedly. "He smells nice, doesn't he?"

Merewin frowned. The crone had no business smelling Hauk. "It doesn't matter. He still left."

"Did he bed you?"

"That is private, crone."

Drakkina's smile faltered, and one of her gray eyebrows rose. "Nothing is private as it pertains to saving this world." She waved her hands in the air. "All the worlds." She pointed a finger at Merewin, jabbing it in the air. "You and your soul mate must be joined and come as one to the stones to fight the last battle."

"So ye've mentioned."

"You have no idea of the hell I'm trying to prevent," Drakkina rebuked, "the vileness of the demons who want to rule this world and all worlds."

"Aye, ye're right, I don't know what ye warn about."

Drakkina huffed impatiently. "Do you remember your parents, your father, Druce?"

Merewin's throat tightened. Images of a large man with laughing eyes rose in her mind. He smiled at her as he tossed her in the air, twirling her around until they both fell in a heap of laughter as her sisters piled on top of them.

"I remember."

"Druce was my most powerful student while I lived in corporeal form, your mother a close second. Their combined power was immense. Frightening, in fact, if they did not honor the Earth Mother with it. Frightening in the hands of darkness."

"The demons killed them." Merewin sat gingerly back on the small pallet and wrapped the fur around her shoulders as a chill infiltrated her bones.

"Your father met them on his own, the foolish, conceited man. Thinking his powers were enough to overthrow them." Drakkina shook her head.

"So they killed him," Merewin prodded. She couldn't remember much before falling from the sky into Navlin's cradle.

Drakkina's sharp gaze stared directly into hers. "They did more than kill him, they stripped his powers from him first, stealing them to use for themselves. Then they killed him for pleasure." Drakkina's expression looked sad. "Such is the way with evil."

"And they murdered my mother."

Drakkina nodded. "But the fight was vastly different. Gilla was wise, wise and cautious. Always had strong wards set around the stones surrounding your house. The wards gave her enough time to transfer her powers to you and your sisters and then hide each of you." Drakkina fluttered her hands around. "Somewhere in time."

"And then the demons..."

"Gilla couldn't hold them at bay, not after they'd absorbed Druce's powers. The demons used the same powers that at one time protected his family against his family. Ironic."

"But my sisters all escaped?"

Drakkina smiled. "Yes, they did. The four of you are spread out across the temporal planes in different places. It could take centuries for the demons to find you." Drakkina let the thin veil over her head fall upon her shoulders and three dragonflies flitted up around her silvery hair. "I've seen it clearly in my scrying bowl."

"And the outcome?"

Drakkina's smile faded. She held out a bony finger and a purple-winged dragonfly lit upon it. "I've scried many outcomes. Some good." She looked at Merewin. "Most horrific."

"Horrific?"

"As I explained before," Drakkina narrowed her eyes in rebuke, "the demons want to break the temporal planes."

"Which means what exactly?"

"The demons will crash all times into one, flooding the Earth with humanity until bodies are stacked upon one another. A sea of people."

Merewin held her breath, listening to the dark prophecy. The seriousness in Drakkina's face, her tone, told Merewin the crone believed the terrifying scene she predicted. And considering who Drakkina seemed to be, her prophecy could come true.

"Most will die," Drakkina said, "suffocated perhaps, fed upon by hungry creatures," Drakkina shuddered slightly, sending more dragonflies to hover in the chilled air. "Semiazaz is a fallen angel and the leader of his demonic brethren. They will take the young, the children, and raise them in fear and torture to be their slaves."

Drakkina clasped her hands before her, raising them until her sleeves slid up to her elbows, revealing thin arms. "I forged a bond, tying them together, long ago when I was full of power. If they manage to break it, they will track you and your sisters down to steal Gilla's powers, combine them with Druce's, and break the temporal web."

Disappointment weighed on Merewin's chest. "Then my sisters and I must stay apart and hidden. For humanity's sake."

Drakkina shook her head. "Semiazaz's demons seem to be growing stronger on their own. Which is why I'm hunting you all down. I must make certain that each of Gilla's daughters finds their soul mate. And then each pair must return to the stones for the most important battle ever waged on this earth."

"And we will kill them."

The crone's lips pressed together for a moment. "If the Earth and all those alive along the temporal webs hope to live."

Merewin let out a long huff, her shoulders rounding as she sunk further into the warm fur. "But you said my mother couldn't kill them. How can we? We only have her power."

"When you form a bond with your soul mate, your power increases, which is why you both must live and battle the demons together."

Merewin nodded slowly, her headache increasing.

Drakkina looked around. "This room is too small. A pallet barely fits in here."

"I'm a thrall. Do ye expect Hauk to give me the largest room?"

"Yes," Drakkina answered pointedly and frowned at her. "Where you should be in his bed with him."

Merewin held her hands up, palms forward. "I do not control his actions."

"You could encourage him. Although, with your beauty, the man must be blind if he isn't enthralled with you."

The ice of Drakkina's ominous prophecy melted as Merewin's temper flared. She stood, her hands braced on her hips. "I did naught to discourage him. Perhaps ye need to be lecturing him," she added acidly. "He saw ye at the healing. No one else did."

Drakkina's eyes widened, and her lips pinched in a look of contemplation. "He has a touch of magick in him, but 'tis raw, and he ignores it. Except in battle if he's survived this long."

Merewin forgot her irritation. "Magick in Hauk?"

Drakkina pulled the light hood up over her hair. "Not much. He probably thinks he has incredible battle instincts, knowing which maneuvers the enemy will use." She shrugged. "When he's not in battle, he fights against his magick."

"He doesn't believe in it," Merewin said. "Won't follow it."

Merewin watched Drakkina begin to fade. "So he's safer then, with these instincts." Her words were quick, trying to catch Drakkina before she disappeared.

"If he trusts them," Drakkina sniffed. "Stubborn men. Women are much easier to work with, although *you* aren't compliant."

"Where are ye going?"

"To find your man, child. To get him back here safely so he can bed you and fall in love with you." Drakkina's eyes rolled skyward, and she vanished. Merewin heard the last threads of her voice as if they came in on the wind. "And watch the girl. Her heart is heavy with stony darkness."

CHAPTER FIFTEEN
DREAMS & NIGHTMARES

Deep brown hair wrapped around Hauk as if it were alive and he could drown in the warm, spicy-sweet scent of it. Eyes, green like the depths of the forest in the waning light, stared into his. Soft skin rubbed along his naked length. The rhythm building, building until he thought he'd explode.

Her rose-hued, full mouth moved, but a garbled string of sounds came out in a husky voice.

"Merewin?" Hauk held on to Merewin's image, but it began to shift within his grasp like sand in the shallows.

The husky laugh returned with more garbled sounds, not his language, not the smooth lilt of Merewin's voice. Grabbing for the soft hair, Hauk breathed deeply. Instead of spicy sweetness, the rank smell of unwashed body assaulted him.

In the space of a heartbeat, Hauk rolled over, pinning the intruder under his hard body. His captive gasped as he opened his eyes to find a woman staring back at him. Not Merewin. This was Garrett's woman, her large breasts naked and pressed against him. She smiled timidly, and he relaxed his hold, sitting back to put distance between them.

She slid her hand boldly down his torso to his erection. Although he couldn't understand her mumbled words, he read the meaning plainly and grabbed her hand, pushing it away.

The woman was a Pict, one Garrett had found and claimed, no doubt for her large breasts and lusty personality.

"Nay," he said, as she stood up, dropping the rest of the clothes from her ample hips. She was shapely and obviously ready for any and all activities Hauk may desire. Did Garrett know his new thrall was hopping from tent to tent?

The woman turned and Hauk thought she might be bending over to retrieve her scant clothing. Instead, she bent over, spreading her legs to reveal herself, showing him she was wet and ready for him. She looked back over her shoulder and touched herself.

Hauk hardened once again, his body responding to his recent celibacy. Before his trip to Northumbria, he wouldn't have thought twice about mounting this willing woman, plowing into her, sating himself. But instead, he found himself lifting her to her feet. He placed a woolen blanket around her and bundled her clothes up, placing them in her arms. She pouted at him, her little nose tilting upward in the air.

Merewin made the same face when she was angry. *Merewin*. By Odin, he missed her.

The Pict woman huffed and stomped out of the tent. He watched her leave, unwilling to call her back. The slap of the flap rang in his ears.

Hauk rubbed hands through his hair and sat back in the warmth of his pallet. He was once again alone. He'd spent many nights alone on missions even when his family was still alive, more so now that they were gone. But he'd never felt lonely before, empty somehow.

He shook his head, feeling very weary. "What is wrong with me?"

Much.

The single word echoed in his mind, and Hauk shot up from his pallet. Naked, Hauk unsheathed the dagger strapped to his leg and turned in a quick circle, scanning the tent. "Who speaks?"

Come to me, Hauk Geirson the Broad, Dane of Spring House.

The voice seemed loud in the silence, yet it felt as if it spoke inside his head, not his ears. Hauk put a tunic and trews on and belted his sword across his back.

"Where?"

Follow your instincts, warrior.

Hauk turned to the left away from the camp. West. Two guards moved to follow him, but he stopped them with a raised hand.

Moonlight lit the woods, and Hauk smelled the sea air. Pushing his way through the undergrowth, he trudged through the forest and across two damp fields, feeling the strange pull. Perhaps he was still dreaming. But the dampness under his bare feet, and the cool breeze tugging his hair, seemed too detailed to be a dream. Dreams often hid in mist, muted and without sense.

Hauk stopped. If this wasn't a dream, was it a trap?

Not a trap, Hauk. I'm here to warn you to return to Spring House. Now.

Hauk's head snapped around, and he leapt into a jog toward the pull. "What's happening at home? Dalla? Merewin? Bera?"

Panic threatened the tight control he kept on the beast within him, the beast that erupted in battle. It coiled up from his gut to squeeze into his chest as his jog turned into a sprint. Trap or not, the thought that something could steal what little he had left pushed him forward into unknown territory.

Fists balled, his arms swinging, Hauk broke through the edge of oak trees and stopped short in the center of a broad ring of tall stones. He turned in a circle, his arms open and ready to fight.

The silver moonlight illuminated a stone table at the center. Was this a place of worship for the Picts? He sensed sacrifice here.

I am here, warrior. An apparition appeared in the ring of stones. Small flying insects, dragonflies, flitted about and through her form.

"You were at Ivarr's healing," he said. "Are you a goddess? Freyja, Iduna, Frigg?"

She smiled. *I have been called a goddess before, but those are not my name.* The spirit touched her hair as if to fluff it.

Hauk's hands clenched and unclenched. "Are you Merewin's god then?"

The old woman shook her head. *I am Drakkina, a Master Wiccan Priestess who is now in spirit form.* The voice threading through his head held pride and authority.

"You helped Merewin heal Ivarr," he said. His gaze took in the entire circle, but they seemed to be alone.

In a way, but the healing magick was all from Merewin and the Earth Mother. Not I, and not Serena.

"The other woman? I heard her call Merewin 'sister'."

Drakkina nodded. *To save this world and all worlds, I need great warriors like you, great warriors like Merewin and her sister.*

"You speak of Ragnarök, the end of the world when the gods battle."

Drakkina inclined her head. *Judgement Day, Ragnarök. You can call it whatever you want. Yes, 'tis the final battle of this earth.*

Hauk stared, judging her. "You said I must return home. Is my family in danger?"

The woman looked at him quizzically, and her voice came to his ears this time instead of playing through his mind. "You knew you should not leave them, yet you went anyway."

Impatience flared inside Hauk, the fire coming out in his tone. "Tell me, witch."

The woman's eyes lifted. "Yes, danger stalks Spring House and those in it. Pain, evil, hatred."

Hauk felt the thrum of his pulse increase. "Who does it stalk? Who is the threat?"

The crone glided over to the table and perched on it. Dragonflies swirled around her like a shield, giving her an unearthly appearance. "Hauk Geirson, look within yourself. You know things, feel things, yet you turn away from what is true."

What madness did she spew? "Answer me about the threat at home."

"Whether you admit it or not, you have magick within you."

Hauk's stomach rolled with her words. He walked over to the table and leaned against the unmovable support.

The spirit's gaze followed him from her seat. "If you ignore it, or worse, disrespect it, you will fail, and your family will perish."

Hauk focused on her filmy blue eyes. "It did perish," he growled. The pain he'd stomped down surfaced with her words. He breathed low to control the beast of rage gnashing its teeth within him.

"Not all, not Dalla. If you continue to turn away from your magick, your instincts, you will lose her, too, and Merewin. Perhaps more."

"I trusted magick once, and it killed nearly everyone I loved. Now tell me, is Dalla or Merewin in danger?"

The woman pursed her lips. "Of course they are," she said with irritation. "Who else would I be talking about? Your sister has her husband to guard her."

"Gamal guards Spring House, too," Hauk answered but his mind swirled around bloody scenarios. Norsemen invading from the north. Another illness spreading from Ribe to the farm. Merewin trying to escape only to find herself face-to-face with a pack of wolves. "They...they should be safe," he said, his words shallow.

"Gamal goes to Spring House every three days, but he misses the undercurrents that threaten. For Spring House to heal, it needs you."

"Spring House is healed," he said, keeping the worry from his voice. The witch talked in riddles and ominous predictions.

She raised one eyebrow. "I've never had a child, but I've seen many. There is something wrong with your daughter."

"We are talking about danger, not child-rearing."

"Do you honestly believe you are rearing your child?"

"Dalla is fed, clothed, and warm. The death of our family was difficult on her. Time will make her forget."

"Time will make her forget?" the witch repeated and looked down her nose at him. "Is that working for her? For you?" She paused as if waiting for his reply, but Hauk remained silent.

"I know a little about grief." She paused, but Hauk still didn't say anything. "To recover requires work, not denial, not forgetting."

Hauk frowned, thinking back over the years from the happy child he remembered to the spiteful malicious Dalla she'd grown into. The witch's words pounded in his head, twisting his stomach. The pain of losing his son, parents, and brother broke open like a fresh wound, making it hard for him to draw in a full breath.

"We're speaking of Spring House and the danger 'tis in," he said gruffly. His sword hand clenched and released, clenched and released.

Drakkina rolled her eyes. "I'm telling you something you already know but refuse to acknowledge." She drifted off the table. "I'm leaving.

You should stay in this circle and think. See what comes to you. Be open to it. Don't dismiss it."

"Wait..."

She held up a hand, and her voice returned to his mind. *You must return to Merewin, bed her, love her. Make her yours in every way, Hauk Geirson. Or you will lose what's left of your family and perhaps the world.*

The witch slowly faded, with her last words ringing through his head like an echo of thunder through the mountains. Hauk stared at the empty night air where she'd stood. Her dragonflies flitted out of the clearing.

Hauk turned in a circle, scanning the soaring stones twice his height. Although the space stood empty, save the stone table and gangly weeds underfoot, Hauk felt a tightness, a pressure. It was as if the space stood packed with power. Hauk began to shake his head and stopped, the words of the witch coming back to him. *Magick?* Was the power he felt in the circle magick?

Hauk leaned against the center table and reached into his pocket, fingers finding the stone Merewin had given him. It grew warm in his hand. Breathing deeply Hauk centered himself as he did before going into battle. He opened himself up to the air, to the earth beneath, to the night sounds. In the blackness behind his eyes, light and color formed. Slowly he unshackled the beast, the power within him.

Flashes of Merewin rolled through his mind, Merewin, her hair tangled in honey. Dalla laughing wickedly, then sobbing. It tore through his chest, and he nearly opened his eyes. Instead, he tried to focus on Dalla, her tears, her hands. A knife lay in her hands. She tested its weight, pricked her finger on the point.

"Nay, Dalla," he called out into the tight emptiness of the circle. Hauk jerked upright, shoving the stone back in his pocket. "I must go home.

Now." Hauk broke through the ring back into the forest. The tightness he'd felt in the space lessened immediately. He looked back over his shoulder at the silvery stones. They seemed to watch him, judge him. "I'll return for your battle," he promised and jogged back to the camp. He wouldn't miss a chance to battle at Ragnarök.

⸺◈⸺

Hauk's hand caught in her hair, and Merewin continued his kiss. Passion pulsed through her body. "Hauk," she said, and the tug on her hair increased. The cool hardness of steel pressed against her neck, and her eyes opened, trying to focus. Hauk's mouth came up from her neck. Had he bitten down? She pulled her face back, and he smiled wickedly. "Hauk?" The dream fogged over.

The bothersome tug began on her hair again, lifting Merewin from the deepness of sleep. Then it stopped, and sleep warred with waking. Merewin's eyes felt heavy, and she didn't want to lose the sensual dream completely. She'd been in Hauk's naked, chiseled arms. She sighed and exhaled back into his embrace, returning to face his stormy blue eyes. They stared at her with such intensity she felt compelled to reach out to him. But he wrapped several lengths of her hair around his hand.

Tug! Merewin gasped, her hand reaching for her scalp. Concern beat away the spell of slumber and Merewin's eyes blinked open.

Dalla's head was bent over her where Merewin lay on her pallet.

"Dalla?"

The girl jerked back, a handful of brown hair in her hands.

My hair? "What are ye doing?!" Merewin yelled as she rolled off the platform to her feet. Her hair sifted to the floor around her, her beautiful long hair. Dalla held a knife in one hand and nearly two feet of brown hair in the other.

"Ye little beast!" Merewin screamed, and the girl's smirk wavered in the presence of her unleashed wrath. Merewin towered over her, using every inch of her great height to intimidate. "What have ye done?" Merewin pulled her hair around. Half of it still reached her hips, while the other side reached only to her shoulder blades.

The control Merewin had kept through these weeks of Dalla's cruel mischief snapped. Forced to the breaking point, the rage and fear and loneliness blasted forward into uncontrollable fury. Merewin used the back of her hand to whack the knife from Dalla's, clipping her hand.

"You struck me," Dalla yelped, clutching it.

Merewin grabbed the girl's hair as Vivien poked through the curtain and gasped, her look going from Merewin's head to the floor. "Ve! What's happened?"

Merewin sucked in air, calming her tone without releasing the girl. "Leave us be, Vivien. Dalla and I have some things to discuss." Merewin's voice seeped venom. She dragged Dalla from her room by her hair, pulling her through the longhouse.

The hellion thrashed and kicked pots and baskets along the way, trying to find purchase. She tried to bite Merewin, but Merewin's strength finally won out, and she thrust Dalla out the door of the house without releasing her.

"You'll die for touching me, you whore!" Dalla screamed as Merewin dragged the kicking, cursing girl toward the stream.

Out of the corner of her eye, Merewin watched Vivien smack a horse on the rump, sending the beast flying with little Diarf on it. Was he riding to Ribe to find help? But she didn't have time to think, to consider; she only had now, and this fighting she-cat in her grasp.

All the anger of being captured, the constant fight to control her temper, the anxiety of trying to make friends and peace here in Denmark—it all rolled through Merewin, giving her extraordinary strength to haul Dalla to the water's edge. Dalla's foot kicked Merewin's shin, tripping her, but Merewin refused to release her hold. She'd rather rip the hair from Dalla's scalp than release it.

Merewin's force pushed them both tumbling into the stream that cut through Spring House Farm. Frantic, wild splashing made Merewin wonder if Hauk had ever taught his daughter how to swim. Icy blades of mountain water stung every part of Merewin's hot body as her bare feet easily found the pebble-strewn bottom. 'Twas cold but not deep, and she hefted a spitting, gasping Dalla onto the bank.

Scrambling up, Merewin pinned the girl on her back in the mud while the sun broke over the ridge, sending its first rays down on them. The girl's wet head rested in the battered grass, her hair still caught on the smoothing surface of the water behind her.

"Let go of me!" Dalla's pale lips grayed toward blue over chattering teeth.

Merewin wasn't about to give into any more demands. She leaned over her, her body pressed against Dalla's smaller one. "How dare ye sneak into my room and cut my hair."

"I could have cut your throat instead," Dalla said, her eyes mutinous, although she wouldn't meet Merewin's gaze.

Dalla wiggled, freeing her hand. She brought it up, and Merewin tried not to flinch, waiting for a slap or punch. Instead, Dalla held a leather cord in her fingers, the green jade stone dangling at the end.

Merewin's hand went to her throat, but she knew it would be bare. Dalla had also cut her mother's necklace off while she slept. A chill squeezed through Merewin, a chill deep inside where the cold hadn't penetrated yet.

Dalla swung her arm back to dangle the jade over the water. "Let me go or I'll throw it."

Merewin pieced together the Danish translation. Without her mother's stone, the words didn't translate easily. "Don't, Dalla!" Merewin's heart pounded. The jade stone was all she had left of her mother.

Dalla's hand moved swiftly. There was no way to catch it as she tossed the cord and pendant far down the stream where the current picked up.

Merewin's heart flew upward into her throat, trying to chase it. Tears ached behind her eyes, as she watched the spot where the stone entered. Would she be able to find it? Merewin's gaze moved back to Dalla who stared upward, head laid back at the edge of the water.

Merewin moved over her. "Ye little bitch," Merewin whispered. "How dare ye take what is mine, take what I love." The girl stared back, brave, defiant. "Ye have no idea what I'm going through. I'm fighting for my life," Merewin said in disjointed Danish.

For the first time Merewin noticed tears swelling in Dalla's blue eyes. Merewin glanced away at the blue sky reflected in the calmed water of the eddy just beyond the girl. With the water once again calm, Merewin's own reflection stared back on the surface.

Merewin's wet hair lay flat and tangled against her head. Her gaze looked back at her with anger, fright, and sorrow. Her lips, open to suck in air she hadn't been able to fully breathe since being captured, trembled. "I'm fighting for my bloody life," Merewin said again and looked down at Dalla beneath her.

Dalla stared back, hair flat and tangled against her head, her eyes wide with anger and fear and sorrow, her lips blue and trembling. Merewin studied the girl, so very much like her own reflection in the water. She looked between the two.

How long it took for Merewin to comprehend what she saw, she didn't know. Was it an instant or a full minute? Time moved at the pace of her pounding heart. The realization ripped through Merewin. It made the tears roll out and her body go weak.

This ten-year-old girl was fighting for life, just as Merewin was. *We are the same.*

Merewin rolled off Dalla onto her back, her body next to the girl's. They lay there, their fast breaths coming out in little puffs of white mist. Merewin spoke into the blue above them. "Ye're fighting for yer life too, aren't ye?"

Dalla didn't answer. Merewin turned her head to see Dalla's profile as the girl stared up at the heatless sun. Tears coursed down the side of her face. This girl had lost everyone she loved too, including her own mother. Like Merewin. Dalla fought to keep her father, keep him from death or from another woman. Dalla fought for life, the life she once remembered, and she fought the only way she knew how.

Merewin stared down into Dalla's eyes. "We are the same."

CHAPTER SIXTEEN
CRY IN THE NIGHT

Merewin rested on the small ledge that was her bed. The press of complete darkness made it difficult to discern if her eyes were open or not. Silently she moved a hand around in search of Ellette. Out again, hunting. Ellette hunted at night and slept all day.

Merewin stilled, breathing even, listening. What had woken her? A quick intake of breath caught on a sob somewhere in the house. It was muted and distant, but Merewin could tell it came from Dalla. She propped up on an elbow.

Hauk's daughter hadn't spoken to her in two days, not since the stream. Merewin fingered her sheared hair. Bera had ridden to Spring House to even out the mess Dalla had made with the knife. Merewin's hair fell a few inches below her shoulders and had much more curl and life in it without the tremendous weight. Merewin shook her head to feel the ends slide across her upper back. *Liberating*. She ran fingers through the mass. What would Hauk think?

Another sob cut through the night. Merewin pushed her legs over the side of the platform, slipping feet into leather shoes before wrapping a woven shawl around her shoulders. One hand brandished before her to stop her from hitting the wall, Merewin stepped through the curtain to stand before the entrance of Dalla's room.

Merewin listened to uneven breathing, punctuated by short, stabbing gasps of air. She pushed through the curtain into the large room that had belonged to Hauk's parents. Coals of a small fire near the far wall lit the sparsely furnished space. Several narrow ledges stuck out from the walls and a lump on one of them shook.

As Merewin neared, Dalla rolled over. Her eyes, wide and terrified, froze on Merewin. "Mama?"

"Nay, Dalla, 'tis me, Merewin. Are ye ill?" Dalla's eyes remained wide and wet with tears. She squeezed them, bringing forth a renewed flood. Merewin sat on the edge of the pallet that was as small as her own and smoothed Dalla's hair back from her face. "What is it?"

She wiped palms over her wet cheeks. "'Tis a dream."

"A dream?"

"Aye, I have it..." she hiccoughed. "I have it a lot."

"Tell me." Merewin continued to stroke Dalla's hair.

"'Tis my mother. She's calling for me, but I can't reach her. I'm almost there when she disappears like a ghost." Dalla's words slurred into sobs again, "...never see her again." The girl's shoulders were rigid against the pallet. She wiped the back of her sleeve against her nose. "'Tis foolish."

Merewin shook her head. "Not foolish. I had similar dreams about my mother."

Dalla blinked, looking up into Merewin's face. "You did?"

"Aye, for a long while, but they faded eventually." Merewin's nightmares about leaving her mother to die had haunted her through her childhood. Navlin helped as best she could, but it was something Merewin had to work through. She still had the occasional tragic dream.

"Did your mother die, too?" Dalla's little voice asked.

"Aye, she did, when I was seven years old."

"I was seven too," Dalla said, her voice growing in strength. "How did she die? Was she sick?"

"Nay," Merewin started, but then stopped. No need to fill the girl's head with nightmares of demons. "'Twas...a storm. She died in a storm, but she managed to get me away to safety first."

"You weren't there when she died?" Dalla asked, sitting up under the furs.

"Nay." Merewin's voice was solemn in the darkness. The fact she had abandoned her mother twisted Merewin's heart with guilt. It didn't matter that she hadn't had a choice, that it made her mother's death mean something, that it would save the bloody world. Guilt's poison still coated Merewin's conscience. "Nay, she sent me away before it happened."

Dalla grabbed Merewin's hand. "Me too. Papa sent me away. I..." She sucked in a sob, "I didn't get to say farewell." Dalla's sobs renewed.

Merewin cradled the girl into her body and stroked the top of her head, rocking her in silence. When the girl's cries continued, Merewin remembered a lullaby Navlin had sung to her when she couldn't settle down.

"Hush, little child, blows the gentle North wind.

Sleep little babe, calls the eastern sea.

Quiet now my love under the twinkling stars.

Rest now knowing you have me."

Merewin sang through another verse before coming back to the refrain. Dalla quieted enough to listen, although Merewin doubted she could understand the English words. The grip the girl had on Merewin's hand relaxed as she lay back in her bed. Her erratic breathing evened out.

It seemed she had fallen back to sleep. Merewin stood, slowly releasing her back to the pallet.

"Don't leave me," Dalla whispered in the hushed room. "Sleep next to me."

Merewin surveyed the small ledge. "There isn't room, Dalla. And the other beds aren't made up."

Dalla pushed up and swung her legs over. "Papa's bed is huge. He wouldn't let them bury it with Mama like they did with all her other things."

"Ye want us to sleep in Hauk's bed?" Merewin asked, as a cool draft filtered up under her nightdress.

Dalla hopped out of bed, her hand finding Merewin's in the dark. She tugged Merewin through the curtain. "I'll get light." Dalla let go of Merewin, running toward the central fire in the long hall. She lit a taper and hurried back, her hand cupped around it. "Come." She pushed into Hauk's room, and Merewin followed.

The circle of light bit into the dense darkness of the large, cold room. Even though Dalla was the one to lead Merewin deeper into her father's room, Merewin felt like she trespassed.

"Are ye sure yer father will not mind us being in here?"

Dalla shrugged her shoulders. "He's not here to mind, is he?" Sarcasm laced her whisper. Dalla led her to the side of the enormous log hewn bed where she set the taper in a holder.

Merewin's gaze followed the lines of the massive piece of furniture, strong and chiseled into beauty like its owner. She glanced around the rest of the room, as far as the circle of light allowed. Two chests and a small table stood on one side of the bed, and a cold fire pit sat farther away.

Dalla crawled up onto the high pallet. She burrowed under the heavy pelts. "Come, Merewin, help me warm the bed."

Merewin pulled back the furs and woolen bedding and climbed in. She sank into the soft down. Not what she had expected from the hardened warrior she'd met. "'Tis quite soft." She rolled back and forth, floundering in the sinking tick. "I'm surprised," she snorted, at last finding a comfortable spot, "someone as," she thought for an appropriate word, "hardened as yer father would sleep in such a soft bed."

"He says he likes it soft when he's home, reminds him he's not sleeping on the hard deck of a ship." The girl looked swallowed up in the furs and darkness. Only her little head peeked out. "But you should know about Papa's bed since you shared it with him before he left." Dalla watched her closely.

Merewin shook her head against the down-filled head rolls. "Nay, I haven't been to yer father's bed, Dalla."

"But Svala said—"

"Svala says a lot that's untrue." Merewin's calm belied the anger Dalla's words had sparked. Svala telling Hauk's young daughter that Merewin had been sleeping with him confirmed the woman was cruel. Although, had they not been interrupted with Ivarr's near death that night over a month ago, she may be familiar with Hauk's bed. But it was not something a child should worry about.

Merewin smiled timidly at Dalla. "Time for sleep, then." The chill under the covers had lessened to a mild warmth as they moved their legs back and forth. She blew the taper out and scooted closer to the center where Dalla lay.

"What if the nightmare returns?" Dalla's voice was small in the darkness.

Merewin moved her hand around until she found the girl's and squeezed it. "I'll be here to wake ye."

"Will you sing to me again? My mother used to sing to me."

Merewin inhaled and began the familiar words, soothing yet sad at the same time. She blinked at the ache of tears in her eyes. The memory of her birth mother was so distant now that she mourned it anew for forgetting.

Dalla shifted, turning her back to Merewin but not moving away. The girl sounded half asleep when her soft words broke through Merewin's song. "I'm sorry I cut your hair."

Merewin said nothing, but stroked Dalla's hair until she was sure the girl was asleep. Lying there in the darkness, 'twas as if she stared at her own back sleeping as a child of ten, listening to Navlin's voice. The sweet woman had raised Merewin as her own, stroked her hair, and guarded her against the nightmares of demons and death.

As Dalla's breath evened out, Merewin sunk down into the feather tick. She inhaled, recognizing the faint scent of fresh soap, leather, and man. As she drifted into sleep, held securely in furs, surrounded by Hauk's unique smell, Merewin knew her own dreams would involve the Dane warrior who liked to sleep on a bed as soft as a cloud.

⬥◦⬥

Hauk stared up at the familiar stars as he lay on the hard deck of the longship. He shifted, trying to find the most comfortable spot. The wind filled the double sails, so most of the crew had taken the opportunity to rest while the tillerman kept the course based on the stars. Clear skies and a strong wind from the west sped them toward Denmark, toward home.

Let me get there in time. The image of Dalla holding a sharp knife played through his mind, followed by Merewin, angry and in tears. The words of the spirit woman, Drakkina, haunted him.

Magick, in him? He didn't know which terrorized him more. The possibility that he possessed a touch of magick or that he believed the dire words of the crone. He believed them so strongly he'd ordered their departure the next day. He'd once invited magick into his house and it tortured those he loved until death had mercifully taken them to Asgard. And now he was putting his trust in it again.

Hauk rolled his head to the side, the back of his skull grinding into the hard boards. Garrett's new thrall sauntered along the boat, her robes whipping around her legs. Bjalki's hand shot up to snake up her thigh. She pulled her robe close around her legs but smiled at him. Hauk rolled his head back so he stared straight up at the inky, star-filled sky.

Garrett would have to keep his thrall close or someone else would claim her. Perhaps Bjalki would take an interest in the Pict woman instead of Merewin. It would solve an immediate problem, yet Hauk still waited for the chance to accept Bjalki's challenge. The man had insisted on returning with Hauk even though half the men remained behind to further assure Danish rule.

The sea air was a balm to his tight lungs, and he inhaled, trying to calm his mind enough to sleep. Three full years it had been since the pox, and yet the words of a spirit woman had brought it all back to him as if it were yesterday. Time healed, time made one forget, he'd always believed that. Ignore it and it vanished, forgotten. Yet the pain of losing his son had crushed him again, sickening his stomach, clasping at his chest.

Was it the same with Dalla? Did the pain haunt her as viciously? His sweet daughter had indeed disappeared over the last three years, becoming openly angry and scornful. So if time didn't heal his daughter, what would? Merewin? Did her magick stretch into the mind, into the nonphysical pain of grief?

Hauk ran his hand through his hair. To ask Merewin would mean asking for magick, again. Nay. He wouldn't do it. "I don't believe in magick," Hauk murmured and closed his eyes. Life was easier if he didn't believe. If he trusted in magick, then he put his faith in hope. And if disaster struck anyway, he would relive the horror of three years ago. Nay, it was simpler to not believe.

Even as the denial faded in his mind and sleep overtook his tired body, Hauk's subconscious conjured the spicy sweet scent and deep green eyes of magick.

Merewin's look snapped fire at the tall warrior standing stubbornly. "Gamal," she said succinctly in his language. Without her necklace to aid translation, she had to concentrate more on the proper words to use. It probably made her sound terse, but she didn't care. "Dalla needs to go to Esbjerg."

"But her mother is dead." Gamal shook his head, sending his shoulder-length hair to slide against his broad shoulders. "She doesn't need to see her."

"Aye, she does. She never had the opportunity to say goodbye."

"She can say goodbye here at Spring House."

"But she's not here."

"And she's no longer in Esbjerg either. Ingun has traveled on to Asgard."

Merewin ground her foot into the frosty dirt to stop herself from stomping. "But her body is there, buried with all her mother's things. And Dalla's grandparents, Ingun's parents must—"

"They have never wanted much to do with us," Gamal said, his face hard. "And I hear they moved to Varde several years ago."

Merewin wouldn't be denied. "Then Dalla and I will leave for Esberg on our own."

Gamal crossed his arms before him. "Nay, I will not let such a thing happen. Hauk entrusted you to me."

"So," Merewin raised her eyebrows and tipped her head to the side, "ye will guard us every hour of every day?" She crossed her arms to mimic his stance.

Merewin caught a glimpse of golden hair along the side of the house. Dalla listened. She'd been excited when Merewin proposed the trip when they'd awakened in Hauk's bed. Since Merewin had realized the similarities she shared with the girl, she understood her better. Merewin still felt the anguish of leaving her mother to save herself.

Gamal let out a labored sigh. "You are a most stubborn woman." He shook his head and Merewin smelled victory. She contained herself, though. This man would dig in his heels if she gloated.

"At dawn, then," he said. "We go, we say goodbye to the land over Ingun's bones, and we return by nightfall. I would not be away from Bera very long."

Merewin grimaced at the crude mention of Ingun's bones and hoped Dalla hadn't heard him.

Merewin understood Gamal's desire to return home. Bera was rounding out more and more each time she saw the woman. Merewin stamped down the familiar unease whenever she thought of Bera's birthing. Bringing a bairn into the world was dangerous, and a newborn wouldn't heal by her magick, not when it had just been plucked from the Earth Mother's warm arms.

She touched Gamal's shoulder. "Thank ye." She smiled. "And ye'll see," she whispered too soft for listening ears around the corner. "'Twill make a difference in our Dalla."

"*Our* Dalla?"

Merewin quirked her lips. "Aye." She nodded. "Our Dalla."

Gamal looked at Merewin's hair. "Our Dalla, who knifed off your hair as if you were a sheep to be sheared?"

Merewin ruffled her fingers through her shorter hair. "I think 'tis rather becoming, much lighter for certain." She shook her mane. It definitely moved with more life in it since she'd lost the heavy length. "I like it."

"It does move." Gamal reached to touch it but paused in midair before dropping his hand. His face grew red, and he snorted. "We'll see what Hauk thinks of it."

At the mention of the Dane's name, Merewin's heart picked up speed and her gaze glimpsed the path down to Spring House, but it was vacant. How long did missions take, anyway?

⚬

The dragonboat scraped along the wooden dock, the familiar creaks of the strained wood welcoming him home. Hauk jumped over the gunwale onto the pier, ropes in hand. Several other men jumped over, with lines to secure the boat to the dock. The night was silent, eerily silent. Only the muffled sounds of his men disembarking with their treasure broke the stillness.

Hauk tied off his lines and spoke with two of his men. "I'll return in the morning to properly dock the ship. Stay with her overnight." He handed them several pieces of Pict gold. Normally he would stay with Gamal in Ribe, make repairs and wash down his ship the following day before riding to Spring House. But not tonight, not this journey. Fueled by the images he'd seen in the circle, Hauk jogged through the night toward his sister's home.

He stopped at the door, and a soft neigh came from the fenced yard. Gamal wouldn't mind if he borrowed a horse.

Urging the sleepy mare into a full run, Hauk came quickly to the edge of the sacred forest. He slowed the horse at the border, cursing the moonless night that made the trees nearly impenetrable. The void of blackness sucked at his torchlight, allowing only a compressed circle around horse and rider. Hauk followed fresh tracks made by other horses. Who had traversed earlier in the day to Spring House?

Why had he journeyed away, leaving Merewin and Dalla? It had seemed easier, an opportunity to escape once again the swollen tension of home. He cursed himself.

The low branches arched over the path like a cavern beneath the earth. In some spots Hauk had to bend low to pass without catching his head on the twiggy appendages. His hands clenched around the reins, and he concentrated on keeping his control, steering the horse through the heavy darkness.

Hauk broke through the tree line at the top of the path leading to Spring House. All lay quiet, dark before him, the smell of hearth smoke revealing life below. Hauk turned to follow the path down when a cracking sound pulled him around in his seat. His sword sang as he drew it. Unfortunately, the torch gave away his position, his disadvantage obvious.

"Who waits in my woods?" his voice carried into the darkness. He'd have dropped the light, but the leaves could catch fire. He could also use it as another weapon. *Crack!* He heard it again, followed by a chattering noise. His head spun in time to catch sight of the pine marten hurling through the air from a perch above the far side of the path.

Merewin's pet landed behind him on the horse's hind quarters, its little claws catching at his cloak for balance. The startled horse neighed, lifting her front hooves to paw the air. Hauk only kept his seat by clamping his iron-like thighs around the beast's middle. He slammed his sword back into its scabbard and grabbed the reins with his one free hand.

"Down." Hauk's calm voice belied the strain he used in his thighs and his arms to soothe the horse. The pine marten jumped onto Hauk's back and climbed up to his shoulder. Hauk pulled the torchlight around to look at the little beast, its blackberry eyes staring at him. It tilted its head to the side, as if asking him what he was doing there.

"Is there trouble below? Do you guard the path?" He stared as the little creature nodded. "By the gods, I'm going mad."

Merewin's pet hopped from his arm, launched itself at a trunk, and skittered down to the path leading below. It looked back once as if to see he followed. Hauk's heart pounded in his chest. The last time he'd been here staring at his home, it had held death. He took a deep breath against his ghosts. What would he find this time?

"Odin, let them be safe," he murmured and tapped the horse into a jog down the winding slope.

CHAPTER SEVENTEEN

PERMISSION GRANTED

Hauk dismounted in the yard, tying Gamal's horse to a post near the stream. All seemed calm. He tried to catch sight of the little pine marten as it scurried past the corner of the house after some meal. Apparently, its watch was over. Hauk tried the door, but it was barred as it should be. He moved around to the back, where the bushes lay thick against the logs to the small inset door. Spring House's secret door. He'd added it as a precaution but had used it more than once when arriving home late after the house had been barred against the night. There was a delicate lever through a hole one had to pull in order to spring the latch inside.

Hauk worked his finger in the hole and felt for the thin rope pull. *Click.* The lever snapped up and the small door swung inward. Darkness and silence sat heavy in the house. He closed the door and trod through the empty great room, the fire reduced to a glow of embers in the center hearth. He breathed in the darkness, but no herbal fumes hung in the air this time, only the gentle smell of wood smoke. He breathed in again, his senses attuned. The embers stirred to life, and a flame rose to light the room.

Hauk grabbed a taper and lit it from the hearth pit. He paused at Merewin's room. Silence. He moved to Dalla's curtain and walked through.

Hauk held the taper high. His gaze moved to his daughter's bed. *Empty.* Unease tightened in his gut and muscles. The small light flickered over the walls of the empty room. "Dalla." His voice rang starkly through the stillness. In two strides he was at her pallet, neatly made. He even pushed at the furs to make sure she wasn't under them. "Dalla, where are you?" Turning on his heel he strode to Merewin's small room and threw back the curtain. Her pallet too lay neatly made and empty.

He drew his sword. "By Odin, where is everyone?" He turned back to the great room, firelight shining along the unmarred walls. Had they been taken? Had Merewin run away? His gut tightened with his fists. *Dalla?* The tightening twisted sharply.

"Master?"

His heart slammed behind his ribs, and he lowered the sword.

"Aye, Vivien." He wished it had been Merewin's voice in the darkness. Although she'd never have called him master.

"You've returned already?"

"Aye. Where are Dalla and Merewin?"

The gruff edge to his voice made her mute. The woman pointed, wide-eyed. Hauk turned, ready to insist he'd checked their rooms, but she didn't point to either. The servant pointed to his quarters. "They've been sleeping in your bed."

Hauk looked back. "They?"

"Dalla and Merewin."

Had Vivien gone mad? When he'd left, Dalla hated Merewin, would barely look at her, let alone sleep next to her.

Vivien nodded. "Since the big battle," she flapped her hands around as if mimicking turmoil.

"Men battled here?"

"Nay," she said in a rushed whisper. "The battle between Merewin and Lady Dalla."

Hauk rubbed a dirt-stained hand against his head. "Between Merewin and Dalla?"

"Aye, 'twas fierce."

Had Dalla held a knife to Merewin's throat like he'd seen in the stone circle? He scrubbed at his face, pushing away the tightness in his forehead. "Who won?"

Vivien smiled timidly. "Both."

Hauk stared at the grinning woman. Perhaps the turmoil had scrambled her thoughts. Turning, Hauk lit a lantern and strode across to his bedchamber. Lanternlight revealed one lump in the middle of his large bed, under the furs. He walked without a sound to the edge. On closer inspection, two distinct shapes comprised the lump, enfolded together.

He brought the lantern around to the other side, illuminating their peaceful faces. A glimpse of the little girl Dalla had been remained in her relaxed expression, and Hauk's heart squeezed. He remembered the carefree child who had hugged easily and laughed with all the wonder of the world, the child before the pox.

Hauk's gaze slid to Merewin, and she turned gently onto her other side, back against Dalla's. He moved around to see Merewin's lovely features, also relaxed. The flamelight accented smooth cheekbones and the perfect slope of her nose. Her lips parted, and Hauk stopped breathing when the tip of her tongue stroked the edge of her bottom lip. Her breathing increased and Hauk saw the flicker of her eyes behind the lids. To slip into her dreams, now that would be magick. He watched.

"Aye, Hauk," she murmured, voice husky with sleep or something else. Hauk froze, his eyebrow raising. *She's dreaming of me?* The thin line of a grin relaxed his face. He turned on silent feet and strode back out the curtained door. He eyed the flimsy wool blanket that covered the arched doorway. He'd have to replace it with solid oak.

Vivien jumped at his quick entrance.

"I must bathe." He grabbed a thin bar of the mint-scented soap Vivien made and headed for the barred door. He'd been at sea for a week. The last thing he wanted to do was crawl into bed smelling of sea slime and fish.

"'Tis nearly freezing out there," she called.

Hauk snorted at the cold and strode across the dark yard. Perhaps a dip in the stream running before Spring House would cool the fire Merewin's simple words had sparked. Her husky voice, relaxed features, hair spilled across the down-filled headrest. Her hair? There was something different about it.

Icy pinpricks shot along his skin on contact with the mountain water, and all other thoughts left as he rubbed the layers of grime from his body. Minutes later, Hauk emerged to dry with a bathing sheet. He shook shoulder-length hair and returned to the house. No Vivien. She must have returned to her sleep in the outbuilding she shared with her son. He tied the bathing cloth around his waist and traipsed back to his room. They hadn't moved. Merewin seemed to have submerged farther into slumber.

Hauk slid the blanket and furs back, and lifted Dalla gently, carrying her back to her quarters. She was warm and smelled of some flowers. No matter what had happened, the child was clean. He found her pallet and tucked her under the furs. She turned several times, but soon her even breathing told him she continued to sleep.

Pivoting on his bare heel, Hauk walked back to his own bed. Merewin lay in the center, no doubt smelling of warm sweet spice and woman. He bent down and inhaled. Aye, that was the scent haunting his dreams. Lifting back the furs, he crawled into the space still warm from Dalla, his own body quickly adding to the trapped heat.

His body sank into the familiar pallet, collapsing it and causing Merewin to roll toward him. Her body collided softly with his, and she murmured without opening her eyes. Instead, she rubbed her face into his bare chest and sighed.

Hauk's body turned rigid, and he groaned inwardly as Merewin's knee rose up to rub against his growing erection. He could only see the top of her head in the dim light of the lantern. *Odin's ballocks.* What should he do?

Hauk lay rigid, his conscience fighting with his base needs. Merewin was his, his thrall by law. He'd claimed her openly, twice. And the woman was in his bed!

Hauk pulled the furs back down her shoulder, exposing her upper arm and the swell of her breasts straining against the thin fabric of the sleeping gown. He ran one finger down the soft under skin of her arm. It must have tickled, because she jerked, rolling away onto her back. Hauk held his breath. Would she wake?

He watched the even rise and fall of her perfect breasts, laid bare save for a film of white fabric lying tight along the twin peaks. Her lips parted again, and he waited for the tip of her tongue to slip out, but it didn't. She rolled again so her back was to him, and he moved closer.

Merewin wiggled in the soft pallet, pushing her backside out and unwittingly into his groin. Hauk groaned out loud and wrapped his arm over hers. Her hair seemed looser, fuller. He buried his face in its fragrance and inhaled, restraining his need to thrust against her arse. By Odin, he might climax right there against her.

"Hauk," Merewin moaned softly, and his head jerked upright, eyes wide in the dark.

He froze, waiting, and then rubbed his lips together. "Aye, Merewin." He rolled her name in his mouth, tasting the syllables, anticipating other delicacies on his tongue. She didn't answer and he realized her breath had become rapid. She was dreaming, of him. Hauk pressed himself against the curve of her back and stroked the slight womanly roundness of her stomach, his fingers trailing down across her woman's mons with each stroke.

Merewin responded in her sleep by pressing back against him, and a natural rhythm began to grind into his palm. He groaned again, realizing his conscience had lost the battle. He draped her hair to the side and ran his lips across her naked nape. She shivered in response and pushed backwards against him.

He had to wake her. Honor meant she must be awake to grant him access to her body.

Edging back, he rolled her toward him until she lay once again on her back. Hauk brushed hair from her face and leaned down to gently kiss her parted lips. Merewin moaned in sleep-induced abandon, clinging, deepening the kiss. Hauk reveled in the response. After all, she was dreaming of him. It wasn't as if he was doing anything she didn't want him to do. Grrr... He shouldn't. He couldn't. Damn but he wanted to.

Hauk pulled back, breaking the kiss, and Merewin's breathing changed. Hauk felt her shift into consciousness, a slight drawing back, a stiffening. His eyes had adjusted to the deep shadows so that he could make out her wide eyes.

"Hauk?" her lovely arched eyebrows drew together.

"I've returned."

She relaxed at his words. "This is a dream."

"Nay." He coaxed her hand to lay flat against his chest. "I am here. I took Dalla to her room."

Merewin glanced around, studying the dark space, then back to his face. "Ye are really here," she whispered, breath shallow.

Hauk wrapped his hand in her hair. "Aye, I'm here, and so are you. We will finish what we started before I left."

She blinked at him, her breath shallow. "Now?"

He swallowed, holding himself in check. 'Twas as if he wore Loki's chain that Odin imprisoned him in. "'Tis dark. We are warm. We are alone." His voice was a low growl. He took her hand, sliding it down the ridges of muscles making up his torso to rest upon his rigid cock. "I would have you know me, Merewin. And I would know you. If you consent. If you don't, I will touch you no further." His stones might fall off, but he'd never take what wasn't given.

He didn't move her hand up and down his length even though he ached to. It was enough that she didn't yank away.

"And this is not a dream," she said, and he groaned as her hand slid along his length as if measuring his cock.

"Not a dream," he choked out.

"Because this seems larger than it should be."

He would have laughed if he wasn't aching so. "I'm a large man. 'Tis in proportion."

She slid her hand along him again, her legs shifting in the warm covers.

"By Odin, Merewin, tell me yea or nay before I reach the end of my control."

In answer she rolled into his body, her lips finding his. He growled, throwing off the chains holding him back and grabbed her soft, warm body against him. He wanted to touch all of her at once.

Hauk wrapped Merewin with his legs and his arms. The darkness muted the shapes around them, making him only aware of the feel of full curves against his hard body. Merewin's kiss was wild. Her hands cupped the sides of his face as if to prevent a retreat, but he had no intention of pulling back.

The heat under the furs grew and Hauk threw back the covers. Grabbing the end of the gown twisted around Merewin's legs, he tugged it upward and off. The infinitesimal light inside the charred wood in the fire pit grew, the thin ribbon of fire catching the fuel left there. Light lifted the veil of darkness in the room, exposing the milky hue of Merewin's nude body, her luscious breasts, and curls at the *V* of her legs. In one motion he ripped the cloth from around his waist, leaving him naked.

Merewin shivered and he gathered her back into his arms, raising the furs. "I will warm you," he whispered at a lovely little ear. Her hands flitted across his hot skin, touching, outlining, exploring flesh. When she reached to grab ahold of his cock again, he caught her wrist.

Eyes, dark in the orange glow, stared up at him. Hauk barely recognized his rough voice. "You are certain?"

She stared at him. "If I wanted to be a maid forever, I wouldn't have dreamt the dreams I dreamt."

Hauk heard her words just under the rush of blood flooding his ears, in his veins. She stroked him, testing his cock's length, its thickness.

With grace born of hours practicing maneuvers against his foes, Hauk lifted and rolled Merewin under him. She moaned softly, rubbing herself against him. Her breasts pressed upward, and he lowered his head to one peak.

Merewin gasped as his hot mouth encircled the bud while his hand palmed the soft flesh. He rolled the other nipple between his thumb and forefinger and felt Merewin's hips rise against him. She moaned softly and it was all he could do not to plunge into her tight virgin's body.

Hauk breathed deeply, reining in his need to ravish her. He returned to her lips, kissing her, tilting her head to slant against his own in deeper union. When he felt her tongue touch the edge of his lip, he lost his mind in the heat of her mouth. She pushed her hips upward in reaction. Hauk leaned to one side, cupping her breast, palming it before stroking the heel of his hand down her soft belly to the curls below.

His fingers parted her, touching her heat, pressing into her. She was drenched with desire. "By the gods," he rasped.

"Aye...there," she cried as he found her most sensitive jewel, rubbing back and forth as her hips rose to meet his hand, her body begging him for more.

Power surged through Hauk. Strength filled him yet strain dragged against him, making a fine sweat break out on his back as if he were locked in mortal combat. The fire behind him flared up and receded. *I must go slow.* By the gods, it would kill him.

Merewin's body was ready, her knees falling open to the sides.

Aye, she was ready for him, but he wanted to make her melt with pleasure before he plunged inside. Hauk worked his fingers within Merewin, making her thrash against the softness of the bed.

His own name on her parted lips resonated within him, tugging at his primal need to imbed himself.

In the distance, Hauk's ears picked up a faint voice. Dalla perhaps, talking in her sleep as she often did. But then the rest of the room, the rest of Denmark, the rest of the world disappeared in Hauk's conscious mind as his only thoughts were of giving Merewin complete pleasure before taking his own.

She smelled of arousal, of need mixed with her unique sweet, spicy woman's scent. The flames danced light and shadows in orange hues around the room. His breath labored as he spied her milk-pale skin glowing in the light against the dark furs as she shifted beneath his hand. "You are a goddess."

"Please Hauk, please..." Merewin's eyes centered on his face as he moved his fingers faster, until she released her pleasure in a breathy moan that he muted with his kiss.

She was ready. Hauk moved over Merewin's straining body, but the sound of steel sang in the primal registry of his mind. In a maneuver born of the overpowering need to survive and protect above all else, Hauk rolled over, grabbed the sword on the ground and stood naked before the bed, in front of Merewin.

A man stood in the dark doorway, his sword catching the predawn light.

CHAPTER EIGHTEEN
JOURNEY

"I will kill you, whoever you are," Hauk ground out, passion and blood lust mingling into a deadly strength he yearned to release. The fire roared behind him.

The sword lowered, and Hauk's eyes focused.

"Hauk, 'tis I, Gamal." His friend took a step backwards. "Dalla saw a man in here and feared for Merewin. And well, then I heard her...well it wasn't exactly a scream. Perhaps a moan."

Gamal's gaze dropped to Hauk's exceedingly aroused cock before rising back to meet his gaze with a growing grin. "Apologies if I interrupted."

"Get the bloody hell out of here," Hauk roared.

But his brother-in-law looked around him to the bed. "Good morn, Merewin, ready to go?"

A muffled "good morn" came from the furs behind him as Hauk tried to control the bloodthirsty thrum coursing through him.

"What, by the bloody holy gods, are you doing here!" Hauk's words blasted into Gamal as he advanced on his friend. Gamal took another step back and held up his hands.

"Would you care for another fifteen minutes to...finish."

Hauk roared. "Get out!"

Hauk heard what sounded like Bera in the outer room. "Tell my brother to stop his vicious yelling. His daughter would like to welcome him home." Her voice was a mix of rebuke and relief.

Odin's stones! He was putting an oak door on his quarters today. His hand went to his aching cock.

"I'll wait out here," Gamal chuckled as he let the curtain fall. "I suppose I can see why you stole my horse."

Gamal poked his head back through and lowered his voice. "And you may want to put something on." Hauk threw one of the pillows he'd kicked off the bed at Gamal, but the man pulled his head back, laughing heartily.

⸺◆O◆⸺

Merewin stood paralyzed behind the curtain, mortified. She'd donned the soft green gown that brought out her eyes. She'd bathed the night before and her shortened hair curled in a wild flow past her shoulders. Ellette chattered at her, hopping into a tight ball to roll on her bed. Usually her wild antics made Merewin laugh.

"Oh Ellette, I can't go out there," she whispered to her pet, her icy palms pressed against her hot cheeks. At this rate she feared her face would stay permanently stained the color of shame. It had all felt so right, so good, as the dream became reality, as she realized Hauk was, indeed, loving her.

In the main room, Hauk's sister talked happily as Gamal explained he'd arrived at dawn to take Dalla and Merewin to see Ingun's grave.

Peeking out, Merewin saw Dalla sitting on her father's lap. Hauk frowned but kissed her head. His searching gaze drifted over to the curtain, and Merewin yanked it closed.

Aye, Hauk had returned, big and beautiful, and more lusty than any dream she had experienced in his absence. And oh, how he'd made her body cry out. As she thought about the exquisite release moments before their interruption, Merewin felt a new wave of heat wash through her like lava. She would incinerate into a pile of ash if she walked out there, all eyes studying her as if they could see the brand of pleasure on her body.

"You are not going." Hauk's words snapped Merewin's gaze back to the slit in the curtain. Merewin centered her eye on the space and saw Dalla's hopeful face fall into defeat. The child's pain squeezed Merewin's heart.

"Which was what I told her," Gamal said, "but Merewin said they'd go on their own if I didn't escort them." He looked at his wife. "And Bera refused to stay home. I was hoping I could convince her to remain at Spring House with Vivien while I took them the rest of the way."

"No one is going anywhere," Hauk said with iron words.

Merewin threw back the curtain and strode out, hands fisted. "This trip is for a great purpose." Lightning-like anger overrode her embarrassment. "We are certainly going."

They all turned. Hauk's gaze raked over her. Was he remembering the way she'd moaned his name? Merewin held tightly to her anger to scatter the heated memories.

"We must go to Esberg. 'Tis part of the healing," she said, glancing at Dalla. "It must happen."

"Your hair." Hauk stood, placing Dalla to the side. "What's happened to your hair?"

Merewin's hand touched her much shorter hair as she caught a frantic look on Dalla's face. She forced a smile and shook the mane out.

"'Tis lighter and free feeling," Merewin said cheerily. "Much easier to wash."

Hauk walked behind as if inspecting, and annoyance rolled through her. "'Tis my hair," she said daring him to contradict her since he had captured her. "And that's not the issue here. We must go to Esberg. Dalla never had a chance to say goodbye to her mother."

Merewin turned to Hauk, and her hair slipped from his fingers to fall behind again. She swallowed, meeting his eyes. With a steadying breath, she softened her gaze. It was the closest she'd come to begging. "It will be a short trip, not even overnight if we leave soon." She must convince him. "Please," she whispered, "by the Earth Mother, we must make the journey."

Hauk stared. "Who cut your hair?"

"The Earth Mother," Merewin said in her native language.

"Why do you use the words of the Picts?" he asked, and his look dropped to her neck. "Where is your birth mother's necklace?" he said. "The one that helps you speak?"

Merewin felt the gasp more than she heard it, and Dalla ran out the front door.

"Dalla?" Bera called and waddled after the girl.

"Where is the necklace?" Hauk demanded.

Gamal cleared his throat. "I'll go help Bera catch Dalla." He strode out the door.

Hauk reached forward to touch Merewin's hair again. "Does it have something to do with the hair?"

Merewin found her voice. "The necklace was lost in the stream," she said in succinct Danish language. "I can speak yer language without it. Sometimes I slip."

Merewin put her hands on Hauk's arms. Dark circles bruised the skin beneath his eyes. There was a strain about him, a tiredness he would never admit. "Will ye take Dalla and me to Esberg tomorrow after ye've slept? 'Tis crucial to her healing."

"She isn't sick." His words lacked emotion as he stared.

"Aye, she is."

"Then cure her."

Merewin shook her head. "'Tis not an illness my magick can cure. 'Tis an illness of the heart, of the soul. She's improving, but she needs to say goodbye. Children need..." She paused over the word and finally said it in her own language. "Ritual. They need to say goodbye as much as adults."

Hauk studied her, weighing her words for truth. Had she killed her own cause by mentioning magick?

Gamal stepped back to the door and Hauk's gaze turned to him. "Take Bera home. I will escort Dalla and Merewin tomorrow."

Gamal stared for a moment, surprise raising his brows, then nodded and turned. "Bera, we are leaving, dearest."

"Thank ye," Merewin whispered on a great exhale.

Bera came in breathlessly and pulled Merewin away from Hauk. "Brother, Gamal wants to talk with you." She shooed him out the door.

Merewin eyed her bulging midsection. "Ye must take care, Bera. The bairn comes soon."

Bera nodded. "I will. I didn't run after Dalla. There was no catching her." She lowered her voice. "She must be upset she threw your mother's necklace in the creek."

Merewin had told Gamal about losing the stone when he questioned why she wasn't talking much. She was able to get by with the Danish words she'd learned quickly when she'd worn the stone.

"Let her be alone a bit," Bera countered. "It will do her good to think on her actions. 'Tis a hard lesson to learn, that acting in passion like she did was wrong."

Merewin felt the fire heating her cheeks again at the innocent reference and Bera smiled, squeezing her hand. "Sometimes, however, acting in passion is wonderful." Bera looked at Hauk through the open doorway. "Even tired, he has more spark in him then I've ever seen, even when Ingun lived," she whispered. "I hadn't realized how empty he'd been before."

Merewin studied Hauk. His frown mellowed into a slow grin, and he laughed suddenly at something Gamal said. He slapped Gamal on the back and then stretched his arms overhead as if shucking a weight off his back. His back muscles were evident through the tunic, bunching in chiseled glory.

Gamal turned, his smile ruining his grumpy tone, "Come Bera, let's reclaim your mare from this horse thief and get you back into bed." His raised eyebrow insinuated that she wouldn't be resting in the bed.

"Very unlikely in this state," Bera teased as Merewin escorted her out the door.

Bera squeaked as Gamal swatted her behind. He took her arm from Merewin. "I'm known for my creativity, wife."

"Don't be gone too long, Merewin," Bera called. "With my husband this randy, I'll be birthing this babe soon."

Merewin waved to them as they rode together on Gamal's gelding, the mare following sedately behind.

She felt Hauk's presence and then a tug as he threaded his fingers through her hair.

"Dalla did this," he said softly.

"'Tis really all right, now." Merewin turned toward him. His face had darkened once more.

"She used a knife?"

What should she say? Should she lie to protect the girl from her father? *A lie pulls darkness to it*, another of Navlin's favorite phrases.

"She was angry. Thought I was taking ye away. She's a child." Merewin narrowed her gaze.

"Did she use a knife?" he repeated.

Merewin swallowed down her worry and nodded.

"A sharp blade of silver about this long?" Hauk held his hands about a foot apart.

He knew the exact knife? She nodded, and Hauk paled, the dark circles beneath his eyes giving him a haunted look.

"Why did ye come home so soon?" Merewin asked. "Were ye warned?"

"Your witch came to me, led me to a stone circle."

The hairs on Merewin's nape rose as if Hauk's unease leapt across into her.

"What did she say?"

"Much." He walked back to the fire pit indoors.

By the Earth Mother, what did Drakkina tell him? And why did it haunt him?

"I see everyone is up and about," Vivien called as she and Diarf came in through the back door with freshly baked bread and a lump of cheese.

Hauk messed Diarf's flyaway blond hair as he passed. "I'm going to my bed." He tore a hunk of bread off the loaf and headed for the curtained doorway. With one jerk he tore the offending fabric off the support above the archway. "And when I wake, I'm putting up oak."

Vivien looked at Merewin, and Merewin, despite her blush, shrugged her shoulders and stepped outside to cool her cheeks.

CHAPTER NINETEEN
GOODBYE

Merewin stood on the hill overlooking the cemetery. Stones of all shapes and sizes outlined each gravesite in the pattern of a longship. Crowded together, some nearly overlapping, they looked like a fearsome fleet of spirit ships. The long waving grass swirled around them like ocean waves.

Mostly women lay there, buried with all their household possessions to take to the next world. Merewin had learned from Hauk on the solemn journey that Ingun's parents wanted her buried in the earth instead of being placed on the ship to burn with the rest of his family. Hauk had honored their request, so he'd carried Ingun and her possessions to Esberg to be buried in the center of a stone longship.

Merewin tugged the woolen cloak tighter as the wind whipped across the ridge. Her gaze trailed Hauk and Dalla as he led her to Ingun's grave. If Merewin had made good her threat to take Dalla here by herself, they would never have found the correct longship. Thank the Earth Mother Hauk had taken them at the next dawn.

He'd spent the night building an oak door for his bedchamber while she listened from her small single room. It was best she sleep alone, she'd told herself, ignoring the hope he'd come to her when he'd finished. But dawn woke her instead of Hauk.

"Hold her hand, ye big barbarian," she murmured. Merewin had privately schooled Hauk on what to do before she'd sent them down together. *Talk to Dalla. Tell her of yer pain and how much ye miss Toki and yer family.* Hauk had looked doubtful. Merewin sighed. He didn't seem experienced with any emotion except anger.

Father and daughter stopped before a large outline towards the middle of the field. Colored leaves scattered with the brief gusts of wind and caught among the rocks. Large crows cawed as they dodged smaller sparrows from shedding trees. Hauk and Dalla stepped into the stone pattern and stood together, their arms touching.

"Put yer arm around her," Merewin said as she focused on Hauk's back. Astonished, Merewin watched Hauk reach to scratch his back where she'd stared and then reach across Dalla's shoulders. Merewin gasped, forgetting to exhale.

Her birthmark burned and tingled against her thigh. "There may be hope for his magick yet." Drakkina's voice caused Merewin to jump and whirl around, hand to her chest.

"Old woman!" She bent forward, hands on her knees, to gulp several deep breaths while she assured her heart that it was best to remain inside her chest.

"Turn and wave to him," Drakkina said calmly, "before he charges up here."

Merewin turned to see Hauk staring, his sword half drawn. She waved a hand and made a shooing motion toward Dalla.

Drakkina stood in her flowing robes of shimmering thin material, a strange sight in the crisp autumn wind. Ethereal dragonflies lit on her silvery hair. She looked along the broad valley where the tombs lay.

"There is magick here." She held out her hands as if feeling the air. "Such as within the stone circle where you're from on the western shore of Pictland."

"My home is in the west." Merewin had always felt drawn to it.

Drakkina nodded. "The stones here vibrate with generations of ceremony, prayers, and spiritual thoughts. It changes the energy flow of the granite." Drakkina moved her hand to indicate the shapes of longships below.

Merewin looked back at the pair. Hauk kept his arm around Dalla's shoulders, their heads bent together.

"The child seems much more restrained, polite. You cured her of wickedness."

Merewin frowned. "She wasn't wicked, merely frightened and angry." Hauk placed both arms around Dalla, holding her while her small shoulders shook with sobs. "She's still healing, but not from my magick."

"If not your magick, what changes her?" Drakkina asked.

"Perhaps understanding." Merewin worried gently on her lower lip. "And love. Love can be more powerful than my magick."

Drakkina's brow wrinkled. "The magick you possess, handed down through the Earth Mother, is more powerful than any force in common men and women."

Merewin shook her head. "Some things can't be healed with anything except love." She indicated Hauk and Dalla.

Drakkina braced her hands on her hips. "Love cannot heal a broken head, but you can."

Merewin shrugged. "Sometimes I can, but if someone doesn't have a love for life, my powers are useless. And a life without love..." Merewin breathed deeply to control the emotional wave washing up. "A life without love is lonely, as deadly as the pox or a broken head."

Merewin wiped quickly at the wetness on her cheeks. "'Tis good she can say goodbye to her mother." Merewin struggled to keep her voice neutral.

"So it seems," Drakkina said, watching Dalla.

Merewin sniffed back her tears and looked at Drakkina. "Where does *my* mother lie?"

Drakkina's eyebrow rose slightly. "Lie?"

"Her body, after the demons killed her? Did they…" Merewin's face pinched, "torture her first?"

Drakkina's form floated closer to Merewin. Her ethereal hand reached out toward her but pulled back into the folds of her robe. "Gilla died quickly, child."

Merewin trembled as relief surged. She closed her eyes and drew a deep inhale.

"They hit her with the force needed to kill a full Wiccan priestess, being unaware that she'd transferred all her protective powers to her daughters. A mere woman had not even a second of pain before changing to dust. Which was a good thing, because evil, when fooled, becomes viciously cruel."

Merewin pushed past the dark words without letting them settle inside her head. "So there are no remains anywhere?"

Drakkina's brow wrinkled again. "In truth, her death occurred in the future of this plane of time." She indicated the area around them. "You will die long before Gilla's birth or death. So no, there are no remains."

"No place to go to say goodbye," Merewin murmured as Hauk walked away from Dalla, toward the slope leading up. He ignored the winding path, his long legs eating up the steepness as if climbing simple steps.

"You can come to the stone circle, Merewin," Drakkina said and Merewin turned, watching the old woman's body fade. "Gilla's soul is timeless even if her body is not."

"The circle to the west."

"Yes." Drakkina completely faded. "Your barbarian knows where it is," Drakkina's voice floated away on the wind. "You will come there together in the future."

Hauk's body emerged from the ridgeline. Merewin rubbed at her cheeks and masked her sadness with what she hoped was a sedate but happy expression.

Hauk stepped up, and his gaze narrowed. "You've been weeping."

So much for her sedate but happy expression. "'Tis a sad place." Merewin motioned toward Dalla. "Yet grieving can heal."

Hauk rested his finger beneath Merewin's chin. Gently, he raised it so she had to look into his eyes. "You are healing then?"

Merewin blinked against the ache of tears. Was she still healing? Hadn't she done that long ago under Navlin's care? Or had she ever really dealt with the pain of losing her family? Seeing Dalla's raw need for closure scratched at Merewin's carefully knitted wound. "So it seems."

"That's why you understand Dalla so well." Hauk reached out to rub a tear that had escaped Merewin's eye. "After the first course of tears and sobs, she seemed..." Hauk glanced down at Dalla's small body still in the gravesite, "better, calmer."

A ball of tight energy loosened in Merewin's chest. She'd been right. The girl did need to say goodbye.

Hauk pulled Merewin in front, blocking her view of Dalla. "You are healing my daughter. Thank you."

The corners of Merewin's mouth turned upward.

Hauk caught one of her curling wisps tugged free by the wind. "She confessed to me down there." Hauk let the wind tease the hair away from his fingers. "Cutting your hair and throwing your stone." His fingers moved to the exposed skin under the clasp of the cloak where the jade had rested most of her life. Merewin still wasn't used to its absence. The feeling was akin to loneliness. Somehow Hauk's touch seemed to lessen the ache of loss. Hauk's thumb caressed a circle lightly along the bare skin.

"She was brave to tell me and has convinced me of her remorse," he added. "You may ask for her hair to be cut as punishment."

Merewin couldn't quite catch her breath with his warm fingers tracing her collarbone. She kept her gaze on the amulet of Thor's hammer resting in the hollow of Hauk's throat. "I...nay." She shook her head and swallowed past the rushing sensation along her skin. "I should go talk to her."

"Mmmm..." His gaze trailed over the same area as his fingers. "Aye, you should. Then we can leave for Spring House."

Merewin leaned away slowly, and Hauk let his fingers drop. She tamped down the immediate feeling of isolation and turned to walk down the path. Merewin filled her lungs with a cleansing breath of crisp air to calm her pulse and release the tension that ached low in her body.

Hauk's voice followed. "Aye, we will sleep under the beams of Spring House tonight. I have a desire to try my new oak door."

Merewin didn't turn, but her heart pounded behind the skin that still tingled from his touch. He couldn't see the hint of a smile on her flushed face. She felt his eyes on her back the entire way down the hill.

Dalla looked up from the grass as Merewin stopped. Red eyes blinked in her pale face. The girl stood slowly, as if she suffered from age.

"Dalla—"

"I'm so sorry I threw your stone. I didn't know it belonged to your mother. I never would have thrown it. I only have one comb from my mother. They didn't take it because I was wearing it, but they took everything else and I'm so, so sorry I..." the rest came out in garbled sobs.

Merewin opened her arms and Dalla fell against her, wails drowning out the soothing words Merewin tried to give. Merewin wrapped her cloak around the girl and hugged her, resting her chin on the child's head. Her own tears poured unheeded, wetting Dalla's golden-colored tresses. Merewin swayed slightly as she'd seen mothers do with their bairns. Dalla's arms gripped with the might of the desperate. As if letting go would allow all the darkness in to crush her.

Merewin swayed until the sobs died down. "We seem to have a lot in common," she said. "We both lost our mothers." Merewin felt Dalla burrow further into her. "And we both survived." Dalla stiffened slightly, and Merewin pulled back to look in her eyes. "I think I have a hard time with that one." She squinted her eyes. "Me surviving when my mother did not." Merewin tilted her head. "Perhaps ye do too?"

"She left me behind," Dalla said, with a new downpour of tears. "I think I was meant to go with her."

Merewin looked down at this young life in her arms and shook her head. She remembered Gilla's assurance. *As long as you live, I live.*

Merewin stared into Dalla's tear-filled eyes. "Mothers die in peace when they know their bairns are safe." Dalla didn't look completely convinced. "Because ye lived, Ingun beat death. Ye're the part of her that survived."

Merewin felt her own tears, hot on her cheeks. "There was nothing I could do to save my mother, but I helped her win by living." Merewin cupped Dalla's cold cheeks in her hands. "And ye will help yer mama to win against death by living, too, living a long life, full of love and happiness."

More tears streamed out of Dalla's already drowned eyes. The girl had stored up three years of them, and now they watered the land over her mother.

"Do ye understand? Ye must live fully so yer mother will win. Live for her, even when ye don't feel like it." Merewin felt Dalla nod as she pulled her back into the embrace. "And I forgive ye for throwing the stone." Merewin felt Dalla's arms tighten. "We will find it in the spring."

Dalla nodded vigorously against her. Merewin leaned back to meet her gaze. "I'm getting tired. Grieving is good for the soul, but 'tis hard work."

Dalla's mouth twitched upward at the corners, and she hiccoughed.

Merewin looked to where Hauk stood. The sun had begun its decent behind him, outlining his imposing stance in golden light. He looked like the giant barbarian full of human strength, but he also resembled his god, Thor, magnificent and all-powerful. A shudder ran down Merewin's body. Her feet seemed rooted to the earth, yet her heart beat fast as if sensing something wonderfully urgent.

Dalla grasped her hand, making Merewin jump. "Time to go home," Dalla said.

"Aye." Merewin walked next to her toward the ridge.

Dalla paused to look at the longship encircling her mother's grave. "Don't worry, Mama. I'm alive, and I'm strong."

Merewin glanced up into the sky. "Goodbye, Màthair" she whispered.

Merewin leaned back against the high edge of the giant bathing barrel. She and Vivien had filled the contraption with steaming water where Hauk had placed it in the center of her small room. They'd returned to Spring House merely two hours ago, and here she was up to her neck in wonderfully warm water.

Before coming to Spring House, Merewin had always taken her baths outdoors in the stream that wound its way to the pond near Navlin's hut. Merewin closed her eyes at the delicious sensation of warmth wrapping around her body, invading every intimate crevice with heat. No wonder Hauk had built the tub, and it was big enough for him to use. Dalla said he loved sitting in it to relax his muscles.

Merewin worked the fragrant soap along her skin. The smell painted images of wildflowers and sunny meadows behind her closed eyes. She ran the refreshing fragrance along her limbs and breasts as they peaked above the surface. She lifted her dripping, washed hair to lie over the back of the tub.

Even though she'd always loved her long locks, she had to admit that the unwanted shearing made washing her hair much quicker.

"Mmmm," she sighed, sinking as low as she could. In the privacy of the water, Merewin ran her hands along her body. The warmth lay heavy along her stomach, her hips and between her thighs. She touched herself.

"Enjoying your bath?" Hauk's deep voice felt like an intimate caress. Merewin gasped as her eyes snapped open. She sank up to her chin. He couldn't see beneath the water, could he? She twisted in the basin to look at him over her shoulder.

Hauk's body engulfed the small doorway. His hair left small trickles of water running down his bare chest to disappear into the cloth loosely tied around his hips.

Heat rushed through her as she noticed the bulge of his pintle through the cloth.

"I…I," Merewin fumbled, "'tis a luxury. I'm not used to heated baths. I bathed outdoors in Northumbria."

Hauk moved closer, and the cloth around his hips dipped lower.

"The heat works on the muscles." He clasped hands together and stretched them over his head.

Though surrounded by water, Merewin's mouth dried up so thoroughly her tongue stuck to its roof. He looked at her expectantly, so she nodded, a nervous half smile on her lips. She pushed up a bit to ease the cramp in her folded legs, and her wet shoulders and the tops of her breasts rose above the waterline.

Hauk's gaze was intense, almost tortured, his hands curling into fists as if to keep them under control. The sight of him so uncomfortable sent a thrill through her. Would they finish what they'd started the night he arrived home? The thought sent a hot ache down between her legs as if the heated water penetrated her.

Merewin cleared her throat. "Has Dalla fallen asleep?"

Hauk's gaze moved back to her eyes. "Aye. She's exhausted from the trip."

"Healing is tiring."

A small pinch sharpened between his brows. "You are tired then?"

She could say yes, shoo him away. So she could what? Toss and turn all night with the carnal ache plaguing her? Or bring herself to climax alone? "I am not tired yet," she said.

An arrogant grin tipped up the corners of Hauk's mouth. "'Tis best to get you out of the warmth before it makes you tired." He stood there for a long moment, neither of them moving.

"I won't get out with ye watching me."

He frowned. "I've touched you, woman. I've claimed you twice."

The flush in her face spread down over her collarbone. "Ye claimed me with words."

"And brought you to your peak before Gamal interrupted."

Merewin drew a breath, allowing it to turn into annoyance. "If ye want to find *yer* peak all on yer own tonight, then by all means, keep standing there."

Hauk stared at her, his hand adjusting the growing bulge beneath his towel, and then he turned. Once she heard the new oak door close behind him, she rose out of the water and wrapped in a linen cloth. The chill of the room cooled her blood, and she stood undecided.

Ellette lay curled in the blankets on Merewin's bed, but she knew her pet would wake and leave soon to hunt. Then Merewin would be alone. Cold wind blew along the floor. She lifted her toes up from the small woven rug and ran fingers through her wet hair. She had no fire, no thick furs, no large body to keep her warm. She stuck her lower lip out in an exaggerated pout.

"By the Earth Mother," she whispered to the mocking curtain. "Where do I really want to lie this night?" The hot ache within her answered.

CHAPTER TWENTY
TEACH ME

Merewin shivered as another breeze blew in, making the curtain move. Had the blasted man left the front door open to sway her toward his heat? She poked her head out of the curtain. Nay, the front door to the longhouse was closed. Even so, Ellette always found a way out.

Merewin looked over at the oak door of Hauk's bedchamber. He'd have a fire going for certain. Plus she'd become accustomed to the deep softness of his large bed and countless furs. The man liked to sleep in luxury. Luxury could be a good thing. So were his brawny body and talented fingers.

Merewin turned to find her sleeping gown and stopped. To don it would make her look shy like the maid she was, weak and unknowledgeable. Merewin raised her chin in the air and tossed the gown back on her frozen pallet. She wouldn't act naïve. Hauk was right. He'd touched her intimately. If he was going to see her, let him see her proud and willing, a slave to no one.

Merewin dropped the wet cloth and grabbed a fresh one, wrapping it around her chilled body. Her hair had begun to dry into long curls that brushed down to the tips of her peaked nipples. Ellette sat up and stretched little paws. "Good hunting," Merewin whispered to her and slid through the curtain.

The smell of freshly hewn wood filled the air, and she pushed through the door into Hauk's room. A comfortable wash of warmth greeted her. She'd been right. There was a bright fire in the firepit, which cast the room in a shadowy glow. Merewin's attention flitted to the large bed covered with soft pelts. She swallowed past the worry in her middle. It wasn't her fault she was unexperienced, but she hated to be ignorant. Of course, she knew how the mating process worked, having watched animals and listened to the couples she helped through infertility. But the pleasure Hauk had brought out in her had been wild and raw like nothing she had expected.

The bed was in shadow, but it looked empty.

"I am here," Hauk's voice came seconds before his body shifted out of the darkness near the window slit and into the glow.

Had he seen her jump? She hoped not. Determination moved her feet, step after step on the cold floor toward him. She stopped before the fire, its heat branding her skin.

Hauk wore only the towel from before, his chest bare with a light trail of hair curling down to disappear below the cloth line. The firelight crested and fell along the sharp contours of his biceps as he folded arms across his chest. His face was unreadable, serious, watchful.

Had he been waiting for her? Was he angry she'd taken her time? There was no way to know. She took a sidestep closer to the heat, letting it touch all sides of her body. Merewin kept her gaze trained on Hauk's piercing stare. With a small tug she dropped the sheet. Despite the warmth of the fire, a draft brushed her bare skin as the soft linen pooled at her ankles.

"And I am here," Merewin said softly, so her voice wouldn't squeak, which would totally dissolve the effect she was trying to deliver. Calm, confident, unafraid of his big, oh-so-seductive body.

Merewin drew a quick breath when Hauk's gaze slid down her naked form. Her glance moved to the fire that suddenly cracked, hissing a stream of heat toward the ceiling. In silence she turned back to him. His expression looked the same, but something had changed. A glint in his eyes, a tensing in his jaw. He uncrossed his arms and took a step closer, raising his open hand to slide down her hair. His finger followed the ending curl where it teased the tip of her breast.

"Beautiful and bold, with the spirit of a warrior." His voice sounded hoarse, controlled. His hands rested on her shoulders, a gentle cloak of heaviness and warmth. He ran his hands down her arms to her elbows. A grin relaxed the hard lines of his face. "We will match well."

Merewin continued to stand there. She wasn't sure what she was supposed to say or do. He stared at her expectantly.

"I..." She trailed off and focused her attention on the scar marking his forehead. "Ye, I mean." Oh, she had to stop this blabbering or she'd totally lose her illusion of bravery. "Ye will have to teach me what to do. I'm a maid."

His eyes held nothing but kindness, mixed with a lustful dose of mischief. He grunted softly and pulled her closer so the peaks of her breasts touched his hard chest. "Of course." He tipped her face up with a finger under her chin. "I will teach you." He ran the other hand down to her breast and rubbed his thumb against its nipple.

Sensation shot through Merewin. It coursed down between her legs to pool with the other delicious feelings his deep voice and open appreciation were creating. "I will teach you to cry my name," he continued while capturing the peak between thumb and finger, drawing a moan of pleasure from Merewin. It felt as if hot sparks from a fire snapped through her.

Releasing her, Hauk smoothed the rough flat of his hand down Merewin's gently curved torso and across to her hip. He pulled her closer to fit against his hard body. "I will teach you to shudder with pleasure under me."

His words were a deep caress. Merewin closed her eyes as he gathered her hair to the side, exposing her neck. His warm breath washed against delicate skin seconds before his lips grazed her rapid pulse. She trembled on an exhale, feeling his hard, powerful body. She was surrounded by his scent, his complete focus, his strength. The intoxicating feel of his lips on her skin, his hands on her body, and his words tethered her to him. An ember burned inside her belly, searing her with building passion. Hot lips scorched a path down to her collarbone.

Hauk's hands came back to her shoulders. Their solidity grounded her as he paused.

Merewin blinked.

Hauk's intense eyes watched her face. There was a question there, lurking, sitting between them. Did he await permission, permission from a thrall? Merewin felt the heaviness of the moment. He had told her what he planned, warned her with his touch and words. But now he waited.

Merewin's heart pounded almost painfully beneath her bared breasts, excitement and passion mixed with denied fear. She abhorred fear. Here she would not hide, not from Hauk, not from the passion that engulfed them before the fire.

"Aye, Hauk, teach me," she breathed and raised her chin to look directly at him. "Teach me to make *ye* cry *my* name, teach me to make ye shudder beneath me." Merewin smiled, and with it, relaxed. She raised hands to his face, trailing a fingernail from his temple down along a stubbled jaw. "Teach me, now."

A low growl rumbled up from Hauk's chest, and heavy hands sloped down her arms and up to capture her wrists. Slowly he raised Merewin's arms above her head, holding them caged in one large fist. Merewin remembered the broad oak tree in Northumbria where she'd first been captured by the Dane warrior, and her blood ran faster, pumping lustful heat throughout her confined body.

In one quick jerk of his other hand, the cloth around Hauk's hips fell free. His mouth descended onto hers, warm and full. The brutal force she'd seen in his eyes and had heard in his growl remained confined, as if he caged himself. Merewin gave in completely, and the tip of her tongue slipped along his lip, tasting him. Hauk growled and released her hands to hold the sides of her face, angling it to seal them together.

The kiss made Merewin's legs wobble, and she leaned into Hauk's body, feeling his arousal against her stomach. Merewin had despised weakness in herself, but somehow she desired this weakness, this giving in to the sensations Hauk's touch provoked. She welcomed the tremor in her muscles, the promise of something more in each stroke of Hauk's fingers.

Hauk's hands slid against her skin. The heat from the fire added to the heat coursing inside her body. Merewin felt Hauk wrap one hand in her hair while the other stroked down her side and hip. His fingers slipped into the curls shielding her core, and her breath hitched as he touched her intimately. Liquid heat pooled there, making her ache for more.

Hauk's breath whispered at her ear. "Soft, wet, hot. Aye Merewin, we will fit well together."

Before Merewin could respond, Hauk lifted under her knees and carried her to the layered furs spread across his massive bed. He sat her on the edge, and Merewin fell back on the pelts, rubbing her bare skin against their softness. The luxurious fur slid a seductive caress on her already tingling flesh. Merewin stretched her arms overhead and fanned out her hair. She felt languid and fluid and very aware that Hauk watched. His intense gaze sent another thrill deep inside her.

The firelight cast shadows along his muscles, accentuating every honed line. Merewin's gaze trailed over the wide stance of his shoulders, down the soft hair across his rippling chest, down to his long, thick pintle. She pushed the maidenly fear aside before it could take root. This was no brute who would hurt her for sport. His hands lay fisted at his sides as if he still held a tight rein over his lust.

"Woman, you tempt me." His face was grave.

Was she acting too wanton? She braced on her elbows. "Would ye have me act the shy maid and curl in a tight ball under the furs?"

Merewin watched him flex his hands and ball them once again into fists at his sides. "I don't want to frighten you." He leaned forward until his fists sank into the furs on either side of her. He was large and hard and exquisitely carnal.

"I don't frighten easily." She inhaled, smelling the alluring scent of clean male and lust between them.

Hauk raised one eyebrow slightly, belying the feral warning in his stare. There was a sense of danger mixed with the intoxicating promise of unimaginable pleasure. Her body was torn between the need to run and the desire to rub against him.

Who would make the first move? She couldn't wait much longer with this lust thrumming through her body. With pent-up energy, Merewin rolled onto her stomach, leaping forward across the bed. Her arms reached in front of her to grab the opposite side of the pallet as Hauk's hands fastened around each of her ankles. Merewin flattened on her stomach across the furs.

With leisurely force, Hauk pulled her body back towards him. "Ah, but your lessons have only begun, my kærasta."

The furs rubbed along her naked body, her nipples teasing against the softness, as he dragged her across the pelts. The delicious friction across her breasts, the sensitive expanse of her stomach and pelvis, increased the pressure building inside Merewin. In this position, she was totally under his control. It excited her since she knew he wouldn't hurt her.

Hauk slowly slid one ankle to each side of him where he still crouched over her on the bed. Merewin gasped as she felt hot breath along her neck. He trailed sensual kisses down her spine, raking teeth across tender skin, teasing with his tongue. When he reached her bottom, he spread her legs farther apart. "Open for me." He kissed and rubbed each of her round cheeks and then slipped his fingers under, parting her from behind.

Merewin moaned and moved against his hand, her fingers digging into the fur pelts as he explored her flesh. She felt his arousal against her cheeks as his thumb began a circular strum against a most sensitive spot. "Hauk," she breathed into the furs.

"Aye?" He leaned down to kiss her shoulder blades.

Merewin felt herself climbing, seeking the climax he'd teased out of her the night he'd returned. She moved against his hand as he lifted her onto her knees. Hauk's other hand moved from her torso to her nipples. He rolled one between thumb and forefinger.

"Hauk, please..." she cried, as she pushed back against him. He leaned low and she felt his naked chest rub against her back, his arousal in the cleft of her bottom, rubbing forward to where his fingers still sank into her.

His lips brushed her ear as he moved the tip of his pintle to her entrance. Merewin nearly begged in frustration. She wanted more, more of him. She wanted him deep within where the heat churned, but she was a virgin with a virgin's tight channel.

With hulking gentleness, Hauk rolled Merewin over onto her back. The look of raw passion on his face nearly made her climax right there. "What—?" she started and stopped as he spread her legs wide, opening her to his view.

Hauk murmured something reverent as his gaze took her in, and then he leaned over her, bracing himself. He stared in her eyes. "I want you to see me when I—"

He cut off his own words by thrusting deeply into her open body. He groaned low, covering Merewin's gasp as the intrusion mingled with her building pleasure. He held completely still, his breath coming hard as he held himself embedded within her. Merewin had never felt so full in her life.

He teased her breasts and kissed her exposed neck. Still he didn't move. When his hand slid down to find the sensitive nub, Merewin couldn't stand it any longer, and she pressed up into him.

"Hauk," she breathed. "I need ye to...to move."

A slight grin softened the tense lines of his face. "Aye woman, I need me to move too, as soon as you're accustomed to me."

"I'm accustomed." She moaned as his calloused thumb rubbed in circles.

He slid part way out of her, and the friction of pleasure tore a moan from her. Hauk braced his forearms on either side of her head and began a rhythm, in and out. Each stroke raked within her, sending Merewin soaring higher. Together they moved, their bodies pressing together in a building tempo. She held tightly to Hauk's broad shoulders, a rock in the storm of passion flooding her, wiping away all reason except this. She wanted this man, wanted him completely. She closed her eyes, her lips parted on a shallow breath as he reached between them to rub her most sensitive nub while he thrust.

Pleasure tightened, and Merewin curled her fingers into the furs as she climbed higher and higher. Legs parted, giving him complete access, surrendering all inhibitions, Merewin felt the coils of her need strain together until, with a cry of exultation, Merewin climaxed. As wave after wave of pleasure rolled through her, Hauk moved faster, his body straining until he too roared, lowering to cover her. She felt his heart pounding against her chest as he hugged her tightly, his forehead resting against her own. They were one.

After a moment, she realized that he was so heavy, she couldn't fill her lungs. She tapped his upper arm. "Can't breathe," she whispered.

Hauk rolled them to one side into the softness of the pelts, their legs still entwined. Drawing in full breaths of air, Hauk and Merewin stared at one another while his hand lazily lifted and stroked her breasts, sliding between the valley and across her stomach as if he were mapping her terrain. Their breathing slowed and exhaustion began to overtake Merewin, making her eyes flutter closed. Her hand rested on his hip. Warm, and utterly contented, she nuzzled into Hauk's chest. His hand had stilled on her back, the heaviness of it like a mantle of security. She felt his deep even breaths. *The beast sleeps.* She smiled against his warmth.

As Merewin let her mind drift and numb, a deep whisper, like thunder across a plain, rumbled from Hauk. "Merewin of Northumbria, you are..." he paused. Merewin waited, barely breathing as she lay completely surrounded by this mountainous man. "Ye are mine, always and forever."

CHAPTER TWENTY-ONE
GIFTS

Hauk stepped out into the cool autumn morning and stretched his arms toward the azure-blue sky. He filled his lungs. "By Thor, what a magnificent day," he said as he walked to the spring, which sparkled with drops of sun. He watched the crystalline water weave its way down the mountain at the far end of the valley.

Hauk whistled a festival tune as he spied some large trout through the deeper channel near the middle of the stream. Aye, they'd have fresh fish for their meal today. *Merewin would like that.* And he wanted to please her. He continued to survey the midday meal still swimming idly under the surface. When was the last time he'd wanted to please someone? His marriage to Ingun hadn't been a love match but an obligation, and love had not grown between them.

Of course he wanted to please his children, but that was different. His song halted as his mind wandered over the thought of his son. His chest tightened as usual, but he didn't thrust the thought away. Instead, he focused on his son's smile, his playful antics, his awkward battle stance. These were memories he'd banished because they were too painful. Somehow, they didn't hurt quite so much today.

"Merewin," he mumbled at the disappearing tail of scales. He frowned slightly. Could the woman be using magick on him? But she said her magick didn't work on him. Hauk shook his head and turned to the shed to collect his fish traps. "And I don't believe in magick," he said with forceful finality.

As he thumped through the grass toward the back of the house, his thoughts remained on the woman still curled within the furs on his bed. He'd left her sleeping this morning after rousing her several times during the night.

His frown dissolved. He should have guessed by the fierceness in her spirit that she would be no fainting lamb in his bed. Nay, she'd been fierce and passionate, pushing shyness aside for the pleasure they could find with each other. Merely thinking about her lush form and wild honey-brown tresses twisting across the pelts made Hauk hard again, tempting him to forgo the fish and return to bed.

He eyed the traps and grunted. "Best let the woman recover." He adjusted himself. He'd asked Vivien to heat more water so Merewin could have another bath when she woke. The heat should help ease the aches in her well-loved body. He could imagine her skin glistening in the tub, her round breasts cresting the fragrant surface.

With a small groan and another adjustment, Hauk got the traps out of the corner of the shed and stepped into the cool breeze. "By Thor, 'tis still hot even as we near winter," he groused, and strode back toward the stream. The chill barely cooled his bare arms.

Hauk rounded the corner of the house and paused. Dalla stood downstream, searching the quick-moving water. She crouched at the edge on her knees. Maybe she watched the fish. Hauk smiled. It would be fun to fish with his daughter today. He hadn't spent enough time with her since the deaths.

"Dalla," Hauk called, as he walked up.

She stood and brushed her knees, her head bent.

"Did you see the trout swimming? I think we can catch..." he paused as he glimpsed her pinched face and wet eyes. Hauk set the traps down on the bank and gently pulled Dalla before him. "What's this, more tears?"

Dalla shook her head but kept her gaze cast down toward their boots.

Hauk tipped her head up. Had she caught Merewin in his bed? Did she not approve? "Merewin is a good woman, Dalla."

Her eyes opened a little wider. "I know, Papa."

"And I have claimed her. She's mine and will be staying here." His daughter stared. "I thought you were learning to like her."

"I am."

"Then you're not upset she's here?"

Dalla shook her head and glanced at the fast-moving water. When she turned back toward Hauk, her eyes brimmed once again with tears. "It was here I...I lost her mother's stone. The one she always wore on a strap around her neck." Dalla reached for Hauk's hand but turned her gaze back to the deep ripples on the water. "'Tis green jade, polished. 'Twas all she had left of her mother."

Hauk looked between his weepy daughter and the rushing water. "Let's try to find it then."

Dalla's crystal blue eyes widened. They were so very much like his son's. The open expression of trust and adoration had also belonged to Toki. Hauk's brow furrowed. Had he been avoiding Dalla because she reminded him of Toki?

"Aye," Dalla said and gave him a quick hug before walking along the bank, peering into the water.

"I'll set these fish traps upstream, and we will look," Hauk called. Pebbles of all sizes dotted the bottom. "A rock among rocks," he mumbled to himself. It would be a long day wading in the icy mountain water.

"Papa."

He looked up at the radiant smile on his daughter's face. "Aye, Dalla?"

"Thank you."

Hauk smiled and nodded. Aye, a day of hunting for a rock among rocks, but he'd be working alongside his girl. It had been a very long time.

⸻◆⸻

Merewin had risen hours ago, enjoyed another warm bath, and helped Vivien with mending, spinning, cheese-making, and various other household chores. Several times she'd stepped outside to look toward the stream where Hauk and Dalla worked. Merewin wasn't quite sure what they were doing, but they were doing it together, and Dalla looked almost happy.

Walking back inside, Merewin rushed over to Vivien to lighten her load of baking stones. They set them amongst the hot cinders of the central fire. "Vivien, do Hauk and Dalla usually spend so much time together?" Merewin indicated the door with a tilt of her head.

Vivien shook her head and dusted her hands. "Nay. Not since before the sickness came. Before then, he spent much time with Dalla and Toki."

Merewin picked up the basket of wool to spin. *I'll leave them alone.* She wasn't sure she could look Hauk in the eye without blushing after last night. Their mating had been intense, and she hadn't hidden any of her reactions. Pure need and attraction had spurred her into actions she hadn't known possible, but Hauk was a gentle teacher.

Merewin selected a tuft of wool and stood above the spindle. She spun the spindle and began to pull the tuft into a strand. It caught onto the end of the wool already spinning.

"And if you're to thank for..." Vivien began. Merewin looked up as Vivien gestured toward the door. "Well, 'tis been different around here since you've come. A good kind of different," she added with a nod. "I believe you're indeed a great healer."

Merewin's smile was genuine, reaching her gaze as well as her heart. She returned to work as Vivien hurried off. Merewin's fingers moved along the wool, the smile still in place.

Dalla had wonderful potential for being a kindhearted girl now she had purged some of her grief. Merewin could help guide her into womanhood, although she'd never be able to explain what she'd learned last night, the positions, the things one could do with one's mouth, the way a pinch of pain could enhance the pleasure. Heat flooded her body, and she worked the spindle faster. By the Earth Mother, she now knew Hauk's smell, his taste, how it felt for him to—

"Merewin!" Dalla flew breathlessly through the door, making Merewin jump. She dropped the spindle as her heart thundered and her face heated. It rolled across the woven rug she'd been working over.

"I am here," Merewin said, chasing it.

Dalla stood breathing heavily. Her soaked dress stuck to her legs, and bits of hair bristled out of her braid. Joy infused her face. "Merewin, we found it! It took most of the day, and Papa grumbled a lot." She waved her hand as if his temper didn't matter. "But we found it, there among the pebbles in the deepest channel."

"You found..." Merewin's voice trailed off as Hauk stepped into the doorway, a half grin on his face as he crossed his arms over his soaked tunic.

Merewin swallowed down the immediate visceral reaction to him and turned back to Dalla who flitted this way and that. "What did you find?"

"Your stone, the jade, your mother's stone!" Dalla held out her palm. Nestled within was the green jade.

Merewin sucked in breath as tears welled up in her eyes. She blinked and picked the icy stone from Dalla's hand, wrapping it in both of hers. "Thank ye," she whispered as Dalla continued to jump around in celebration. Merewin looked toward Hauk. His eyes connected with her gaze. "Thank ye." She held the precious rock to her heart.

He nodded and walked forward. "This chain is stronger than the leather cord you wore." He let the length of gold dangle from his fingers. His fingers brushed Merewin's palm as he took the jade and slipped the chain through the bit of silver fastened onto the stone.

Merewin pulse ratcheted up as Hauk moved her hair aside to fasten the stone back in place around her neck. His fingers teased at her nape, a sensitive spot he'd discovered last night. Pleasure trickled through her body.

His lips came near her ear. "There. Now I know you can understand every word I say," he whispered, his breath kissing the ridge of her ear, once more reminding Merewin of their first encounter at the tree.

"Isn't it wonderful!" Dalla cried as she grabbed her hand, pulling her away from lustful thoughts. Hauk stepped back, and Merewin could breathe once more. She smiled at Dalla and touched the stone.

"Aye, ye must have worked very hard to find it."

"Papa did most."

Hauk snorted as he strode toward his room.

Merewin saw the soaked fabric sticking along his frame. She frowned. If he caught an illness, she wouldn't be able to heal him. He was immune to her powers. Drakkina had said it proved he was her soul mate.

"Dalla, ye should change into dry clothes," Merewin said and followed Hauk.

Dalla skipped after her and shot off into her room.

Hauk's new oak door stood half open. Should she knock? Call to him? Or just enter? Merewin hesitated. "Shall I send for warm water for a bath?" she called through the crack. She heard footfalls, and the door swung inward.

"Aye, a warm bath," he said, his glance light. He stood without his tunic, only wet trews sucking at the hard lines of his thighs, molding against his body. His bulge was easy to see. "And a warm woman." He drew her towards him. His lips met hers for a kiss, a slow, thoroughly sensual kiss that melted along her tongue and down her throat. Merewin shivered, half from the kiss, but more from his icy skin.

"Steaming water," Vivien called from behind them. Hauk released Merewin and stepped to take the heavy bucket from her.

"Thank you, Vivien."

"Diarf will bring another bucket."

"Aye, thank you," Hauk repeated, without taking his eyes off Merewin. His gaze captured her, and she couldn't look away.

"Vivien, there's fresh trout near the door, for the evening meal."

"A treat," Vivien said.

Merewin barely followed her words as her world narrowed down to Hauk's two blue eyes.

"I will have Dalla help me prepare the meal." Vivien backed away. Diarf hurried past Merewin, and Hauk took the bucket in his other hand, setting them down.

With one last smoldering look, Hauk walked past Merewin to retrieve the large bathing tub from her room. He must have emptied it that morning, because he carried it into his room with little effort, setting it down near the fire pit. He picked up both buckets of steaming water, pouring them into the tub and retrieved one more of cool water. Merewin watched his biceps grow like mountains as he lifted them.

"Come Merewin, help me with my bath." His voice and the display of strength flowed through her like warm wine.

Merewin swung the oak door shut behind her and watched as Hauk untied the lacings of his trews. She tried not to stare, but it was nearly impossible as he slid the clinging material from his body. Merewin knew for a certainty that the look he had given her had not been a ruse, for he was fully aroused and ready.

For the space of several heartbeats, Hauk stared at her as if deciding whether to forgo his bath. He sighed deeply and stepped into the water.

"I would not smell of trout when I give you your next lesson."

With his naked lower half covered by water, Merewin silently chided herself for her sudden inability to concentrate. She walked over to the tub and dropped an oval loaf of goat's soap into the water, splashing Hauk's face. "Perhaps I have some lessons to teach ye."

Hauk wiped a hand down his dripping face and glanced up. "And what would this freshly consummated woman teach a man of carnal pleasure?" A teasing light to his eyes softened the arrogant expression. He began to rub the soap across his chest and down over a taut stomach made of ridges of muscles.

She tilted her head, suddenly feeling ire. "And where did the teacher learn about pleasure?"

He continued to rub his chest, his eyes narrowing. "I am not foolish enough to answer."

Her lips tightened. "'Tis obvious ye've known many women to become such an expert."

The water sloshed as he sat forward, his brows raising. "You are angered I can tease out your pleasure until you explode like a carnal volcano?"

Feelings mixed and were piqued by her embarrassment. Merewin turned away, but Hauk caught her wrist. "Merewin, your form is the loveliest I've ever seen, the softest I've ever run my hands along." Merewin turned back to him as he continued, sincerity in his voice. "You are round in all the best places and your skin smells of fresh flowers and mysterious spice." She met warm, serious eyes. "And your passion is like fire."

Merewin's flush prickled along the sensitive skin of her neck and chest.

His voice lowered. "You branded me with that fire last night and this morn." He pulled her closer until her thighs rested against the wet edge of the wooden tub lined with a linen sheet. "Aye," he nodded slowly, "I did learn last eve from you. And as soon as I rid myself of trout," he grinned and dropped her wrist to pick up the soap, "I plan to learn even more about you." He smiled wickedly. "I will seek out any new spots that make you howl. Aye, I can learn a lot from you." He dipped his head under water, his knees poking up.

Merewin's heart beat steadily, the ache of want already pooling in her pelvis. Bubbles broke the surface of the water, and Hauk reemerged to rub soap through his hair and short beard.

"I should help Vivien with the meal," Merewin said.

Hauk frowned. "Nay. Then *you* will smell of trout."

He stood, the water sloshing off him in a wave that sent some over the rim onto the floor. He grabbed a linen nearby, wiping away the droplets.

They both paused at the sound of horse hooves outside, and Hauk moved swiftly to a trunk, grabbing a fresh tunic and trews.

Merewin moved to the door.

"Nay, stay here until I know who comes," Hauk ordered. He grabbed his war axe near the bed, and Merewin followed him out of the room.

Gamal slammed the front door open, causing Dalla to jump and the dog to bark. Gamal's wild look surveyed the room. They fastened on Merewin, and she knew.

The tight knot of panic pulled at her stomach, and she rubbed a hand across her midriff.

"Bera," Merewin whispered on an exhale.

"'Tis time," Gamal said. "Come."

"Is there no midwife here?" Merewin asked, desperation trapping her next breath. Bera had told her one traveled between the villages.

Hauk's hand closed on her cold fingers. His grasp was warm, solid.

"Bera wants you," Gamal said. "She worries about the babe."

Merewin shook her head. "Ye know I can't heal wee bairns, Gamal. If there is a problem, I can do naught to save yer child."

"But you could save my Bera." Gamal's eyes bored into her with such intensity that Merewin felt certain the man wouldn't leave without her.

Hauk squeezed Merewin's hand but didn't demand she go, though she felt his support and worry for his sister.

"I will get my stones." Merewin turned.

⁐◆⁐

The moon slanted shadows from the bare limbs of the sacred trees as they rode through the cold night. Lines of darkness and moonlight sliced against them. Merewin rode with Hauk, cradled against the warmth of his chest. It was almost surreal, the chill on her face, the splashes of moonlight and the warmth at her back. Yet she felt numb. Perhaps this was a nightmare. Perhaps she didn't really ride toward her greatest fear.

Visions of the toddling boy she'd tried to heal years ago came unbidden, stinging her eyes. She'd been so sure of herself then, so arrogant. She'd channeled her energy into him and felt the cracks in his back, the twisting of his neck and spine, the bleeding beneath his still-soft skull. Merewin had mended injuries like this before, worse even, on men in town. "Don't worry so. I can heal him," she'd boasted, but then she'd hit the wall of his apathy.

She'd been able to heal Ivarr because he was old enough to have favorite things in this world like his mother's song and his father's sword. But a newborn babe would know nothing of this world except cold and fear.

Merewin wiped at a tear as it leaked out of her eye. She drank in the chill. It snaked around her tongue, cooling the inside of her cheeks. *Numb.* She was numb and had no idea what she would do if something in the birth went wrong.

She swallowed. *Bera is healthy. The bairn is on time.* Perhaps all would go well. Merewin glanced at the trees as they swayed, bending their arms down as if to snag her, stop her. She took another deep breath to quell the foreboding that throbbed in her chest.

Bera and Gamal's home stood bright against the darkness. The glow of firelight beaconed out under the door and around every window slit tightly covered against the cold. The trees leaned over the dwelling, as if to listen in on this crucial moment in time.

Gamal jumped off his mount, striding into the home. Merewin took it all in as if she watched a painting come to life, sat apart from it, her own breath in cadence with her heart. The trees swayed. Several women stood in a group outside, praying to their gods.

"You'll pass out if you keep breathing so fast." Hauk's words brushed warmly against her ear. "Breathe slow and steady."

"Do none of them know the ways of birthing?" she asked, trying to breathe more evenly.

"Gamal told me that Bera only wants you. After all your healing in the village, they agree that you're the best to help her." Hauk's arms wrapped around her like a heavy cloak. Warmth and the fresh smell of soap and man surrounded her. Merewin concentrated on Hauk's strength and slowed her breathing.

Bera's guttural moan leaked out into the night. The entire dwelling pulsed with swollen anticipation.

"Come," Gamal demanded from the open door.

The warmth and strength of Hauk's arms suddenly felt like an iron cage. Merewin pushed against them, and Hauk released her to dismount. Before she could jump down, Hauk plucked her from the war horse's back, setting her next to the statue-like beast. Only its ears twitched toward the sound of Bera's cries.

"Now, Merewin!" Gamal yelled before heading back inside.

Hauk dropped the leather pouch into Merewin's numb hands. The heaviness of the stones grounded her, and she took a full breath, then a step toward the dwelling. Bera needed her, sweet talkative Bera. Merewin took another step. Hauk stood somewhere behind. She felt his presence, like a silent mountain in the darkness, a stony rampart, guarding her, supporting her.

Stagnant heat prickled against Merewin's face as she pushed into the dwelling. The sweltering room swirled with body odors and smoke. She choked. "Gamal, air the room. There's too much heat and smoke in here."

Without hesitation the man leapt into motion. *Give the worried something to do* had been Navlin's sage advice.

Hauk went to his sister. Bera lay on the central platform made up as their bed. Furs surrounded her, matted with sweat. The woman's look flashed wildly up at Hauk.

"I will die." Pain flicked across her face, and she swallowed hard.

Another lesson from Navlin. *Give the ill hope.* Merewin stepped over rags and thrown linens tossed carelessly on the floor around the platform. *Realistic hope*, Merewin added.

"Do ye wish to die, Bera?" Merewin asked, voice calm, positive.

"Nay!" Gamal yelled, and she saw Hauk catch Gamal's arm out of the corner of her sight.

"Nay!" Bera groaned low, wailing the denial out on the crest of pain.

Merewin nodded and smiled. "Then ye will not die. I won't let you." Merewin touched Bera's chin so Hauk's sister had to stare back into her eyes to see the conviction there. Merewin nodded. "Ye will live." She wiped her cool hand across Bera's slick brow, nudging back the tangled mats. Bera mimicked her nod and took a deeper breath. The panic ebbed away from her stare.

"And my babe?"

The panic that had left Bera, like a serpent pushed from its hole, dove under Merewin's skin. Merewin continued to stroke Bera's hair aside, calming the woman. "Ye will live, Bera. I will do everything for yer bairn that I can. Let's work together now to bring him to Midgard."

Merewin felt the pain cross through Bera as the woman squeezed her eyes tight. The turmoil twisted inside Merewin, but she kept a serene expression. If the bairn died, would Bera not want to live? If so, she could lose them both.

Merewin took a deep breath and stomped the panic deep into her stomach. "Breathe deeply, Bera. It helps to move ye through the pain." Bera nodded as she whooshed in a breath. Merewin couldn't take the pain from her. To do so could stop the contractions that would bring the babe through her body. "Gamal, keep her hand and remind her to take long deep breaths, in and out." Gamal hurried to his wife's side.

Merewin looked at Hauk, still silent but waiting for her orders. "Too many furs," Merewin said, and the two of them peeled the skins away from Bera's straining body. Merewin draped her form with linens, bending beneath to roll up Bera's gown to check if her body was opening. Merewin swallowed hard. She'd helped Navlin with births but had never delivered a bairn on her own.

Bera began to pant low.

The sound of progress. "Do ye feel a need to push, Bera?" Merewin asked, relief relaxing her chest as she saw Bera's body was opened.

"Aye!"

Merewin looked to both men. "Help her move her body to the edge of the bed before ye leave."

"I'm not leaving her!" Gamal yelled and wiped a hand over his pale face.

Merewin didn't have time for dealing with a panicked bear. Gamal resembled one bent on attack, with his hair sticking out and his face in fierce lines, his lips pulled back as if to bite. She waved her hand at Bera. "Help move her. I want her secure on the edge with her legs down. The bairn will come easier that way." Merewin's gaze ran up the wall to the ceiling where supports continued across in equally spaced rafters. She pointed to one over Bera. "And throw a rope over the beam."

Gamal moved Bera to the edge while Merewin re-draped her figure. Hauk grabbed a braided rope from a pile circled near the hearth.

"Gamal." Merewin caught the wild gaze of Bera's husband as the rope dropped like a heavy snake from the beam above. Merewin grabbed the two ends and knotted them together. "I need clean cloths, a sharp, clean knife and warm, clean water."

He stared for a moment, blinking, then nodded and turned.

Merewin glanced at Hauk. His eyes were on her own. The effect grounded her.

"Brother, you should leave," Bera yelled as Gamal ran back inside, holding things the women of the village no doubt heaped on him as soon as he left.

It was true that only women attended births. Men weren't usually strong enough to handle the pain and smells. "I stay!" Gamal growled, as he held a knife blade in the fire.

Hauk moved toward the door. "I will stay on the other side of—"

"Nay!" Gamal ran over to Hauk, his eyes wild. "But she yells at you. 'Tis strengthening." He lowered his voice, but Merewin still heard. "I would have her angry instead of weeping."

Another woman came in. "Bera, please let me help." She glanced at Merewin. "I'm Minerva and have six children of my own."

"Aye, come," Merewin said. "These two don't know about bringing life into the world."

"She's right," Hauk said, tugging Gamal's arm. "We should wait outside."

Bera panted, her words coming out on a shrill note. "Get this babe out of me now!"

Touching her very large belly, Merewin could feel the granite-hard contraction. "Bera, I will look to see if yer bairn is coming." Merewin waited for the panting woman to nod before ducking under the draping.

A little head crowned between Bera's parted legs. *Thank the Earth Mother!* The bairn was turned the right way. She came back up and smiled at Bera, pushing back her own sweat-sticky hair.

Gamal hesitated by the doorway, torn about remaining by Bera and retreating with Hauk.

Merewin smiled at Bera. "I see the bairn's head. 'Tis coming out the right way." She nodded to emphasize the good news. "Time to push, Bera."

CHAPTER TWENTY-TWO
FREEDOM OR EXILE

"Aye," Bera breathed through clenched teeth. "'Tis time."

"Take the rope," Merewin instructed. "Pull down on it as the pain grips. It will help."

Gamal lurched away from Hauk. "I'm staying." Merewin actually appreciated his strength as he climbed behind Bera, lifted her up so Minerva could guide her arms into the hanging loop.

Minerva counted out loud while Bera pulled her body upward on the rope and pushed. A deep groan ripped from her.

Merewin watched Gamal's face turn a sickly shade of white. "Gamal, sit down."

"Nay," he said, breathing like a dragon from his flared nostrils.

Each series of counts seemed to last forever as Merewin concentrated on the little skull edging out of the woman. Finally, the head came free. The heavy umbilical cord lay around the child's neck. Merewin pulled gently on the cord and kept her voice even. "The head is out, Bera." The cord was required for life, but in some cases, it also brought death.

Minerva glanced at Merewin, but she had no answer for the woman's silent question. They must get the bairn out quickly. Merewin watched Bera's body tear on a scream. With one more count the wee bairn slid free of its mother. "'Tis a boy," Merewin called as she pulled the bairn completely out under the sheet.

"A boy." Gamal's voice echoed marvel and joy. "I have a son."

"Blessed be." Bera began to cry. "A sweet boy."

"Gamal, hold her." Merewin instructed. "A clean linen, the knife!"

Hauk brought the supplies over. He'd probably stayed to catch Gamal if he passed out. "Here," he said beside Merewin, but she was staring down at the bairn. A prickle ran up her back. The bairn made no noise. Merewin worked at the thick cord, cutting through the fibrous length and tying it off.

"By Thor, nay," Gamal whispered between his teeth as he watched Merewin unwind the cord from the fragile neck of the blue-tinged bairn.

"What?" Bera called, panic edging her voice. "Why does he not cry? Where is he, my son? I want to see him."

Merewin wiped the birth fluid from the wee boy's face and mouth. Despair gnawed its way up through her stomach. The bairn didn't move. No breath came from him. Merewin funneled her healing powers into him, hitting his still body hard, forcing him to take the energy, forcing him to want to live. *Nothing.*

In a split second, her fear crushed inward. The memory of sorrow when she couldn't heal the other child racked her body, sucking the breath from her. She staggered backward, and Minerva took the bairn.

Merewin couldn't breathe. Anger at the Earth Mother for luring the bairn back, fear Bera would fall into despair... It all slammed into Merewin. She had to get away.

Merewin heard Bera scream as she turned her back and ran for the door. But before she could escape into the night, out and away from the suffocating pain, a hand closed around her wrist. Warm and solid.

Hauk's voice penetrated the blood rushing in her ears. "She needs you. The babe needs you." Merewin turned back and saw Bera lean over her son and moan. Merewin's eyes flooded with tears. She shook her head at Hauk.

"I can't help the bairn. I tried. My magick doesn't work on bairns." Merewin sobbed once and looked down at the floor where their boots nearly touched.

Hauk's warm fingers caught her chin, gently forcing her to look into his hard eyes. "Merewin." She focused on the blue-gray flecks of his irises as he shook his head. "I don't believe in magick." He paused, his stare becoming more intense. "I don't believe in magick…but I believe in you."

Was it the words or the tone or the intensity of his eyes? Merewin wasn't sure, but she knew she had to try something. It had been less than a minute since the bairn had come into the world. There was still time to try something.

Merewin raced back across the room and pulled the wrapped bairn from Bera's chest.

"Nay!" Gamal roared, grief evident in the dangerous strain across his face.

Merewin ignored him and laid the bairn on the bed, unwrapping the little limp body.

"My stones!" she yelled. Minerva stood back, staring. Only Hauk moved, bringing her sack to her. But then she shook her head. They would be useless. Merewin ran her hands over his body, massaging, pushing at his chest that wasn't filling.

Breathe! He has no breath. She would give him hers.

Merewin put her mouth over the little nose and mouth and gently blew her breath into him. His chest rose. She drew back and watched it go down as the air escaped. Again, she breathed into him. And again.

Please Earth Mother, give him breath. Make him take mine.

She rubbed his head, his little body as she continued to blow all her hope into him. *Let him live, oh please let him live!*

Her thoughts screamed through her head as she breathed. The quiet sobbing beside her fell away as she concentrated on his little form. The nightmare she'd lived with from years ago faded. Everything left her except for the wee life she tried to coax back from the Earth Mother.

The movement was faint at first, really nothing more than a flutter, a slight warmth her keen powers recognized as a life force. The tiny sound of trapped fluid gurgled.

"That's it wee bairn, cough!" Merewin cried, and tipped the infant on his side, wiping fluid desperately from his mouth, her finger swabbing inside the small opening. "Cough!" She lightly thumped him on his back. With her words came the smallest cry, a whimper. "Aye. Live," she gritted out.

The little chest swelled with breath on its own, and with the exhale came a loud cry that flooded the room with miraculous joy.

"He's alive!" Merewin yelled, gently moving the bairn's arms and legs as if teaching them how to move. "He's alive, Bera!"

Gamal bent to peer into his son's face, his mouth slack as he looked between him and Merewin.

"But..." Minerva said, her eyes wide, "he wasn't breathing. He was tinged blue. I checked him."

With each cry the infant's face grew rosier. Bera threw her arms out, sobbing through her joy as Merewin swaddled the bairn and set him in her arms. Tears flooded out of Merewin's eyes, hot and sticky down her cheeks. Gamal's tears caught in his beard, and he laughed hard, kissing Bera hard on the lips.

Merewin backed away, her legs numb. She rubbed her face and jaw that ached. She must have clenched her teeth through the entire ordeal. The room began to turn, but she didn't care. All she cared about was saving the bairn, and she had. Without her magick.

I did it. I made the Earth Mother listen. Thank ye. Merewin felt herself fall, but she didn't even try to catch herself. She waited for the impact of the hard floor against her body. Instead, she fell into the familiar warmth of Hauk's arms. She smiled as the world slipped away into darkness.

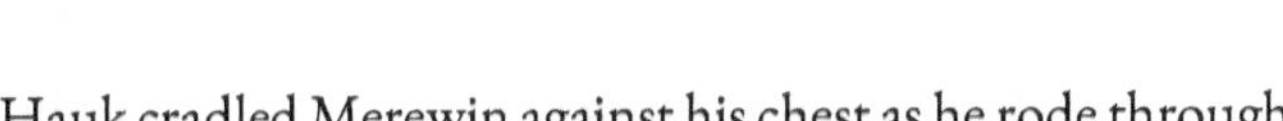

Hauk cradled Merewin against his chest as he rode through the predawn light. He guided his horse with his knees while he stroked Merewin's hair back from her face. The large war horse picked his way gently through the grove as if he too sought to give Merewin an easy ride while she slept.

Hauk watched the fading shadows tilt across her soft features. He'd never before seen anyone more beautiful than Merewin. *My Merewin.* In her sleep she looked fragile like a woodland flower, yet he knew there was a fire burning behind her deep green-gold eyes. A grin relaxed his jaw as he remembered that fire they had shared among the furs of his bed.

There was so much more to his woman. She cared for Dalla yet didn't let his daughter trample her. She stood against Svala and made Ragnar and Gamal hop to her bidding. Hauk ran a finger along the soft skin from her ear, around her jaw to her chin. Strength and courage lay behind the softness. Merewin had a warrior's heart. Terror had weakened her when the babe came out unmoving, yet she'd overcome it, breathing life into him without the use of magick.

Magick. He frowned, exhaling. *I am stubborn.* Could he not admit that Merewin controlled magick? Hauk watched her sleep against him. Had she used those powers to ensnare his heart even though she said he was immune? Perhaps she lied.

He pulled her closer as if she might disappear from his grasp. Her hair smelled fresh from the wind, with a hint of flowers and her own woman's scent. He buried his face into its dark softness and inhaled. Perhaps he didn't care if she'd used magick on him. Perhaps all he cared about was keeping Merewin close to him, loving her, and making her a permanent part of his home.

Home. He hadn't thought of Spring House as home for a long time, but somehow this quick-tempered, infuriating, chaos-churning woman had brought it back to life. Aye, Merewin had brought life back to his home, back to Dalla, and even back to his stony heart. The woman must possess amazing magick.

Merewin's breathing changed as she stirred. "Hauk?"

Hauk smoothed her hair. "I'm here." His voice sounded stark against the quiet of the spreading dawn.

Merewin blinked and tried to sit upright. Hauk helped her lean into the breadth of his chest. Merewin turned her head to look up at him. "The bairn?"

Hauk smiled and nodded. "He is well."

Merewin relaxed with a sigh. "And Bera?"

"As talkative and loud as usual. Minerva helped her when I carried ye out."

Hauk felt Merewin tense in his arms. "I should check on her."

"After you've rested."

She relaxed into him again.

"The healing...your magick," Hauk said slowly. "It drains you, makes you faint."

Merewin stared straight ahead in silence for a long moment. When she turned to him glittery tears were in her eyes. "Ye said 'yer magick'."

"Aye," he frowned. "It weakens you."

Merewin's smile transformed her face. The tiredness that marred the smooth skin seemed to vanish. Light shone in her eyes and color infused her cheeks. He would do anything to keep her happiness in place.

She nodded. "None of my magick worked on the bairn." She glanced down at his chest. "More likely my terror exhausted me."

She leaned against his chest, and he brushed a hand along the side of her face. "You overcame your terror, Merewin." Her skin felt cool and smooth like marble overlaid with the softest doe hide. Thin splashes of gold radiated out through the warm green irises staring back up at him.

"By the gods, you are beautiful." His words seemed thick in his throat. "So beautiful and strong." Overcome, Hauk closed his eyes for a moment. "When I breathe you in," he said on an inhale, "I breathe in your courage, your magick." He opened his eyes and kissed the top of her hair. "You fill me with strength and clarity."

Hauk felt a tremor run through him. He forced himself to breathe in slowly. Hauk's father had been a mighty warrior. The most important fact he taught Hauk was risk. Nothing is gained without risk. Calculated, wise risk of course, but risk nonetheless.

When Merewin looked at him, there were unshed tears in her eyes. She opened her mouth to speak, but Hauk started again. He'd never talked so much in his life. "So I'm releasing you." He pushed it out before he could stop it. *Nothing is gained without risk.*

Merewin's mouth clamped shut, her brows pinching.

"On my honor before Thor, I release you. You are a thrall no more." There. It was done. He'd never rescind an oath on his honor. He'd released the bird. Now would she fly away?

Hauk's horse stopped on the ridge overlooking Spring House. He looked down on the sprawling homestead. Smoke wisped up through the central opening of his longhouse. A few chickens pecked around the yard. The wide spring rippled in the dimness of the early morning.

It was as if his mouth moved on its own. "I will return you to your Northumbrian woods if you wish." The thought of leaving her there unprotected tore through his stomach. He tried to soften his clenched jaw. "Back to your massive oaks, your acorns." *Nothing is gained without risk.*

They sat in silence. Hauk's heart beat hard in his chest, making it hurt. A bird swooped low before them and then soared into the growing dawn. "Or I will set you up here as a free woman. You can heal the people of Port Ribe." The thought of men coming to her door, perhaps in the middle of the night, made Hauk clench his fist. There was risk and there was foolishness. "Perhaps you can live with Bera and Gamal."

She didn't respond except to somehow grow stiffer in his arms. She may have moved apart from him by the width of a hair, yet it felt like a huge gap. But...it was done. Now he must wait. Hauk drew her back into his chest and kneed his horse down the steep path to Spring House.

———◆O◆———

Merewin slept into the early afternoon. She woke alone on the very edge of Hauk's enormous bed. The last numbness of sleep left and memories of the day before reminded Merewin why she felt queasy.

"'Tis the thought of riding those horrific waves again," she whispered as she clung to the edge of the bed, unwilling to move yet. But she knew it was more than that. Hauk's words haunted her. *I'm releasing you.* Like she was a hawk set free by its master. Merewin had heard tales of tamed hawks who would sit by a dead master on the battlefield until they too died.

"Humph." She pushed herself upright to look around the room she already knew was empty. "Like I'm some tamed bird." But he was master here, and he had released her. Merewin's shoulders slumped. She could go back to the familiar oak woods, back to the small cottage amongst the ferns. She could go back to the suffocating loneliness.

"I could stay." She tugged a fur from the bed around her shoulders and stood. "Have a cottage near the sea." It sounded better but still lonely. The third option Hauk hadn't mentioned. To stay at Spring House. The option had hung there between them as they'd sat upon the ridge, but he hadn't given it. She could go to Northumbria or to Port Ribe. Merewin's spine stiffened. She frowned and pulled on a gown, clipping it at the shoulders.

"Has she risen?" Gamal's deep voice seeped through the door. Vivien's softer tones barely penetrated the heavy wood.

"I have." Merewin stepped out into the great room.

Gamal's huge smile hit her a brief moment before his chest did. Gamal picked Merewin up into a vicelike hug. Her feet dangling, Gamal squeezed, laughing, and then set her back on the ground.

"Merewin of Northumbria, you gave me my son last night. A healthy, feisty, hungry little man with the lungs of Thor." He held her shoulders and bent to smile into her face. "You saved my life in Northumbria and now you've saved my son's life." He bowed low, nearly scraping the ground. "I repay you with my service."

Vivien let out a little squeak behind Merewin. "But she's a thrall, a slave."

Gamal's eyes twinkled as he stood straight again. "Nay, Vivien, Hauk released her."

Vivien's hand flew to her mouth, a smile spreading behind it. It looked sincere.

"He told me this noon as he stopped in before heading toward the docks. Said he was leaving it up to Merewin as to where she wanted to go."

"He released you?" Vivien questioned again, this time hugging Merewin.

"I'm sorry, Vivien." The woman was still a thrall to Hauk.

Vivien waved away Merewin's concern. "I'm more family than thrall to Spring House, but you've had such a terrible time here. Your spirit is too strong to be tied here against your will. He saw that." She nodded to emphasize her point. "He was right to release you. Now you can go home."

"She is home," Dalla's voice choked. "Merewin is home at Spring House." Tears in her eyes, she stood in the doorway holding a bouquet of winter berries. "She won't leave." Her pale face turned to Merewin. "You won't leave me."

No one said anything for a long moment. Merewin took a deep breath. "Your father released me, Dalla. He's given me the option to go back to my land or to have a home in Port Ribe."

"Or stay here," Dalla insisted. The winter berries scattered across the floor. "Or stay here with me!" she yelled.

"He didn't mention Spring House to me, Dalla." Merewin took a step toward the child, but Dalla shook her head, tears now running freely. Merewin took another step, but Dalla raced through the long room to the back and into her room. Merewin turned to go after her, but Gamal's hand shot out.

"Let her calm down," he said. "I was hoping to bring you to check on Bera."

Merewin shook herself mentally and forced her own tears back into place.

"Go on," Vivien said, setting her mending aside. "I will check on Dalla. You two can talk when you return."

Merewin's gaze moved back and forth between Gamal, Vivien, and Dalla's curtained door. She nodded. "I must check on the new mother."

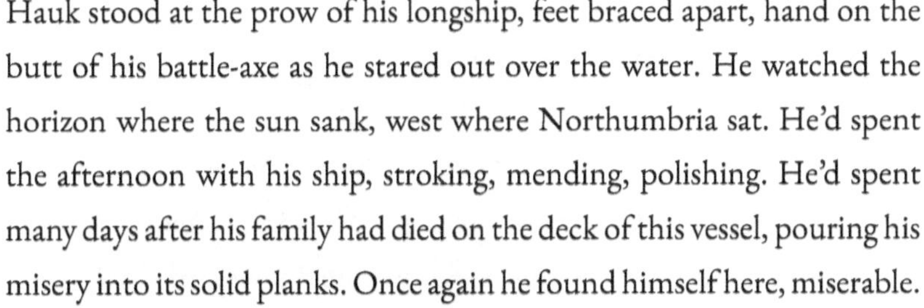

Hauk stood at the prow of his longship, feet braced apart, hand on the butt of his battle-axe as he stared out over the water. He watched the horizon where the sun sank, west where Northumbria sat. He'd spent the afternoon with his ship, stroking, mending, polishing. He'd spent many days after his family had died on the deck of this vessel, pouring his misery into its solid planks. Once again he found himself here, miserable.

By Loki's stones! What in Midgard had possessed him to release her? There was risk and there was foolishness. Had he played the fool this morning?

A sea bird dipped down suddenly, skimmed the water, and ascended with a good-sized herring. Hauk watched the bird soar until it was only a small dot vanishing above the trees. Free, the bird had disappeared, leaving nothing visible. No one would ever know it had been here gliding above the water line, no one but the fish.

Hauk cursed under his breath and huffed. "So I'm reduced to the status of dead herring."

"Hauk." Gamal strode across the wooden dock.

Hauk turned. "Is all well?"

Gamal smiled. "Aye, except for my lack of sleep. Little Alrik likes to keep us awake."

Hauk's frown broke. "Babes like to make sure you know they're in charge." Gamal chuckled and quickly hid a yawn. Hauk jumped down from the boat, his weight thumping along the floating dock. "And how is my sister?"

"Merewin has given her some herbs to help her heal inside."

Hauk nodded, his frown returning at the mention of Merewin. "Did she lay her stones on Bera?"

Gamal nodded.

"Did she faint?"

"Bera or Merewin?" Gamal smiled.

Hauk frowned harder. "Merewin."

"Nay, but she seemed tired. I took her back to Spring House."

Hauk turned back to the ship. "Bera will be fine. Merewin's stones are powerful." How easy it was now to accept Merewin's magick.

Gamal walked closer to where Hauk coiled a ring of thick rope. "Hauk."

Hauk glanced over his shoulder at his friend and brother. Gamal's smile had slipped away, and he rubbed at the back of his neck. "Aye?"

Gamal dropped his hand and met his gaze. "Dalla heard about you sending Merewin away, so you should be warned. She's not taking it well. I haven't mentioned it to Bera yet because honestly, I'm not certain why—"

"Sending Merewin away?" Hauk's hands clasped the rope and spoke slowly. "I did not send her away."

"Releasing her so she can leave."

"That's different." Hauk's face darkened. He dropped the heavy rope, and it thudded hard against the dock. "Merewin is free, she has the option to stay."

"At Spring House?"

"Or Port Ribe, or even at your place if we build on. She could take care of Alrik as he grows."

Hauk walked off the dock. Gamal followed him, taking wide steps to keep up. "Aye, we would be happy to have her." Gamal reached his side. "Uh, Hauk, did you mention Spring House? As a place she could stay? Because Merewin doesn't know Spring House is an option."

"Dalla misunderstood," Hauk said.

Gamal caught his shoulder, stopping him. "I was there when Merewin explained it to her. She said you didn't give her the option to stay at Spring House."

Bloody stones! Hauk turned on his heel to stare at Gamal, trying to remember exactly what he'd said or apparently didn't say. He'd been focused on releasing her and praying she'd decide to remain. He took long strides toward his horse tied in Gamal's side yard. "Blessings to you and Bera," he called and threw himself up onto the warhorse. "I will visit my nephew tomorrow."

Gamal grinned, his brows raised in merry question. "Blessings to you too, Hauk. I think you'll be needing them."

Hauk plunged down the path leading out of town.

CHAPTER TWENTY-THREE
ACORN FOREST

"Release me," Merewin sneered the words like they were a condemnation. She'd been stewing all day on Hauk's words. "Throw me away is more like it, like I'm some slave to be kept or sent away." *Actually you are.* The thought ran through her, adding to her fury. She huffed out loud at it and stomped through the long room to her original small room. She barely noticed Vivien moving about.

Dalla was not there. Vivien said she'd run out after Merewin had left with Gamal. At least Dalla wanted her at Spring House. A small sob caught in Merewin's chest. *Oh no! Not self-pity.* She wouldn't give into that. Fury is what she needed to hold on to. Fury at Hauk.

He'd merely used her for his pleasure and now that he was done, he would push her out. *Barbarian!* Merewin sat down hard on the small ledge in her closet. The tears could not be stopped, and since no one was about except for a sleeping Ellette, she let them flow. Merewin leaned back against the wall, exhaustion rolling over her, and pulled her sleeping pet into her lap to stroke. Ellette nuzzled into her as she had many times after Navlin died, when Merewin had sat alone sobbing in their small hut amongst the oak trees.

"I don't want to go back there, Ellette." It came out as a whisper, but the admittance felt like a dam breaking. Anger, loneliness, and sadness infused Merewin. There was nothing for her now in Northumbria. She had no family there, no real friends. All she had were the trees, the giant oaks that kept her company. Here she had the beginnings of friends, Bera for one. And then there was Dalla, so fragile and finally beginning to heal from the trauma of her family dying.

"Dalla needs me, Ellette." The little pet squinted and rubbed into Merewin's hand. "And Bera and little Alrik, they could be friends. Gamal too." Merewin wiped at her tears. "'Tis settled then, I'm not returning on the bloody boat." But where would she live in Denmark?

"Somewhere close so I can see Dalla every day. She needs a mother. I could act as one." Ellette seemed to nod, her beady look flicking around the room, then she yawned, and settled back down into Merewin's lap as if all had been decided. "And Vivien could surely use some help around here. 'Tis a big homestead. And Hauk should get some more livestock, a milk cow to start with."

Merewin set Ellette on the fur covering the ledge and pushed to her feet. New determination dried her tears, and she rubbed the old ones from her cheeks.

Merewin looked under the ledge where she'd put the few things she'd brought with her from Northumbria. Up against the wall sat the little bag of acorns that Vivien had retrieved from the floor. Stretching, Merewin grabbed it and marched out of the closet, a shawl over her shoulders.

Outside, the early evening light hovered like a sleepy child ready to be put to bed. Dalla stood by the stream throwing rocks into it. Merewin stopped next to her. *Plip. Plop. Plip. Plip.*

"Can ye help me with something, Dalla?"

The rocks continued to break the surface of the calm water, sending circles outward. Merewin grabbed Dalla's hand and pulled her toward a sunny little patch of land on the far side of the house.

"Let me go!" Dalla tore her hand from Merewin.

Merewin bent down to meet Dalla's red, puffy eyes. "I'm not the one who wants me to go, Dalla, so there's no need to be angry with *me*."

Dalla's eyes filled with tears, and she blinked, the anger in her face melting into despair. "Things were..." Dalla paused and swallowed, "better. Better than they'd been for a long time."

Merewin took a deep breath. "Dalla, I'm not going anywhere."

Dalla's gaze snapped up to Merewin's. "You're not?"

Merewin shook her head and smiled past her own sadness. "Your father may not want me here, but I'm staying." Merewin stroked a hand down the side of Dalla's head. "You're too important to me to leave," Merewin said.

With a choked gasp, Dalla threw herself into Merewin's arms and hugged her hard. "I won't let him send you away either."

Merewin took her hand. "Let's start making Spring House my home." She poured some acorns into Dalla's cupped hands. "Where I come from there are a lot of oak trees. I lived amongst them. I think Spring House could use some good sturdy oaks to guard it."

Hauk leaned forward over his horse's neck as he raced toward the sacred grove, urgency tugging at him. Of course Merewin had the option to stay. Why hadn't he mentioned it?

Hauk pushed his horse along the winding path, his mind still on Merewin. If she didn't know Spring House was an option, she'd already be making plans to leave, perhaps packing right now. Would she hike away on foot? He cursed under his breath and spurred the charger into a slow run. The stubborn woman might strike out on her own. Why hadn't he said she could stay at Spring House?

Because she might have said no.

The truth nearly knocked the breath out of him, and he let his horse follow the familiar trail without guidance.

If Merewin had said no, if she *says* no, what would it do to him? Cold sweat beaded on his face as his heart pounded like hooves in his chest. The thought of losing someone he...cared about, again, made his solid stomach clench.

"By bloody Odin," he cursed as he headed down the slippery slope to Spring House. He didn't see anyone outside. Could Merewin have already left? She couldn't have gotten far. He'd find her. But then what? He'd freed her from being his thrall, would he haul her back after that? *Nay, I cannot.* He would let her go.

His jaw firmed. "But she can't stop me from following." One way or another, he'd be with her. But how could he make sure she'd never leave him? His mind churned.

Hauk galloped into the yard before Spring House like he was a warrior leaping through a breach in a castle wall after a long siege. Hens scattered, clucking the alarm. The dog barked viciously as the war horse pawed the air, trying to stop his mad dash.

Vivien poked her head out of the doorway of the longhouse, terror in her eyes and a large knife in her hand.

Hauk jumped down from the lathered horse. "Which way did she head?"

"By Odin, you scared me," Vivien stammered as she stepped out.

"Merewin, which way did she go?" Hauk all but growled.

Vivien's eyes widened farther, and she took a hesitant step back toward the house. She pointed to the right, "back that way."

"How long ago?

"Not too long."

"On foot?"

"Aye." Vivien took another step backwards into the safety of the dwelling.

"Daft woman," he swore. "She probably didn't take any food."

"Nay." Vivien's voice called from inside the house.

Hauk's long strides tore across the packed dirt into the grass that grew beside his house. He'd check the telltale markings she would have left to determine her direction, then he'd go back for his horse. She must be hiking out across the clearing that sloped gently upward behind Spring House.

He rounded the corner and took several long strides before stopping. He blinked, trying to make sense of the scene before him. There in the middle of the clearing crouched Merewin and Dalla. They were laughing, and... Hauk took two steps closer. They were digging.

Dalla saw him first and stood up, defiance hardening her angelic features. This was the temper she'd always hidden from him, the temper others had warned him about. She placed her small fists on her hips like a grown mother would do before giving a good scolding. His daughter opened her mouth, but then Merewin stood next to her and caught her arm.

"Dalla, this is between yer father and me. Go on down to the house."

"But Merewin..."

Merewin leaned down and whispered something before straightening. "I promise, now go on down."

Dalla made a great show of stomping past Hauk. He turned back to Merewin. "Why is she angry with me?"

Merewin pushed hair back from her face, which smeared some dirt across her lightly freckled cheek. "I'm not the one who made her angry."

Hauk looked at Merewin's dirty skirt and then where she was digging. "What are you doing?"

She raised her chin even higher as if she were the most royal queen, her hair tousled around her shoulders, her hands caked in dirt, her look snapping with defiance. She was beautiful, so beautiful that Hauk was having a hard time understanding what was going on.

"I'm digging," she said.

Digging? Her grave? His grave? "Has someone died?" He stepped closer.

Now she looked confused. "Nay."

"Then why are you digging?" One more step and he stood before her, close enough to grab her if she bolted. His chest unknotted enough so he could breathe again. She was within arm's reach.

Merewin opened a fist to show him a handful of acorns. "I'm growing oak trees here," she said as if daring him to contradict.

"Oak trees?" He studied the warrior's spark in those lash-framed green eyes.

"Aye, ye have no oaks here, and I live where there are oaks."

The wind teased a strand of hair so it moved like a little serpent against her bare throat. Hauk watched the pulse in her neck and swallowed. He remembered how her pulse jumped as he ran his tongue along it the other night. "Aye, I have no oaks."

"Well ye will, I'm planting them right here."

"Because I don't have any."

Merewin huffed in frustration. "Nay ye don't, but ye need oaks. They're strong and wise and..." She paced before him and then threw her arm out toward the hill. "Ye bloody foolish man, don't ye see that ye need them here?"

"Oaks?" Hauk said and placed his hands on her shoulders to stop her.

"Aye." She tipped her face up to glare into his eyes. "And I will tend them."

Hauk blinked. "Here? At Spring House?"

Merewin's face reddened as if he'd slapped her. She reared backwards out of his hands. "Aye, at Spring House. Ye can't throw me out. Dalla needs a mother, and I'm the closest one she's got. I won't destroy her by walking away."

"And what about me?" he asked, following. His hands fell once again on her shoulders. He stooped slightly so he could look straight into her lovely, snapping eyes.

"What about ye?" she yelled.

"Will you destroy me by walking away?" There was no humor in his face. He wanted her to see he did not jest, that he was fully serious. "Because I won't allow it." He straightened to his full height so Merewin had to tilt back to still meet his gaze. "I may have released you, but I don't intend to let you go."

Merewin opened her mouth to reply but nothing came out.

Hauk continued. "I gave you options, but no matter what option you chose, I would follow you. All the way back to Northumbria if I must."

Her lips came together and opened twice before she said, "Spring House wasn't one of yer options."

Hauk exhaled. "If I'd suggested Spring House..." He looked away, "you might have said nay."

She stared, her brows furrowing.

Smack. Her open hand slapped his chest. "I thought ye didn't want me here, ye oaf."

He grabbed her hand, pressing it where she hit his chest. "If I'd suggested you stay, you would probably have said nay to be contrary."

They stared at one another until the edges of Merewin's mouth turned upward, seemingly against her will. "I'm not always contrary."

Hauk leaned in slowly, and she met him halfway. Their kiss was full without reservation, as if they'd been starving and afraid they'd never see food again. Hauk poured all his worry and vulnerability into it. He drew her hard up against him. He had her, there in his arms. *I'm not letting go.* She responded, kissing him back with growing fervor.

Merewin's hand unclasped, and the small acorns tapped on the ground as they fell. She wrapped arms around his back, molding her body against his. He ached to consume her, absorb her. Hauk ran his hands down her curling hair, gathering her softly rounded body into him. If he could make Merewin a part of him, he couldn't lose her.

They broke the kiss slowly, breathing hard. Hauk leaned his forehead against Merewin's. He bent, picked up an acorn, then straightened. "You aren't leaving Spring House." He put the acorn back in her hand.

Merewin shook her head. "I am not."

Hauk closed his eyes and breathed in her warm scent. "I released you, Merewin, because I had to." He opened his eyes to study hers. "I cannot wed a thrall."

Merewin stared into his eyes. She blinked once, twice. "Wed?"

He nodded. "Wed me, Merewin. Stay with me and your new family. And we can plant your oaks."

Merewin ran her hands up his arms and tugged on the war braids hanging from his temples so he'd lower his face. There was a shine to her eyes and a smile on her lips. "Aye, Hauk of Spring House. I will wed ye." She kissed him, and the ice that encased Hauk's heart cracked.

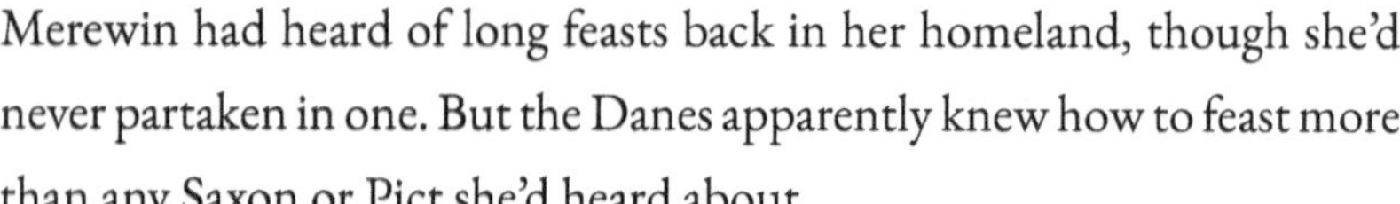

Merewin had heard of long feasts back in her homeland, though she'd never partaken in one. But the Danes apparently knew how to feast more than any Saxon or Pict she'd heard about.

"The feast will last a full week," Bera commented, as she wrapped a swath of finely woven cloth around Merewin, while rocking little Alrik's cradle with her foot.

"A week?" Merewin asked. "Where exactly will we feast for a week?"

Bera brushed her fingers through Merewin's hair. Merewin would wear it down to symbolize her unmarried state. Bera smiled brightly. "King Lothbrok is so thankful that you'll be staying near Port Ribe he's offered to host your wedding feast. We will dance and eat, drink, and jest merrily at his grand dwelling."

Alrik fussed softly, and Bera nudged the cradle again with her toe.

Merewin watched it rock gently as her mind drifted over the mountain of details of the wedding later in the week. Everything had been in a whirl since she and Hauk had announced their intent.

Bera and Queen Aslaug advised her on food and drink, clothing and jewelry. Normally there would be years to sew the right linens and to dream about flowers, but Hauk had insisted on a quick wedding, once Bera insisted Merewin stay with her and Gamal until the wedding.

Merewin sighed deeply and rubbed at a nagging ache at the back of her skull.

Bera stopped in mid-sentence. "Merewin, it will be splendid. Leave the food and drink to Aslaug. She's entertained visiting nobles for years. And she has honey enough to make bridal mead to last the whole month after the wedding as required." This was an important part of legalizing the Danish marriage. Bera patted Merewin's hand. "And I've already shown you the beautiful crown you can wear."

"Thank ye again, Bera."

"It was my mother's and then mine, and it shall be yours to wear. Although, you're so beautiful you could wear a circle of dead leaves and my brother would still fight any warrior who tries to take you." She shook her head. "I've never seen him so besotted."

"Besotted?"

Bera nodded as she tried pinning several broaches on Merewin. "He's smiling all the time, even when I talk at length. Gamal told me Hauk was humming while he worked on his ship." Bera stopped and looked up, her eyebrows raised in shock. "Actually humming." Bera shook her head. "Unheard of. Aye, my brother is besotted."

A slow smile relaxed Merewin's face as the ache ebbed away.

"And Dalla. She smiles and talks of happy, young girl things." Again Bera raised her eyebrows in exaggerated shock. "She's actually pleasant." Then she smiled at Merewin and squeezed her hand. "You've done wonderful magick here, Merewin, in all our lives." Bera glanced at her sleeping infant. "Truly wonderful."

"I didn't use my magick for any of those things." Merewin corrected and smoothed the lovely material over her body. She glanced at herself in the polished sheet of metal Bera had against a wall.

Bera's face popped up over her shoulder. "There was definitely magick involved, perhaps not the magick gifted to you by your mother, but the magick from your heart."

"Thank ye, Bera. Ye've made me feel at home here."

"This is your home now." Bera gave her a hug.

"Nay," boomed a voice from the doorway. "Spring House is your home, woman." Hauk walked into Bera and Gamal's dwelling.

Both women jumped at his voice, Bera laughing, and then frowning and shushing as Alrik woke.

"My pardons, sister." Hauk took Merewin's hand, tugging her outside. She laughed as he caught her by the waist and swung her around. The warm sun belied the late fall day.

"Bring her back here soon, Hauk. You know she's staying with me until she's wed to you." Bera called over Alrik's wail. "Hauk? Did you hear me, brother?"

Hauk pulled Merewin along until they reached the edge of the woods behind Gamal and Bera's dwelling. He stopped inside the shadow of trees and leaned Merewin against a tall birch. Without a word, his mouth claimed hers. Merewin's smile was lost in his kiss, and she rested her arms over his broad shoulders.

"Mmmm." Hauk inched back so they could catch their breaths. His forehead met her own. "I've missed ye," she whispered.

Hauk growled low in his throat causing Merewin's heart to hammer inside her chest. "I don't like this custom of keeping you from me. We've already…"

Merewin placed her finger on his lips. "'Tis important to yer people. I need them to accept me."

Hauk nuzzled the side of Merewin's neck, causing gooseflesh to run down her side. "But if they do not know..."

Merewin's breath was hoarse in her throat as Hauk's touch lit through her body. "Do ye have a plan, barbarian?" Merewin smiled coyly.

Hauk pressed a small bundle into her arms. "Wear this and meet me here tonight. No light except for the full moon." He grazed her neck with his teeth.

"Merewin!" Bera stepped around the house.

"One hour after the house settles down. Here on the hill." Hauk jogged away, leaving Merewin breathing hard, clutching the soft sack.

Trudging up the slope, Bera looked around. "He disappeared already? Just as well." Bera wagged her finger at Merewin. "I may not abide all the old traditions, but I do believe in keeping the two of you apart until the wedding. Mostly because 'tis driving my brother as insane as Loki." She pointed to the sack. "What's that?"

Merewin didn't know, but instinct told her she may not want Bera seeing what was inside. "Hauk left it with me. I think 'tis some of my clothing from Spring House."

Bera looped her arm in Merewin's. "Back to work." She tugged Merewin toward the homey dwelling. "Like I said, we'll most likely feast for a full week. Hmm, I should stop eating now so I don't outgrow my gown by the end of the feast." Bera laughed.

Merewin smiled at her new friend. These were good people and most treated her better than any back in Northumbria. Where the Northumbrian townspeople were suspicious of her abilities, the Danes seemed to embrace the magick. Except, of course, Hauk, who still seemed grumpy whenever Merewin tended an injured person. If she had herbs simmering, he wouldn't even come near. Merewin smiled, thinking of him. His short visit had filled her with energy.

"Aye, Bera, let's get back. We have lots of work to do." They strode back down the hill. Merewin hugged the bag against her still-hammering heart. Anything to make the day pass quickly.

CHAPTER TWENTY-FOUR
MOONLIGHT HUNT

The moon sliced silver blades of light through the molting limbs of the trees. There was a bite in the air, but no frost even though a wet snow had fallen the day before. Most of it had melted away, leaving a perfect night. Hauk stood in the shadow of a tall birch, watching his sister's dwelling below. *There!* He smiled, feeling the blood race through his limbs. A black silhouette slinked gracefully along the side of Gamal's house.

Merewin. And she wore what he'd brought for her, the black, tight apparel he'd first discovered her in when he'd chased her through the Northumbrian forest. As she jogged up the hill towards him, her sleek body wrapped in the fabric as if she wore nothing, Hauk was glad he'd asked her to wear it. He smiled. It would make running easier.

She stepped up the rise silently and stopped near a tree. Hauk emerged from the shadow, and Merewin sauntered toward him. Hauk pulled her to him as soon as she was within arm's length. He held her with one arm and stroked her soft waves of hair.

Hauk's voice sounded harsh in the silence. "Such softness. Tell me..." Hauk looked down into her eyes. "What color is your hair, woman?"

Merewin's gaze narrowed, and her mouth turned into a sly grin. She'd probably known what he was about from the moment she saw what he'd brought her to wear. His future wife was clever.

"Speak, woman."

She crouched before him, and his breath caught. Would she take him in her mouth right there? Was her lust for him so intense she—? But then she stood, remaining silent with a challenging smile on her lips. They would continue their play.

Hauk cocked an eyebrow, allowing his gaze to run the length of her form. "I know you understand me." He captured her head in his large palm. "Such beauty. I think you will be mine."

Pain shot through Hauk's foot, making him look down at the small boulder she must have picked up when she bent. It was enough of a surprise to allow her to twist away from him. Hauk cursed, a smile on his lips, as Merewin sprinted into the woods. Aye, Merewin was his match. But these were his woods. He knew them, where his sleek minx did not.

Hauk turned toward the trees, his ears picking up her footfalls along the common path. She crunched through some of the remaining snow on the ground. He breathed in deeply as he began a slow, silent jog after her, like he'd done while trailing her among the oaks of young King Æthelred's forest in Northumbria. His blood pumped, warming him as he watched her dodge between the moonlit trees ahead. She glanced back. He heard her gasp and curse. His smile widened. He breathed deeply, imagining he could already catch her scent. Spice and sweetness wrapped in warm woman. Hauk pushed his pace forward, closing the gap, craving her aroma.

He'd guessed right, she was staying along the trail, unlike the chase she'd given him before. Merewin wanted to be caught this time. This would be easy. He slowed his pace.

Merewin ducked off the trail around a large tree. Hauk followed into the winter-plucked forest. The moon filtered down through the skeleton branches.

Snap! A branch cracked ahead to the left. He caught a glimpse of her hair as she flew around a tree. She'd picked up her speed. "So it *is* a chase," he murmured, as he adjusted his course, leaping over a fallen trunk. He chuckled. His prey wouldn't give up easily. A sharp twig sliced along his cheek. "By Loki's stones," he swore, dodging more low branches.

Hauk ran for some time along the snow-dusted scrub, stopping to redirect after a scant *crack* gave Merewin away. Dodging and leaping, he'd grown warm. Luckily he'd chosen not to wear the heavy wraps, leaving his large arms bare, free to slap away branches. Hauk stopped, his breath in little white puffs before him. Listening.

A wolf crooned from far off. Hauk looked up, the moon in a full circle above him. He cocked his head, turning it this way and that. His eyes strained to catch a hint of movement ahead. He frowned. "Where are you now, woman." His words were as soft as the casual night wind. He turned slowly around. Had he run past her?

Splat! A ball of snow hit his right ear. Turning to the right, he ran before he even saw her. Growling, he wiped the side of his wet face with a bare forearm. "I think there was ice in that ball," he yelled.

Merewin shrieked softly and ran, like a doe sprinting away from the wolf. She took arching, graceful leaps over brush, her legs long in the tight-fitting trews. Hauk was tempted to pause and watch, but he dare not lose sight again. Time was up in this merry chase.

Hauk closed the distance in less than a dozen strides. He lunged, catching Merewin around the waist and pulling them to the ground. He twisted in the air so she landed on his chest. Before she could speak, Hauk pulled her up and pinned her against a towering pine tree. "Injure me again, woman, and I may take out my revenge on you."

Merewin grinned at him. He waited but she remained mute.

"First the rock and then the snowball." Hauk held her two hands together, pinned above her head against the tree. He rubbed the wet side of his head. "I think you put ice in that ball."

Merewin's brows pinched. "I didn't throw a..." but the rest of her words were cut off as Hauk's mouth descended, leaving no room for words or thought. Long minutes later, Hauk trailed his lips down her neck.

"Aye, woman, what color is your hair?" At Merewin's silence, Hauk growled low, his hands running down the landscape of her waist and hips. "Stubborn then. Let me tell you all I intend to do with you." He looked into her eyes. "Because you are mine."

Hauk scooped Merewin up in his bare arms, like she weighed nothing more than a lamb. He walked under the moonlight, talking in detail of all the varied things he wanted to do to her, like he had back in Northumbria. How different things were now. Then he'd been so empty of love, letting bitterness and sadness squeeze out everything else. Then he'd tried to distance himself from the tempting Witch of the Woods. But now as he spoke of nibbling and licking, kissing and rubbing, thrusting and surging, now he didn't have to keep away. Merewin was his.

The pallet of furs Hauk had left seemed like a league away. During their walk, Hauk described every image of lusty play of which he could think. Merewin's lips parted, and her breathing quickened. His mighty erection proved his words had teased him as well. Hauk lowered Merewin onto the soft pelts laid out in a secluded burrow away from the main path. Hauk lay down next to her and ran his hand through her hair.

Merewin looked up at him. She traced the scar above his brow with her finger. It felt hot against his cool skin. Her gaze smoldered as she stared into his. "Brown." Her voice escaped on a tremor. "A medium brown with some traces of gold, from what I've been told." Merewin ran her fingers down the side of his jaw and back into his hair to pull his face closer to her own. "Now barbarian, tell me what ye are called, so I will know what name to moan."

His lips fell on hers. Hauk took a breath against her. "Master, you can call me master."

Merewin laughed huskily, moving her hand down to cup his huge cock. "Hmm, now who would be master of whom, here?"

Hauk laughed and poured the rest of his attention and energy into making all his previous words come true.

⎯⎯⎯◆O◆⎯⎯⎯

Drakkina cackled softly as she floated above the crystallized earth. Her snowball had found its mark perfectly. Even without a corporeal body, she could still wield power. She hummed a little song she'd learned from an Egyptian princess long ago and floated up above the tree line. No need to follow Merewin and her mate now that they'd found one another. Best to give them privacy. They were well on their way to love, and without much of her interference at all. Drakkina had learned something from her last adventure turned near disaster with Merewin's sister, Serena. Best not to push soul mates together too fast, just little nudges, nudges like getting Hauk to go to Northumbria.

The barbarian had seemed so morose then, so dark and angry, but Merewin had changed him, healed him. Even if her magical powers could not work on her soul mate, the power of love had. Merewin had used love to heal the man's daughter of bitterness. The girl seemed happy now, rather pleasant from what Drakkina had observed.

Drakkina snorted as she wafted past the bright moon on her way to a timeless plane to rest. Love. She hadn't believed it was more powerful than magick to heal, as Merewin had told her at the Dane cemetery. But Drakkina had to admit, love was very powerful, indeed.

"It still can't mend a broken head," she quipped to the stars as they faded from her sight. Drakkina lay upon the fog, closed her eyes that weren't really eyes, and fell into sleep that wasn't really sleep.

⊷◯⊶

"So he will marry his slave." Svala seethed as she stirred the pot of gurgling brew over the cook fire in the small outbuilding in which she now lived. Without her husband, she no longer held a place in the much larger royal abode. "That little whore." She ground her teeth together in fury, her stomach tight. "He was my chance to get back my status, my life." Angry tears gathered in Svala's eyes. "So be it. If I can't send her away, and Bjalki can't challenge for her, then she'll have to die." She shrugged past the tension in her shoulders. "She had the chance to leave. 'Tis her own fault for staying." The words barely sounded like her own. When had her voice become so shrill and hateful?

Svala uncorked a small clay jar and shook the powder into her pot with more honey. "But first I must kill Hauk's love for her, else he'll pine away. And I don't have time for him to get over her." Svala smiled and inhaled, pushing away any niggling guilt.

"They will all think she made them sick. She didn't fix their pains, merely hid them like an illusionist." Svala stirred with the long wooden spoon, a sweat breaking out on her pale forehead. Pieces of hair poked out of her usually perfect braid as the steam billowed. All the planning and work would be worth it when Hauk and she married. Hauk would be Ragnar's successor when his son finally succumbed to some illness. Then her child would be king.

Svala rubbed a hand across her damp forehead. "Aye, it will all be worth it. I will have my throne, my respect, and a talented warrior in my bed."

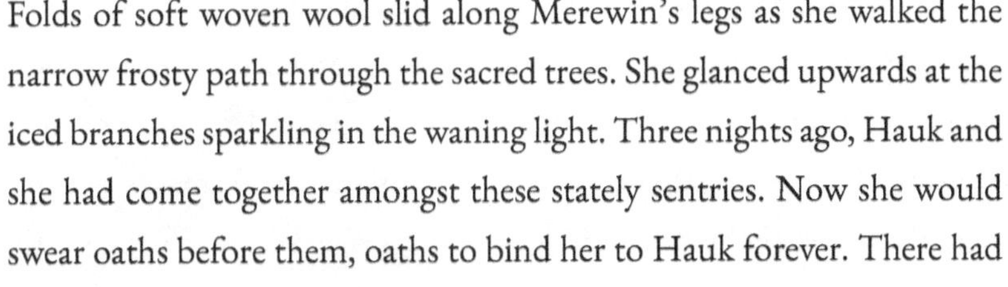

Folds of soft woven wool slid along Merewin's legs as she walked the narrow frosty path through the sacred trees. She glanced upwards at the iced branches sparkling in the waning light. Three nights ago, Hauk and she had come together amongst these stately sentries. Now she would swear oaths before them, oaths to bind her to Hauk forever. There had been no words of love between them, but their bodies had spoken of their mutual respect and trust. 'Twas a good start.

The day bore the early winter chill, but the flawless sky and radiant sun were good omens, said Bera, when she had fastened her own kransen on Merewin's wavy hair. The circle of silver, dried flowers, and wheat, intertwined with her curls, made Merewin look like a mythical fairy.

Merewin watched the lowering sun reflect against all of nature, captured in crystalline glory. Her feet, bound in soft leather slippers, crunched on the bright white snow. Her heart raced at the feel of the heavy sword against her side. Gamal had found a lovely groom's sword for her to gift to Hauk, as was customary.

Bera walked alongside Merewin, for once silent. Occasionally she squeezed Merewin's hand, a sign all would be well. Ellette had risen for the occasion and scampered amongst the trees. Merewin smiled and breathed deeply of the cool air. Her creamy cloak of soft leather was lined with fur. Its softness rubbed against Merewin's neck, reminding her of the furs Hauk had arranged for her here in the woods. She blushed softly.

She and Bera continued toward the onlookers ahead. A boar had been sacrificed and would be roasted for the feast. The ceremonial blood was replaced with bridal ale. As Merewin approached, Eldgrim made the sign of Thor's hammer in the air with a fir branch, misting the couple with the ceremonial ale.

Merewin turned to her once captor. Hauk stood tall, decked in rich woolens and furs. His arms remained bare where circlets of gold wove tightly around his muscles. His shoulder-length hair hung in wild, soft waves. His hand grasped her cold fingers, and she looked up into his face. Merewin's breath caught. His blue-gray eyes held such life, such promise. He smiled at her, looking totally at ease with all the formality around him. Dalla stood at his side, as well as Gamal. Dalla held her hand covertly before her and waved.

Merewin barely had time to smile at her as the elder began his blessings and questions. Hauk presented a bridal sword to Merewin, which she would give to her son someday. Merewin presented her sword to Hauk. Hauk held the tip slanted downward, the hilt toward Merewin.

"Place his ring on the hilt," Bera whispered near her ear. *So many details.* Merewin laid the band of gold on the end of the sword. Hauk removed it and placed it on his own finger.

Several men from behind him, including the king, grunted in approval. Gamal slapped him on the back. Hauk looked at her sword, and Merewin raised it in the same fashion, though she had to use two hands and a leather cloth to hold the massive blade. Hauk laid a ring on the hilt. Merewin took the intricate rope band of gold off, lowered the sword, and placed the band on her own finger. It was as if the whole community let out a sigh of relief. They were happy. They wanted her here. Even if it was because of her powers, it didn't matter. They accepted and wanted her.

"Merewin of Northumbria," Eldgrim's nasally voice broke through, hushing the quiet celebration. "You are now Merewin of Spring House, wed before us all, and the gods of Asgard, to Hauk Geirson of Spring House. May Frigga, the goddess of marriage, bless this union."

Merewin stepped into the warmth of Hauk's strong arms. She melted into him as his lips found hers. The remaining words were drowned out by the shouts and laughter of those around them. Hauk's warm masculine smell surrounded her, making a rush of heat flow all the way down her body.

Gasps broke into their kiss. Merewin opened her eyes, glancing up to see hundreds of diaphanous dragonflies flitting around above them. They zipped amongst the trees over the heads of the shocked audience. Merewin felt her birthmark grow warm. Drakkina was close.

Very good, Gilla's daughter. You've secured your soul mate. Drakkina's words wove through her mind. *When I call, he must take you both across the sea to the stones in the west. The fate of the world depends upon it.*

Merewin felt Hauk's arms tense, and he glanced around. He'd heard Drakkina's command. His gaze fastened on a branch high up.

I have felt evil threading through this time, searching.

Merewin's breath caught. "The demons?" she whispered.

They feel my power. I will lead them away. The pine needles dipped and bowed, fluttering and coming together into the outline of a woman's body.

Bera gasped, and slowly the celebration and wonder at the dragonflies quelled, as those gathered stared at the strange image in the pine.

You hear me, Hauk Geirson. Drakkina's words remained within Merewin's head and apparently Hauk's as well. Hauk gave only the slightest tilt to his head in agreement. *We had an agreement.* Again Hauk nodded.

The priest bowed low. "We honor your presence, great goddess." His voice quavered.

The tree shook, and the dragonflies flew off. "I bless this marriage." Drakkina's voice rang out majestically as a wind blew through the trees, causing the pine needles to dance back into their natural state.

Merewin looked at Hauk, one eyebrow raised. "Agreement?"

"Later." Hauk brushed a kiss over her lips. "Now we celebrate."

People gawked at the once again normal fir branches. They glanced around as if expecting a goddess or god to be amongst them.

Hauk squeezed Merewin's hand. His voice boomed through the awkward stillness. "Let us away then! To Ragnar's to feast!"

"Aye!" called Gamal, with an uneasy smile. "To the feast and to the ale," he joked, breaking the unease. Several men agreed heartily, though their gazes still watched the trees.

Bera grabbed Merewin's other hand as Dalla snatched the one away from Hauk. "By Freyja, Merewin, you're a friend of the gods," Bera whispered loudly. Dalla's eyes looked round as moons.

Merewin put her arm around the child. "'Tis a blessing on all of us." She didn't have the heart to tell them Drakkina was a meddling and possibly dangerous witch who predicted Ragnarök instead of one of their gods.

Merewin glanced over at Hauk who gazed at her even though the men had surrounded him with raucous chatter. A tender smile played across her lips, and she tucked a loose strand of hair behind her ear. His look was only for her, and fire smoldered below the surface.

Following Ragnar and Aslaug to the great hall, Merewin's smile slipped away upon seeing Svala and Bjalki. She glanced behind, but the men had detained Hauk.

"I'll be right back," Bera said and released Merewin's arm.

Merewin watched her hurry back the way they'd come. "Where's she going?"

"To bring Papa," Dalla said, eyeing Svala.

Merewin patted Dalla's hand. "We will do fine on our own until he catches up."

"You should wait," Dalla said.

"Is the mighty warrior woman afraid to enter the hall on her own?" Svala taunted. She placed her arm across the doorframe, barring Merewin's way. "You better wait for permission."

Cac! Merewin wasn't about to let the viper think she scared her. "Dalla and I will await my *husband* inside."

Fury twisted Svala's face. "You aren't allowed without Hauk. Once a thrall, always a thrall."

"Merwin, we should wait," Dalla said as she let go and glanced back at Hauk striding out of the forest.

He called out to Merewin, and she waved calmly to him. But she was determined to enter Ragnar's hall on her own, right past Svala.

Merewin pulled her long skirt higher and stepped over the raised wooden door jam. As she set her foot down, Svala's leg shot out. In an instant Merewin fell over the threshold into a puddle of fine wool and fur.

"Merewin!" Queen Aslaug called and rushed to her side. "Svala, what is the meaning of this?"

Svala grinned wickedly. "I guess she thought she was too good to follow our customs."

"Customs?" Merewin asked, as she ignored the sharp ache in her ankle. She'd known about the sprinkling of ale, the weeklong feasting, the trading of weapons as gifts, the traditional headpiece, but no one had mentioned not walking into a building.

Hauk stepped past Svala and lifted Merewin into his arms. "The groom is supposed to carry you over the threshold of the feasting hall," Hauk answered. "Are you hurt?"

"My ankle." Merewin blushed. "I'm not usually clumsy."

"Svala tripped her," Dalla interjected, with a defiant glare at the woman.

Svala *tsk*ed. "Such bad luck, tripping over the threshold."

"Bad luck?" Merewin asked, as Hauk set her down on a bench and felt her ankle.

Svala slinked into the hall with other guests. "To trip over the threshold on your wedding day means ill fortune for the marriage."

Bera stood before Svala, hands on her hips. "Her marriage was blessed by Frigga herself, we all saw it, we all heard it."

Merewin winced as Hauk found the muscle that had been strained. "'Tis in need of wrapping and rest."

Svala shrugged her thin shoulders. "Still don't understand why the woman can't heal herself if she's really a healer." She sauntered away.

Hauk set Merewin on a bench at the head table, and more people from the town began to filter in through the doorway. Food was being set upon a runner of colorful woven threads spread down the center of the table. Roasted venison and duck wafted mouth-watering aromas throughout the room. Roasted winter vegetables, at least six different types of poached fish with herbs, and silver bowls of dried fruits were heaped on the many tables set up in the great hall. Cooks had used the finest herbs to tempt the tongue in each recipe. Three musicians struck up a lively tune near the door. Their lyres and flute lightened the atmosphere.

"A drink for my wife." Hauk handed Merewin the silver-rimmed horn filled with bridal ale.

"I believe I'm the one who is supposed to serve my husband," she retorted, smiling up at him as he sat down heavily.

"Aye, but you are injured."

"By not following tradition," she replied wryly, and handed the horn back to Hauk. "So there, husband, drink of the bridal ale so I can appease yer gods."

Spirit sparked in his deep gray-blue eyes, and he laughed before drinking from the horn.

"And so Merewin plies her husband with bridal ale!" Ragnar called from his station near his wife on the other side of Merewin. A roar of approval shook the walls as heavy tankards and horns thumped on the wooden tables. Merewin laughed. Danes knew how to throw a party. She took a sip then of the bridal horn, letting the honey ale sweep away the dryness from her throat.

The night flew by with dancing and feasting. Merewin's ankle felt better, but she sat out most of the dances due to the slight swelling.

Aslaug and Bera remained close to her, talking and laughing, while Hauk talked amongst the men gathered in small clusters.

"Now, sister." Bera patted Merewin's hand. "Queen Aslaug and I should explain to you the delicacies of the wedding bed since you are still a maid."

"But we, I mean, ye know that we..." Merewin began, but Bera's wink stopped her floundering response. Her new sister had downed several cups of bridal ale.

"Aye," Aslaug started in, quite serious but a bit slurred in speech. "We need to tell you of your duty to your," she held out a rather limp hand in Hauk's direction, "your big man warrior husband there." Merewin hid a giggle. Perhaps she had imbibed a bit too much herself.

"My brother is a large man." Bera winked. "Not that I've seen him naked since he was a lad swimming in the lake, but I'm sure he's grown quite large."

"Bera!" Merewin laughed.

Aslaug looked serious and leaned forward. "You mustn't scream when you see it." She looked reflective for a moment, setting a slender finger against her pursed lips. "Although he may like that."

Bera and Merewin broke into laughter.

"Ye two are terrible at this," Merewin said. "Aren't ye supposed to be making me feel less nervous?"

"And miss making you squirm like our friends did us?" Bera said.

Aslaug nodded vigorously.

Bera squeezed Merewin's hand. "Don't you fret. My brother will take care of you." She winked again.

Aslaug leaned in. "But still, he may like it if you scream a little at it. Makes him feel bigger," she whispered.

"Don't worry, Hauk is plenty big—"

"Aye, I'm big," Hauk said, stepping up to the clustered ladies, who raised their eyes to him in unison. They erupted into laughter so hard Aslaug fell off her seat. Bera scrambled to help her up while Merewin tried to catch her breath. Hauk frowned at her, but she waved her hand in the air.

"Don't fear. 'Twas foolish drunken talk, Hauk, nothing serious." Merewin wiped her eyes. She tugged him down closer so she could kiss him. His lips were warm and tasted like sweet ale. "I was but complimenting ye, husband," she breathed against his lips.

Hauk kissed her once more and straightened. "I fear nothing." He seemed more relaxed as he shook his head at his sister and Aslaug. "Except the giggling of drunken women." He grinned.

"When are we allowed to go home?" Merewin moistened her bottom lip with the tip of her tongue. Hauk stared at her mouth. She could still taste him there.

"Soon." His gaze glided down Merewin's form. It was as if he'd stroked her, and Merewin felt her nipples harden through the fabric. "We have more nights of feasting," he nodded. "I wouldn't want to tire you out the first night." He gestured to Bera and Aslaug, "nor let those two get you too drunk for my bed."

"Yer bed, milord?" her innocence an obvious ruse.

Hauk leaned in toward her ear, propping his hands on the bench so his bare, muscled arms bracketed her. "Aye, woman, I will have ye naked and thrashing in my bed," his finger rubbed against her bottom lip, "very soon."

Merewin's breath quickened, and she felt a flush creep into her cheeks. Her lips closed around his finger, sucking along it.

A fire grew in Hauk's eyes. He growled, scooped Merewin up, and tossed her gently over his shoulder. His large hand rubbed her arse.

"We leave now, wife." He headed toward the door. Merewin managed to look up as she heard Bera and Aslaug calling out. They leaned together as if holding one another up and waved.

"Good luck," Bera yelled over the melee.

"Remember to scream a little," Aslaug called and then shrieked as Ragnar picked her up much the same way. As Hauk carried Merewin out through the door, she saw many husbands picking up their wives to carry them out on their shoulders.

"Seems the festivities are ending early tonight," she called to Hauk as she pummeled his back. Once outside he pulled her around and carried her in front of him.

"Nay, woman, the festivities are only beginning."

CHAPTER TWENTY-FIVE
PARTY TRICKS

The gods were pleased with him once more. Hauk smiled and relaxed into the walking rhythm of his horse through the sacred grove. Merewin dozed in front of him, her soft body warm against his chest. The poor woman was tired, he thought and smiled. If he were a whistling man, he'd whistle. He'd brought her to Valhalla time after time until she'd begged him to let her rest. Hauk felt more alive than he'd ever felt before.

He splayed his fingers down through her hair and brushed his lips against the top of her head. She murmured and curled in tighter against him. They rode toward another night of feasting. Perhaps this time they'd actually make it through dinner. As long as she didn't wrap her hot little tongue around his finger again. If there hadn't been an audience, he'd have pushed her onto the table and buried himself within her sacred body. Merely thinking about it made him shift in the seat. Perhaps Bera would take Dalla in next week, and he and Merewin could check the strength of the table at Spring House. The newly married should have some time alone together, after all.

The trees overhead swayed in the breeze. Crisp sun dotted down through the branches. Some were tipped with dormant buds waiting for spring. Had he ever noticed signs of new life before? His life had always centered on war, conquering, proving himself, and death.

He looked down at Merewin's parted lips. What was important to him had shifted. This magnificent, brave, warrior woman curled so trustingly in his arms made him stronger, more powerful than he had ever been. His chest filled until it ached, and he pulled her closer to him to inhale her spicy flower scent. She was magick.

Hauk let her sleep until they came into Ribe. From the sounds coming from Ragnar's hall, they hadn't waited for the couple to arrive before the party commenced. "We are here," he whispered in her ear, and Merewin stirred. He marveled at her long lashes as she blinked.

"More celebrating," she said, running fingers through her hair.

"Aye, but we don't have to stay for long." Her smile grew slowly, and she nodded.

⬥◦⬥

"Here Wise Eldgrim, sit here," Svala crooned sweetly to the old seer, indicating a seat near the fire pit.

"Thank you, Svala." Eldgrim accepted the tankard of ale she handed to him.

"I know how your joints ache so." She patted his arm.

"Nay, Svala, Merewin has put an end to those aches," he chuckled.

Svala put on a sweet yet skeptical smile. "Of course she did."

"Nay, really, Svala. She wields the gods' magick."

Svala leaned in toward the old man. "I hope you're right and she isn't an illusionist who cast a spell making you all feel fit again when you're not."

Eldgrim frowned and rotated his shoulder. "I certainly feel fit."

Svala shrugged. "Hopefully when the bride begins to feel the effects of the bridal ale, she can keep her illusions up."

"Svala, I don't think that's how—"

"Excuse me, Wise One, I must speak with Aslaug. She looks pale to me." Svala walked quickly away from Eldgrim as he took several sips of the ale she'd brought him. "Aye, drink up old man."

Svala wound her way through the guests to Aslaug. "Queen, how do you fare today?" She furrowed her brows, searching the woman's face.

"Fine, Svala, how are you this eve?"

Svala waved her hand to indicate Aslaug sit back down. "I'm fit, but you look pale." Svala touched Aslaug's forehead. "Has your heart been heavy again, beating fast?"

Aslaug's eyes rolled up toward Svala's hand. "Nay, not since Merewin helped Ivarr, and then me. I'm quite sound."

Svala put on a bland smile. "Aye, you all seem quite happy now that Merewin has rescued you."

Aslaug took Svala's hand from her head and held it. "Now Svala, you must let go of your bitterness toward Merewin. She has become part of our community now."

Svala smiled but had to take several breaths to calm the hatred burning the back of her throat. "I admit I was angry with her initial treatment of me, but I have a large, forgiving heart."

Aslaug patted her hand. "'Tis easier that way."

Svala motioned to one of the ladies carrying drinking horns out with ale. "May I get you a drink?"

"Aye, something to relax my spine a bit. Whenever all these big men cram in here and then get drunk, it makes me jittery that something will be ruined. I had all the costly rugs rolled away and put down some older ones." She leaned into Svala. "I hope none will notice."

Svala took the drink. "I'm certain none will. Look Aslaug, here comes your handsome king." Aslaug turned to wave at Ragnar.

In a quick gesture seen by none, Svala lowered the drinking horn beneath the edge of the table. She opened the top of her large ring and poured half the powder into Aslaug's drink.

"Here Queen, your ale."

"Aye, thank you." Aslaug sipped.

Svala's smile was tight. "Let me know if your heart begins to race again. I still worry about Merewin's abilities. I hope she isn't a terrible illusionist whose power will run out."

"Your suspicion will only torture you, Svala." Aslaug frowned but took another drink.

Svala walked away, her head held high. *Two done. Eight to go.* Svala smiled at some other women who walked in. She made her way around the room, stopping only to refill her hollow ring with a different powder. Each powder had side effects. She didn't plan to kill anyone, only emphasize the ailment that they'd sought out Merewin to cure.

Bjalki was taking care of everyone else by putting the required low dose of hemlock in the haddock chowder, its flavor hidden by the strong onions the cook liked to use. Unless someone was to eat several bowls, they should recover after a bout of vomiting. She needed these people sick for her plan to work. *It must work.* This was Svala's last chance to turn Hauk away from the whore who'd ruined all her plans. Her life depended on it.

Svala's fists tightened as Merewin and Hauk ducked through the doorway. Cheers and greetings, sprinkled with a few lewd jokes, flew around the filling room. Slipping into a small room off the main hall, Svala filled her ring one last time with a powder for Merewin. *Bloody cow!*

Svala breathed deeply to control her anger. She snapped the ring shut and blended back into the throng, whispering brief misgivings about Merewin's abilities about the room. She stopped toward the back of the room, readying herself for the final part of her plan. Svala gasped as heavy hands clamped down on her shoulders.

Hauk. A rush of excitement leapt into her heart. He'd sought her out. Her stomach, already nauseous, flipped at his closeness. She raised her gaze and smiled casually.

"I didn't expect you to attend. You caused enough mischief yesterday." Hauk studied her. "What are you up to tonight, Svala?"

She blinked with what she hoped was a most innocent expression, even though she felt her face flush. "Mischief? I but reside in Ribe, Hauk. And there seems to be a feast so I will attend."

He stared at her, his blue-grey eyes piercing. "I haven't seen you smile for a long time," he commented. "You are comely when you aren't angry, Svala. Let your anger go, and you'll find another mate soon."

Svala's heart thumped painfully in her chest, and she felt tears well up in her eyes. She was so emotional these days. "'Tis you I want, Hauk, no other."

Hauk released her shoulders. "You can find love and be a vital part of this community if you would stop battling against fate's path." His look softened with sympathy.

Svala's anger surged back into the pit of her belly. "Don't pity me, Hauk. I'm much too clever to be pitied." Svala made her face relax back into something of a smile. "I pity *you*."

"How so?" Hauk's gaze scanned the crowd again, and Svala knew he'd be leaving her side soon.

"When you realize you've been tricked again by a false healer, I will be here to comfort you, like before."

Hauk's stare swung back. "Svala, I regret our one night together. It was just after their deaths. I should never have—"

She put her finger against his lips. "I will be here when the truth comes out." Svala sauntered away before he could.

She maneuvered gracefully through the throng and grabbed a goblet of ale from a serving thrall. She took several long breaths of the stuffy air to compose herself. The timing was imperative.

Svala stepped up to where Merewin sat laughing with Bera. Both women turned to look. Svala smiled nervously. "I wish you well, Merewin." She spoke as convincingly as she could, while her stomach roiled.

"For once, I think I'm speechless," Bera replied and Svala laughed, flopping down on the bench beside Merewin, shoving against the table hard enough to make the goblets pitch. Bera's tipped into her lap. She screeched and jumped up as the cold wet mess washed down her gown.

Merewin turned to help her friend, and Svala caught Merewin's drinking goblet as if to steady it while jumping up to help. With one push of a clasp on her ring and a tilt to her hand, the powdered hemlock fell into Merewin's goblet.

"Oh Bera, I am so sorry. I came to toast Merewin and Hauk's union, and I've ruined your gown."

"I must run home and change," Bera gritted out.

"Again, I am truly sorry."

"Of course you are," Bera mumbled and stepped away from the table, plucking at the stained gown.

Svala waited until Merewin turned around. "Now that I've made such a mess, I should finish what I started. I toast you, Merewin." Svala held her own goblet high. "May you and Hauk have a long and fruitful marriage," she called out loudly, so those around could hear her good wishes.

"Thank ye, Svala." Merewin tipped her head slightly, studying her with stiff composure. "I hope one day we can move past any hostility." With so many others raising their goblets with Svala's to toast her marriage, Merewin raised her own and drank.

Svala smiled a bit too much and covered it with a little hiccough. Without any further words, Svala stood and walked away, her business done. The whore didn't deserve any type of farewell. Now to watch all the pots she'd set to boil.

Aslaug was already complaining to her husband about chest pains. Eldgrim rubbed at his joints. Svein pushed his fist into his stomach. The soup had been served. Luckily, Hauk seemed too busy amongst the guests and fawning over his whore to eat the soup.

Bjalki came from the kitchens adjusting his trews. One of the kitchen thralls followed him, her cheeks reddened. He ran a hand familiarly over her round backside as she walked by.

Svala elbowed her brother. "You are supposed to be working here," she hissed.

"I put the powder in the soup, sister dear. But there was such a lovely new kitchen thrall I had to have a taste of," he drawled. He looked to where Merewin sat sipping her bridal ale. "Just looking at her makes me hard again." Svala rolled her eyes.

Bjalki moved his lips close to her ear, his hot breath pungent with ale and woman. Svala's nose wrinkled. "For my help in this, you promised

I could have Merewin tonight, Svala. Remember that. I want her alive enough to fok."

"Crude."

"You call me crude when you poison the entire village."

Svala bit her fingernails into his bare arm. "Shut your rank mouth," she hissed, and glanced around, but no one was close enough to hear his words. The musicians started up again and a few people began to dance. "You will have her, Brother, as much as you desire, as long as she's dead by morning."

Bjalki frowned and rubbed his jaw. "Let me take her away from here. You can say she's dead, but I would keep her away with me. No one will know."

Svala looked down her nose at him. "You would leave your home to keep the whore?"

Bjalki adjusted his obvious arousal. "Aye, for day and night of her flesh. I'll take her overseas and start fresh with her as my thrall on one of the northern islands."

Svala seemed to consider it. "Nay, I need Hauk to see her dead."

Bjalki growled low. "That bastard needs to die."

Svala rounded on her brother. "Do not touch him, else you find yourself dying in your own puke," she threatened.

Bjalki frowned, returning her stare until he finally looked away. "Make sure she's not dead when I get to her tonight."

Svala smiled tightly and patted his arm. "All according to plan."

— ◦ —

Merewin was tired of raising her goblet for yet another toast. Svala's insincere little speech had started off a series of happy toasts to her and

Hauk, and with each one, Merewin took another sip of her bridal ale. Now the goblet was empty, and she felt strange, tired, and a bit queasy. She shouldn't have drunk it so quickly.

Merewin looked about the room for Hauk and noticed that many people were grabbing their stomachs. A prickle ran under her skin. *Something's wrong.* Merewin tried to stand but found she could hardly move. 'Twas as if she were in a dream where her body wouldn't obey.

"Are you well, Merewin?" Svala's voice hissed near her ear, but Merewin wasn't able to turn her head. She was paralyzed, the wall behind the bench the only thing holding her up. "Nay, I suppose you aren't. Just sit tight and watch the show, my snared little sparrow."

Merewin's heart pounded in her pained chest. Svala had poisoned her. She concentrated on keeping her breaths coming in and out, her gaze searching for Hauk. *Hauk!* Merewin screamed in her mind since her lips were too numb to move. She huffed, trying to get a word to form, but nothing came out but air.

Someone toward the door vomited, causing several people to yell and more to run out of the hall. Then another vomited, and several doubled over, holding their stomachs.

Svala's voice rang out over the noise. "We have been tricked!" She stood up next to Merewin.

Hauk came to stand in front. "Svala, what have you done?" he asked evenly, and looked at Merewin. Merewin could only stare at him. Could she even blink? She was trapped, her eyes pleading with Hauk to understand.

Svala kept her voice loud to be heard. "Merewin has confessed to me that she doesn't really know how to heal people." This got the attention she wanted, as several people turned her way. "She is an illusionist and has hidden your ailments from you."

Hauk kept looking at Merewin, but she couldn't say anything. *Earth Mother, help me.*

"I don't believe you, Svala. Why would Merewin say that, especially to you?" Hauk glanced between them.

"She feels guilty about her tricks making you all sick," Svala yelled and opened her arms to the room. Hauk looked behind him at the attendees, most of whom were vomiting in the rushes.

"My joints hurt so bad I can't stand," Eldgrim yelled. "She tricked me," he shouted and pointed to Merewin.

Svala forced a concerned look. "Aslaug, you look unwell." Hauk turned to look at the queen, where she stood by a very pale Ragnar.

Aslaug clutched at her chest. Had Svala poisoned her? "My heart."

"You had better check poor Ivarr." Svala shook her head with mock concern.

Merewin twisted and turned inside her paralyzed body, trying to find a way out. The hold on her was too thick. Her breath came rapidly as she tried to say something. Anything!

"Why would she do this?" Minerva yelled, a moment before retching.

"Loki is her partner," Svala answered. "She wanted to gain your trust, Hauk's trust, so he would free her."

"Lies!" Hauk thundered. "Merewin, say something."

Merewin mustered what she could, willing her lips to move. "I...c...can't—"

"She can't because she's guilty," Svala interrupted.

Hauk began to move toward Merewin, when Dalla's voice called out behind him. "Papa...I'm sick." Hauk froze, his face paling.

He spun away from Merewin. In two steps away from her, he picked up Dalla. The girl looked pale and shaky.

Hauk turned toward Merewin with Dalla in his arms. His face was tight with anguish as he held his only child. "Merewin, you need to heal her."

Merewin tried to lower her head toward them but couldn't. "I...c...can't—"

"She can't because she's no healer. I'm sorry, Hauk." Svala spread her arms, indicating the room. "You've been tricked again." Svala's voice dripped with syrupy compassion. Couldn't Hauk hear the triumph behind Svala's words? Merewin could. Her words were thick with it. Inside, the woman was gloating.

"Merewin?" Hauk yelled again, and the sound nearly tore her heart from her chest. There was anguish in the question. Betrayal tightened all the planes of his face. Hauk had begun to accept her magick, to trust her, and Svala was shredding the fragile fabric they'd woven.

Merewin fought against the heaviness imprisoning her body, fought against the sickness rolling through her stomach and mind. She had to help these people; she had to get to Dalla.

Gamal came to Hauk's side. "Let's take Dalla to our house, away from this mess." He indicated the foulness in Ragnar's hall.

Merewin watched with tears blurring her eyes as Hauk turned away and headed out into the night. *Hauk, Dalla!* Merewin screamed inside her mind. She began to sway in her seat and felt the vomit creeping up her throat. Perhaps she would die by choking. Death would be an escape from the damning look in Hauk's eyes.

"Ve! She's puking!" Bjalki's voice came from behind her.

"'Tis good," Svala said, "else she'll die before you've quenched your lust."

Bjalki grabbed Merewin off the platform. He held her head down as the vomit poured from her mouth. Blood rushed to Merewin's head and blackness closed in.

Dear Earth Mother, help me.

CHAPTER TWENTY-SIX
CHANGE OF PLANS

Cold water smacked Merewin's face, followed by the burning fire of being slapped. Her eyes cracked open slowly, her vision blurred and wobbling.

"Wake, woman!" Svala shouted in her face. Another cold smack of water hit Merewin. She blinked to clear the sting of it from her eyes. Two blurred visions of a fire condensed back into one. Merewin sat on the ground against a tree. The chill of damp soil seeped up through her gown, and the darkness of the forest surrounded them. Svala bent by a pond to bring up another bowl of water.

"I'm awake," Merewin muttered, relieved she could form words. She slid her weak arms to her lap. Thank the Earth Mother, she wasn't paralyzed anymore. Since she wasn't tied, she slid her hands back to their place on the ground. Her tormenter might not realize she could move yet.

Svala cursed, dropped the bowl, and walked toward her. The firelight cast Svala's huge shadow along a large rock outcropping. They were alone in the forest.

As the scene and Merewin's mind cleared, fury sparked up inside her. "Svala, what have ye done? Those people, me. Ye've poisoned us." Her teeth clenched as if ready to bite into the she-devil.

"It had to be done," Svala stated. "Without them ill, they wouldn't have let us take you, nor would they believe that you tricked all of them."

"And innocent Dalla?" Merewin yelled.

"Don't judge me, whore," Svala spat back, taking full advantage of Merewin's position on the ground. "You don't know anything about me, what I've suffered, what these *good* people have done to me." She spat on the hem of Merewin's dress.

Svala's frown cut deep lines across her face. How could Merewin have ever thought the woman attractive? The ugliness of her soul claimed her features. Svala turned away from her, glancing out into the night.

"Then tell me yer charges against these people ye've tricked, sickened, and perhaps killed."

Svala turned back to Merewin with tears swelling out of her eyes, but they didn't soften the horrific visage. "They turned away from me when my husband died. I was part of the royal household, but when he died, they sent me to live in a small house, fit for a commoner."

I'd have sent her away, too. Merewin watched her as she dug her fingers gently into the earth beneath her. She needed the Earth Mother's strength. Merewin still wore the jade stone and felt it warm.

Svala squatted in front of her and grasped her shoulders, shaking Merewin until her head snapped back and forth. "Everyone knew Aslaug couldn't birth a healthy child. It was to be my son to take Ragnar's place one day, my son. But Gorm died before he could get me with child! Then, they threw me out."

"I can't imagine why," Merewin said, ignoring the sharp headache.

Svala shoved her backwards, knocking Merewin onto the hard ground. Merewin's teeth clanked together as her head hit the packed dirt. She rolled to her side.

Svala pulled out a long dagger. "I had no one!" She stood over Merewin. "And if you hadn't come along, I would have caught Hauk. He came to me one night." She smiled wickedly, the look maniacal. "And how I made him moan with pleasure." She turned, her gaze going back to the dense blackness around them. "But then he went off on raid after raid for years. He'd finally returned when Ragnar sent him after you." She spun, pointing the dagger's tip at Merewin.

Merewin had no weapon. She moved her fingers in the dirt searching for anything sharp. She tasted blood and licked her cracked lip.

"And now you're going to kill yourself, Merewin. Kill yourself over the shame you feel, a sacrifice to the gods to repent for tricking the village, for tricking Hauk." Svala smiled and grabbed Merewin's hair. Pain, sharp and bruising, tore along Merewin scalp. Svala pulled her back up into a sitting position then released her, turning to the woods.

Merewin pushed her hair from her face, and some wisps came out in her palm.

"Where are you, Bjalki?" Svala asked, stamping her foot. She curled her lip when she looked back at Merewin. "Bjalki has some fun planned for you tonight before you kill yourself. I pity you really. He can get rough when he takes his pleasure on a wench, and he's quite lusty for you."

Merewin swallowed against the fear that caught like thick syrup in her throat. Torture, rape, and death. For the first time in her life, Merewin had found a community who accepted her. She'd found a new family. And this madwoman planned to steal it all.

Hauk's love gave her the strength to try. Fear of failure no longer gripped around her throat, no longer plunged its ice-cold blade. No longer would she hide away from trying. She was a fighter, a warrior. She wouldn't give up. Hauk hadn't said he loved her, but Merewin had felt it growing between them, like a freshly budded flower. But Svala had trampled it tonight. Merewin had seen the pain and confusion in Hauk's eyes when he'd held Dalla in Ragnar's hall, begging Merewin to heal her. And then he'd turned away, left her with this killer.

If I die, Hauk will believe I lied.

Merewin took a deep breath. She needed anger, not sorrow. *Focus. What can I do?* She harnessed magick to push into people to heal them. Could she pull out their energy to harm them? She'd never tried or even contemplated it before. It went against her education, her character, her nature, but she had to try something. *I'm not giving up. I need to heal Dalla. And Hauk...*

One hand half buried in the earth, Merewin grabbed Svala's ankle as she walked near.

"Let go of me," Svala yelled.

Closing her eyes, Merewin imagined sucking the light out of Svala. Svala's lifeforce was yellow like sickly bile. And then— Holy goddess! Merewin stopped, her eyes snapping open to look at Svala.

"Svala! Ye...ye're carrying a bairn? Ye're with child?"

Tears flooded Svala's large eyes. "How do you know?" She glanced around and lowered her voice.

"I feel it growing in ye."

Svala's hand went to her belly, hidden by the gown.

"Who is the father?"

Svala rubbed a hand over her face, still clutching the knife with the other. "I'm not certain. There were two or three men in the village."

The bairn growing in the woman was innocent. Merewin couldn't hurt it. She let out a whispered curse.

Svala sneered at Merewin. "If you hadn't been here, I would have found a way to bring Hauk back into my bed. He would have married me once I told him I was with child. His honor would have demanded it."

Svala started pacing again. "If I go to him after you've been found dead, I'll comfort him again with my body, and then in a couple of weeks I'll tell him I'm with his child. The child will be born early." She nodded vigorously and wiped her tears with the back of her arm. "The plan can still work." Sanity had surely left the woman.

Svala stared out at the night. "I only need you out of the way."

A small skitter sounded behind Merewin, and she felt Ellette creep up under her hair. Svala continued to watch the surrounding forest. Ellette's soft fur rubbed against Merewin's neck. She turned her lips toward Ellette and whispered. "Get Hauk; lead Hauk here."

"What are you saying?" Svala screeched, and ran behind Merewin, her look frantic.

Ellette scampered down Merewin's arm and leapt past the fire, darting out into the night. "I was but praying to the Earth Mother."

Svala looked uneasy. "The illusion you cast with Ivarr won't save you."

Hooves thudded from the direction Ellette had run. *Hauk, please be Hauk!* Merewin held her breath.

A horse stopped at the edge of the woods, and Bjalki jumped to the ground. Merewin's heart struck hard against her chest. Pain gripped and she took slow breaths to release it. She dug her fingers in the dirt, trying to find a rock. She would try her reversal healing on him, but she feared it would take all her strength to affect him. Which would leave her immobile. And if she didn't harm him, she'd not be able to fight at all.

He strutted into the circle of light, already stripping his shirt over his head. His large torso was covered with scars and a lawn of hair growing over his shoulders and down his back. He stretched his arms overhead like a great beast. "I've been looking forward to taking a bite of you for a long time, Merewin."

"Has Hauk returned to Spring House?" Svala demanded.

Bjalki didn't even look at his sister but went to stand over Merewin, his legs braced apart. Merewin stared at his knees, her back as straight as the tall trees. She would never cower. "Nay, he's at Gamal's," he called casually, a leer sharpening his features into that of a predator already tasting his prey.

"Did you tell him you saw Merewin running away?" Svala asked impatiently.

Bjalki pulled Merewin up. His foul-smelling tongue ran up the side of her throat. She gagged.

"Mmmm...open your mouth, thrall."

"Did you tell him, Bjalki?" Svala demanded.

"Aye, but he didn't believe me. He went into the hall to see for himself. Now leave us or join in, dear sister."

Bjalki held Merewin's face. She tried to move her head, her nails biting into the backs of his hands. He squeezed harder as if to pop her brain out. Merewin's strength dulled with the pain, and she dropped her hands to dangle limply. Bjalki ran rank lips over Merewin's face. His tongue pushed between tight lips. "We can make this easier on you, or harder," he whispered pulling her hair so hard it threw her head backwards.

"Didn't believe you! How could he not believe you? She wasn't with you. She wasn't in the hall!" Svala pulled her brother's arm. "Go back, don't let him find us. Convince him you saw her leave in the other direction. Send him east."

Bjalki grunted, releasing Merewin's hair to grab at her skirts. *Rippp.* The skirt tore, exposing her legs. He wet his lips, leaving spittle. He closed in on Merewin again, but Svala's knife stopped him.

Svala stood behind Merewin, her blade against Merewin's throat. Merewin could feel its cold sting against her pulse. Dying this way would be better than facing Bjalki. But no, she wouldn't leave Hauk without a fight.

"I will kill her before you've had a chance to yank your trews down, Brother."

Merewin closed her eyes. *Drakkina! Where are ye!?* Where was the witch? She said she was leading the demons away. How furious she would be to find Merewin dead upon her return.

Bjalki dropped the rags of Merewin's skirt. "My balls are going to fall off, Svala, with all this waiting." He huffed. "I'll go back," he said, the words grinding out. He pointed at his sister, "but you better have her here, alive, when I return."

Svala lowered the blade. Bjalki tied a leather strap around Merewin's wrists and stomped off to grab his tunic, throwing it on.

"I'll make sure your Hauk doesn't come charging in here." He looked at Merewin. "Feel free to make yourself ready for me, sweet. It will go easier for you if you're already juicy. With all this teasing, I won't have much patience when I return." He looked at Svala. "I won't be long."

"Don't kill him, Bjalki," Svala said.

"Aye, I know. You get yours alive. I only get mine for one night," he muttered as he mounted.

Merewin had to remind herself to breathe. How much time did she have before he returned?

"Don't think about running, Merewin," Svala said. "I'll be forced to kill you then, tell Bjalki you were escaping, and I had no choice. He'll be angry, but he's scared of me. Always has been, because he knows I'm the clever one. He wouldn't live a day if he beat me." Svala pointed to the ground. "Sit, rest yourself. You will need your strength when he returns."

Svala tended the fire while Merewin sat at the edge of the deep pond against the tree, her hands tied.

"You know, Merewin, I'm doing this all for my babe." Svala ran a hand over her still-flat belly. "When Hauk marries me, this child won't be a bastard. It will have a strong father and a throne when Ivarr ends up dying early. My plan is working." She smiled over at Merewin, her look pitying. "Here dear Merewin, have some hot wine. 'Tis not poisoned." She took a sip herself. "I think you should have something before my brother returns, to fortify yourself."

⸺⸻◆⸻⸺

Hauk stood inside Gamal's house next to Dalla's nearly unconscious figure. What in the name of Odin was he supposed to do? Merewin was gone. He'd looked all around the village. Nearly everyone who'd been at the celebration was sick and moaning around the hall or had dragged themselves home. His daughter seemed the worst. What was making her so ill? She'd purged numerous times. A curdled fishy tang filled the air, like it had with his family when the healers poured poison down their throats.

Hauk stood over Dalla in a warrior's stance, ready for battle, yet the foe of illness was one he couldn't strike down. He clenched and unclenched his fists.

Bera ran a soothing rag along Dalla's brow. She'd sent her son to stay with a friend who had not been at the celebration to protect him from the illness.

"Merewin did not do this," Bera said, looking at him.

"Aye," Hauk said, as he stared down at his daughter. "But where is she?" He rubbed his bristled jaw. "Bjalki says she's run away in shame."

Bera snorted and washed the rag out in a bowl of water. "The man has never told the truth in his life unless it somehow benefited his own cause."

"I didn't say I believed him." He leaned near Dalla, listening to her breathe. "But she's gone. He's the only one I could imagine taking her, but he was still here, and she was gone."

Hauk looked back up at Bera. "You didn't see the look on her face when Svala yelled accusations. Merewin didn't say anything to defend herself, would barely look at me. She wouldn't refuse what Svala said."

"Svala!" Bera spat. "That mathkr! I tell you, Hauk, that she-snake is behind this. I feel it in my spine."

"Papa?" Dalla murmured, and Hauk crouched low, taking her hand. "Papa, I want Merewin. Where is she?"

"I don't know, sweet one."

"She can help me."

Hauk took a deep breath, doubts twisting in his chest. What if Svala's venom had truth to it? What if Merewin couldn't heal like she'd promised? But had Merewin ever promised to be able to heal? Scenes tumbled through his memory. Nay, she'd never promised healing. She'd only ever said she would try. But then why would she run away?

Hauk covered Dalla's folded hands with one of his own. "Sweet one, Merewin may not be able to heal you."

Bera *tsk*ed under her breath and laid another rag over Dalla's head.

After a moment Dalla moved her lips again. "It doesn't matter, Papa. I still want Merewin. I love her, and she loves me."

Hauk's eyes dimmed and then closed. He took a deep breath and glanced up at Bera. The innocent words of a child were so plain, and yet he'd forgotten them in the chaos of the night. No matter what, he needed Merewin, because he loved her. And he'd felt her love for him in every touch and tease and glance. That was truth; that was her promise.

Hauk stood. "I will find her, Dalla. I'll bring her home." Hauk stepped out into the night and began to study the ground near the exit of Ragnar's house.

"Looking to see which way she ran?" Bjalki's voice broke his concentration. The man stood in the empty road watching, his arms crossed.

"I don't have time for you unless you have information regarding Merewin." Hauk looked at him. "True information."

"Check the tracks if you'd like, but I tell you I saw her run off." Bjalki pointed east toward the rocky shores that lined Denmark. "I'm thinking she stole a horse because Ivan told me his is missing from its stall." Bjalki shrugged. "Perhaps she'll hide out in one of those caves along the shore and try to find a boat to take her back to Northumbria."

Hauk looked down at the haphazard display of tracks. "She wouldn't voluntarily get back into a boat." The bloody saklauss was trying to confuse him with lies. Hauk looked back up at Bjalki. Why would the man be trying to confuse him? If Bjalki thought he knew where Merewin was, he'd be tracking her himself.

Hauk's gaze narrowed. His lips curled back to show white teeth. "Where is Merewin, Bjalki?" Hauk's blood raced. Warrior instincts sharpened his mind. He stared at the enemy.

Bjalki uncrossed his arms slowly, hands flexing. "I told you she went east."

"And you have nothing better to do than give me ideas of where I might find my wife?"

"I'm being helpful."

Hauk took two full strides and grabbed the front of Bjalki's tunic, pulling him close so he was right in the warrior's mottled face. "Bacraut! You are never helpful. Where is she?" Hauk stopped then, the roar of blood rushing through his ears. He sniffed, and the faint scent of spice and flowers drifted under the man's foul odor.

With the might of his warrior's arm and the strength of cold fury, Hauk shoved Bjalki back as if he weighed nothing and pulled his sword. "I smell her on you. What have you done with her?"

Bjalki drew his own sword and shrugged. "Looks like we'll have to go with my plan, Sister Dear. Yours dies and mine lives, at least as long as I want her."

The cryptic message infuriated Hauk. *Svala.* She was helping her brother kidnap Merewin. The beast within Hauk demanded justice, revenge, death of his foe. He swallowed hard against it, stomping it down deep into his chest. He couldn't lose himself in it or he might not find Merewin, and everything within Hauk screamed that she was in need. He'd been too confused and worried about Dalla to pay heed.

Hauk swung his sword, not with blind rage but with precise execution. Bjalki met the blade with his own, the clang ringing out in the eerily silent night. They both pulled back to circle one another, anticipating, planning. Low sounds of moaning still came from Ragnar's hall, but all else lay still. It was as if the wind, the darkness, and the very trees watched.

Hauk had left his battle-axe at Gamal's house. He held the double-edged long sword that was Merewin's wedding gift before him with one hand, parallel to the ground. The moon sliced through the trees, casting strange shadows downward and making it difficult to see the slight changes in Bjalki's eyes. Eyes told Hauk a foe's plan for attack. Hauk inhaled the chilled air like water, cooling the fire in his belly. Battle energy, the beast, surged through him, boiling close to rage.

Must keep control. If he had a plan, he was in control. *A plan.* He'd cut off Bjalki's arm first. He wouldn't kill him, for he knew too much. He needed to carve the information out of his flesh. Where was Merewin?

"Skin so sweet," Bjalki taunted, his large tongue hanging out as he grinned. "Such a lovely neck I licked from her ear down to—"

Hauk roared, swinging a mighty blow, but Bjalki had been ready for it and easily side-stepped the passionate strike, coming back with his own. Only Hauk's strength held Bjalki back as his sword took the advantage. Hauk struck again, desperate to keep the beast tucked deep inside. To let the rage out would disorder his reactions, ruin the attack. He needed to win, he needed to get to Merewin. Hauk exhaled the hatred fogging his mind as he parried against Bjalki's strong thrusts.

"And those breasts," Bjalki grunted out, between blows. "So round and soft, I will suckle them well."

Step, turn, strike high, strike low, turn, thrust. Hauk blocked out Bjalki's words with his own, letting calm control harness the beast. Hauk had prepared for this his whole life, enemy after enemy. The movements were like a familiar dance. Slowly Hauk began to lead the dance, pressing ever so slightly at his foe so Bjalki wouldn't notice how the tide of the battle turned. Tire your enemy first, then surprise them with your strength.

If only the enemy who had taken his family had been of flesh and bone. He'd have battled them, hacked them, spilled their blood for daring to touch his son, his brother, his family. *Swing. Dodge. Turn.* But the enemy had been elusive, a disease that ravaged their bodies before his eyes. He'd paid huge sums of gold to the healers for help, help they'd provide for the right price. But they had lied. Hauk growled low as his swing dripped with emotion. Bjalki nicked him and smiled as he circled, sweat trailing down his face.

And once again, an enemy sought his family. But this time, the enemy stood before him.

"She was panting when I left her," Bjalki taunted, and threw his bulk against Hauk, knocking him off balance for a moment. He swung towards Hauk's sword arm.

Clang! Iron against iron, brute strength against cold power. Round and round Hauk moved, meeting each thrust, each angle, pushing, always driving forward. As Hauk came down hard, Bjalki's other hand twisted and plunged a blade into Hauk.

Burning seared through Hauk's sword arm as the dagger lodged in the flesh of his shoulder. Hauk pulled the dagger out of his arm and whipped it through the air. Bjalki dodged and the blade sliced through the cloth sleeve that hung from his arm, clattering to the solid ground. Bjalki laughed and lunged. Hauk grabbed his sword with his other hand and met Bjalki's attack. There was a good reason why Hauk trained with both his arms.

Bjalki grinned. "You're losing blood, Hauk. 'Tis only a matter of time before you fall." Bjalki thrust again, a renewed energy making him almost giddy. "And then I will ride back and fok her." Bjalki breathed hard, spitting out the last two words. "I think I'll ride her from behind like an animal first." Bjalki swung around with all his strength, his foul teeth showing in his feral smile.

Time slowed as Hauk's muscles revolved around bone, aligning and honing his strength, his warrior power. Hauk sliced downward, the wind whistling along the fine edge of iron.

Bjalki's laugh turned into a deep guttural grunt as Hauk's sword cleaved down through muscle, sinew and bone, carving through Bjalki's neck.

A war cry, born of desperate need, raged up and out of Hauk. "Change of plans, Bjalki!" Hauk roared as he pulled his sword free. Bjalki's head thumped to the churned-up dirt as his body toppled over into a growing pool of blood. "Change of plans," Hauk said, his chest heaving, his sword outstretched. "You die."

CHAPTER TWENTY-SEVEN
BATTLE FOR THE INNOCENT

"By Odin, where are you, Bjalki?" Svala hissed toward the darkness.

Merewin twisted her hands in the leather binding while Svala's gaze searched the dark woods. Merewin sat on the other side of the fire, her bare legs as close to the heat as she could get without being hit by the sparks that spit out wildly into the darkness. The wind pushed the smoke around the clearing. Could Hauk smell the smoke? Was he even looking for her?

Svala paced on the other side of the fire. She mumbled to herself and wiped her eyes and cheeks. Svala turned a tear-streaked face toward Merewin. "Whore, this is all your fault," she said and kicked a jagged rock. Merewin ducked her head as the stone skidded past and plopped into the murky pond. Had the woman gone completely mad? Of course she had. A sane woman wouldn't poison half the town and kidnap a woman she planned to offer as a sacrifice to her brutal brother.

A twig cracked in the woods. "Bjalki?" Svala called, turning toward the noise. Merewin's heart raced, but she took a deep breath and worked at the leather binding her hands together. "Bjalki?" There was no answer. Perhaps it was some wild animal. A crazed blood-hungry wolf would be better than Bjalki.

"Something's wrong," Svala whispered and swore into the night. Her hands clenched and unclenched. She stomped against the packed dirt. Svala glanced back and forth between Merewin and the surrounding darkness. Hair from her normally kempt braid stuck out at odd angles, and her eyes were wide open, wild. She breathed hard through her mouth and swallowed several times before slipping her dagger back out from its sheath.

"He's taking too long," she said, and her face swiveled toward Merewin. "I can't have someone find you still alive." Svala's hands trembled. "I will have to kill you now."

"Svala," Merewin said with her hands still tied. "I can help ye."

"Help me? You can't help me. I'm with child and not married. My child will be a bastard. We will be shunned!" She shook her head. "Nay, not my child. My child should be treated as royalty." She poked her chest with her finger. "*I* should be treated as royalty." Svala came closer, and Merewin backed toward the pond from her position on the ground. Outside the circle of warmth, Merewin's bare legs grew goosebumps as she shivered. "Nay," Svala continued. "The only thing you can do to help me is to die so Hauk will marry me and be a father for my child."

Merewin felt the edge of the pond with her foot and stopped. There was nowhere else to go. "Surely Ragnar will help ye," Merewin insisted, trying to distract the crazed woman from her advance.

"Ha! Ragnar. He hates me." Svala stopped and looked at Merewin's hands. "If you were to kill yourself, where would you slice?" She paused and stared at Merewin, as if expecting her to answer. "I think your wrists, but you wouldn't have them bound if you were killing yourself. Foolish me." She shook her head in a gentle rebuke. "Then they'd know someone else sacrificed you."

"Svala, Bjalki will kill ye if I'm not alive when he returns." Merewin swallowed, watching Svala as if she were a stalking beast.

Svala rolled her eyes. "Nay, he knows I'm in charge." She huffed, glancing behind her but then shook her head. "He's taking too long." Svala jabbed the point of the blade into the ground, making Merewin flinch.

Svala opened a sack and withdrew several vials, setting them on a flat rock. "These are the poisons I used. I'll leave them here to be found with you, so if people don't believe it was the lack of your healing that hurt them, then they'll believe you poisoned them." She nodded and smiled. "'Tis really a clever plan," she said delightedly and yanked the dagger back out of the ground. "I'll kill you and then cut your wrists apart, leaving the knife in one hand."

"Svala, don't do this. Think of yer bairn. The child will have a murderer for a mother."

Tears washed out of Svala's eyes. "Don't speak of my babe. You know nothing about the love for a child."

"I do. I love Dalla as my child. She needs my help." The frozen mud at the edge of the pond gave way, and Merewin's foot slipped, making a small splash through the thin layer of ice.

Svala grabbed Merewin's bound hands, trying to slip the knife past her bonds to slice her wrist. "Don't struggle now, Merewin. Be a good woman for once and stop fighting. Hauk doesn't want you. He walked out on you."

Tears blurred Merewin's vision, and they washed hot down her cold cheeks. She didn't believe it. *He will come.* He'd released and married her. He'd sworn to protect her. "He loves me, Svala." Saying the words out loud made them feel real. Hauk did love her. She'd felt it. When he held her, she was filled with his strength. "He loves me," she repeated, "and I won't let ye take me from him and Dalla."

Svala pushed against her as Merewin twisted, grasping Svala. Merewin dug her heels into the earth and pushed. Their combined weight sent them tumbling into the freezing pond.

Needles pricked along Merewin's skin as the biting water stole her breath. It was so dark, she couldn't tell which way was up. She twisted, her wrists bound, her eyes wide and stinging. A flicker of firelight drew her, and she threw all her energy into kicking.

The water filled her ears, mixed with bubbles. Its stagnant essence filled her mouth and nose as she fought to surface. She broke through, gasping and spitting. *So cold.* It hurt as if she were crystallizing, but she kicked through the aching pain.

Behind her Svala surfaced and resubmerged, then came up again flailing. "Help!" she screeched. "I can't...can't swim."

Merewin's feet struck solid ground near the muddy edge. She glanced back at Svala as she splashed, breaking the thin ice farther into the pond. The woman would die. There was no way to save Svala with her hands bound anyway.

"My babe," Svala spluttered. Merewin stilled in the icy water and slowly turned toward the splashing. The bairn, the innocent child nestled in Svala's womb, would die with the mother.

"By all that is holy," Merewin cursed through chattering teeth. "I'm foking daft." Merewin's toes squished down into the mud as she lurched off the solid edge, kicking back out to the floundering she-devil.

Svala grabbed her, dragging them both underwater. The frantic woman would drown them both. Merewin fought, kicking them to the surface. When they broke through, Merewin struck Svala's chin hard with her bound fists. It stunned Svala enough that Merewin could grab the woman's long braid with her fingers.

When she ducked under water, Merewin realized her feet could touch the bottom of the pond. She anchored her toes into the rocks and hauled Svala by the hair toward shore. Merewin kicked twice to bring her back to the surface for air. Svala continued to flounder and scream, but her hair was long enough that Merewin could stay in front of her wildly swinging arms. She towed Svala with every bit of strength she still possessed. With each step, Merewin's pain numbed along with the rest of her.

"Earth Mother, lend me strength! I beg ye!" Merewin called out. Her toes dug into the deep pond mud, and a small burst of warmth shot up inside her to reach the jade stone resting on her collarbone. Warmth and power spread through Merewin's core. Prickles of feeling returned, and she trudged forward. Thin ice ringed the lip of the pond, sharp and brittle. Merewin used her bound hands, still holding onto Svala's braid, to chip through it.

Svala's heavy floundering ceased. Merewin crawled up the edge, hefting Svala's unconscious body half out of the freezing hole. Merewin hadn't the strength to pull her free completely. She lay on her side, bare feet lodged under one of Svala's arms to keep the woman from falling back in the pond.

It felt as if she would freeze to the ground. Merewin could see the fire flickering in the clearing, but she couldn't move to it. Numbness wrapped around her body. She trembled as her eyes shut.

"Hauk! Help me!" Merewin screamed into the night. But all that came out of her frozen lips was a whisper that the wind carried away.

⸺◦⸺

Hauk's battle cry brought several men running with battle-axes. Gamal reached him first.

Hauk breathed hard through his nose. Steam rolled off his bare arms. The sight of Bjalki touching Merewin still tortured him. The faces of his dead son, dying parents, and crying Dalla seemed to float before his eyes. Enemies surrounded, and he held his bloodied sword in his uninjured hand.

Power radiated through him, pulsing with the beat in his blood, pent-up despair and fury. The beast had found an outlet. It poured from him now, mixed with the raw energy he'd always had but had squelched with self-control. Control was gone and power surged like a sun burning deep within. He let the blinding power emerge. Throwing arms wide, his chest flexed as he stood over Bjalki's twitching body. A roar of rage bellowed out into the night, and he swung his sword down to strike against the man who had become the symbol of Hauk's enemies.

"Hauk!" Gamal's voice barely registered in Hauk's bloodthirsty mind. A solid hand fell upon his shoulder, and he turned toward it, ready to strike. "Hauk, 'tis me, Gamal." Gamal's hand clenched Hauk's shoulder. "You are," Gamal started and hesitated at the look in Hauk's cold eyes. "You're arm, 'tis sliced." Gamal grabbed a rag from one of the onlookers and wrapped it around Hauk's shoulder.

Hauk stood tall, breathing deeply, warring against the berserker in him to regain control. But his mind continued to picture the leer on Bjalki's face. Hauk snarled and raised the sword once more toward Bjalki's body.

Gamal's words came low. "Hauk, it will show weakness to chop up a slain man. Rest your sword. There's more urgent things. Merewin."

Merewin. Her name poured through Hauk, drawing him back from the darkness, taming the fire. Hauk took several full breaths, caging the berserker. "He took Merewin."

"Where?" Gamal asked and put pressure on Hauk's arm to get him to point the blood-washed sword towards the ground.

"He said things...what he'd done," Hauk began.

"You killed him before you found out where," Gamal said nodding. "I'd most likely do the same." Gamal turned to the small crowd held back by the intensity in Hauk's stance. "Merewin's been taken against her will. This whole night was a trick on us by Bjalki."

"And Svala," Hauk said. "He said that much before..." he looked around. "Before I lost control." Hauk wiped the blade on the grass. "We must find her," he paused, hearing...something. *Hauk. Help me.* Hauk turned in a circle, but the words were in his mind without direction. "We must find her now!"

"Can she heal us then?" One man spoke out.

"She already has," Hauk murmured, and ran to Gamal's house to retrieve his war horse.

Gamal followed Hauk into the sacred trees, watching the ground for tracks. They walked, leading their horses behind them.

"This is taking too long," Hauk growled, as he held a burning torch over Bjalki's tracks. "I need to find her now. I feel..." He looked at Gamal. "She needs me."

A screech peeled out from the bushes as an animal leaped in an arc toward them. Hauk held the torch higher as Gamal pulled his short sword. Merewin's pet stopped before him chattering and jumping.

"What is it?" Gamal asked, bringing his sword around.

"'Tis Merewin's beast from Northumbria." He bent down. "You know where she is." The little beast continued to leap and chatter. "We'll follow," Hauk said, and mounted his horse.

The dark, long body darted ahead amongst the trees. Hauk pushed his horse after the animal. They dodged branches and flew over fallen logs. Whenever he'd lose track of the pine marten, it would chatter loudly. Hauk used attuned senses to track it. As they approached a large outcropping of stone, Hauk smelled the fire. "Merewin!" He leaned forward, and his horse burst through the brush.

"Merewin!" They plunged into a clearing lit by a small fire. "Merewin, where are you?" Hauk jumped down and pivoted in a tight circle searching the space, but it was empty.

"Ye came." The small voice caught him, and he dropped to his knees before the edge of a black pond. He felt more than saw her, lifting Merewin's bound arms up and hauling her away from the frozen water. Her body was stiff and cold, like the dead.

"Nay, Merewin!" he yelled. Frantic lips moved over her pale face as he wrapped her in his arms. She was too cold, stiff. Was he too late? Hauk carried her over to the fire, rubbing arms and legs, turning her this way and that so the fire heat could sink in. The flames rose as he wished, bigger, stronger. Sweat beaded on his forehead. "You are ice," he whispered into her hair.

Gamal charged up behind him. The little pine marten chattered and leapt up Merewin's clothes to nuzzle the back of her neck under the wet tangle of hair. With a quick slip of a dagger, Hauk cut through the leather bindings around her wrists. "My love, Merewin," he said as he rocked them. "Do not die."

She sighed against Hauk and began to shiver. "Ye're here." The happiness in her voice tugged at his guilty heart. The pine marten jumped down from Merewin and ran chattering toward the pond.

"Merewin, I'm so sorry." Hauk brushed soaked hair back from her forehead and looked into her half-open eyes.

"But ye came for me. There is no need to be sorry."

"I left you there, for that bastard to take. I doubted—"

Merewin put a finger against his lips. "Later. Now we need to save Dalla."

Gamal dragged Svala from the water. "What should we do with her?"

"She was going to kill you, wasn't she?" Hauk asked, his face once more of stone. "She's responsible for the sickness, too. For Dalla."

Merewin nodded.

"We leave her, then," Gamal said, stepping away from where she lay on the cold ground. "Justice."

Merewin grabbed Hauk's arm. "She carries a bairn, Hauk, an innocent life. 'Tis why I saved her from the pond. Don't condemn the child for the madness of the mother."

Hauk exhaled and then nodded toward Svala. "Take her."

Gamal wrapped Svala in a blanket and mounted his horse. "I'll take her to Ragnar's. She can see the sickness she's caused."

Hauk settled Merewin before him on his horse. Her pet wrapped its thin body around her neck.

"Take me to Dalla," Merewin murmured.

CHAPTER TWENTY-EIGHT
THE GREATEST HEALING MAGICK

"By the love of Freyja, you are frozen through!" Bera ranted as she stripped Merewin down and cocooned her in warm blankets while Hauk held her standing.

"Where is Alrik?" Merewin asked, as she glanced between Dalla and Bera. "Was he poisoned?" Needles of pain stabbed along Merewin's extremities as the warmth battled against the sharp cold still claiming her skin. Hauk helped Merewin sit in a chair next to Dalla's bed.

Bera's eyes teared slightly. "Nay, he was not. I sent him to a girl in town who watches after him sometimes. I thought he would sleep better there."

Merewin nodded, head feeling twice as heavy as it should. Some of the potent poison still sat within her, muting her own powers. The fight for survival, even with the gift from the Earth Mother, had drained her strength.

She searched Dalla's white face. Tremors ran through the young girl. Merewin glided fingertips along Dalla's forehead and cheeks. "Dalla," she whispered.

Dalla's eyes flitted open. "Merewin. You came."

Merewin smiled reassuringly. "Everything will be fine now."

"Even if you can't heal me, I want you here."

Merewin glanced around. "Even if I can't heal ye?"

"Svala said you couldn't heal anyone," Bera supplied but glanced at Hauk.

Merewin's gaze followed.

The apology, the guilt lay there amongst the gray in his eyes, muting the usual spark. Hauk had believed Svala.

Merewin's eyes teared up. A heavy pressure sat in her chest, making it difficult to breathe. Her voice was small and laden with emotion. "Yet ye still came for me."

Hauk looked startled, but he nodded.

Merewin squeezed her eyes and then wiped away the swell of tears. She blinked, keeping him in view. "I love ye, Hauk, with my very soul."

She didn't wait for his reply but turned back to Dalla. "I will make ye well."

Gamal rushed in. "Aslaug's heart is pounding so hard, she can't stand. Ragnar is purging but refuses to leave his wife's side." Gamal looked at Hauk. "If Aslaug dies, I don't think anyone will be able to save Svala or her babe from Ragnar's wrath."

There was too much for Merewin to do to succumb to Svala's deathly mischief. Merewin's voice rose stronger. "Bera, grab my bag of stones. Hauk, ye must carry me to Ragnar's."

Bera ran across the room to grab the bag tucked away in a bucket near the pallet where Merewin had slept. "Gamal, bring Dalla," Merewin ordered softly. She looked straight in Hauk's eyes. "Svala lied about everything."

"I know…" he tried to interrupt, but Merewin held up a hand.

"I am a powerful healer, regardless of the outcome. I will not fail to save yer people." She squeezed his large hand near her shoulder. "Our people." She would give her life for them if she must.

Hauk's stare was intense. "'Tis too dangerous for you."

Merewin's face hardened into the mask of a warrior. "I will not fail, Hauk." She pointed to the door. "Help me."

Dalla moaned low, pushing Hauk into action. He helped Merewin out into the night toward Ragnar's. "Ye're hurt," she said.

"Not much more than what you did to me back in Northumbria. You concentrate on helping the others."

They stopped in the entrance of the Meeting House, the tang of curdled vomit hitting her fiercely.

Hauk's lips whispered hot breath near her ear. "I believe in you, Merewin. I believe in your magick."

"Good," she said. "I'll need yer faith, every bit of it."

Hauk's body tensed around her as if he feared she might slip away from him.

Merewin called out as she pulled farther into the hall. "Throw open the doors and windows."

"Do it," Hauk said, and the kitchen thralls lifted flaps along the walls to circulate the air.

"Everyone has been poisoned," Merewin said. She looked to the startled women. "Get rid of the rest of the food. Don't eat any of it." Merewin squeezed Hauk's arm. "I need to be in contact with the earth."

"Move the rushes and the rugs out of the way," he said and several people who had not eaten the poison cleared the middle of the room.

Some of them were children who hovered near their parents on the floor. Merewin's heart pounded for them. *I can't fail.*

Merewin moved to the center of the room and lowered to the dirt floor. She cradled her green jade in the palm of her hand and felt the heat pulse out from it.

"Bera, pull out the green stone, moss agate, and give it to Aslaug. Have her lay on the ground near me," Merewin instructed, and Hauk went to lead the queen. Merewin let her bare calves and feet rest on the dirt. She closed her eyes. "Pass out the grayish-silver, long crystals to those very ill and have them lie down. Keep one for Dalla." Merewin breathed deeply. Tentatively she pulled at the energy beneath her, from the earth. It came slowly, sluggishly. After several moments of breathing she said, "place Dalla on me, her back against my chest."

Dalla's slight weight covered Merewin, and panic began to well up. Dalla was still young, and she was still so weak. What if she couldn't heal her?

"I will not fail," Merewin enunciated softly.

"Aye, Merewin." Hauk's voice was close, so close she could feel his breath on her cheek. "You will not fail." His words were intense, solid, as if they held substance she could grab onto. His trust shot another wave of heated energy up from the ground to engulf her and Dalla. *Magick?*

Merewin opened her eyes to look into his. "Ye have yer own magick, Hauk. I feel it." Silence hung between them. "Help me save her." Merewin studied his eyes.

"Tell me what to do."

Merewin's heart beat with renewed hope. "Take the purple amethyst and put it into one of Dalla's hands." She waited until he found it. "Place the yellow citrine in the other. Close her hands around them. Aye, like that." She watched around Dalla's hair. "Lay the long silver one on the hollow of her throat."

Merewin closed her eyes and drew at the energy trapped in the earth. It came easier, up through the stones she used. The jade that lay between them grew hot. A chattering sound came close. Ellette crawled into a ball near Merewin's ear, sending another jolt of earth energy. She smiled. "Even ye have a bit of magick, Ellette."

Merewin channeled the power gently into Dalla, feeling for the poison. It lay like a bitter river along the conduits controlling all body functions. The damage was extensive. Merewin tugged at the poison. It shifted, lessened, but did not leave the girl. Merewin squeezed her eyes tighter. Her hands fisted so hard that nails dug into her palms.

Merewin concentrated, pulling desperately through the stones at the power from the earth beneath her body. "Dearest Earth Mother, lend me yer strength. Use me to flow into this child." Merewin felt a rush of heat as she opened herself to the earth's power, but her own body wasn't strong enough to hold it all. She felt it drain away back into the ground.

"Nay!" she yelled. "I will not fail." Tears trickled out from beneath her shut eyes.

She felt Hauk's warm, strong hands grip her shoulders on either side of Dalla. He kneeled over them, straddling them. "You will not fail us, Merewin. We will save her." His voice, deep with raw emotion, shook Merewin. She opened her tear-blurred eyes. His were stormy blue, narrowed with concern and something more. "I will roll you two to your sides so we both touch the ground."

"Why?" She could lose herself in those eyes. She didn't want to look away, didn't want to break the connection.

He rolled them gently over. "I don't know," he said. "But whatever you're doing, we'll do it together to save our daughter."

Our daughter. More tears spilled from Merewin's eyes, and she squeezed Dalla. This young girl was now hers to love and raise, and she wouldn't let her go. Hauk and she would work together to save her.

Merewin's voice calmed. "Close yer eyes and concentrate on the heat ye feel from the earth beneath yer bare arm. Pull at it, draw it into ye." They both closed their eyes, and Merewin once again began to channel the Earth Mother's energy up and into her own body.

Dalla jerked and trembled. A quick internal read of her condition caught at Merewin's chest. "Hauk, we have to do something now!"

"What do I do?" he said low, as if he were in battle.

Merewin reached and grabbed Hauk's arm, feeling the strong connection he had with the elements. The energy she felt in him would have killed a lesser man. It was raw and rich, not of earth but of fire.

"Ye hold fire magick, Hauk." Together they pooled fire and earth energy together, ready to use. She drew the earth energy up and he held it with his own. His body burned like an iron, but Merewin held tight.

"That's it, Hauk, hold onto it. Don't push it all into her else ye kill her. Let me guide it," she whispered, their mouths nearly touching over Dalla's head. They hugged her between them, their own bodies cocooning the girl within their immense power. The combined strength of their love for her and for each other intensified their own abilities.

Merewin absorbed a thin ribbon of energy from Hauk, channeling it through Dalla's heart, stripping the dark sludge from around it. The hemlock disintegrated at the touch of their combined love. Hauk's energy was pure power while Merewin's was finely tuned healing energy. Her magick was dampened by the poison within her body, but Hauk's rejuvenated it. They worked together. He supplied the energy, and Merewin used it like a fine blade, slicing the poison from Dalla's young spine and organs.

The tremors quelled. The taint melted, vanishing.

"Hauk, ye can stop drawing the energy," Merewin's shallow breath sounded far away in her ears. Dalla was safe, which was what mattered. She felt consciousness melting away. But before she gave into the relief of darkness, Merewin pushed away from Dalla's back so she lay flat on the ground. Merewin sucked Hauk's energy into her and threw it out with the last bit of strength she possessed, out to the other people spread upon the ground. The mix of Hauk's strength and her healing flowed from her like a brilliant light of hope.

As darkness carried Merewin away she heard a collective sigh as poison dissolved. She smiled into oblivion. She hadn't failed. Their love had saved their people. But would it be enough to save her?

⊰O⊱

"Bloody kerling!" Hauk swore at the image hovering over them as he carried Merewin through the night back to Bera's house. "Where in Midgard have you been? She needs you."

"I'm not an old hag. I am Drakkina, great Wiccan priestess and one of your goddesses if you believe those attending your wedding." Worry marked her tone. "What's happened? I thought I left her in capable hands."

Hauk stared straight ahead. "She's been poisoned, hemlock. She used her last strength to save Dalla and the townspeople." Hauk's heart pounded against his ribs, where he cradled Merewin. His breath hitched up high in his throat.

She was so pale, pale like death. Hauk ducked into Bera's empty house and dropped to his knees, lowering Merewin gently to the bare ground. He moved his lips over her forehead, her cheeks, her mouth. She was too cold. He vaulted up, grabbing furs from Bera's bed to cover Merewin's still body. The fire in the central pit flared and snapped. He could warm her from the outside, but she was cold in her core.

Hauk glared at the apparition floating nearby. "Help her."

Drakkina hovered over Merewin, touching, feeling. The witch's eyes grew round.

"You must save her," she said. "And quickly before she passes."

"How!" Hauk roared, his arms outstretched, his powerful hands in rock-hard fists.

"Your magick." She flapped her hands toward him. "You know you have magick."

"What do I do with it?"

"Everyone's magick is different," Drakkina clipped impatiently, moving hands around and scattering the dragonflies that lay against her diaphanous body.

"You are useless," Hauk yelled as he pulled off his blood-stained shirt and tossed it. He threw off the heavy furs and scooped Merewin into his arms. He held her, stomach to stomach against him, and lay back along the ground. To Drakkina he demanded, "find her stones in Ragnar's hall. Bring them. Can you do that?"

"I'll make it happen," Drakkina vanished.

Hauk was alone with Merewin in the house. He wrapped his large arms around her slender frame, cradling it, loving it. "Take my strength, Merewin." He ran his hand down her mud-caked hair and along a soft cheek. "My beautiful warrior." He lowered his mouth to her head. "Fight," he breathed into her hair. "Fight and live. Fight to stay with me, Merewin." He pressed his mouth to speak against her head. "I love you."

Bera appeared in the doorway, gaze narrow, arms stiff against her sides. She held Merewin's bag of stones in one hand. "Which stones?" Bera said with a demanding voice.

Hauk narrowed his eyes. Something was odd with her. "Bera?"

"It was the quickest way to get the stones here," Drakkina said through Bera's lips. "Your sister will be fine when I leave her body." She held out the bag. "Which ones?"

"You choose, else dump them all on top of her back." Hauk pressed his lips again to Merewin's head. He rocked her in his arms as he held her against him and closed his eyes. He breathed as Merewin had instructed before. He imagined a flame above his stomach, deep in his body near the heart. As he inhaled, the flame grew. He felt the fire energy growing, fed by his lungs like great bellows. The fire in the central pit sparked, flaring high up into the air, mimicking the energy flowing inside him.

Hauk focused on the image of the flame. She'd called it fire magick. The hot power was familiar, the same energy he felt in battle, the same energy that made him invincible against foes. Pure strength, raw power, the beast. If he didn't control it, the beast would destroy them both. Hauk's muscled shoulders twitched as he held the immense weight of his power from crushing into Merewin.

"If you have any magick, witch, use it to funnel this energy into her," Hauk gritted through clenched teeth.

Hauk watched Drakkina stretch out of Bera. Bera blinked and looked around. "What happened?"

Drakkina flew over to Hauk. She hovered over Merewin, ethereal hands washing down Merewin from stone to stone laying randomly on her back. Hauk envisioned his power wrapping around Merewin, a bath of warmth to soak her in. Drakkina pulled from it.

In the background, he heard Bera crying and Gamal shouting. He continued to focus on the energy crushing in on them while Drakkina worked to cleanse Merewin inside. Sweat broke out along his forehead, and he took short, controlling breaths, as if he held the weight of the world.

"Are you nearly done? Have you helped her?" He huffed through his teeth under Merewin's length.

Drakkina continued to move her hands, chanting something he couldn't hear.

"Witch?!" Hauk yelled.

"Hold your tongue, man! I'm working!"

Hauk kissed the top of Merewin's head, her face pressed against the hollow in his throat. He felt her mother's icy cold jade stone against his chest. "Merewin," he mouthed against her hair. "I love you! I believe in you. I believe in us, in the magick we have together. Live!"

The stone against his skin warmed. Was it just the heat from his own body?

"I need you," he whispered roughly into her ear. The stone grew warmer still. "Merewin." He drew her face back to his.

Merewin's eyes moved behind her lids. Long lashes twitched. Hope thrashed through Hauk, scattering his concentration. Energy flew outwards from him, causing the fire in the central pit to soar and scorch the ceiling. Voices shouted. Feet ran past, but Hauk cradled Merewin closer.

"Open your eyes, Merewin. Come back to me."

Her parted lips closed, and the tip of her tongue touched their dryness. "Hauk?"

A multitude of ethereal dragonflies buzzed around them, but Hauk closed his eyes, closed out everything but the feel of Merewin gathered in his arms.

Hauk breathed and crushed her to him. "I am here." He held her, rocking back and forth where they lay on the ground. "I will always be here."

She moved and tipped her head back to meet his gaze. Her eyes were clear and focused now. "I love ye too."

<hr>

"Ye are certain we are really alone for the whole week?" Merewin asked as Hauk ran the scented oil down her spine. She lay naked on the furs of their large bed. The fire cast shadows to dance along the walls.

Hauk leaned in, sweeping her hair to the side, and kissed the nape of Merewin's neck. "Aye, all alone for the week. Dalla is with Bera and Vivien and Diarf went, too. Even your pet has gone with Dalla. We are completely alone. You may scream in pleasure all week like you did earlier. No one will hear you." Hauk couldn't see the blush creep up Merewin's face as she buried it in the furs.

"And Drakkina?" she asked, her words muffled in the thick pelts.

"We have an agreement," Hauk said, rubbing his hands together. "She leaves us alone, and I promise to bring you to the stone circle in the west when she calls us."

Merewin groaned tersely, "not overseas again." She flicked her feet upwards, tapping his naked, toned backside with her toes.

Hauk caught a foot and rubbed it before letting it fall back to the bed. "We will work on finding a cure for your sickness."

Hauk ran his large hands down the sides of Merewin's back, massaging her muscles. Merewin moaned into the furs.

"Where did ye learn to do that?" She turned her head to the side, so her cheek rubbed against the softness of the furs. "Nay, perhaps I don't want to know."

Hauk chuckled deeply and pulled her hands up over her head. "My war horse likes me to rub his legs down after a long, hard ride." He leaned forward until his breath tickled Merewin's ear. "You deserve rubbing down too after my long, hard ride."

Merewin neighed from her position on the bed, and Hauk laughed deeply. He ran his strong hands down her arms and along the sides of her breasts before continuing on to her buttocks. He massaged and rubbed, kissed and nibbled until Merewin felt her body relaxing into a sensual puddle of feminine softness.

Hauk's fingers traced the dragonfly birthmark on her inner thigh. "It doesn't tingle right now?"

Merewin rolled over, stretching languidly upon the pelts. "Oh I have tingling, but not on my birthmark." She spread her bare toes, letting the fur tickle between them. Merewin let her own hands rub down her warm, curvy, well-loved body. He groaned and the fire behind him surged upwards.

Merewin smiled saucily. "Ye best learn to control yer fire magick, husband, else ye burn down the house."

Hauk straddled Merewin, breathing deeply for control, and the fire returned to normal.

"I've always been in control before." He frowned. "Until you came along."

Merewin pushed up and looped her arms around Hauk's neck to pull him to her mouth. She kissed him as she snaked her hand down his muscled chest and taut belly. Boldly she stroked his thick pintle. "I like ye out of control, like when ye scream my name, husband."

"You may call me master," he taunted as he ran his hand through her hair.

"Master of piquing my ire."

Hauk chuckled and leaped up.

Merewin rose onto her elbow. "Where is my barbarian going?"

Hauk picked up a bucket of melted snow and dumped it on the fire. He followed it with another until only moonlight from the smoke hole in the ceiling kept the room from complete blackness. He returned to the bed. "I plan to get out of control," he growled at her ear, sending shivers along the whole side of her body. "If there's a fire already started, I might burn the whole dwelling to ashes."

Merewin laughed. Hauk rolled them and settled her, sitting straddled across his naked hips. He ran both hands through her hair, fanning it out around her shoulders. "What color is your hair, woman?"

Merewin leaned forward so her tresses brushed his chest. "Brown with a touch of gold," she said with a smile in her voice. It seemed like a lifetime ago when he'd chased her between the soaring oaks of Northumbria.

Hauk twirled a lock of her hair around his finger. "Do you miss your forest?" His words were cautious.

Merewin leaned forward and kissed him gently. "I thought I was free then, but I was trapped in loneliness. By capturing me, ye've freed me, Hauk." She kissed him long and slow, stroking his face. As her eyes adjusted to the darkness, the bright moonlight filtering down through the smoke hole in the ceiling showed the strong outline of Hauk's face.

"I captured your body," he said, "but it was my soul that was trapped. Trapped in fury and suspicion." He ran his thumb over her cheek, over her full bottom lip. "You have freed me, Merewin." He cupped her face as if he were holding a most precious gem. "You used your magick to heal me and my family."

Merewin shook her head, still held in his hands. "I used no magick on ye."

"Your love, Merewin," he whispered, his eyes catching the spark of moonlight. "Your love healed me."

Merewin leaned forward, her soft belly against his hard stomach, and stretched out her long legs against his. Hauk's arms came around her, adjusting her so she lay intimately on top of him. Merewin traced her fingers over his firm jaw and leaned in until their noses touched. "I do believe," she said, her lips against his, "love is the greatest magick of all."

CHAPTER TWENTY-NINE
ONE YEAR LATER

King Ragnar's Meeting House

"I charge you with attempted murder, Svala Lothbrok," Ragnar declared and indicated the hall of onlookers, "attempted murder of nearly everyone in this hall."

Merewin watched Svala from her place next to Hauk. She stood on the platform holding her infant boy in her arms. Merewin had helped her through the last stages of childbirth six months ago. Svala had named the child, Bjor, after her father.

Since Bjor's birth, Merewin had visited Svala and her son each week to ensure he progressed under Svala's mothering. The woman had been held captive in her small house. She'd been so weak after her near drowning and then the birth that Merewin had funneled healing magick into her several times. During these times, Merewin had felt and tried to alleviate some inner imbalances in Svala's brain. She seemed calmer now, healthier in spirit.

Now Svala cradled her son in her arms, staring down at his little rosy cheeks as he grinned back up. Tears ran down her face, but she forced a smile for the child so as not to frighten him. She ran a finger through his little patch of red hair and over his flawless features as if memorizing them.

"I call for a sentence of death by fire," Ragnar said grimly. "The child will be cared for by Minerva until he can walk on his own. Then Aslaug and I will raise the boy."

Svala cooed softly to her son and cuddled him to her chest. She closed her eyes and nuzzled the soft hair, inhaling the scent like it was the most precious experience of her life. She said nothing to the people. She knew her guilt and the law.

Merewin moved her hand to her expanding abdomen as she felt the little kick from inside. She was six months along with Hauk's child. The bairn turned and twisted gently in her womb. Merewin sang and spoke to it daily. She was steadfastly, absolutely, already in love with their bairn.

"Is the babe bothersome?" Hauk asked with a gentle smile as he rubbed Merewin's lower back and placed one hand across her belly.

"Nay." A tear trickled down her cheek as she watched Svala whisper to her own bairn.

"I will find you a stool to sit upon," Hauk whispered. She stilled him with her hand, but looked at Ragnar, who continued the sentence.

Merewin stepped forward. "King Ragnar Lothbrok, I would address ye and these good people of Ribe." Ragnar paused and then nodded. Merewin walked to the center of the room and turned toward the people, her people. Hauk moved up to stand beside her, his support evident.

"I understand yer laws decree that Svala be put to death for her crimes." Several men nodded firmly. Merewin noticed Svein, his red hair the same shade as Svala's bairn, did not. Merewin glanced at Svala who continued to cuddle the boy. "I have spent much time with Svala and Bjor." She paused, knowing the people weighed her words. "People change. Their troubled minds heal." She looked at the woman who'd tried to kill her, but she was a different person now.

"Love," Merewin said and felt Hauk squeeze her shoulder lightly. "Love changes a person, heals a person." She nodded to Svala. "And she loves her bairn with all her heart." Svala looked at Merewin, and big tears gushed out of her eyes as she nodded. The small crowd mumbled, but Hauk held up his hand, and all quieted so Merewin could continue. "'Tis my opinion, because I am a healer and I am a mother," she said, moving her hand to her stomach and her gaze to Dalla near the back. "I know Svala is a healed woman. She should be allowed to live."

Whispers and comments broke out like leaves whipping around the room from a windstorm. It took Ragnar several shouts to calm the outburst. "Merewin," Ragnar said, his voice still raised from overriding the crowd. "You have become an important part of our community, and I respect your thoughts, but this is our law, a law we have honored for a very long time."

The room quieted, curious to hear Merewin's response. She took a deep breath. "I understand that yer ancient laws also decreed a virgin girl be sacrificed in the sacred groves." The crowd murmured. Merewin noticed several mothers and fathers pull their daughters closer. Ragnar looked like he was thinking of something to counter when Merewin continued. She shook her head. "I don't ask ye to dishonor yer ancient laws, but to look at each incident, and weigh the evidence and details with clear sight." She indicated Svala loving her little son. "I ask for mercy. Exile Svala. Do not kill her."

"Nay," Svala said, her voice cracked with tears. "I cannot bear to live without my son. If we are to be separated, let it be by my death." Svala hugged her little boy so tightly he began to squirm and fuss. She put him against her shoulder and rubbed his little back until he settled. The bairn must have smiled at Aslaug where she sat behind him, because she smiled and flicked her fingers at him.

Merewin's voice rang out, once more strong with purposeful resolve, even though tears brightened her eyes. "Death is less cruel than separation from one's bairn, I agree." She raised her hand up to quell the room quickly. "Exile for Svala and her son, away from Ribe, but let them live together. Do not drive a knife between the bond of mother and child."

"The child will be punished for his mother's crimes, then?" someone called out.

Merewin shook her head. "When Bjor grows to be a man, he may come to Ribe if he desires, but without his mother."

Aslaug stood frowning. "How could you be sure she will raise the boy right, without hate and malice in his heart? She could mistreat him."

"Never," Svala stated, turning to look at Aslaug. Tears rolled freely down Svala's face, and she didn't try to stop them. She kissed her bairn's soft cheek. "I did not know what love was until I held Bjor in my arms."

Aslaug inhaled with a brief nod and took her seat.

Merewin looked at Ragnar. "Ye could send someone to keep an eye on her, one of yer men who wouldn't mind adventuring west, perhaps to where yer ally settles with the Picts." Merewin looked around the room until her gaze fastened on Svein. "Perhaps Svein Balthor. He is without family."

Svein stood tall and looked at Ragnar, waiting.

"Would you be willing to take Svala and her son west, to watch that the boy is raised properly? Would you take him back here if he is mistreated?" Ragnar asked.

Svein looked at Svala where she wiped her eyes while hugging the wiggling bairn. He nodded slowly. "I would."

The room waited while Ragnar rubbed his jaw through his beard. He finally nodded. "Svein will take Svala and her babe into exile until the boy is a man."

Svala looked between Svein and Ragnar, and a new bout of tears poured from her eyes. She clung to her wee boy. "Thank you," she choked out with a half smile, half sob. Svala turned her red eyes to Merewin. "I... Thank you." She wiped at her face. "How can I ever repay you?"

Merewin inhaled and blinked against the ache in her eyes. "True love is the most powerful magick there is. Just love Bjor well. 'Tis payment enough."

Hauk pulled Merewin up against his side so she could relax into him. Her body shook slightly.

"Your words have wisdom, Merewin," Ragnar said. "To take a mother from her son is not something Freyja would support." He looked out over the gathering. "I declare Svala Lothbrok exiled with her son to Dalriada, in the care of Svein Balthor. Svala is to be watched to make certain her son is raised well. If the child is brought back to Ribe, my queen and I will raise him as our own."

Nods and "ayes" filled the room. Merewin took a deep breath and tugged gently on Hauk's tunic. He leaned his ear to her lips. "Take us home, Hauk. To Spring House."

◆

Drakkina floated overhead without using energy to make herself seen.

Merewin glanced around as if wondering about the tingle that probably infused her dragonfly birthmark, but Drakkina hid, watching.

Merewin relaxed into Hauk on his war horse as the girl, Dalla, ran up ahead. Burnished golden leaves still held tightly to the trees, creating an arch over them as they rode through the Dane's sacred forest. Splashes of sunlight slanted down through the maze of slender branches. Drakkina wished she could still feel the warmth of the sun, but alas, her body was lost to time.

Drakkina heard Merewin sigh. "How did I get so lucky?" Contentment relaxed her face and her body as she snuggled into her barbarian husband's arms.

Merewin tilted her face up to his, and their eyes met. "I have a family," she said, "a wonderful husband, and a bairn on the way."

Drakkina remembered the ice in the warrior's eyes when she first identified him as Merewin's mate. The feelings that had grown between them had melted away his fury.

Hauk kissed Merewin's forehead. "And a fledgling forest of tiny oaks to tend."

Merewin laughed. "Aye, my acorns have certainly taken to yer soil."

They continued moving together in the gentle sway of the horse, wrapped in each other's arms, toward Spring House and its grove of finger-length oaks.

Drakkina floated higher above the trees, up within the clouds. "Guard her well, Dane. Love her well," she said into the breeze. She tilted her head slightly, watching Dalla run to them laughing. Hauk tipped back his handsome face, and laughed, too.

Drakkina's brow rose. "It seems love can heal some things better than magick." Shrugging, she closed her eyes and allowed her ethereal body to elongate into a thread, a thread that shot off into time.

Continue the adventure of THE DRAGONFLY CHRONICLES with Book #3: MASQUERADE as Merewin's younger sister is sent to current day England to be raised in an orphan's home. Burned in her youth, Kat uses her glamour magic to cover the scars on her face. As an adult, she steals from the rich to keep the orphaned children's home going until she's caught by a Highlander who can see through her magic. When they are sent back through time to Toren MacCallum's century, Kat finds herself in 16th century England. Can she escape Queen Elizabeth's court? Will Toren ever let her return to her own century?

Subscribe to my Newsletter

Be the first to know when Eleri Drake has a new cover reveal, release, sale, or giveaway! New subscribers receive a FREE download of THE BEAST OF AROS CASTLE! Sign up for my once-a-month newsletter at:

Newsletter

Did you love Merewin and Hauk? The way love could heal even when magick could not? If you did, **please leave a review where you purchased this book or on Goodreads**. In this vast ocean of publishing, please help this guppy find the people who love my stories. Thank you! Eleri

ABOUT THE AUTHOR

Eleri Drake is the penname of Heather McCollum, a *USA Today* and *Publishers Weekly* bestselling author of Scottish historical romance. Books written under the pseudonym Eleri Drake contain fantasy elements to make the adventure and passion even more fun.

Growing up, Eleri/Heather dreamed of fairies and magic. She would swim in her family swimming pool with her legs together, hoping they'd fuse, and she'd turn into a mermaid. Her favorite television show was *Bewitched* where she wished to be Tabitha, the playful, trouble-making little witch child. Now she can funnel all her whimsy into these romantasies set back in time.

Social Media Links for Eleri Drake

Follow me for book info and writer-life fun!

Let's stay in touch!

Join my once-a-month Heather/Eleri newsletter at:

https://www.heathermccollum.com/about/newsletter/

ACKNOWLEDGMENTS

Thank you, awesome readers, for continuing your reading journey in my new writing sub-genre, Historical Romantasy! Your support means the world to me.

Also, thank you to my wonderful editor, Melinda DeJongh! Here's to many more projects together. And to my family and friends who never cease cheering me on. Love you all so much!

At the end of each of my books, I ask that you, my awesome readers, please remind yourselves of the whispered symptoms of ovarian cancer. I am now a thirteen-year survivor, one of the lucky ones. Please don't rely on luck. If you experience any of these symptoms consistently for three weeks or more, go see your GYN.

- Bloating

- Eating less and feeling full faster

- Abdominal pain

- Trouble with your bladder

Other symptoms may include indigestion, back pain, pain with intercourse, constipation, fatigue, and menstrual irregularities.

GET THE OTHER BOOKS IN THE DRAGONFLY CHRONICLES

Prophecy – Book #1

18th Century Scotland
Forbidden Love * Dark Prophecy * Telepathy

Serena Faw must shut out the barrage of thoughts from everyone around her. Her telepathic powers reveal the darkness and true intentions behind every false smile. When her adopted brother is accused of murder, the only man who can help her is the one person she cannot read. Can she trust the Highlander with the life of her brother? Can she trust him with her heart?

Keenan Maclean, the younger brother to the new chief of the Macleans, has grown up in the shadow of a dark prophecy. It is said that one Maclean brother will live, wed to a witch, and one will die. Keenan has grown into a fierce warrior while accepting his fate to defend his clan and die with honor.

Serena and Keenan hunt a loyalist murderer before the Battle of Culloden while trying to deny the attraction growing between them. Despite the prophecy's warning that she heralds his death and Keenan's need to protect his brother and family, the passion becomes too great to ignore. Will their lives be the penalty for their forbidden love?

Prophecy

OTHER SERIES BY HEATHER MCCOLLUM

HIGHLAND HEARTS

First Book – Captured Heart

Enemies to Lovers

Captured Heart

Set in the early 16th century Highlands. A Scottish Historical Romance series, spanning generations, with a touch of magic. The women in the Macbain Clan have the power to heal, a "gift" that gets passed down through family lines. Those with the gift must evade witch hunters and deal with suspicion. They harness herbal lore and learn to use their magic to help those they love.

HIGHLAND ISLES

First Book – The Beast of Aros Castle
Marriage of Convenience

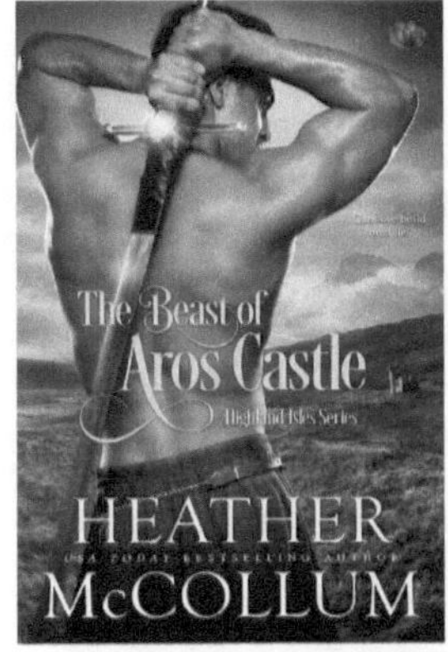

The Beast of Aros Castle

Set in the mid-16th century on the western isles off Scotland. Fun banter and laugh-out-loud adventures with the broody chiefs of the clans and the feisty women who find their way into their lives. Mysteries and secrets abound!

THE CAMPBELLS

First Book – The Scottish Rogue
Enemies to Lovers

The Scottish Rogue

Set in the 17th century in Scotland. Two English sisters journey to Scotland to start a school for the local people in a castle that their brother bought (or so he thought). They quickly realize that on top of learning to read, cipher numbers, and serve tea, the girls need to learn how to defend themselves against both Scottish and English villains. The school becomes a self-defense school, and the pupils are called the Roses (beautiful but with dangerous thorns).

SONS OF SINCLAIR

First Book – Highland Conquest
Enemies to Lovers

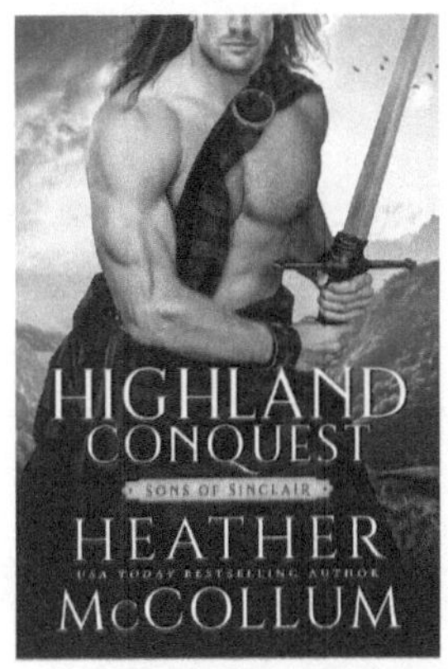

Highland Conquest

Set in the late 16th century northern Scotland. Four brothers were raised by a mad, war-loving father to be the biblical four horsemen of the apocalypse. They are mere flesh and bone, but they were raised to be Conquest, War, Judgement, and Death. Learning to love, the most powerful prize of all, challenges all their beliefs.

BROTHERS OF WOLF ISLE

First Book – The Highlander's Unexpected Proposal
Marriage of Convenience

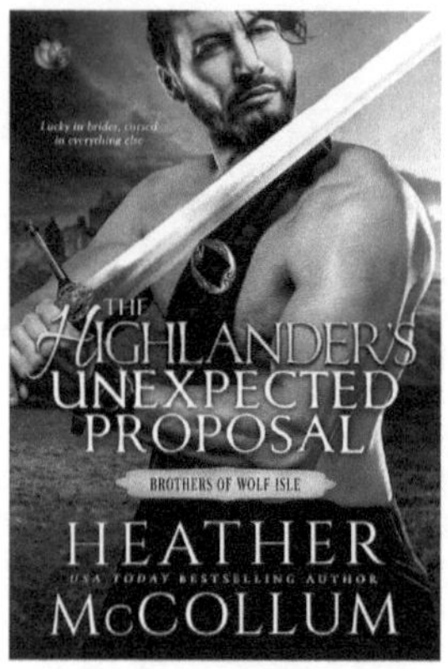

The Highlander's
Unexpected Proposal

Set in the 16th century off the west coast of Scotland. Five brothers are trying to rebuild their clan on their ancestral isle, but the isle is said to be cursed. To break the curse, they must learn truths about love. The original idea for this series was loosely based on the musical *Seven Brides for Seven Brothers*.

THE QUEEN'S HIGHLANDERS

First Book – The Highlander & the Queen's Sacrifice
Secrets, Body Guard, Tudor

The Highlander & the
Queen's Sacrifice

Set in 16th century London at Queen Elizabeth's court. Three of the queen's ladies get mixed up with visiting Highlanders to expose assassination plots. Poisoned gowns, a chastity belt, and masquerade fun!

BROTHERHOOD OF SOLWAY MOSS

First Book – The Highlander's Wild Flame
Enemies to Lovers

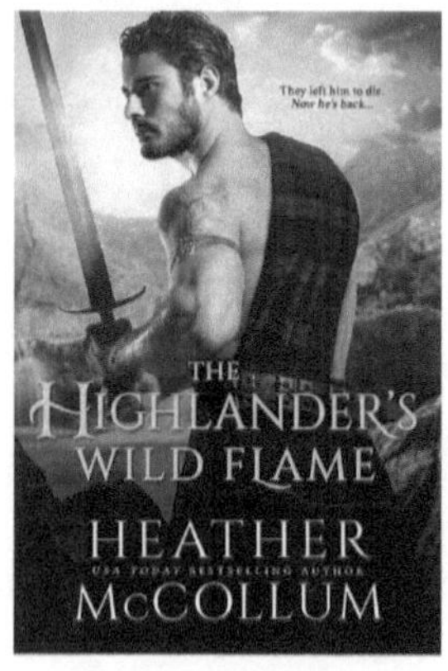

The Highlander's
Wild Flame

Set in the mid 16th century Highlands. Four Highlanders, who were raised as enemies, escape an English dungeon by working together. When they return to the Isle of Skye, they pledge to convince their feuding families to unite to strengthen Scotland. Alliances are only as strong as the emotions behind them, love being the most powerful. Strong women and a witch work to bring elements of fire, air, water, and earth together to strengthen their isle.

Rohaise the Red (novella ghost story)

Rohaise the Red
Novella Ghost Story

Based on a true haunting in Scotland.

The troubled spirit's name is Rohaise, and her yearning to live once again is fierce, fierce enough to kill for love and freedom.